The Hangman's Fracture

Books by the same author

What's Truth Got To Do With It?
ISBN: 979-1904440802

The Molecule Man
ISBN: 978-19044440963

In Death We Trust
ISBN: 978-1906775117

Published by

Librario Publishing Ltd.

ISBN: 978-906775-24-7

Copies can be ordered via the Internet
www.librario.com

or from:

Brough House, Milton Brodie, Kinloss
Moray IV36 2UA
Tel/Fax No 00 44 (0)1343 850 617

Printed and bound in the UK

Typeset by 3btype.com

Cover design by Melissa Thomas-Anderson

The Hangman's Fracture

by

David Crigman

Librario

Chapter 1

Manchester, England. 1963.

On a cold Wednesday morning the hangman's assistant weighed Henry Stanton in his prison clothes. At one hundred and ninety pounds that meant that the drop would be set at exactly five feet three inches. Whilst the executioners busied themselves testing the gallows beam which had been brought up from Pentonville on the morning train the Governor allowed Jane Stanton a final visit conducted through the bars of the condemned cell. The Home Office had ordered that he was to be hanged on Thursday at precisely eight a.m.

Her forlorn face was white and drawn, the lines of her body drooped in hopelessness as she stared through the bars at her sobbing husband. There was neither room nor time for any attempt at stoic dignity. A prison warder without a soul stood alongside her, preventing her from crossing the yellow line, so that the condemned man could never again know the touch of his wife.

"I swear on the life of our unborn child that I never killed her," he cried in despair. "If I'd done it I'd tell you. To save you more pain."

The woman's hands went instinctively to her swollen belly as if to protect the life that lay within from being exposed to this spectacle of agony. "I've always believed you," she whispered softly, "and, when the time is right, our child will know."

"Is the lawyer still trying?" he asked plaintively.

"The latest petition to the Home Secretary is being presented this afternoon by our MP. There's still hope," she answered flatly, knowing that these eleventh hour bids were no more than hollow gestures of despair.

On the far side of the cell stood a broad and battered wardrobe, incongruous in the spartan setting, but she knew the grotesque secret that lay behind that ugly piece of furniture. Tomorrow morning the warders would drag it aside to reveal the steel door which led directly into the execution chamber. The condemned man took a pace towards her, causing a momentary stiffening in the body of the warder alongside her, but the prisoner posed no threat. He simply wanted to deliver his final message, designed to endure over the decades to come; decades of which the rope was about to cheat him. His sobbing had stopped now and his voice had grown firmer.

"The truth is out there, Jane," he began. "The real murderer has buried the truth. Helped by someone else. Maybe someone in authority. Don't let the truth die with me. I'm begging you. . ."

His voice trailed away and was consumed again in misery as the wretched woman offered him the only consolation that was left before he departed this earth.

"I promise you the truth," she breathed. "Even if it isn't in my lifetime, I promise you the truth."

* * *

Outside, in a thin rain, a crowd had started to gather shortly after midnight and, by the time a grey dawn had broken over the industrial eastern horizon, two distinct factions had been formed. Those baying for blood and those repulsed by the concept of State-sanctioned murder.

By seven o'clock the prisoner had been dressed in his civilian clothes and the priest had offered him absolution. Now shaking uncontrollably, the doctor had authorised a glass of brandy. The Governor had led the hangman into the condemned cell as two warders heaved the wardrobe aside and threw open the heavy steel door to the chamber beyond.

As soon as the hangman had bound his hands behind his body with a leather strap the warders walked him into the chamber and on to the trap door. Stanton staggered and then almost fainted as he set eyes on the rough timber of the gallows beam and the dangling noose with its brass eyelet. Supporting arms held him upright as the hangman slipped the white linen hood over his head and Stanton returned to full consciousness with the sickly smell of the linen in his nostrils. His legs were pinioned with leather around the ankles before the noose was lowered over his head and the eyelet anchored under the angle of his jaw. He had rejected prayer until now, convinced by the barbarity of his fate that no divine force could exist but, as he felt the hangman's fingers position the noose tightly beneath his left jaw, he screamed to some obscure deity to save him, before vomiting into the cloying white linen. His last act on earth was to soil his grey flannel schoolteacher trousers that his wife had been allowed to bring into the prison.

When the lever was thrown the body dropped like a stone and, as the rope reached its full extension, the head snapped backwards and the spinal cord was wrenched asunder beneath the brain stem, fracturing the neck at the second and third vertebrae. The classic *Hangman's Fracture.*

Other prisoners, with cold hearts and dead eyes, had buried him in an unmarked grave inside the prison walls. Even his spirit in eternity was incarcerated unless the truth was ever allowed to set him free.

* * *

On Friday Frederick Walgrave sat at his desk, head in hands, staring at the morning edition of *The Times,* which carried grainy pictures of the young victim, alongside the stark inquest verdict recorded by the Coroner.

"Henry Francis Stanton. At Her Majesty's Prison. Male. Aged 32 years. Schoolteacher. Cause of Death : Injuries to the central nervous system consequent upon judicial hanging."

Walgrave had not slept for three nights, helping to draft the last minute petitions to the Home Office, denied even temporary respite from the anguish generated by the fear that an innocent man may be going to the gallows. Two years National Service had toughened Walgrave up, but not to the extent that he could easily handle the injustice wrought upon Stanton.

In November 1956 he had been part of the 3rd Battalion's parachute drop at El Gamil Airfield in Egypt to establish a secure base for incoming support aircraft engaged in the Suez Campaign. One of his men had been hit in the chest by a sniper's bullet in an ensuing skirmish and Captain Walgrave had carried him, under enemy fire, across the airfield to shelter. It was only when he gently lowered the blood-drenched body to the floor that he realised he had been carrying a corpse. Sitting at his desk in his Hampstead home, reading the Coroner's verdict on Stanton, produced the same churning feeling, deep inside his stomach, as he had experienced on that dreadful Egyptian day.

On completion of the Suez Campaign he had been discharged and returned to London, completed his studies for the Bar and begun work as a barrister in a small set of chambers in the Temple. Work was scarce, and most mornings he would position himself on the front row in one of the Courts at the Old Bailey, alongside numerous other fresh-faced barristers, hoping that the Judge might allocate him an unrepresented defendant as a dock brief.

Such morsels as were thrown out to new boys like himself were invariably the small fry. The Cockney pickpocket, the local brawler or the shiny-suited pimp. And so it had come as an enormous shock, both to him and all the other barristers sitting expectantly on the cab-rank, when Mr Justice Vishney allocated him the case of Regina against Stanton. A case of murder. He was too young. Too inexperienced. This was a case for a QC. But the Judge had cast his eye along the row of seated wigs and, espying the new, white wig and obvious inexperience had picked him out. Vishney despised child murderers.

"Mr Walgrave," the Judge had intoned on that fateful morning. "Are you professionally available to conduct the defence of this man?"

"I am, My Lord, but, respectfully, is it not appropriate for a defendant charged with a capital offence to be represented by Queen's Counsel?" he replied nervously.

"Not necessarily," the Judge snapped back. "The facts of this case are very straightforward. The witness statements amount to less than thirty pages. Other than the pathologist, there is no expert evidence. The public purse need not be constrained to provide Queen's Counsel in such a case. The brief is yours. The trial will begin next Monday morning in this Court in front of me."

Known to the Bar as "Vicious Vishney", Mr Justice Vishney was an autocratic, self-satisfied despot, with an acid tongue and a fierce temper. In his Court he controlled everything; the witnesses, the barristers, the staff and, most importantly, the jurors. Tall, haughty, long-faced and always wearing pince-nez spectacles, he presented as the patrician, born to rule and issue orders. Acquittals in his Court were a rarity.

For the five days that Vishney had allowed him to prepare the case, Walgrave had gone over every detail a thousand times and spent several hours in the grim prison, trying to take instructions from Stanton who was manifestly in a state of clinical depression.

Louise Donovan was a sixteen year old pupil at the school where Stanton taught mathematics. The school took children from all across the social spectrum. Louise was from a poor family. Rather plump, but flaxen-haired with a pretty smile, she was well-liked at the school. Particularly by the boys, as she was promiscuous. The school drive ran alongside a golf course and in a small copse separating the drive from the tenth hole her body, crudely covered by a few twigs and leaves, had been discovered by the greenkeeper refreshing the out-of-bounds line on a warm summer afternoon. She had been raped and strangled. Still clothed, except for her navy blue knickers, which had been found by the police stuffed in the saddlebag of Stanton's Raleigh Lenton Sports bicycle in the school bike sheds later that day. When the police questioned him, Stanton admitted that he had taken a walk on the golf course during the lunch hour. Alone. They arrested him and took him to the police station where he was medically examined. His back bore scratches which were consistent with having been caused by fingernails.

The first witness on Monday morning was the girl's distraught mother who, between outpourings of grief, identified the knickers as her daughter's, both by brand and by a pink motif of a lily on the left leg. She was followed into the witness box by Walter Mangan, the green keeper, a whippet of a youth with darting eyes and a stutter, who described the isolation of the copse and the heavy cover provided by the trees and bushes. As he detailed his gruesome discovery, the mother, seated in the public gallery, wept audibly and uncontrollably. Vishney made no attempt to stop her and watched with satisfaction as Walgrave cringed in his seat, knowing the damage that this heart-rending distress was doing to his client.

Amy Beckett had been a class mate of Louise Donovan and they had eaten their sandwiches together, sitting on a wooden bench on the perimeter of the playground at lunchtime. She told the Court that Louise had bolted her sandwiches down, before hurrying away in the direction of the golf course, saying that she had arranged to meet someone. Walgrave tried to prevent this prejudicial hearsay being admitted, but the Judge had waved him to sit down and the girl was allowed to blurt it out. She went on to tell the jury that just before school started again at two o'clock, having spotted William Hollister from the Sixth Form surreptitiously smoking a cigarette behind the old horse chestnut tree on the edge of the school drive and the golf course, she had then observed a male figure emerging from the course, disappear from view alongside the bike sheds and then reappear on the school drive, heading in the general direction of the school buildings. She believed that person to be Mr Stanton.

Walgrave may have been nervous and inexperienced, but he cross-examined this witness with great skill and determination, pointing out that she had not been sure it was Mr Stanton when making her witness statement to the police as the figure was so far away, and that it would have been very difficult to see what she claimed from the vantage point that she described. His attack on her credibility was aided by the potent sentiment that he didn't believe a word that she said. As he sought to decimate her evidence, "Vicious" Vishney came rushing to her assistance.

"I will not have a young witness bullied in my Court," he barked.

"I am just trying to challenge her evidence, My Lord. To show it does not bear close scrutiny," Walgrave responded bravely.

"No doubt the jury will scrutinise your proposition that a sixteen year old girl, whose friend has been murdered, has seen fit to invent a sighting of your client," came the crushing reply.

Concluding the evidence of the first day, was the young Police Officer who had searched the bike sheds and discovered the incriminating knickers in the Raleigh's saddlebag. Open-faced and polite, he readily conceded that the sheds were not locked, and that anybody could have slipped in discreetly and hidden an object wherever they chose and that the Defendant had seemed shocked when the discovery of the knickers was put to him.

"You can't say if he was shocked that they were in his saddlebag or shocked that he had been found out, can you?" Vishney had interjected in irritation at the Officer's candour.

"No, My Lord," the Officer mumbled in embarrassment.

"But you can say that the Defendant appeared to be co-operative with the police, can't you? asked Walgrave.

"He came with us willingly enough. He answered all our questions. That's all I can say," came the frank reply.

"But you are in no position to say whether his answers were true or false," came back Vishney in exasperation. "Really, Mr Walgrave, confine yourself to questions of fact, not ambiguous opinion."

By lunchtime the following day the evidence was over. The Home Office Pathologist confirmed that death was caused by pressure to the neck, which had not produced any fracture of bone or cartilage, suggesting that the victim had suffered a vagal inhibition. This, he explained, did not require great force, but occurred when pressure was applied to the vagal nerve, provoking severe interference with the rhythm of the heart, sometimes stopping it, as had happened here. He declared himself satisfied that the girl had been raped because of signs of trauma to her genitalia, explaining the absence of semen by either non-ejaculation or the use of a contraceptive.

The Police Doctor had produced his medical notes detailing the scratches he had seen on the Defendant's back. There were only two scratches, one inch long and so minor that they were barely discernible on the body sketch drawn up in the Doctor's notes. In cross-examining him, Walgrave pointed out that the post mortem notes on Louise Donovan had stated that she appeared to have fingernails that were habitually bitten, but the Police Doctor refused to accept that she was incapable of causing such scratches.

The Defence case was short and powerful. Henry Stanton, though depressed and terrified, gave a clear account of his short walk on the golf course at lunchtime, later speaking to a school prefect, Thomas

Littleton, in the corridor of the Mathematics Department at a quarter to two, as he returned to the classroom to prepare for the lesson on Pythagoras, eating an apple in the classroom and then conducting the class with good humour and enjoyment. His clothes were, as always, in pristine condition and, at the end of the school day, he had walked down to the bike sheds where he was pounced upon by a Police Officer from the shadows as soon as he touched his Raleigh bicycle. It was obvious, he suggested, that the real murderer had stuffed the knickers in the saddlebag out of malice or panic. Thomas Littleton gave clear evidence in support of his meeting with Mr Stanton and Jane Stanton, nervously, but, in Walgrave's opinion, with patent honesty, related that in bed the previous night she had caused the two minor scratches to her husband's back in the throes of passion which, with excruciating embarrassment, she had to spell out before a public court.

So often it was the little things in a case that provided the key to the truth. In Walgrave's view it was the apple. Unless Stanton was the Devil incarnate there was no way, having just raped and strangled his sixteen year old pupil, that he would be sitting at his desk ten minutes later preparing Pythagoras and eating a Granny Smith. He beseeched the jury to set aside all emotion, bias and thirst for revenge and see the evidence for what it was, namely quite incapable of convicting a man of murder. When he sat down, exhausted and drained, many of the jurors smiled and nodded their approval at his words and argument. Walgrave felt the beginnings of great relief. All would be well. But he had not bargained for "Vicious" Vishney's assassination of the Defendant; his moral outrage at the death of an innocent girl in such hideous and evil circumstances, the devastating impact of the evidence of Amy Beckett and the discovery of the knickers.

At ten to four he sent the jury out to consider their verdict with his contemptuous dismissal of the defence case ringing in their ears.

At five o'clock they returned and convicted Stanton of murder and, with the black cap atop his wig, Vishney sentenced him to death.

Under The Homicide Act, murder in the course of rape could not attract capital punishment, although murder where a theft was committed, could. The Judge ruled that the motivation was not only rape, but a sexually deviant theft of the victim's underwear, thereby making the case eligible for the ultimate penalty.

The Appeal against conviction and the sentence of death was heard six weeks later and dismissed. A five-judge Court upheld the view that the theft of the knickers brought this case within a category where execution could be justified. Four months later Stanton went to the gallows, leaving Walgrave haunted for the rest of his days by the deployment of such savagery and hurried justice on an obviously innocent man.

Chapter 2

Taunton, England July 1988

Over the first weekend of July a ridge of high pressure had settled over the West Country and the day had dawned with a sky that was breathtakingly blue, lifting the spirits of Frederick Walgrave. Bolting down a bowl of cereal, then kissing his wife fleetingly on the cheek, he jumped on to his 1963 Norton Dominator 88 motor cycle, gunned the 500 cc engine and raced down the country lanes to the small airfield where he kept the single-engined light aircraft he shared with the neighbouring farmer across the valley.

An outdoor life raising white Charolais cattle had provided some degree of fulfilment after his few years at the Bar. Marrying a farmer's daughter with a great appetite for life and being blessed with two daughters, one outgoing and with a love for animals and another rather introspective, had helped him create a new and successful career in a world far removed from wigs, gowns and injustice.

By the time he had unmoored the plane and conducted his pre-flight check he could feel the sun beating down on his back and he threw the weathered brown-leather flying jacket into the cockpit. He'd won that jacket in a game of poker with a couple of pilots after the drop into Egypt and it had seen him through many a frosty Somerset dawn, tractor-towing fifteen hundred pound cows out of deep, muddy ditches.

Today he was flying to a grass airstrip just outside Carlisle to meet a cattle dealer for lunch in the hope of buying a new bull. Prices were high at the moment and he'd suffered a disaster, in that a bull he'd purchased in the winter from Scotland, had sired three fatally defective calves from three different cows. Some obscure genetic flaw had produced joints in the animals that went into immediate dislocation rendering them unable to stand and leading to rapid death. It had been an expensive and distressing episode and he needed a sound and healthy replacement. But the magnificent weather, and belief that he could strike a satisfactory deal in Carlisle, had lifted his spirits and a sense of liberation filled his soul as he powered the craft faster and faster down the tarmac until that critical moment when he would pull back on the control yoke and soar into the heavens above.

But this time, as he hit his optimum take-off speed, the cockpit seat sheared from its latch, rocketing him backwards and causing such a sudden pull-back on the yoke that the aircraft pitched violently at a height of only about thirty feet in the air, before stalling and hurtling him back towards the ground and violent, flame-engulfed death. There were but a few terrifying seconds between his realisation of the inevitability of his fate and death itself. In those few seconds he thought of only one thing. He thought of Henry Stanton.

Chapter 3

Searchlight, Nevada, USA June 1989

102 degrees and rising. She was sizzling like a greasy sausage in a frying pan. Inside the trailer was worse than outside. Despite making as much noise as a steam locomotive going uphill, the air conditioner crudely lodged in the window of the sitting area just couldn't cope. It had been on its last legs for a couple of years now but she had never seemed to have the funds to replace it. Tonight she was working, so she'd call in at Artie's Electrics on Paradise Road and see what was on offer. This was the first really hot day of summer and she wasn't ready for it. Stripped down to her bra and panties, she lay slumped on the lawn chair that she'd placed in the open doorway of the tin-can trailer that she now called home. Her heavy breasts were covered in a sheen of sweat and she ran a tea towel over them to wipe it away, admiring the fact that despite the passing years she'd kept her body in the kind of shape that had never left her short of customers. The belly was still flat, the beam was not too broad and the legs were as shapely as the girls in the big Hotel chorus lines. But the face was another story. As hard as a slab of concrete. Dyed blonde hair. Fleshy cheeks. Cash register eyes you couldn't see behind and a cruel mouth. Reaching for a can of Mountain Dew she'd just taken from the fridge, she poured half of its contents straight down her throat in one hit, enjoying the cooling sensation of the sticky overflow running down her chin and in between those generous breasts that still kept her in business.

There were only half a dozen trailers on this site. All permanent. Well spread out. Fixed on bricks. No wheels. Tucked up against the side of a rock face on the outskirts of the few shanty buildings that the few hundred locals called town. At the beginning of the century it boasted a population bigger than Vegas, but that was when the mines were producing and the Barnwell and Searchlight Railroads connected the town with the main Santa Fe Line. By the time of the Depression the railroad was a washed-out ruin, the mines were gaping holes in the barren terrain, rusting machinery lay abandoned across the landscape and most of the people had left. Now there was a sprinkling of bars, a couple of excuses for casinos and a paved road with little traffic that took you to Vegas in less than an hour. Strangely, for such a hard-bitten woman, she took pleasure in the isolation and enjoyed the eucalyptus and oleander trees, the coyotes and the desert tortoises. They were so alien to her upbringing, but somehow she related to them. Although she plucked her dollars off the lonely strangers on the Strip, she preferred to live well away from the relentless bright lights. A loner now. Neither desire, nor need, for any permanent man.

Taking another swig from the can of Mountain Dew, she thought about the men that had brought her down to where she was. Every downward step had involved a man. None more so than Jerry Mandolay. She'd run into him at Toot's Place on 56th Street in Manhattan. It was her first time in New York. A one week trip with a couple of girlfriends. It was electric. Throbbing. Exploding with energy. And, back then, wow, was she a looker. Jerry was at least ten years older than her, although she never learned his exact age. From Baton Rouge, Louisiana. A charmer. Jet black hair. Moustache. A touch of Creole in his dark, olive looks and a voice to die for. When Jerry sang, the world stopped. He only ever got lounge bar spots because he was a waster. Completely unreliable. A womanizer. A drug taker. And free with his fists. Of course, she knew none of the down-side when his eyes picked her out in Toot's Place, as he stood in the spotlight on the tiny stage, displaying that soft voice of magic. He seduced her that same night. Minimal token resistance. Begged her to leave her life in the land from where she came and team up with him.

At the end of the week she'd gone home, thought about nothing else but Jerry Mandolay and, three months later, she was back in America living with him, moving from town to town. He got a spot in the Lounge Bar at the Sands in Vegas. Only the early evening spot, but a big break. They'd got married in the Chapel of Love on Sahara Avenue. Then he re-christened her. She became Tammy. And that's when she learned he was a pimp.

"Adult rattler sitting right under the front of yer trailer," a husky male voice called out, interrupting her reverie. "You want me to take his head off, Tammy? I like doin' that."

Jumping up from her chair, slipping on a pair of flip-flops, she came straight down the three-step platform and on to the rock-hard ground, making no attempt to cover up what she had on offer. Old Pete Hatcher had seen it all before, but that didn't mean he didn't like looking. Or thinking about it. He'd lived in some shack out on the edges of Searchlight for over fifty years, since the days when the population was less than a hundred. For as long as anybody could remember he'd been the town weirdo, the grave digger at the small cemetery out in the desert and eking out a few dollars selling Indian artifacts and jewellery from a small hut perched right at the crossroads, where the road to Vegas hit the downhill paved track to Lake Mojave bursting with its bass, bluegill and catfish fourteen miles away. A massive lake in the middle of the desert. Only in America.

"Can you fix him, Pete?" she asked anxiously. Whilst she'd grown to like the wild burros and the roadrunners, she'd never got used to spiders and was terrified of snakes. The gnarled old man looked her up and down, lizard eyes lingering on the parts just about covered by the damp underwear, then parted his lips in what passed for a smile, thereby exposing his four remaining yellow teeth, well aware of her feelings towards snakes.

Gingerly picking her way behind the bearded figure, in his dusty blue denim coveralls and faded Giants baseball cap, she heard the rattler before she saw him. He'd emerged from underneath the trailer and was coiled on the worn dirt path that led from her trailer to her battered Ford F-150 pick-up truck. She'd heard the noise before, when the adult was frightened, and was preparing to strike. Whilst it rattled its tail segments together, the actual noise it produced wasn't so much a rattle, but more like the sound of static electricity crackling in the still air.

"Six foot if he's an inch," grunted Pete, now armed with the razor-edged spade that had been leaning on the side of the trailer. Yellowish-brown with speckled banded markings. Heavy-bodied and as thick as her arm, the rattler had now lifted his large triangular head on its thin neck and was making his decision. Elliptical pupils in the eyes. The really dangerous type. Strike or retreat? But wily old Pete made the decision for him, moving with surprising speed for an old man, he drove the edge of the spade straight at a point about six inches below the open mouth and exposed fangs and sliced the rattler's head off its body. Not quite off in one clean hit, but good enough. Grinding the spade through the remaining muscle, tendon and skin on the rocky ground, he separated head from body whilst she watched the six feet of headless creature continuing to writhe, contort and twitch.

"He'll twitch for a couple of hours yet," muttered the old timer, relishing the killing. "Nerves. But he's as dead as this shitty town." Still muttering, he levered the spade under the body and catapulted it into the brush, quickly followed by the head. "Dinner for the coyotes," he added, scraping the slimed edge of the spade in the dust before leaning it back against the trailer.

"I hate those mothers. I owe you, Pete," she said with a sense of relief to the disappearing back of the old man. "Call by for a beer sometime. Gotta make it into Vegas right now."

Such was life in Searchlight, Nevada in the summer of '89.

A couple of hours later she was bowling along a deserted US 95 in the old, brown Ford truck towards Vegas. Stick shift. She'd never got used to automatics. By the time she reached *Artie's*, at the Airport end of Paradise Road, the thermometer had hit 105 degrees and, now she was amidst all the concrete and glass, it felt even hotter. Dusk was still a while away, but the neon was rippling and crackling across the panorama. Searing, relentless heat. Walk half a dozen paces and you were soaked. One hundred and forty dollars for a new air conditioner. She sure needed to make some money tonight. Artie heaved the heavy box into the cab of the pickup, cussing and whining at being dragged out into the Nevada sun. About the only reason she missed having a man on the scene was to do all the shifting and carrying but, she reflected, before Jerry had moved on to a newer model, he had seldom lifted a finger anyway, except to trouser the night's takings.

Even though it was a Monday night the Strip was already heaving. The neon was exploding across the vision, high into the sky, whilst the traffic was solid in both directions and the people, a dozen deep on the sidewalks, sweltered as they guzzled their long margueritas and gawped amidst the fleshpots, green baize and armies of flashing and bell-ringing one-arm bandits.

Ellie's Exotic Escorts Agency rented a small office in a side street, west of the Union Pacific Railroad tracks off the back of Industrial. Swinging the Ford into a parking place in the alleyway at the side of the office, she reached in the back for her holdall containing the work uniforms of the night. Two short length skirts, two low-cut blouses, two sets of underwear, three pairs of tights and a few miscellaneous gadgets of the trade.

"Got ya a nine o'clock at The Riviera," Barbara announced as soon as she put one foot through the door. Given the nature of the business, it was hard to imagine a more incongruous manageress. Mid-fifties, operator's headset and mike worn over the grey tied-back hair, tortoiseshell glasses and as seemingly prim and proper as a hick town librarian. Barbara arranged the girls' encounters with the same bureaucratic efficiency as she would catalogue the romantic fiction. All business was done over the phone. The spot men on the strip dished out the flyers, advertising girls with bodies and faces that didn't exist, lured in the phone calls, allocated the escort according to the age, colour, gender and speciality requested, all openly discussed by Barbara as if she was discussing the week's new book arrivals. Payment up front by credit card. Half of it to the escort, the other half to the House. Gratuity in cash at the rendezvous. "No gratuity accepted less than a C note." That's how Barbara put it.

"Has he got a name?" Tammy asked, as she headed towards the relaxation room and showers where the girls got changed and prepared for the night's assaults.

"Graham Chauncey. Room 1642. Riviera. Usual arrangements," Barbara replied as the phone rang again and she moved on to the next cattle sale.

By the time that she sidled into the back room at the Riviera she'd worked the war paint as best she could but the face had grown no less hard. Crimson, low-cut blouse, slinky black skirt, black stilettos and fish net tights. Whilst the woman was expensive to hire, she remained inescapably cheap to look at.

The trick duly arrived. Early sixties. A full head of iron grey hair. Well worn face with plenty of creases. Generous mouth. Just under six feet, fifteen pounds overweight but solid build. Wearing a mass-produced, badly cut lime green linen jacket and light blue Dockers that didn't go with the jacket, he homed in on the only table occupied by a solo woman.

"Are you Tammy?" he asked politely enough.

"Sit yourself down, honey," she replied, slipping easily into the synthetic patter that passed for a third-rate mating dance.

Security had toughened up in the big hotels. They were looking for the family business. Theme parks on the roof, tigers in the lobby, circus acts overhead. Whilst they wanted the raunchy image and the big dollars from the men in town on their own, they had become nervous about upsetting the wives and mothers. Any idea of hanging out in one of the bars displaying enough flesh to make a catch belonged to yesterday. Security would throw them out. So now, it was a touch more discreet. Meet the guy in the restaurant. Make him buy dinner. More of a full service than fifteen minutes in the hay. Pushes the prices up at the same time. Up to his room with him so as to get past Security at the elevators. Plus, the men behind the agency paid the Security at the main hotels a retainer to look the other way. The room number was logged back at the office and the girls wore an alarm bracelet which they could activate if they were in trouble and a couple of heavies could be at the door within a few minutes. A new way of operating, but the merchandise on offer was as old as the purple mountains that surrounded the Vegas basin.

"Where you from?" she enquired over the two Jack Daniels that had quickly arrived via the cocktail waitress. If he was disappointed that the face didn't seem to match up to the quality of the body, then he was making a good job of disguising it.

"England. Near Canterbury. You heard of it?"

"Course I have. It's got a big cathedral. Long way from the Riviera Hotel."

"I like this place," he answered. "Says in the book that they used to pay Liberace $50,000 a week to play here over thirty years ago. I'm into stuff like that."

"Yeah. Now they got *Crazy Girls*. Topless. Tastes change. Next week they're filming a Mickey Spillane movie just outside on The Strip. Anything you want. It's all here. So long as you got the necessary."

"Money counts," he agreed. "Same in England."

"But you don't get rattlers in England," she laughed nervously. "Had one on the porch today. Makes my skin creep. Took his head off."

Empty talk, between lonely people, over mass-produced food thrown on the griddle by immigrant fast-food cooks, served by waitresses with aching feet and brains addled by the heat and the grim realisation that they were never going to make it. Reduced to carrying fodder to a couple more losers. Just glad to have a job that wasn't on the graveyard shift.

Then came the time when Tammy had to deliver the goods. Just last year the Riviera had added the Monaco Tower, a new 24 storey extension costing nearly $28 million and taking the number of rooms in the hotel to over two thousand. Room number 1642 was a generous sized room on the 16th floor of the new Tower, looking out over the Strip which was now ablaze with a million lights forever screaming out where to stay, who to see, what to eat, who won how much and where to gamble. The King size bed was on a raised platform in the centre of the room with a bedcover of hideous purple velvet.

Undoing her blouse all the way down without words or ceremony, she turned on her hollow smile of invitation, patting the bed alongside her and crossing her legs so that the skirt exposed the requisite expanse of inner thigh to start the bidding. For the first time in the evening Graham Chauncey began to look uncomfortable. She knew nothing about him and the less she knew the better. That had been the first lesson that Jerry had taught her. This was the stage of the proceedings when she called the shots and clawed in the roubles. She was already a hundred and forty dollars down on the air conditioner. Throwing his jacket over the armchair in the corner of the room, he sat himself on the bed where directed, but his eyes weren't on the cleavage or thighs where they were supposed to be. They were fixed on the floor.

"I guess the office told you a C note for the basics," she began in her softer voice, well practised as an opening. "Make it a couple of hundred, honey, and you'll get a lot more than that."

"We're not here for that," he replied sharply. "I'll pay you the couple of hundred alright. But not for sex."

"What the fuck are you saying here?" she barked, seeking to retain the initiative. "You into violence or summat?"

"No," he replied vehemently, getting up off the bed and marching over to the armchair. "All you have to do is talk. Talk to me about certain things."

"What the hell you mean? Talk sex? Talk dirty? What you saying?" she snapped. "Don't you like what you see?"

As her tone stiffened, she watched his demeanour change. Now perched on the arm of the chair in the corner of the room, he was seeking to take charge. Make the demands. His eyes were straining to see behind her mascara and false eyelashes and there was a look of determination about him that unsettled her. Graham Chauncey was starting to give the impression of a man accustomed to getting what he wanted.

"I like what I see, Tammy. It's nothing to do with your looks. And the talking is just that. Talking," he declared, fishing out two one hundred dollar bills and holding them up for her to see. "It's yours," he added, "won't take long, once you agree to talk."

From his angle, the harsh overhead lighting in the room was picking out some of the lines in her face that the cheap make-up was designed to hide. Small vertical lines over the upper lip and a narrow furrow above the bridge of the nose from too many years of scowling and screwing her eyes up at the grubby people with whom she'd had to deal.

Uncrossing her legs and leaning forward, so as to reveal even more cleavage, she reactivated the techniques which usually secured the transfer of the dollars from the man's hand into her purse. "Let's be having the money then, honey," she cooed, "then we'll talk about any goddamned thing you choose."

The man walked slowly and deliberately over to the writing desk to the side of the picture window, picked up the heavy green ashtray emblazoned with Riviera Hotel in red lettering and placed the two hundred dollar bills underneath it. "All yours," he announced. "When you talk to me. About murder."

"Murder! So you're just a fucking crazy, are you?" she shrieked at him, jumping up from the bed, grabbing her bag and heading for the door. When he moved quickly towards her she surreptitiously pressed the alarm on the wrist band that the Agency provided.

"Calm down, Tammy," he demanded, cutting her off from the door but being careful not to appear to threaten her physically. "I'm not crazy and you're not in any danger. I'm a retired Police Officer. I used to be Detective Sergeant Chauncey. That's what I mean when I say I want to talk to you about murder."

Still clutching her bag and struggling to button up her blouse with one hand, the woman stopped dead in her tracks and stared at him long and hard. Just like that rattler had stared at old Pete a few hours earlier. Far from calming her down, his words seemed to drive her to a new intensity. Sweat had broken out on her forehead and the corners of her mouth were twitching. Underneath the war paint he could see that the blood had drained from her face and lips. Even the two hundred dollars seemed to have taken a back seat as she suddenly lurched for the door, scrabbling to open it before he had time to react. But, even in retirement, he was too quick for her and grabbed instinctively at her wrist, wrenching it off the brass handle.

"I haven't travelled all this way for nothing," he spat out. "You just sit down, talk to me about murder and collect your two hundred dollars. Treat it as a bit of business."

"OK. OK, you bastard," she breathed. "OK. Let go of me first and then we'll talk."

As he released her wrist from his grip his shoulders dropped a touch and he started to relax. That's when she lashed out at him with all the venom of the alley cat that she had become and probably always had been. She didn't hit him with an open hand but with a clenched fist, straight in the mouth and he wasn't expecting it. The imitation emerald ring that she sported on her right middle finger split his lip. At the same instant the bedroom door flew open and two burly Latinos burst in, bowling him over on to the bed. While they pinned him down the woman walked deliberately over to the green ashtray. She wasn't intending to talk about any murder but she still had an air conditioner to pay for.

Chapter 4

Tanna Island, Vanuatu, South Pacific October 1989

There were no paved roads on Tanna and for most of the twenty five miles across the island he was forcing the old Land Rover Series 111 across fertile bush, rich in kava, copra, yams and coconut, through ancient rainforest of palm and banyan trees, over raw rock and then out on to the lava ash plains that surrounded Mount Yasur. The final ascent up the side of the volcano was the most demanding of all as he fought to get the vehicle within a couple of hundred yards of the crater rim, crunching over chunks of rock and around reformed boulders that the rumbling monster had spewed out into the sky.

It was already dusk by the time he came to a halt with the vehicle anchored at a precarious angle, leaving his passengers only a short climb to the edge of the rim. There had already been a couple of eruptions as they had battled up the southern side of the volcano and he warned his tentative group that they must not venture beyond the outer edge of the rim as further eruptions would occur with unpredictable degrees of ferocity. Right on cue, as they clambered out of the Land Rover, the mighty rumbling began again from deep within the bowels of the earth and glowing ash and showers of rocks the size of basketballs were hurled a hundred feet into the sky, before thudding down on to the edges of the rim and beyond, still glowing bright red before beginning to cool and reform into new shapes.

With the acrid smell of sulphur in their nostrils and the sensation in the soles of their feet of the heat simmering below the thin crust, they picked their way upwards in single file following his every turn and command as they neared the crater's lip. A long plume of grey ash lingered above them and the thunderous booming began anew as they finally peered over the edge into the three cavernous mouths that lay below. Within the central crater there was a sea of bright orange, a seething mass of churning lava, so primeval and overwhelming that it almost seemed to call for human sacrifice in recognition of its terrifying power. It always reminded him of looking back to the creation of Earth itself. As the blackness of the night descended, the colours from within the monster took on ever more fiery shades of red and orange.

Despite the spectacular display that Mother Nature was providing, he was unable to prevent his eyes from wandering away from the fire below to steal glances at the only young female in the party. On this trip to the volcano he was in charge of five people. Two retired Australian businessmen from Adelaide, a middle-aged couple from Auckland and this fair-skinned, wildly attractive girl from somewhere in England. He had been captivated by her as soon as he had picked the party up off the boat at Lanarkal yesterday morning but, other than basic introductions on the short journey to their accommodation, he had had little chance to talk to her as she had set off snorkelling on the coral reef as soon as he had delivered the party to the small inn where he was working for the summer. From fifty yards away he had observed the lithe, long-legged figure in a turquoise bikini, confidently heading for the beach carrying snorkel and goggles. Any expectation of seeing her at the one large dinner table where all of the guests dined together had been thwarted by the generator breaking down as soon as the dinner gong had been rung. There was no electricity and the generator was vital. It had taken him two hours to fix it and, by the time he had emerged from the shed, all of the guests had retired to bed. There was no light provided after nine o'clock, and the guests were always exhausted by then anyway, after their nine hour journey on the old rust bucket from Port Vila on the main island and the day's activities.

It was only when she clambered aboard the Land Rover the next afternoon that he had any real chance to talk to her. She had sat in the back, but he could see her face clearly in his driving mirror as they set off for the volcano. Her complexion was text book English rose. No make-up. Her hair was light brown, worn carelessly and long. But it was her eyes that dominated her whole being. They were almond-shaped and as blue as the South Pacific seas that surrounded the island. In a yellow T-shirt and tailored shorts, her full figure and sun-tanned legs completed the picture. By the time the vehicle had travelled from the Inn to the first section of bush, he'd learned she had an easy manner about her, was quick to laugh, and, most importantly, was travelling alone. Crossing the lush White Grass plains, three magnificent wild horses had run alongside the vehicle and she had asked him to stop so that she might take photographs of them, explaining that horses were her passion. After that the tracks became so rough and the driving so demanding that conversation with anyone other than the immediate neighbour became virtually impossible.

Once on the rim his small party stopped and found rocks upon which to sit and watch the show. The older members of the group were still panting from the exertions of the climb, but she appeared untroubled as she settled on a smooth-sided boulder and pulled her camera from a small rucksack.

"Like me to take a picture of you sitting on top of one of the world's most active volcanoes?" he enquired with a smile.

"Yes, I would. It's one of the drawbacks of travelling alone. You get no photographs of yourself," she laughed as she handed him the camera and smiled easily when he pressed the shutter. The flash of the camera coincided with another convulsion from below and a fountain of fire exploded across the sky lighting him up against a stunning backdrop. He wasn't handsome in any classic sense, but so very dark with crinkly black hair, worn too long; his nose had been broken twice at Australian Rules, and he had a noticeable overbite where the lower jaw protruded slightly beyond the upper. Picked out by the weird lights of the show that nature was providing, he seemed to present as a solid and comfortable young man.

"I don't know your name," he continued, after handing back the camera and then perching himself alongside her, waiting for the monster to perform its next act.

"George," she answered. "Really Georgina, of course, but everybody calls me George. I've heard that you're Cal."

"Yeah, Cal Stewart," he replied. "From Sydney. Just got my degree in mechanical engineering. Got a job for six months out here on Tanna. Maintaining all the gear at the Inn, doing the volcano trips. That kind of stuff."

"It's a strange place to spend six months," she volunteered. "No electricity, no proper roads, no TV, very few white people."

"Well, until relatively recently, they used to eat white people," he answered. "Many a missionary ended up in the cooking pot. Man Tanna is still a pretty ferocious warrior, but if you respect their ways it's an interesting enough place. Time enough for a more conventional life when I get back to Oz."

"When did the white man first come here?" she asked, listening with interest to the strong Australian accent with the typical throw-away delivery.

"Limey. One of your lot. Captain Cook. 1774. He was sailing by in HMS Resolution and saw Mount Yasur exploding into the sky. It's been erupting for over eight hundred years. Cookie landed and tried to take a closer look at the volcano. But in those days there was a taboo on climbing it and Man Tanna stopped him. Didn't have him for dinner though."

At that moment the other four members of the party moved over to join them, seeking the assurance of the proximity of their guide as full night descended and the eruptions seemed to grow even more intimidating. Their arrival inhibited any further private conversation with the girl. After two hours and dozens of photographs he announced to the party that it was time to head back to the Land Rover and the three hour drive that awaited them. Leading the way with his torch he suddenly felt a soft hand slip into his right hand as, without embarrassment, she asked for some assistance over the ash and loose rock. On arriving back at the vehicle, the old Aussie who'd sat next to him on the journey out, told George to take his place in the front and so, with her bare leg pressed tightly against his own, he had set off on the precarious drive down the side of the volcano and back across the island. Driving in these conditions at night was extremely dangerous and required all of his concentration, leaving little opportunity for idle chat and, by the time that he was back on the flat lava plains she, like all of the other four, was fast asleep, her pretty head frequently coming to rest on his broad shoulder as he steered them home through the darkness. A sandwich and a cold drink were set out on the communal dining table awaiting the party on their return and then he was required to refuel the Land Rover from the heavy oil drums in the maintenance work shed so that it would be available for the morning's errands. By the time he got back she had gone to bed.

* * *

Marilyn Monroe didn't turn up for work the next morning. She was one of the two local girls employed on waitressing and housekeeping duties and was just about as reliable as her namesake. Whilst there was no television on Tanna, most of the inhabitants had, at some stage in their lives, made the nine hour boat trip to Port Vila on Efarte, which was the main island of the eighty three islands that made up the archipelago of the New Hebrides, latterly known as Vanuatu, since it gained its independence in 1980 from the territorially acquisitive French and British Colonialists. Port Vila might not boast a traffic light or a proper Police Force, but it had television, beamed in from the Australian mainland and replaying all the old Hollywood movies night and day. A constant diet of Burt Lancaster, Kirk Douglas, Katherine Hepburn, Humphrey Bogart and numerous other legends.

Such a cultural tsunami had an immediate and major impact on the given names of the native Ni-Vanuatans and this overnight breakthrough soon found its way to the neighbouring islands. The three young deckhands on the Port Vila-Tanna ferry were Happy, Lazy and Grumpy. The Tanna Post Office was manned by Spencer Tracy and Lauren Bacall. In the midst of the Tanna bush you were just as likely to happen across Tony Curtis as you were to bump into Kalcot Keaspaka. And so it was that Marilyn Monroe waited table and made beds at the Tanna Inn, at such time as she remembered to walk the four miles from her thatched hut in the bush and turn up for work. Her absence meant that Cal had extra duties that day and would not be free until late afternoon.

Running backwards and forwards from the kitchen to the communal dining table on the open veranda with plates of pineapple, banana, paw-paw and mango and cups of full strength Tanna coffee left little opportunity to speak to George but, when she and the lady from Auckland set off for a walk along the beach he took the bull by the horns and he asked her if she might be free to do some diving later in the day. With an open smile she agreed to meet him at the Green Lagoon on the eastern beach at four o'clock.

By lunchtime, Marilyn Monroe, attired in the loose, floral *Mother Hubbard* type dress with billowing shoulders that the native women wore had bothered to show up and enabled him to finish his chores earlier than expected so, armed with reef shoes, snorkels and masks he wandered along to the cluster of small, thatched guest bungalows which were set amidst the lush green vegetation and surrounded by rubber and palm trees. From the raised porch of each bungalow there was an unobstructed panorama across the white beach to the stunning South Pacific waters. At the shoreline the water was still and translucent as it ran over the coral before the reef fell away into deeper waters and the surface colour changed to varying shades of electric blue.

Two native-carved rocking chairs were positioned at each end of the porch and, as he came out of the trees, he could see her gently rocking backwards and forwards, her head, covered by a fashionable straw hat, angled downwards indicating that she was immersed in some book.

"Good story, lady?" he chirped out in an overblown Aussie drawl which caused her to look up and smile in his direction.

"The best there is," she replied. "Written by a free spirit."

Leaning on the wooden support of the porch he looked up at her. Wearing the same turquoise bikini as he had seen her in before, with bare feet and the dashing hat, she looked stunning. Being an Aussie, he told her.

"You look a million dollars, George," he exclaimed. "And, you're right about the book. Jack Kerouac. *On The Road.* I've read it half a dozen times."

Nodding approvingly, as if he had gone up another notch in her estimation, she slowly rose from her chair and disappeared into her bungalow, emerging a minute later with her own diving gear in a raffia shoulder bag and minus the hat. Her long hair was now tied tightly back and the full shape and softness of her face became even more striking.

"He died at 47, you know," she remarked, as they set off down the path towards the Green Lagoon. "I mean Kerouac. Alcoholic, conservative and disillusioned."

"That's because the America he wrote about ceased to exist. It left him with nothing," came the perceptive answer, prompting her to nod again in the same approving manner as before.

The narrow path ran through frangipani and hibiscus, growing denser as they neared the beach. At one point they had to squeeze their way past an enormous banyan tree with its scores of intertwining trunks. As she stopped beneath its vast canopy she was suddenly aware of a scuttling noise in the vegetation beneath her feet when, in an instant, Cal ran towards her and stamped half a dozen times with all his weight on whatever creature had been heading towards her.

"Handradlegs," he exclaimed breathlessly, when he was sure that it was dead, picking up a stick and parting the foliage to reveal a giant black centipede squashed on the ground. About six inches long, with the circumference of a broom handle, it lay about two paces from where she had been standing.

"Vicious bite," he explained. "Can kill a child. Would have made you very ill and hurt like hell."

"Why's it called handradlegs," she asked, far more alarmed now she knew what it was and what it could do than she had been on first becoming aware of it.

"Bislama. Vanuatu pigeon English. Giant centipede. A hundred legs. Get it?" he laughed as they continued down the path, now emerging on to the wide beach of magnificent, soft white sand which fell gently away to the waters of the Green Lagoon.

"Do they still really use pigeon English?" she asked.

"All the time," he replied, stripping off his shirt and pulling on the reef shoes necessary to protect his feet from the razor edges of the coral, acutely aware of her watching him, assessing the sun-darkened skin, the cut of the muscles, the narrow waist and the obvious power of the frame.

"OK, George. I guess you've been in already, but let me give you an idea of what you'll see. Brightly coloured tropical fish. Nearly all harmless. A dozen different types of coral. Elkhorn fire, branch coral, brain coral. Don't touch it. It'll cut you to shreds and likely give you a serious infection."

Since they'd arrived on the beach, she had remained silent and seemed to be taking his measure in all he said and did and, as they picked their way cautiously into the crystal-clear green waters, masks and snorkels now in place, she was observing his sure-footedness and self-assurance.

Vanuatan coastal waters are as warm as the European's bath. The mass of coral reached to within six feet of the surface. Sometimes mountainous with overhangs and caves. Sometimes long tunnels leading into gardens of acropora. Myriads of amazingly coloured fish darted hither and thither, within an arm's length of her mask, but so quick and elusive as never to be within grasp. There were fish that had the exact appearance of leopards, covered with black and yellow spots, some that were the colour of the red molten lava she had seen erupt from within the volcano the night before and even small brown sharks which seemed far more afraid of her than she was of them. With a nod of his head, Cal communicated to her that they were harmless.

For two hours they swam, dived, rested on the beach and then swam and dived some more. She saw more varieties of fish in those two hours than she had ever seen in her whole lifetime. When they lay chatting on the beach, he would explain to her what they had seen and she would listen and observe some more. He spoke with authority of squid, cuttlefish and nautiluses. Creatures that they had seen that had adapted to the sea. Molluscs that had acquired flexibility. Fish that could change their colour or had developed a form of jet propulsion and even cephalopods that had learned to grow three hearts.

Occasionally he tried to prompt her to talk about herself, but she would gently deflect the conversation away from anything too personal and bring it back to him. When she felt she had had enough sun for the day, they wandered slowly back up the path and, on the steps of her bungalow, she thanked him for such a wonderful experience. She meant what she said and he knew it and liked it. The staff were not allowed to dine with the guests, but she asked him to come and join her on her porch after dinner and share a bottle of Australian Chardonnay that she had brought with her.

And so it was, on a remote island, later on during a balmy tropical night, that she changed his life for ever.

Sipping Chardonnay from their thick bathroom glasses, as they sat lazily on the porch rocking chairs, he was choosing his moment to try to kiss her. Meanwhile, she was choosing her moment. To drop a bombshell. It was so dark that he could only just make her out a few feet away from him, so he could not see her eyes when she spoke.

"I have a very big confession to make," she began nervously.

"What?" he asked, interest now well aroused.

"Up on the volcano last night," she continued, her voice thin and anxious. When you told me your name was Cal Stewart."

"Yeah?"

"I already knew."

"You knew my name?"

"More than just that. I knew exactly who you were. You're the reason I came to Tanna."

"Hang on a minute," he exclaimed as interest gave way to concern. "We've never met before. We're complete strangers."

"I had to come and see you for myself. Before deciding whether I should tell you or to just let it die," she said, ignoring his response.

"What the hell are you talking about, George? Let what die? You're getting really creepy here. I don't like what you're saying."

"I know things which may change your life. I had to meet you to decide if you could handle it. My judgement is that you can," she announced, using words that seemed carefully selected and rehearsed.

"Stuff the melodrama," he protested, pulling his chair even closer to hers in an attempt to see her features and read the expression in her eyes. "If you've got something important to say, then say it. Or are you just some kind of drama queen?"

"Just hold fire. This is a tough call for me. I risk damaging your relationship with your mother and I risk knocking you sideways. That's why I've travelled ten thousand miles to see you. To observe you. And then make the decision. I suspect you'll hate me forever once I've told you." The words were now tumbling out, with increasing urgency as spontaneity took over and previous rehearsal was abandoned.

"There's only one way to find out, isn't there? You're frightening me. So just spit it out," he demanded.

"OK. Here goes," she sighed. "Your mother lives in Sydney. She's a nurse. Her name's Jane Stewart. You're an only child."

"So what? Any of the other staff here could have told you that. We spend hours together every day talking about ourselves. There's not much else to do out of working hours."

"You've never met your father," she continued, paying no attention to his responses. "I suspect that your mother has told you little or nothing about him."

"Ma told me that she had a brief relationship with some guy in England. I was the result. It didn't work out. She came to Australia and she heard soon after I was born that he was dead. That's all I've ever known," he replied.

"The fact is that your mother has protected you from the truth. I've agonised for nearly a year over what to do. In the end I decided that I must find you. Watch you. And make a judgement. I hadn't bargained for you being in such a remote place and forcing me to make a judgement so quickly."

"Bloody Hell, George. Are you going to tell me that my father is alive? That you're also his child? That you're my sister?" he shouted.

"No, Cal. Nothing like that. Your father is dead. He died before you were born. There's just no easy way of saying this," she continued, biting her lip as her voice wavered and a tear ran down her cheek, although he could not see it in the dark. "Perhaps when you've heard it all you'll understand why I'm doing this and will forgive me for telling you. Your father was convicted of murder and hanged. In England."

"Jesus," he exclaimed. "Holy Jesus. Where on earth did you get that from?"

"From my own father. He's dead now. Killed in a plane crash last year. But your father's death haunted him. He used to talk about it. To my sister, mum and me. He also wrote it all down. I found it in his papers after his death. He never got over it. You see . . . and this is the hardest part of all. My father was convinced that your father was innocent. He was hanged for a murder he never committed."

"Jesus," he kept repeating. "Jesus. Hanged? How did your father get involved in all of this?"

"My father was the barrister who defended him. And lost. It drove him to such despair that he gave up being a lawyer. Became a farmer in Somerset. He never came to terms with what had happened."

"So why have you come here?" he demanded to know.

"Because you and I have a joint burden to bear. Your father was wrongly convicted of murder. It wasn't my father's fault. He did everything he could, but it wasn't enough. But my father had a conscience and such a burning sense of injustice that it plagued him until the day he died. You and I have got to put this right. Until we do, neither of them can rest in peace." Her voice had now regained its composure and her words carried purpose and authority. This was the announcement of her mission. These were the words she had reflected upon for the best part of a year, formulated in ignorance of what kind of person she may be addressing them to. Now she had seen him, she had no doubt.

"Put it right? Put it right? How can we put it right over twenty five years later if your father never could at the time or soon afterwards?" he asked angrily.

"I don't know. Obviously, I've thought very hard about it. I've got some ideas. We'll have to develop a plan once you know the whole story. I've got my father's actual notebook from the trial. He kept a record of everything. Every piece of evidence. Every answer from the witnesses. Most of the Judge's summing up. He kept all of the original case papers. The photographs of the scene. And all his Advices and Appeals and Opinions. His own notes. I've got copies of it all in my bag. So long as you agree, I'm going to leave it here for you to study and then we'll have to decide the best way forward."

"Oh no! It's not as easy as that," he responded aggressively. "You can't drop a bombshell like this on me and then expect me to come to decisions just like that. I need time to think and you'll be gone tomorrow."

"I told you. I hadn't realised you'd be stuck out in the middle of bloody nowhere. I'd hoped for more time. To come down to Sydney. Make a decision. Spend a week or two with you and then work on it together by phone and letters. It's going to take a long time. It'll have to be fitted into our lives, as and when we can arrange things."

"How did you ever find me?"

"Actually it was very easy. After the execution your mother decided to leave England immediately. She got a ten pound assisted passage to Sydney. Changed her name from Stanton to Stewart. So when you were born in Sydney you were registered as Cal Stewart. Once she'd settled in Sydney she wrote my dad a letter. You can read it. She wanted him to be able to contact her if ever anything turned up which might clear your father. Whenever you moved address she let dad know. It's all in his file," she explained carefully.

"But I'd left Sydney."

"Yes. So when I eventually decided that I had to meet you, I phoned your mother. I just said I was an old friend from school and were you at home."

"And what did Ma say?"

"She laughed. Said you'd gone off to some tiny island where they grew coffee and lived underneath a volcano. Tanna. Gave me the name of this place where you were working. You wouldn't be back in Sydney for six months. The rest was easy."

"Do you have this letter Ma wrote after I was born? I want to see it."

"I've only got a copy. It's in my case," she answered, getting up off the rocking chair and touching him gently on the shoulder, before disappearing inside the tiny bungalow.

When she returned she was holding a large buff folder from which she extracted a single piece of paper and handed it to him. He switched on his torch and sat poring over a letter which seemed destined to change his life.

Dear Mr Walgrave,

As I promised you before I left England I would let you know my whereabouts. My address is as set out at the top of this letter and if I move I will let you know of any new address. I beg you to get in touch immediately if any fresh evidence emerges which we can use to get the case reopened. It is too late for Henry but never too late for his name.

My son is now six months old. His name is Cal. Despite my promise to Henry, I don't know if I shall ever have the strength to tell him the truth. That is a decision for the future. At the moment I live from day to day and have just started a job at a small cottage hospital on the outskirts of the city.

Not a day goes by without my thinking of Henry. I shall never get over it. We both know he was innocent and no-one could have fought harder for him than you did. It is important that you understand that I do not blame you in any way. I read in the newspapers that there may soon be a debate in Parliament about abolishing the death penalty. It cannot be soon enough. I can only pray that no other woman ever has to suffer what I am enduring and that one day Henry is pardoned.

I have changed our family name to Stewart.

God Bless you, Mr Walgrave. You are a good man.

Yours sincerely,

Jane Stewart

"You've got one hell of a nerve to do this to me," he eventually whispered. "What am I going to say to Ma? How can I look her in the eye and know she's got this terrible secret without telling her I know?"

"I've agonised over that for months," she replied. "But imagine if the positions were reversed. If it was my father who'd been wrongly convicted. What would you do? Just write him off?"

"That was a judgement for my mother. Not for you," he barked back at her.

"I told you that you'd hate me for doing this," she answered sadly.

"I'm not sure what I think. Perhaps I will hate you. Who is he supposed to have murdered?"

"A schoolgirl. He was her teacher. The murderer raped her," she added almost under her breath.

"Jesus. As if it wasn't bad enough already," he winced.

"I don't think it's sensible for me to give you little snippets. You need to read the file. And, when you read it, you need to remember that both my dad and your mother were absolutely convinced of his innocence. The man who did the things you'll read about was almost certainly not your father. You need to read it with that at the forefront of your mind."

"But you leave tomorrow. There'll be no time for me to read it, take it all in and then talk to you about it," he declared.

"There are only two ferries a week back to Port Vila and only two flights a week out of Port Vila back to Brisbane. If I don't get tomorrow's ferry I'll have to wait the best part of another week before I can get back to Brisbane. I didn't know just how remote this place was," she answered.

"Then you should have told me why you were here as soon as you arrived," he growled back at her.

"How could I? Until I was sure about you. You might have been a wimp. A whiner. Not up to it. I had to get your measure. Anyway, here's my idea. Take the copy file away with you now. Take a look at it. Sleep on it. In the morning tell me how you feel. If we can work on it together I'll stay another three days, work out a plan with you and I'll get the later ferry. If you decide you don't want to get involved, or don't want to have anything to do with me, then I get tomorrow's ferry as planned. Your call."

He got up, clutching the file in its large buff folder, and walked slowly down the crudely carved steps which led from the porch to the rough ground below. It was so dark that she lost sight of him within a few seconds, but his voice passed clearly enough through the blackness of the South Pacific night.

"I don't hate you, George. I guess I'd have done the same thing if the positions were reversed."

The girl sat back in the hard rocking chair and relaxed for the first time since she'd embarked upon this fateful conversation. Smiling to herself, she reflected with satisfaction on her judgement of character. Cal Stewart was a tough guy.

One minute he had been looking to kiss her and the next minute she had undermined his whole existence. The documents felt like a ton weight in his hands as he headed back to his hammock in the workers' quarters. Reading by torchlight, he ploughed incredulously through the file. Whilst it contained absolute dynamite it consisted of less than two hundred pages and, within a couple of hours, he had acquired sufficient understanding of the case to form a tentative view. His mother must have endured an ordeal of such cruelty that she had determined to protect him from ever being exposed to any awareness of her suffering. Now, some well-intentioned but naïve girl from a far off land wanted to introduce the ghosts of that dreadful time to the next generation. The prospects of identifying the true killer or of obtaining a pardon for the man now revealed as his father would be negligible. Terrible, ill-healed wounds would be reopened and he would taste the brutality and empty despair that his mother's stoicism was designed to save him from. As sleep gradually dulled his teeming brain he had little doubt that George would be getting tomorrow's ferry.

At first light he awoke, his eyes falling immediately on the buff folder, its contents spilled carelessly on to the floor beneath the hammock. Long ago, his mother had taken him to a museum in Sydney, where the hideous leg irons that had shackled an English convict transported to Australia two centuries previously, were housed in a glass case. The prisoner had been subjected to three hundred lashes by order of the vicious Master of the ship and had arrived in Australia with festering wounds and typhoid which killed him within a week. Cal had never forgotten the feeling of revulsion that had welled up inside him as he had stared in grim fascination at those wicked rings of iron and heavy chains. It was exactly the same feeling of revulsion that he felt now as he stared down at the case papers beneath, telling their own equally gruesome tale. The convict had been "transported beyond the seas" by order of a Judge at Cambridge Assizes for stealing a Cheshire cheese. He, too, had been innocent.

Pulling on his running kit, he set off for his customary five mile pre-breakfast jog. He could think so much more clearly when his body was put to work. Unusually, there was a thin mist across the hill which the warm breeze from the ocean was not yet dislodging. His route took him across a verdant coffee plantation, along the edge of the middle bush and out on to the open plain where he would normally increase his pace and put in a mile at under six minutes. But this particular morning he stopped, seating himself uncomfortably on a fallen log which lay alongside the crazily intertwined roots and limbs of a giant banyan tree. Staring out across the plain, its grass and vegetation displaying so many shades of vivid green that it seemed like the uninhibited handiwork of a child with a new set of paints, he slowly regained his breath and realised that he had, almost subconsciously, come to a decision. George must exit his life as abruptly as she had entered it, taking with her that sad file of papers and all the human misery that it contained.

With the decision made, a weight lifted from his shoulders and he started to raise himself up from his position on the log, when he suddenly became aware of a chestnut stallion which had appeared silently from behind the natural screen provided by the banyan. It was a quite magnificent creature, muscles rippling across the flanks, veins standing proud within the powerful chest while the massive head was held high, eyes gazing across the plain and down towards the turquoise Pacific. The wild stallion was surveying his realm, like a tribal warrior king.

As Cal watched, a Tanna man, roughly hewn and naked except for a pair of ragged khaki shorts, appeared from the edge of the bush, walking purposefully towards the horse, calling softly to him in some language to which a white man would always be a stranger. Neither the horse nor the man seemed to have been aware of Cal and they performed their ritual in the belief that they were alone. The man lovingly rested his head with its untamed hair on the horse's flank and stroked the shining coat, constantly reassuring him in that secret tongue. The creature responded, nuzzling the man's body and preening itself in the beauty of their friendship. Then, in an instant, the black body swung itself up on to the stallion's back, gripping the mane and using thick, powerful legs to achieve the leap, while the horse seemed to lower itself to welcome the union. Throwing its head back in pleasure the horse simply took off, thundering across the plain, its native rider, bareback and without reins, shouting out in elation, his cry piercing the early morning air. They scorched across the plain, thudding hooves echoing back to the bush, while the rider bent low across the animal's neck and celebrated the only riches he possessed. Freedom.

Circling back towards where Cal still stood, obscured from their view by the foliage, the animal slowed while the man straightened and looked towards the far side of the banyan, quickly spotting that for which his eyes strained. A small boy, no older than five, emerged from the trees. Bare-chested, thin legged with a clear black skin that glistened in the early rays of the sun that had now burned off the mist. The child ran eagerly towards the horse and the man thrust out his leg so that the boy might climb up on the adult's bare foot to be swept up by a strong right arm on to the animal's back where he clung to the man like a limpet as the horse began to accelerate away with his increased load. The whole process had taken but a few seconds and throughout Cal had been unable to take his eyes off the face of the child. What he had observed was wonderment at this priceless gift by father to son. He had witnessed a joy which, for him, had been forever denied by the hangman's rope. In those few seconds his destiny changed. George would not be catching tomorrow's ferry.

Chapter 5

Warwick, England December 1989

When the saliva of the infected female mosquito is injected into its human prey it contains microscopic parasites which travel to the liver, incubate and multiply before entering the red blood cells where they mature, rupture and attack. These parasites may lie dormant for months or even years before the internal explosion occurs which leads to the manifested symptoms of chills, nausea, fever and seizure. Assuming the patient recovers, the parasites may subside for further months or even years before striking again.

It is in this way that he viewed his own disease. As something as randomly inflicted as a mosquito bite. As something of which he was the victim, not the perpetrator. As something over which he had no control and as something which only manifested its symptoms very occasionally, leaving him, for the rest of the time, seemingly normal and healthy. Unlike malaria, which might prove fatal to its host, his disease proved fatal to young innocent women. Half a dozen so far. Over a quarter of a century. After the third slaying he began to welcome the outbreaks, for the killing liberated him and he began to crave the taking of life. Now the symptoms were upon him again and a seventh victim was within his sights.

Science and technology in crime detection had moved on from when his illness had first struck all those years ago. Death had been a mistake the first time. He hadn't pressed very hard on the girl's fleshy neck, yet she was dead in a few seconds. In the later episodes he had intended death. Relished the prospect of taking life. It had all been so easy so long as you were careful, but now DNA research was threatening to make its way into the forensic field, transfer of clothing fibres from killer to victim and vice-versa was securing convictions and even a hair or a spot of blood on his clothing could lead to catastrophe.

But he was so cautious. So meticulous in his planning. And so quick in the execution. This was the third time he had driven up to Warwick and, although this stretch of river was less than three miles from the town centre, it was lonely and remote. Last time he had seen a chance. Concealing himself in the small copse that ran down to the river, he had observed her looming silently into view, jogging along the path that would take her within thirty yards of where he hid, assessing every line and curve of her body through his binoculars. Like malarial parasites, his illness was about to explode from within and his senses were so heightened that, for the first time ever, he nearly made a mistake. In those exquisite few seconds immediately before the strike, he caught a glimpse of something moving in the grass some way behind her and, in an instant, a large black mongrel dog bounded on to the path, accelerated and caught her up. He even heard her call its name as they passed him, now running in tandem. "Indigo" she called him, her soft voice breathless from her exertions, to remain forever in blissful ignorance that Indigo had just saved her life. Anger and frustration that he should have been thwarted, developed into a cold fury as he slipped stealthily away to drive the ninety miles back to his home.

But tonight he'd moved another half a mile down river to a better spot. Overgrown. Long grass. Thick gorse bushes. Clusters of willows and elms. Dusk. Not a soul in sight except for her. A fat girl, poorly dressed, probably only about seventeen or eighteen with the untidy gait of someone who didn't care too much what they looked like. Some kind of dark anorak and a scruffy skirt over bare legs and grubby trainers. In the last of the fading winter light she was hurrying towards the town, but her weight and lack of fitness slowed her down. Checking and double-checking for any other sign of life, he knew that tonight would take away the fever and the chills. Remedy was within grasp.

Waiting until she had just passed where he crouched, invisible and motionless, enabled him to come up from behind so that she never knew he was there until he was on her, like a lion pulling down the antelope. Gloved left hand straight over her mouth, no noise. Right forearm across her throat. So tight it snapped her hyoid. Whimpering, ineffectual kicking, terror. Dragging heels. Overweight and weak. Within twenty seconds she was on her back in the dirt, deep within the trees and he was straddling her, pressing ever harder across the delicate structures of the neck. The hyoid, the trachea, the windpipe, the jugular, the vagal nerves, he just wantonly crushed them all as he stared in fascination at the terrorised bulging eyes beneath him.

Lank unwashed hair. Heavy-featured. Face now purple. Mouth open to scream, but, denied even an atom of air, soundless. Small, stained teeth. Then no movement. Death. So quick. The sexual ecstasy of wielding power that could extinguish a life within half a minute stimulated his whole being, like the sting of heroin racing to the brain. Wrenching every item of clothing from her lifeless body, he quickly stuffed them into the rucksack he had secreted in the foliage. No bra. Dirty underpants. She smelled. He didn't care. Then, slipping on a condom to ensure he left no biological trace, he raped her. Twice. In a state of excitement that no ordinary sexual encounter could ever hope to rival. His face buried in her hair which smelled of stale tobacco smoke. At last the symptoms of the illness abated and he felt whole again. Ensuring that no-one was in sight, he quickly dragged the naked corpse to the cold, black river's edge and levered it in, watching as the swift current caught it and carried it away. No DNA or hairs or fibres would survive the water when the bloated carcass was recovered downstream after some unfortunate child or angler spotted the apparition. Picking up his rucksack, he disappeared into the night, slipping unobserved into his car, on false plates, for the drive home, disposing of her clothes and his own en route, except of course for her pants, the parasite now dormant again within his liver, but not so deep as before, the illness nearer the surface, ready to break out again.

Chapter 6

Wakefield, Yorkshire, England late February 1990

Lanny Creane was the youngest of ten children. Six boys and four girls. The oldest brother, Benjy, had been the gypsy bare-knuckle champion of Northern England for a couple of years until, in a drunken depression, he had blown his own head off with a twelve bore in one of the family caravans. Lanny, then thirteen, had found the body, brains splattered over the walls and furniture, grotesquely slumped over the kitchen table. After that, nothing ever mattered to Lanny again. He became dehumanised. No act of violence or betrayal caused him any concern. Stealing, cursing, stabbing, beating, all became his natural bodily functions.

The caravans would be towed by heavy lorries from encampment to encampment, fighting eviction to the last and then lurching on to the next area of grassland to defile. Filthy kids, mean dogs, ferrets, litter, scrap engines, abandoned hulks of metal were all his playthings. In the evenings, the group would descend on a pub the men had selected as their temporary base and, terrorizing the locals, they would take it over. Fist-fights, robberies and menace became the norm for as long as they remained. Lanny had a favourite party piece when the families invaded a new patch. Arriving in the pub in his old brown trench coat, rope tied round its middle and poacher's pockets within, he would lean against the bar downing pints of beer while he chose a suitable group of victims. Once selected, he would approach them, open the coat and reveal a brace of hare tied to his belt which he would demand that they buy. No-one ever stood up to Lanny Creane and they would pay up. Then, pulling a knife from the foul recesses of the coat lining, he would slit one of the hares open straight down its belly, plunge his hand deep into the carcass and wrench out the innards. All the guts, organs, intestines and tissues clenched in his bloodied hand. In one move he would thrust it all into his mouth, chew it, swallow it, spit some phlegm on to the floor and then wander back to the bar and down another pint.

Before he was thirty he'd served time in most of the mainland prisons. This last stretch had taken him to one of the hardest in the land. Wakefield. Some bruiser in a Barnsley pub had made the mistake of standing up to him. Lanny had only needed to deliver one blow. It was a full-blooded kick with his steel-capped pit boot directly on to the shin. Lanny's steel on the bruiser's bone. Smashed the tibia and fibia and scattered shards of bone on the filthy floor. It had taken five police officers to arrest him and two of them ended up in hospital but Lanny ended up in Wakefield Gaol with a five year stretch. Given his record it was cheap at the price.

"Here we go round the mulberry bush,
The mulberry bush, the mulberry bush.
Here we go round the mulberry bush,
On a cold and frosty morning."

That was the joke at Wakefield. The mulberry bush, around which the inmates used to exercise, still stood in the prison yard and had produced a dirge recited by them each morning which had passed into folklore. A chant of despair had given birth to a nursery rhyme of innocence. Lanny enjoyed the irony of that. Wakefield housed hundreds of lifers, many serving two or more life sentences and what did they sing? A nursery rhyme. But he hadn't seen much of the mulberry bush in the last six months of his sentence as he'd been banged up in the Segregation Unit. Senior Prison Officer Noone had reported him to the Governor for stealing some cash. Lanny put the word out on the outside. Noone was attended to in a dark back alley and was off work for three months. Everybody knew that Lanny had set it up, but nobody could prove anything. So they trumped something up and chucked him into the Segregation Unit for six months. With the Madman of Wakefield in the adjacent cell. The Madman who attacked anything that moved and had to be caged twenty three hours a day. Some neighbour.

Today was release day. Out into the "cold and frosty morning." HMP issue transparent plastic bag over his shoulder containing a few clothes. A leisurely saunter down Love Lane. He'd told Bev, brother number two after Benjy, not to come to the gaol, but to meet him on the bomb site car park at the back of the cinema. The noisy diesel engine of a battered lime-green Volvo estate spluttered into action and moved in his direction as he walked on to the rough ground of the car park. No road tax, bald tyres, a thick-set bald-headed male with pebble glasses at the wheel. As the vehicle drew alongside him the driver leant across and threw open the front passenger door and Lanny slipped into the seat, throwing his bag into the back.

"So where we going, Bev?" he asked in that rasping accent that took the worst out of peat-bog Ireland, urban Liverpool, the raw North-East and mixed them all up into a guttural, Neanderthal means of communication.

"East Devon. Got a set-up by the River Culm. So what's the crack in Wakefield?" his brother responded in an identical accent, but with an added lisp due to the fact that he didn't have a tooth in his head.

"The bastards segregated me. Six months next to a fucking psycho."

"'Cos of the screw we done?" Bev asked, as he drove straight over a red light in the middle of the town nearly hitting a double-decker bus. A blast on the horn and two fingers from Bev.

"Of course. Worth every day of it," he muttered with what passed as a laugh. "I did get one visit though last week. From Dyer."

"What's that shit want?"

"Got a little job. Put a few quid in me pocket to get me going again, like," said Lanny.

"How much?" Bev barked. "He's a mean twat. Runs none of the risks, but keeps the biggest cut for himself."

"Two grand. Just for a pasting. I ain't complaining," Lanny answered.

"When?"

"Next week or so."

"You want me in?" Bev enquired hopefully.

"Nah. One man job. I got the info. Got an address."

"Where?"

"Near Taunton. P'raps you could be the wheels. A ton to drive me."

"Taunton. Ain't that far from the camp. You could make it a couple of ton, though," came the response.

"Done," laughed Lanny, as they both spat on their palms before slapping hands. "Get the stink of the nick off me first. Maybe tomorrow night."

Bev turned and stared hard through the thick glasses at his younger brother, offering him a toothless grin. 'Lanny was a great guy. Good to have the bastard back,' he thought to himself as he barrelled the hefty Volvo into the outside lane of the Motorway, oblivious to the vehicles he cut up in the process.

Chapter 7

Bristol, England Early March 1990

Two days in a flea-pit hotel in freezing Earls Court had allowed Cal to throw off the primary waves of jet-lag before he met up with George and, despite the macabre nature of his mission, he had done some red-bus sight-seeing. After all, he now knew that he was of full-English stock, although he felt like a stranger in a strange land.

When the mid-morning train drew into Temple Meads Station in Bristol she was waiting for him on the platform. Although they had corresponded at length since her departure from Tanna, it had all been very formal and business-like. Seeing her again was a poignant reminder of why he'd been attracted to her in the first place. A sky-blue bobble hat and long matching scarf framed her pretty, smiling face, the cheeks lightly coloured by the March wind that blew across the cold iron tracks. A loose-fitting suede jacket and ecru corduroy trousers tucked into polished brown knee length leather boots completed the picture. Where he was awkward, she was now at ease, comfortable on her home turf and seemingly pleased to welcome him.

Leading the way to a silver 1987 Mercedes 560SL convertible in the car park she linked her arm in his and made small talk while he tried to assimilate the alien colours, noise and atmosphere of a provincial English city.

"It was Dad's Merc," she volunteered sadly as they eventually emerged out of the urban traffic and on to the M5 motorway and a freer passage.

"Does your Ma know who I am?" he responded, unsure of just how forthcoming George might have been at home.

"Of course," she answered immediately. "Even though I'm qualified now and working, we still live at the farm together. She knows the score. But she's not keen. Better to keep your distance. My sister knows everything, but you won't be meeting her. She's at College in London."

"How are we going to handle this?" he asked. "Vets' jobs are hard to find. We'd planned this thinking you wouldn't be working full time, but now you've landed this job we may have to make some changes."

"I do large animals. Predominantly cattle. So most of the time I'm travelling from farm to farm. No set timetable but available at any time. Twenty four hours a day. So we'll fix our appointments around that. If I suddenly have to go off and visit a sick cow you may have to see some of these people without me. You'll handle that. The guest room is over the barn, but you can use the farmhouse office to do the research and make the phone calls."

Cal gazed out of the window as they glided along the motorway and into Somerset, taking in the shape and texture of the fields, so green after a particularly wet English winter, while the early lamb arrivals seemed to be absorbing this new world with the same interest as him. Perversely, now he'd actually met up with George and she was talking about hard, practical steps for them to pursue, the whole venture seemed to have lost all sense of reality. The identity, personality and agony of his unknown father had felt tangible in Tanna and even more so back in Australia, when he'd eventually had that excruciating conversation with Ma, as she did everything in her power to dissuade him from going to England and facing the heartache and anguish that she believed it would involve. Her strained white face had revealed the pain. How, so as to protect Cal, she had broken her own solemn promise to her husband to seek the truth. But, now he was actually here in England, where it had all happened, it was more like stepping into the pages of a book, observing a fiction.

"In the glove compartment," George was repeating, snapping him out of his reverie.

"What?"

"The list. I've written out how far I've got," she explained patiently. "In the file in the glove compartment. Take it out and we'll go through it."

Everything was efficiently arranged behind brightly coloured dividers in the green ring binder. Names, phone numbers, enquiries made, ideas to follow up, all set out in her neat feminine hand together with all of the letters he had written to her.

"Behind the yellow divider," she said. "That's the important part."

"Officer in charge of the case. Detective Inspector Yarnell. Kenneth Yarnell," he read out loud from her notes.

"Yeah. The school was near a place called Batford, just outside Luton, so I wrote to the Chief Constable of Bedfordshire, asking where Yarnell was. You'll see his Secretary's reply on the next page. Retired in 1979. They don't give out details of private addresses of any Officers, active or retired. But the letter says they are prepared to disclose that he is now deceased."

"A promising start," he sighed, turning on to the next page.

"And it got worse," she replied. "Is the next page Amy Beckett?"

"Yes. Louise Donovan's friend who claimed she saw my father come off the golf course and walk towards the bike sheds. She's very important. We've got to find her," he answered.

"Well, she's not easy to find. I went up to Luton, checked the electoral roll, went to the local libraries, tried to get the school records. Nothing. The school's been knocked down. There's a row of shops and a pub where it used to stand. Beckett's a common name. I got nowhere. Same story with the green keeper, Walter Mangan. And the golf course is long gone. A housing estate now."

"And, of course, Amy Beckett is probably married and got a different name," he added thoughtfully.

"But I have found the other two schoolboys, Hollister and Littleton, she reported. "I fancy stopping for a bite and I can give you the details while we eat. We get off the motorway here and head west on the A358. Our place is a few miles outside Bishop's Lydeard, so it's still quite a way yet. There's a pub just down here on the main road. I'll stop there and we can take the file in with us."

In a soulless roadhouse, over a roast beef sandwich, thin on beef and heavy on English mustard, she explained that Hollister had been easily located as he had a senior position in a Merchant Bank in London and she'd seen his name in the business sections of the papers and had written to him a few weeks ago, explaining that Cal was coming over to try to reopen the case. However, his secretary had replied rather curtly to her request for a meeting, saying Mr Hollister regretted that he was far too busy to discuss matters from so long ago and couldn't help. She had then telephoned him, using a different name, and got through to him. As soon as she said why she was phoning he'd slammed the phone down. Littleton, on the other hand, had been located on the Luton electoral roll, had proved absolutely charming and would be quite prepared to meet them.

"You'll never guess what Littleton's job is," George laughed. "He's a vicar. There, at the head of his letter, look," she added, turning to the appropriate page in the binder. "St Dunstan's. If he's a vicar he should at least be honest."

"Don't bank on it," he replied. "But he was on my father's side. So it's a start. Who else have you managed to track down?"

"Next shot was the barrister who prosecuted. Lumley. That was easy. I looked in Dad's old Law List and got his chambers phone number. Spoke to a young clerk there who said he'd check it out and come back to me. Called back within the hour. Lumley's been dead for fifteen years."

"What about the Judge?" he enquired. "Didn't we decide that we should try to see him."

"Yes. There's an old barrister friend of Dad's called Tim Sprackley. Still practising. I got on to him. Very hush-hush because the Lord Chancellor's Department treats Judges' addresses as confidential. Even retired Judges like Vishney. But Tim liked Dad a lot and he knows what we're doing, so he managed to get it for me. Told me the Judge was a bastard. Over eighty now. Very unlikely to co-operate. Almost certain to ignore any letter. Best idea was to go and knock on his door and confront him. Expect trouble, but take him by surprise. He's seeing out his days in some retirement home near Brighton. The address is in there."

Cal leaned back in his chair and looked across the table at the earnest face opposite him, reflecting to himself what a remarkable young woman she was. Having travelled half way across the world to a remote island stuck in the middle of the South Pacific to see what he was made of, she had written letters, made phone calls and beavered away at a probably hopeless cause that was ancient history whilst, at the same time, finishing off her studies to qualify as a vet.

"You're one determined lady, George," he observed swigging back the last of his warm, insipid pint of English beer. "You've got far more energy and enthusiasm for this than I have."

"Of course I have. I've listened to my father talk about this injustice for years. I saw with my own eyes what he felt about it. Although it's all about your father, you never saw him, never heard him, your mother never mentioned him. You come to it as piece of history. I've lived with it as a reality. Real people. Flesh and blood."

"A dog with a bone," he grinned.

Half an hour later she swung the Mercedes off the country lane, reaching for a remote control which activated a sturdy, six-barred wooden gate, across a cattle grid and on to a dirt track which cut across gently sloping pastureland where a couple of dozen Charolais cattle were grazing. White coarse hides, heavily muscled, horned and long-bodied, Cal had never seen cattle like this before and, as she steered the Mercedes slowly along the rough track, the bull broke away from the herd and moved aggressively into a position which would directly block their path. As an Aussie male he wasn't intending to let George realise that he was getting a bit nervous about the impending encounter.

"That's Nero," she laughed. "He weighs in at two thousand pounds and could turn this car over with one shake of his head. Purebred. The breed comes from south-eastern France. His bloodline goes back to before the French Revolution. Nero was the bull Dad was flying off to buy in Carlisle when he had his crash."

As the car crept to within a few feet of the hulking beast, he suddenly lurched to his left, the enormous muscles rippling across the flanks and neck as he lumbered off to rejoin his harem, pride satisfied that he had made his stand. With the way ahead now clear, Cal got his first glimpse of the old farmhouse nestling at the foot of a tree-covered hill and set behind a rectangular, well-manicured lawn. Half-timbered, covered in wisteria, two storeys with stone mullion windows, imposing hand carved oak front door and, on its western side, a courtyard with a duck pond and a well. On the eastern side were loose boxes, tack and feed stores, stabling and a brick-built barn.

"This is home. Mum's out 'til this evening," George said softly, bringing the Mercedes to a halt at a side door near the pond and switching off the ignition. "Like I said, Dad converted the top floor of the barn to our guest room. I'll walk you over. But one more thing before we go in."

"What?"

"I deliberately kept the best news until we got here," she replied excitedly.

"So let's be hearing it," he replied, turning expectantly in his seat towards her.

"The police officer in the case," she said, taking his right hand in both of hers.

"Yarnell. You told me he's dead," Cal responded, intrigued at what she was about to reveal whilst his heart beat faster at the touch of her hand and he stared at the pretty, animated face just inches away.

"Yarnell's dead," she continued. "But the young constable who worked the case with him. The one who arrested your father in the bike sheds. He's alive and kicking. I found him last week. He's retired and lives near Canterbury. You saw his name in the case papers."

"Chauncey," Cal snapped back immediately. "Detective Constable Graham Chauncey."

"Exactly," she answered. "And I've spoken to him on the phone. He's very interested. Very interested indeed. Apparently, Dad wrote a letter and left it with our family solicitor. To be sent to Chauncey in the event of Dad's death. Setting out all his worries about the case. Asking for his concerns to be placed with the police records. The solicitor sent it to Bedfordshire Police and it eventually got passed down to Chauncey. And here's the best bit of all," she added, her eyes alive with excitement. "Chauncey had never been convinced that your Dad did it. So he started poking around."

"And what did he find?" demanded Cal.

"Not what. Who. He found her," she replied.

"Who? Who is 'her'?"

"He found Amy Beckett," said George beaming with pleasure. "He found Amy Beckett."

Chapter 8

The barn was an open-ended working barn, crammed with farm machinery, heavy equipment, bales of hay, ropes and a Massey Ferguson 590 multipower tractor with enormous muddied wheels and a flat bed trailer hitched up with more bales of hay on it. Farming tools were stacked around the walls and a straight wooden staircase took him up to the second storey which had been converted into a guest bedroom with a separate bathroom. Inside the farmhouse itself there were large but low-ceilinged rooms with original beams everywhere, flagstone floors and open fireplaces. The kitchen had a range of bread ovens, copper pots and pans hanging from ceiling racks and a steep flight of stone steps running into a wine cellar below. While they were having a cup of tea, poring over the ever-growing murder file, the house phone rang and George was summoned away to a suspected case of obstruction colic in a horse on a farm near Cothelstone and, as the sound of the Mercedes receded over the hill, he wandered slowly around the farm, reflecting on the bizarre circumstances that brought him here after all the planning with George and the money that Ma had come up with to help pay for the trip.

Despite the magnificence of the countryside and the borrowed Barbour Wax jacket that George had explained once belonged to her father, the damp air began to make him feel chilled as the sky turned an even duller grey and the last half-hour of daylight arrived. Heading back to his room in the barn he paused to examine the Massey Ferguson tractor. Nice cab, well-maintained, four wheel drive, four cylinder, eight forward and two reverse gears. Keys were in the ignition. He was tempted to give it a whirl. He'd driven one just like this back in Australia last summer. A bird fluttered in the high roof of the barn and momentarily startled him whilst some brown creature scuttled away across the straw. In the dying light he couldn't judge whether it was a large mouse or a rat. He decided it was a bit of a nerve to go for a spin so he turned away from the cab and began to walk towards the stairs. That was the instant when something struck him with enormous force across the face and left hand side of his head. It came from nowhere. Unheralded by sight, sound or smell. Cal had played Aussie Rules and Rugby League. He'd been concussed more than once and had his nose broken twice but he'd never been struck like this. The shock and the pain impacted in equal measure and everything went jet black. The very edge of consciousness. Then, from within the blackness, he saw the bright flashing stars he'd seen before when taking a heavy blow to the head and he realised instinctively that, in a nano-second, he was passing from consciousness to unconsciousness and then back again. Hovering between a barn in Somerset and some dark bottomless void. His strength, fitness and instinctive resilience fought desperately to stop him from falling into that void.

Then he became aware of the rafters in the roof of the barn and dim shafts of light peeking through the slats. Unable to regain his physical bearings he realised that his brain was telling him that he was on his back, yet he couldn't feel his back in contact with the barn's floor, although he sensed the straw and dirt under his hands. His head was filled with the noise of blood rushing through cranial arteries but he had no sense of external sound. He knew that his airways were clear and yet he was struggling to breathe. All of his senses were fighting in unison to bring him back from the void but, strangely, it was his sense of smell that provided the beginnings of explanation. A foul stench of long-dead animals, human body odour, diesel fuel and stale blood. His sense of touch kicked in. A coarse, rough, heavy material pressing against his face and neck. Lanny Creane's brown trenchcoat.

"It's gonna be a hospital job when I'm fucking done with ya," Creane spat out. He was straddling Cal's chest and leaning so close to his face that Cal could now almost taste the stink of his fetid breath yet, beyond the lank hair falling over the eyes and a bulbous nose, Cal could not get a clear picture of him. The man's full weight was on him, rendering him incapable of moving his upper body and there was a bone hard knee pinning each arm directly on the bicep.

"This is just a fucking taster. If ya ain't on yer plane home by Friday I'll cripple ya," he swore, now swinging his arm and crashing a backhanded blow across Cal's numb left cheek. The arc of the swing was restricted by his position and its force reduced by being backhanded but Cal's head and neck snapped to the right, causing him to cry out in terror.

"No more fucking detective work. You get my drift?" the man shouted, suddenly jumping up and delivering a kick straight into the kidneys. Not just an ordinary kick. Lanny had dug out his steel-tipped boots for the occasion and, through the searing pain, Cal was aware of him drawing back his leg for the next one. But this time the man was aiming for his head.

Instinctively, trying to roll away and pull his head away from the impending blow, he sensed something touch the fingers of his right hand. A hard object hidden under the straw that lay on the barn floor. His fingers grasped at it. A wooden handle attached to a half inch diameter steel rod bent into a hook. A baling hook used by farmers to slam into a heavy bale of hay and provide the purchase to hoist it up on to the trailer. As Lanny unleashed his kick, so did Cal swing that vicious steel hook with all his might at the leg, jerking his head away from the arc of the boot. The hook slashed its way through sinew, nerve and tissue into the back of the knee and kept travelling, only losing its momentum when the point of the hook hit the internal underside of the knee cap. Lanny Creane might have known every trick in the book but there's nothing anyone can do if they pass out. Crashing to the ground with an almighty thud he lay in the dirt, twitching and groaning, the hook still embedded in his right leg. Now Cal could see what had smashed into his face. Heavy industrial gloves. Steel-ribbed to protect the backs of press workers' hands from being crushed in machinery. Blood was flowing freely from his face and he realised that his left eye was closing but he had the initiative and, despite the pain and nausea, he had to use it.

The thug was starting to come round, cursing and hyperventilating and pulling ineffectually at the steel that was tearing him apart. Cal reached for the wooden handle, now saturated in sticky blood, and eased it out, noticing the rope that was tied like a belt around the man's coat. He pulled at the rope and it came away. Before the man could fully regain his senses Cal tied the rope as tightly as he could across the area of the wound and then, lugging him across the floor by the collar of his coat, he dragged him to the flat bed trailer attached to the Massey Ferguson. Straining every sinew he somehow manhandled the body on to the trailer, staggered to the tractor cab, hauled himself up, slumped into the seat, fired the beast up, slammed it into first forward gear and lurched out of the barn. Down the drive, head splitting, but the bleeding from the face lacerations had slowed. It was nearly dark but, turning his head to look through the cab's rear window, he could see the body was still lying on the trailer, thrashing about. When he'd been in George's car earlier he'd noticed a public phone box positioned at a junction about three quarters of a mile up the road to the left. If he could get there, make an anonymous 999 call for an ambulance and dump the man alongside the box, he might get out of this without having to deal with the police. How do you explain putting a baling hook into a man's leg without interviews, suspicion, Court cases and hell knows what else?

Fumbling in the various recesses in the console he located a remote control for the gate and slowed to allow the heavy six bar to fully open. Hopefully, there would be little or no traffic but, as he nosed through the open gate, he immediately spotted a stationary vehicle pulled up on the right hand verge. A lime green Volvo estate. Leaning on the boot was a large man. Bald. Thick glasses. And a long dark coat tied round the middle with a piece of rope.

Cal inched the tractor forward until he was about twenty yards from the Volvo and cut the engine so that the man would be able to hear him. The bald man had already started to walk menacingly towards the tractor when Cal threw open the cab door, and, standing with one foot on the sideplate, he brandished the baling hook. The sight of a man, gashed and bleeding down the left side of his grotesquely swollen face, waving a bloodstained baling hook stopped Bev dead in his tracks.

"The bastard's on the trailer. He's had this hook in him and so will you if you try anything," Cal shouted. "Get him to hospital fast and you may save his leg."

Bev ran to the trailer and cried out in anguish when he saw the white face, covered in a sickly sweat and whimpering in agony. "It's OK, Lanny," he whispered. "Just hang on." With an enormous heave he lifted him off the trailer with his hands under Lanny's legs, feeling the trousers saturated in arterial blood as he lurched back to the Volvo and eased his brother into the cargo space of the estate car, lying him flat out.

Racing to the driver's door, he looked back at Cal and spat on the ground. "You're fucking dead meat, pal," he roared from his toothless mouth. "Dead meat. No-one does that to a Creane. We'll be back for you."

"Then you'll waste your time. I'm leaving here now. For good. I'll be at an airport tonight. So no chance, mate," Cal screamed back as Bev gunned the diesel, spun the wheels and tore off down the road towards the nearest hospital. Whether he believed Cal or not remained to be seen.

Chapter 9

Brighton, England the following day. Early March 1990

For the first two hours of the journey he lay back in the passenger seat in a deep sleep as George pointed the Mercedes towards Brighton. The eye was completely closed, the side of the face swollen and black and three lacerations ran vertically down the cheek. When George had returned from Cothelstone she had found him sitting at their kitchen table holding a bag of ice cubes to his battered face and shaking like a leaf. At first she had insisted that she drive him to hospital but, after examining the injuries, she conceded that they couldn't go to Taunton Hospital as the thug would likely be there, so it would mean a long drive to Bristol. And the Doctors would be obliged to report those type of injuries to the police which would prompt the kind of enquiry Cal was so desperate to avoid. Her veterinary skills led her to believe that the zygoma was fractured but there was a good chance that the bone had not been displaced, in which case it should heal without any surgical intervention. The cuts needed stitching or would leave noticeable scars. He settled for the scars, her strongest painkillers and a tumbler of brandy. Neither of them could fathom out who was trying to warn him off, nor what to tell her mother, so she gently helped him back to his room, insisted that he keep the door locked at all times and armed him with one of the family's shotguns with two cartridges in the breech.

In the morning, with a steam-hammer pounding inside his head, they'd waited until her mother had gone out and then set off to track down the old Judge, making sure that Cal slid down in his seat as they came through the gate and on to the road in case anyone was checking to see if he was still around. There had been no sign of any car or any person. That's when he'd fallen asleep.

On the outskirts of Winchester she pulled off the road at a grubby café and shook him awake. They'd be there within the hour and their plans needed adjusting in the light of his appearance. Taking him by the arm she led him inside the almost deserted coffee shop, deposited him at a corner table and went off to the counter.

"Get that down you," she told him on her return, pushing a steaming mug of black coffee and a fat sugared doughnut under his nose. "How's your head?"

"Better for the sleep, ribs ache like hell," he acknowledged, shovelling a couple more painkillers in his mouth and forcing them down with a sip of the coffee. "That guy was a pro."

"Then someone's very keen to stop us if they're hiring pros. That's good news in a sense. Someone's got something to hide. And it has to be someone within the few people I've written to or phoned. So we're spooking someone pretty bad," she said as she munched her way through a doughnut of her own.

"Yeah. But the question is who. Hardly likely to be the old Judge, is it?"

"No," she replied, "but I think I'll have to see him alone." The staff at the Home will take one look at you with those injuries and think you're some ruffian with a score to settle. We'd never get near him."

"I thought about that," he replied. "I've brought a pair of sunglasses and a baseball cap. It might hide a bit of the damage."

"No. It's going to be tough enough to breach the defences as it is. And once I get to speak to him I'm going in strong, so we don't want to make him nervous even before we begin. And take it from me, looking at you now, you'd make most people nervous," she laughed.

"So where do I fit in?" he asked.

"You're the maintenance man. That's where you fit in."

"Cryptic's your style, isn't it George?" he smiled.

"I've put Dad's three foot spirit level and electrics tool box in the boot. I'll try to get to see the old boy in one of the communal rooms. You'll ferret around. Carrying your tools. Find his room. Get in. Bedrooms in old peoples' homes are usually kept unlocked. Any problem and you're the maintenance man," she explained.

"And what do I do if I get in?" Cal enquired wryly.

"He was a Judge for donkeys years, Cal. He'll have kept stuff. Ordered. Filed. You look for it."

"Seems to me you've got more of an appetite for all this than me," he observed. "Sure, I've read the stuff. I've come to England. But I doubt it's going anywhere. I'm just discharging some kind of duty. But you, George, you're driven."

"I knew my father," she replied fixing him with a steely look. "I've read what he felt about this. He was a sound judge of character. I intend to put things right. And today, you're the maintenance man."

Dolphin Glen consisted of three imposing Edwardian houses converted into one inter-communicating residence with thirty five en-suite bedrooms, a large ground-floor reception room with armchairs positioned around the perimeter like wall-flowers at the local dance, a TV lounge and a dining room. One block from the Brighton sea front it was as good a place as anywhere to wait to die.

A young girl in the hallway explained to George that the residents were presently taking lunch but if she signed in and waited outside the dining room then she had no doubt that the old Judge would be delighted to see his granddaughter. The dining room had double doors with porthole windows. George sneaked a peek at the spectacle within. A sea of white and grey. Seated at tables of four. Some with a limb in plaster where they had taken a fall. A leg on a stool or an arm stretched out straight ahead. Some at odd angles where a back or a neck had calcified, freezing the owner into permanent contortion.

But all of them, to a man, still managing to shovel school lunch quality food into that hole in their face which kept them alive and which had become their only remaining reason to live. But, to George, the most depressing feature of all was the total silence. Only the sound of the knife and fork. Not a word of conversation. For none of them had anything left to say to each other.

The girl had told her that her granddad always sat at table eighteen and her father's notes had made frequent references to the Judge peering down his pince-nez spectacles and so, after all these years, she first set eyes on the patrician who had presided over this story of misery. A long head, deathly-white skin, sour expression and deep downward lines at the corners of the thin-lipped mouth into which he was now thrusting some stodgy pudding and custard.

Slipping back outside to report to Cal who was waiting on the pavement she steered him into the building. On the wall at the bottom of a wide flight of carpeted stairs was a notice board setting out the residents' names and their room numbers. George spotted it first and pointed it out to Cal.

Sir Eustace Vishney. Room 9.

As Cal made his way up the stairs, baseball cap pulled down, spirit level under an arm and carrying his wooden tool box, George headed back towards the dining room from where the troops were now making their exit, some in wheelchairs, some on sticks and some tottering along unaided, all homing in on the particular chair over which they had claimed territorial rights. Although they had just had lunch it was still only a quarter to twelve and Vishney was clutching a copy of the morning's *Times*. Reaching a winged armchair with faded floral upholstery in a spot by the window he slowly lowered himself into it and looked disdainfully around the room as if it were his Courtroom long ago. A few staff were wandering about, levering bodies into chairs here and there and making cursory checks on the odd protester. No-one paid any attention at all to George as she picked up a stray dining chair from the hall, crossed over towards the old man scouring his newspaper through those absurd pince-nez and sat herself down immediately opposite him. Green cardigan, food spilled down it, buttons in the wrong holes, crumpled grey flannel trousers and plaid carpet slippers.

"How are you, Judge?" she began, turning on her best smile and behaving as if she had known him for years.

"Am I meant to know you?" came the acid response as he eyed her up and down.

"I recognised you. I know you were very important," she said politely, looking at the parchment skin decorated with occasional clumps of grey whiskers which he had missed when shaving.

"I've been retired over fifteen years. Who are you?" he replied putting his newspaper down on his lap.

"My granddad lives here. He'll be down soon. But I noticed you. You were a famous Judge."

"How do you know that?" he barked.

"Grandad told me."

"Oh, I see. Yes. I was a High Court Judge for twenty-nine years," he said with what was meant to pass for a smile, letting the pince-nez drop from his nose and dangle on the green cord around his neck.

As George warmed to her task, Cal had already located Room 9. It was unlocked. No-one was about. With a final look over his shoulder he slipped inside. Single bed, white bedspread. Walnut desk under the window with papers in neat little piles. Phone. Paper-weight. A couple of framed amateurish oil paintings on the left hand wall. A sunset at sea and a thatched English cottage. Probably painted by the old codger himself. No family photographs. Obviously no-one cared. But the whole of the right hand wall was bookshelves. Five shelves, ten feet long. Laden with books. That was where to look.

Four of the shelves were all books but the top shelf was a row of box files. Stretching chronologically from left to right, they were labelled on the outside from 1946 to 1975. Cal was now sweating. How long did he have? Breaking into a Judge's bedroom may not go down too well. Standing on the toolbox he had put down on the floor, his arm reached out for the box labelled 1963. As his hand touched it he suddenly heard voices in the corridor outside. Getting closer. Two voices. Females. Now right outside the door. Stepping off the tool box, he scurried into the small bathroom. Razor, shaving cream. Pair of dentures in a glass tumbler. Smelled stale. A knock on the bedroom door. A few seconds pause and then the bedroom door opened and he froze. A female voice "Oh! This is a deluxe. You wanted to see a standard." The door gently closed and the voices faded away down the corridor.

Back to the task. 1963. He pulled it off the shelf and sat down on top of Frederick Walgrave's mahogany tool box, finding comfort in it, as if knowing that George's dad would have approved of what they were doing. Somehow he felt quite close to Fred, while feeling little if anything for the man who was his father.

Inside the box files were Vishney's souvenirs. Notes on loose pieces of paper in an educated fountain pen hand. Press cuttings of his cases. Each case separately tied up in pink tape. Photographs of him in his wig and robes. Photographs of men he'd tried. The material Cal was seeking was near the bottom of the box. A clutch of press cuttings about half an inch thick. No personal notes. Cal pulled them out, closed the box file and put it back in place. No time to go through them now but he just wanted to double check he'd got the right ones. The top cutting was a report of the murder itself. Flicking through the bundle he saw the progression towards the day of the execution. And it was then that he was struck with a thunderbolt every bit as powerful as the jack hammer blow Lanny Creane had landed on him yesterday evening. In all of his discussions about his father Cal had never seen a photograph of him. Ma had not kept one. His physical appearance until this fateful second had been a complete unknown. But there, on the day that the State carried out the hanging ordered by the dreadful stranger in whose bedroom the son now stood, was a picture of his father on the front page of The Manchester Guardian. Henry Francis Stanton. The newspaper was yellowed and brittle to the touch but there was no room for any mistake. His father was black.

Downstairs, the old man was slowly responding to the flattery of the pretty young girl, seemingly so much in awe of him. No-one had any time for him nowadays. Nobody appreciated him.

"I'd like you to tell me about one of your cases," she continued. "The case about the schoolteacher who murdered Louise Donovan."

Vishney's demeanour changed in an instant. Behind the pince-nez the milky eyes flashed with the venom that had earned him his title of *Vicious Vishney.* "Stanton. He did it. Jury got it right."

"But he didn't, did he? You know he didn't. You know more about that case than has ever surfaced. Now I'm asking you, before you die, what else did you know?"

"Who are you?" he barked aggressively.

"My name is Georgina Walgrave. My father defended Stanton. He never forgot him. My father knew he was innocent. So do you. Now tell me, if you want to meet your Maker with a clean slate. Tell me what you know."

"I'm going to have you thrown out of here," he shouted angrily, struggling to get out of his chair and on to his feet.

"Why did you give the case to such a junior barrister?" she demanded.

"Get out. Get out. Maureen," he called out to a middle-aged lady pushing a vacuum cleaner towards the dining room. "Maureen, put this young woman out of here. Immediately."

"I think you'd better leave, my dear," said Maureen who came straight over and took George gently by the arm and started to lead her away. "He does have a bit of temper," she whispered conspiratorially. "Come back another day."

As Maureen ushered George towards the hallway she saw Cal, standing stock still, staring at Vishney as he continued to spit out his fury towards the staff, moving his head about in angry little jerks, replacing his pince-nez when they fell.

"I had to see him George," breathed Cal. "I just had to look at him with my own eyes. The man who sent my father to the gallows."

"He's a bastard alright," she replied. "But, more importantly, a bastard with a secret."

"Best you and your friend left," said Maureen, who was now observing this bizarre exchange between some girl who'd apparently upset the old Judge and a young man who looked like he'd just been hit by a double-decker bus.

As they hurriedly made their way back to the car Cal seemed in a state of shock and, as soon as they'd got to the end of the street and turned the corner, George stopped and pulled him into a shop doorway.

"Did you get in?" she asked anxiously.

"Oh, yeah. I got in alright. And I've pinched his cuttings of the case. I've got them here in the tool box. He'll realise it was something to do with your visit. Does he know who you are?"

"Yes. But it doesn't matter. He won't report it. He's hiding a secret. He thought it was buried forever. He'll do nothing which risks it creeping out of the woodwork," she assured him.

"He's not the only one with a secret," said Cal.

"What do you mean?"

"Ma. She had a big secret."

"We've been through that. She didn't want you to know your father was hanged. It's understandable enough," observed George.

"No. George. I don't mean that. She had another secret," he said quietly.

"What?"

"My father was black. Not African black, but definitely part black. Probably mixed blood," he answered. "There's a picture of him in the newspaper."

"I've never seen a picture of him," said George. "There were none in Dad's file. Why didn't anyone tell us?"

"I don't know. Do I look black?"

"No, not really. You're very dark. But you're an Aussie. I met you on a Pacific island. You're as dark as anyone who lives under that kind of sun," she replied candidly. "Does it make you feel different about yourself?"

"As a matter of fact I think it does," he replied softly. "But that isn't the point. You're thinking 1990. Think 1963. Black teacher. White pupil. Murder. Rape. He didn't have a chance."

They stood in silence in the shop doorway of a Brighton milliner's absorbing the latest bombshell. Suddenly, she leaned forward and kissed him softly on the lips. But Cal didn't respond. The kiss felt like a vote of sympathy.

He broke the moment of embarrassment by leaning down and opening up the tool box which he'd placed on the ground.

"There's something else, George," he remarked, bringing out the sheaf of cuttings. "These cuttings are filed in date order. The top one is a report of the murder itself. The second one reports my father's arrest and so on."

"So?"

"Well, on the second one, written in pencil, there's a phone number. *Batford 789657*. In those days they must have still used telephone exchange names."

"Batford is near where the school was," she responded immediately.

'Exactly. Somebody, presumably Vishney, has written a local phone number on a Press cutting that would have come into existence before Vishney ever knew the case was coming his way. On the day of that newspaper report my father hadn't even been charged, let alone been brought before the High Court Judge. Why was Vishney already writing a Batford phone number on it?"

"So we need to find out whose that number was," said George, as he put the cuttings back into the tool box and they continued towards the car.

"Yes. How?" he responded.

"Easy," she said. "Tomorrow. I'll have to work. But you'll borrow the car. And you'll drive to Canterbury. You're going to visit Chauncey. He'll know how to crack the number. And he'll fill you in on Amy Beckett."

"OK, George. Good work. We're making progress. And one more thing."

"What?"

"Sorry about the kiss," he smiled.

"Bad timing," she replied. "Timing's never been my strong point."

Chapter 10

The Black Belt, Alabama, USA 1963

A few miles from a bend in the Alabama River, where it swings south- west heading for its eventual union with the Tallapoosa and Coosa rivers, rich white men have benefited from the fertile topsoil, the sweltering summer humidity and an endless supply of subjugated Negro labour. Slavery was abolished, but only by giving it another name. Sharecropping. A pernicious system designed to keep the white man obscenely rich and the black man dirt poor. Assigning his selected Negro family a portion of land in return for half of the produced crop, the plantation owner could rest in his hammock on the porch, sipping his long mint julep, while the entire Negro family, including small children, would toil in the fields from dawn to dusk to sow, tend and harvest the crop. Any equipment required, any seed, any staple of life would be made available on credit to the Negro at the local store in town. A store which also belonged to the plantation owner and so he ensured that, by control and fraud, the sharecropping family never got out of debt, leaving little prospect of escape. An illiterate Negro confronting a white land owner in Alabama over the annual accounts left room for only one winner.

Such is the resilience of the human condition that, now and again, someone got out. Like Eleazer Wallen. The eighth child of Hezekiah and Sarah, the fourteenth grandchild of second generation slaves and, when his turn came, sharecropper forty six on the Dodds plantation. Eleazer saw beyond the cotton boll, the dirt of the furrowed field and the blazing sun. He saw the azaleas blooming in the spring, the miles of pine forests, the fine antebellum architecture of the old house and the world of books. Painstakingly, Eleazer taught himself to read and then taught his wife Martha. After five years of breaking his back for Edwin Dodds he walked out of the field cabin carrying everything he owned in a cardboard suitcase, knowing his credit at the store was clear, although the Manager claimed otherwise, and set off with Martha on a bus to Brantley, over a hundred miles away.

Brantley was a new world. Parks, libraries, museums, schools, fancy stores, a cinema, soda fountains, tree-lined streets and walkways. Mainly for the white man of course, but there were little corners where Martha and Eleazer could taste the better life. Destined to be childless, they had only themselves to think of and Martha got employment as a maid in the home of a Doctor and his family while Eleazer worked in the kitchens of the Madison Hotel on Main Street. Renting a one-bedroom wood frame cabin in the black section of town they rejoiced in their escape.

On that sultry Friday afternoon in August the temperature in the airless kitchens soared to over a hundred and ten degrees as Eleazer scrubbed the vast copper pans from the luncheon service and wheeled the cartloads of dirty dishes from the collection point to the deep stone basins where each of them would be hand-washed and dried before racking them back up on the shelves ready for dinner. Hands that had been torn apart by the Alabama cotton boll and calloused by the tools that turned the land were now chapped and sore from the harsh detergents and wire cleaning brushes that formed part of his daily chores. But he was not complaining for, tonight, after he and Martha had finished work, they were going to *Carter's Electric Re-Sales* on Albany Street to buy a television. They had talked about little else for the last month. Back on the plantation the notion that black folks would ever own a television set would have been treated with laughter but here in Brantley it was actually going to happen. Second-hand. A Zenith 12 inch. Black and white. They had left five dollars on it and Mr Carter's clerk had told them that they must come in with the rest of the money on payday or lose their deposit. Today was payday. This very evening Martha and he would be sitting in their cabin, drinking a mug of coffee watching Jed Clampett on *The Beverly Hillbillies*.

At three o'clock he was allowed to take a thirty minute break. By then he had already put in nine hours and had another two to go. It was his custom during this precious rest time to leave the kitchens and cross the street to Lomax Park, taking his latest library book with him. The walkways in the park were lined with silver maple trees but, on the west side, they had developed a disease and had to be felled, leaving half a dozen wooden benches that no longer had any shade from the sun and were therefore not used by the white townsfolk and so the whites were not bothered if black people chose to sit there. Eleazer, protected by his wide-brimmed straw hat, was a regular frequenter of the west park benches and today he was engrossed in every word of William Faulkner's *The Sound and The Fury*.

The Carters had lived in Brantley since shortly after the Civil War. Once wealthy landowners, succeeding generations had dissipated the family fortune. Walter Carter was the latest waster. He had inherited five stores from his father. *Carter's Electric Re-Sales* was the only one left. Walter had gradually drunk and womanised his way through the other four, with remortgages, refinances and eventual repossession. Thin strands of fair hair stretched flat on a balding pate, always scowling, heavy-jowled and over-weight, he usually took lunch on a Friday with Aubrey Hardy, President of the Chamber of Commerce and Deputy Sheriff Marty Pope in the Grill Room of the Madison Hotel, purporting to discuss municipal business but in fact talking hunting, fishing and women while drinking too much whiskey.

Walking back to the store across Lomax Park he went as far as the stone War Memorial before cutting along the western walkway and out into Albany Street through the West Gate. As he passed through the Gate he put his hand to his rear trouser pocket and realised that his wallet was missing. He knew that he'd had it when he'd left the Madison because Aubrey had given him the business card of the new Manager of the First Capital Alabama Bank and he remembered tucking it into a flap of the wallet as he had passed the War Memorial. His driving licence had been in it, plus a few bits of paper with names and phone numbers on and maybe fifteen dollars, so he was cursing out loud as he turned back to retrace his steps to see if he could find it. Large sweat stains spread from the armpits of his fawn, cotton jacket as he propelled his bulk back across the park to the Memorial. Nothing.

Wiping his brow with a spotted red kerchief as lunchtime's whiskey leaked through his pores he became increasingly incensed. Someone must have picked it up and there was as much chance of them handing it in as either of his former wives ever resuming cohabitation. Walter Carter was an angry man and, spitting a stream of Tiger chewing tobacco through his yellow stained teeth on to the path, he headed back towards the West Gate. The property taxes on the store were due next month, Perry was pressing him hard for his five hundred dollar gambling debts and that bitch last night had eaten her way through the menu at *Indigo's Southern Fayre* before passing out dead drunk at the table, having to be manhandled into the back of a cab and leaving him to pick up the tab. Then he saw his wallet.

It was in the hands of a Negro who was standing on the edge of the path near the benches. A hard-backed book was tucked under his arm and in his hands was Walter Carter's pig skin wallet. The man was just beginning to open the wallet as Carter approached.

"Get your filthy hands outta my wallet, you thieving sonafabitch," he ranted, coming right up to the man and snatching the wallet from him.

"I jus' this minute find it, Sir. Jus' this very minute," the man replied, shocked at the intensity of the anger that was coming his way.

". . . I bin reading on the bench, gets up and sees it, lying in the grass over there. I was jus' seein' if the owner's name was in it, that's all, Sir. I'd have take it to the owner or the Sheriff's Office," he continued, his voice now shaking as he sensed the accusations that may follow.

Carter's fat fingers were rifling anxiously through the contents, checking to see what was missing. Driving licence. Bits of paper. Bank Manager's card. All there. Counted the money. Fourteen dollars.

"There's a dollar bill missing, boy. You helped yerself already," he spat out.

"I ain't taken one cent, Sir," the man protested vehemently. "I ain't even got a dollar bill on me. You can search my pockets," he added, stepping forward and putting his right hand in his trousers pocket to demonstrate that his pockets were empty.

As soon as he made that move Walter Carter pulled a Ruger's single-action .22 revolver from the inside pocket of his jacket and pointed it at the man who stood frozen to the spot.

"No Nigra steals my money and no Nigra goes for a blade against me," he growled, the sweat pouring down his face and the hand holding the gun shaking in the intensity of his fury. "No fuckin' Nigra puts his black fingers in my goddamned wallet," he continued. Then he pulled the trigger.

Eleazer Wallen never got his television. He got a pine casket, a pauper's funeral with a grave in the black cemetery out by the sawmill and a grieving widow who, after the funeral, returned his overdue book to the library and paid the thirty cents fine that the white librarian demanded.

As Eleazer hit the ground with a bullet lodged in his spine which had ripped its way through the aorta, Carter became aware of a whimpering noise behind him and turned to see a young black boy, barefoot and dressed in rags, maybe eleven or twelve years old, standing watching the callous act of murder. Carter swung the gun on to him. The sound of the shot would bring people on to the scene within a minute. He needed to act fast.

"What's yer name, boy?" he demanded, pointing the gun directly at the boy's head.

"Glover, Sir," the thin voice piped back in terror.

"Glover what?"

"Glover Higg, Sir."

"You see what happen here, Glover Higg?" growled Carter.

"I ain't sure," the boy whispered.

"You see the thief with my wallet in his hands?"

"Oh, yes, Sir," Glover replied, catching on quickly.

"You hear that sonafabitch threaten me that he had a knife?"

"I heard it."

"You see him going to his pocket? You see all that?"

"I saw it."

"You ever say any different boy and I'll have you tracked down by the KKK and hanged from a tree. You got all that?" Carter barked.

"Yessir."

"Unless that's what you saw, you'll have a rope round your scrawny black neck, Glover Higg."

"That's what I saw, Sir."

"And that's what you'll say?"

And that's what I'll say."

"Right." Carter nodded, now putting the gun back in his pocket. "So run and get Deputy Marty Pope up here now. That's who you ask for. Deputy Marty Pope."

As Glover Higg's thin trembling legs sped off to summon Marty Pope, Carter looked back down the path to see if anyone was approaching and saw a knot of people running towards him, about sixty yards away. They'd be on the scene in a few seconds. But Carter only needed two seconds to slip a dollar bill and his penknife into the dead man's trousers pocket.

Two days later, in the one-cell gaol at the rear of the Sheriff's Office, Marty Pope brought in a brown paper bag containing a big, juicy cheeseburger and fries and put them on the table in the centre of the cell. Walter Carter got up from the bench where he'd been lying, sniffed the inside of the bag, extracted the burger and started to devour it while the Deputy broke the news.

"Looks like we're going to have to have ourselves a trial, Walt," he sighed.

"Shit," grunted Carter, his mouth full of half-chewed burger. "You said there'd be no fucking indictment."

"Nah. We gotta have a trial. Too much pressure. National papers got hold of it."

"I don't want no trial."

"Formality, Walt. Formality. The Deputy DA's gonna call by any time and spell it all out," Pope assured him.

"Shit, Marty. I didn't want no trial. I gotta business to run."

"You'll be back at the store by Friday. A Grand Jury indictment in the next day or two and then we'll get yer bond fixed real low. I've already spoken to the Judge. Trial in October."

"Where?"

"Here in Brantley. In front of Judge Sanborne Relford. Your daddy knew him real well."

"Have you seen to the evidence?" Carter enquired, momentarily switching his attention to the mound of French fries he'd tipped out on top of the brown bag."

"Pretty much done. No worries," Pope confirmed, now taking a seat alongside Carter and helping himself to a handful of fries.

"That black kid, Glover Higg?" Carter whispered.

"Yeah? I seen him. He backs up your story."

"And you wipe the penknife good?" Carter asked, taking another enormous bite out of the hamburger as the grease trickled down his chins."

"Sure. No prints."

"And the jury?" Carter breathed.

"You just leave the jury to Jacy Kanade."

"You know what I mean, Marty," Carter persisted.

"White, Walt. White as a Klansman's hood," he laughed. "You don't get no whiter than that. And here's Mr Kanade right on time. I'll leave you two to have a chat."

As Pope squeezed out of the cell the tall figure of Deputy District Attorney Jacy Kanade slipped on to the bench alongside the scowling, sweating prisoner who was now noisily licking his fingers having devoured his lunch. Kanade chose to avoid a handshake in the circumstances and Carter chose to come directly to the point.

"AYAK?" Carter demanded.

"AKIA," Kanade replied immediately.

Carter smiled. Marty was right. No worries. It was one of the first codes they taught you. "Are You A Klansman? A Klansman I Am."

Chapter 11

Wealdstone, England 1963

Slamming the front door of the Victorian terraced house behind him, Bob Lancaster strode through the front room and into the scullery at the rear of the house where his wife, Liz, was standing over the sink, scrubbing the pans from their earlier meal with her red, chapped hands, trying to eke out the hot water from the antiquated and inefficient Ascot heater.

"No need to slam the door, Bob," she observed quietly. "It won't get you your job back."

Last week Goldberg had taken on a new warehouseman. Leroy Dexter. Straight off the banana boat and into a white man's job. At the meetings the speakers had always said that the Jews and the Negroes would never help each other out and now Goldberg had hired one without a word to the other men. Yesterday lunchtime Bob had decided to take his own action and, collecting a couple of the labourers from the yard, they had cornered Dexter in the area behind the giant bins. No-one came out there during the lunch break and Bob had taken his legs away with a piece of four by four, allowing the other two boys to pin him down on his back on the filthy floor. That's when Bob had produced the fitter's knife and pressed it to the black, palpitating throat.

"There ain't enough fucking jobs for us," he snarled. "So no black bastard's moving in 'ere. You walk out on this job at the end of the week. Or else," he threatened, pushing the edge of the blade into the rough unshaven skin, but holding short of cutting and drawing blood.

Leroy Dexter didn't answer. He didn't have the chance, for it was another older voice, coming from behind Lancaster and his cronies who answered for him.

"Go get your cards, Lancaster," shouted Len Goldberg, who had watched from his office window overlooking the yard as Lancaster had gathered his troops. He'd suspected for months that he had a serious bigot on his staff but this was the confirmation he needed.

"We're just funning, Mr Goldberg," he replied nervously, jumping up and shoving the knife back into his overalls pocket. "Just funning."

"Get your cards. Get out. All three of you. He's black and he's worth a hundred of your kind."

Lancaster had just reported the details to the members at the meeting tonight and they had taken a serious view of it. Goldberg's factory was going to have its windows put in. And Johnny Weldon had volunteered to sort out Dexter. This had made Lancaster appreciate the comradeship of the members but, of course, none of it would get him his job back and so he was still in a foul mood when he got home.

"What did they say?" asked Liz anxiously, never quite sure how much of the truth her husband gave her about these meetings which he was attending with increased regularity.

"Goldberg'll be needing a glazier come Thursday morning," he grunted, not prepared to tell her what lay in store for Dexter because she had no real idea yet of what the arrival of these people meant for England and the lengths it may be necessary to go to in order to keep them out.

"And how's that going to help us put food on the table?" she retorted in exasperation. "Can't any of them help you get a new job?"

"No, but there's to be a meeting this weekend. At some old barracks near Gravesend. We stay overnight and there's speeches and a film. I've signed up for it. Means I won't be here on Saturday night."

She walked away from the sink, drying her hands on her apron and staring at him as he carefully laid out a sheet of newspaper and prepared his shoe-cleaning ritual. It was an oddity about him that she'd never understood. Often his behaviour was rough, his language was coarse, he was as sensitive as a hunk of scrap iron, yet he always insisted on keeping his boots highly polished. "Shining boots. The measure of a true Englishman," he used to say.

"What exactly are you getting into here?" she demanded. "Speeches, films, nights away from home. What do you really know about these people?"

Putting down his tin of polish on the newspaper, he turned to face her. "They care, Liz," he responded. "They care about our country. Jobs for the future. Not having bastardised kids. Keeping our women safe." As he spoke she could see that his eyes were blazing with the intensity of what he felt. She didn't like it. He was frightening her and, as she walked out of the scullery into the front room, his words were getting more impassioned and his voice was growing louder. ". . . fight to keep them out, fight to keep them down . . ." she heard him shouting as she closed the door behind her.

The weekend gathering had exceeded all of his expectations. There was even talk of starting a new Party next year and there had been lectures on structuring a civil defence unit to protect members on the streets when public meetings were held. But the highlight of it all had been the film on the Saturday night. It was a sixty minute collection of news footage from a trial that had just taken place in Alabama. As the final black and white images had faded from the screen and the reels on the projector were spinning round empty the whole audience had risen to their feet as one and broken into wild applause at how the Alabama State system was warding off the evil that threatened. When he lay in the camp bed in the dormitory that night Bob Lancaster had played the scenes over in his mind time and time again. He had been inspired.

Back at home in the sitting room on the Sunday afternoon he

had tried to explain to Liz what strength the white population in Alabama was displaying to maintain standards, jobs and public safety.

"Walter Carter's family had lived there for centuries," he began. "This black bloke, Elizah or summat like that, pinched some money from his wallet and threatened Carter with a knife so he shot 'im. The Judge really told them. Self-defence, he said. Jury was white. You know how long they was out, Liz?" he asked in a voice brimming with admiration. "Forty-five minutes. Not guilty."

His wife had listened in silence as he recounted details of the evidence and the TV interviews of the jury after returning their verdict. Soon she found herself thinking that perhaps her husband and his friends were right. Society had to protect its own. It was her husband who was out of a job as a result of these people. It was her family who would suffer. His hatred and bigotry were becoming contagious.

"There was a little black kid gave evidence," he continued. "Claimed he'd seen it all. Told the jury Elizah just found the wallet, made no threat to Carter at all and that Carter just shot him stone dead 'cos he was black."

"Well, the jury couldn't have believed him, could they?" his wife retorted.

"You're missing the point, Liz. Missing the whole bloody point. They did believe him. And he was telling the truth. Carter admitted as much after the verdict," he explained.

"So what's the point I'm missing?"

"Protecting ourselves from these people. Protecting our race. Gotta be ruthless or die, that's the point."

"I see," she answered, although she wasn't really sure that she did see. But it was the next remark of her husband that really shocked her.

"And do you know what happened next?" he continued. "A couple of weeks later they found the kid. Naked. Beaten. Hanging from a tree on the edge of the town. His bloodied clothes was lying in a bundle by the trunk of the tree. They'd horsewhipped him first."

"That's just terrible," she blurted out involuntarily.

"No. It's not. They'll not have no more trouble off the blacks in that town. The lesson's been handed out. Two deaths'll probably save countless more lives, black and white," he explained, jabbing his finger forcibly on the table to emphasise his point.

The next morning he intended to leave the house early to walk to the Labour Exchange to see if any jobs were available. "The early bird catches the worm," he remarked to Liz as he had drunk his cup of tea in the scullery. His boots were shining and he wore a tie. As he opened the front door he bumped straight into the postman who handed him the one letter that he had been about to put through the letter box. Bob Lancaster looked suspiciously at the official looking buff envelope and tore it open clumsily as he set off down the road. Stopping in the middle of the pavement to make sure that he had got it right he mumbled the contents of the letter out loud to himself. *"Robert Lancaster. You are summoned to jury service at the Old Bailey on the first Monday of next month. Please bring this letter with you."* There was a renewed purpose in his stride as he headed for the Labour Exchange.

* * *

"The Judge told us that the first thing we must do is elect a Foreman," intoned an earnest, bespectacled man, who had lived his life terrified of his own shadow. He certainly didn't want the job.

"Foreman. Seems you have to leave my name out of the hat," piped up the lone female on the jury. A spinster in her fifties, still living in the house where she was born.

"And you can count me out," volunteered the man with the ruddy complexion. "I'm a gardener, not a bloody lawyer."

"None of us are lawyers," said Bob Lancaster. "I'll do it. It's going to need someone with balls. Any objections?"

There were no other takers as the group of twelve strangers took their seats in the alien atmosphere of the jury room. The case had only lasted two days and in that time they had only spent a few minutes together out of the Court room. They knew absolutely nothing about each other and, even more importantly, no-one, not even the Judge, knew anything about them.

Lancaster reflected on the Alabama trial. Every juror had been questioned by the lawyers before they were eventually chosen to sit on the jury. Not that they had answered the questions truthfully about their ability to be impartial in trying a black man, but at least they had been asked. This Judge and the lawyers had no idea that the Foreman of the jury was a racial bigot of such extreme prejudice that the accused's prospects of acquittal had plummeted to zero as soon as his face had appeared in the dock. The evidence would be rendered as irrelevant as that of Glover Higg. None of this troubled Bob Lancaster. If the English judicial system could be as disingenuous and foolish to believe that, in any given set of twelve people, there wasn't a serious risk of a personal overriding prejudice outweighing the justice of the case, then they deserved what they got. Verdicts of prejudice.

"If we do him," said a young man in a broad Cockney accent, "what happens to him? Does he definitely swing?"

"I thought that the Judge told us that's his problem, not ours," declared an elderly grey-haired man wearing a large, flesh-coloured hearing-aid in his left ear and who had missed half of the evidence.

"It seems to me that the Judge doesn't see any problems in this case. He couldn't have made it clearer that he thought Stanton was guilty," remarked the only male in the room not to have troubled to wear a tie. "The Judge sees this kind of stuff every day of the week. He knows who's guilty and who isn't."

"But I didn't trust that Amy Beckett. Something about her didn't ring true," observed a rather scholarly looking middle-aged man in an out of date and tired grey flannel suit.

"And what about that Hollister kid the girl mentioned. What was he doing? Why didn't the Prosecution call him?" added another.

"None of that matters. Like the Judge told us. The knickers. So how's he explain the knickers in his saddlebag? They grown wings or summat?" said the Cockney.

"But the prefect, Littleton, if his timing's right, it doesn't tie in with Amy Beckett," retorted the man in the grey flannel suit. "And that Mr Walgrave. I liked him. And what he said about Stanton sitting there, munching on an apple. I'm with Mr Walgrave on that one," he added.

"But the wife was lying wasn't she? Scratched his back in bed the night before. Load of cobblers if you ask me. And what kind of a woman marries one of them anyway?" the loud Cockney accent declared, bringing into the open the issue that was dominating their thoughts, but, until this latest intervention, had remained unspoken.

After a momentary silence others took up the theme.

"I've read that they're very highly sexed," said the gardener.

"And rough with their women," added the spinster.

"They don't see things like us."

"Or have our standards of decent behaviour."

"And," announced Lancaster emphatically, contributing for the first time, "they take our jobs. In Jamaica, if the woman doesn't do as she's told she's beaten or worse. That's the attitude they bring here. That's the attitude Stanton would have had if Louise had said no. Then he'd have lost his rag."

For a further half an hour the discussions continued until the Cockney demanded that a vote be taken. "It's getting late," he said. "I've got my verdict. Let's see where we stand."

"What happens to us if we don't reach a verdict today?" asked the spinster.

"Then we have to trek off to some cheap hotel together and come back tomorrow," answered the gardener. "I can just see my missus's reaction on hearing that. I agree, it's time to vote."

"Right," said Lancaster. "We'll go round the table. I'll start. My vote's for Guilty. Who's next?"

"Guilty," said the Cockney.

"Guilty," said the gardener.

"Guilty," said the man with the hearing-aid.

"Not Guilty," whispered the scholarly man and then shouting it out loud and clear. "Not Guilty. There's at least a reasonable doubt."

"Not in my mind there isn't," retorted the spinster, not relishing a whole evening and night in the company of these men in some second-rate hotel. "Guilty as charged."

Six more votes for "Guilty" shot out across the table like bullets from a machine gun, followed by a complete silence, before Lancaster turned on the bully-boy tactics that they'd taught him to use at the meetings. The technique was to address the mob as if the scab wasn't there.

"We got to all agree. That's what the Judge told us. But we got one do-gooder amongst us who doesn't want to see Louise Donovan get justice. We got one who can't see what these people are like. Ignoring the knickers, Amy Beckett and all what the Judge explained. We got one who thinks he knows better. Stanton likes white women. He's got a white wife. But that ain't enough for his sort. But our friend here just can't see it."

As he continued his diatribe, several of the other jurors shifted uncomfortably in their seats. This man was founding his decision on Stanton's colour more than anything else in the case. They were getting increasingly uneasy. But they were all weak and, in any event, their discomfort was quickly eased by the total capitulation of the lone juror. Harangued, belittled and ineffectual, he simply whispered, "Alright, Guilty." And thus it was, on the stroke of five o'clock, that Henry Francis Stanton was condemned to the gallows.

Chapter 12

London, England. Early March 1990.

In the event, Cal did not drive to Canterbury the next day. Instead he took the train to London to rendezvous with Graham Chauncey in *The Masons Arms*, a grubby, spit and sawdust pub in the back streets of Wandsworth which Chauncey had suggested when George had telephoned to set up a meeting.

Even though Cal had arrived well before the early lunch trade the atmosphere was heavy with smoke as he carried his pint of Old Speckled Hen ale across to a small, round table, scarred by years of abuse and slipped on to the bench seat running along the back wall. The majority of the customers were gathered round the bar, obviously from local warehouses and factories and devoid of any likely looking candidate for a retired copper. As he sipped his beer Cal reflected grimly on the fact that the man he was waiting to see was the only person he had ever met, save for his mother, who had actually talked to his father.

"She said I'd recognise you by your shiner, but I didn't reckon on it being that bad," announced a booming voice, "I'm Graham Chauncey."

Cal looked up at the bulky figure with the creased features and smiling eyes and held out his hand. "Cal Stewart, good to meet you," he replied as Chauncey, already clutching a pint pot containing orange juice, lowered himself on to the chair opposite, staring intently at the young earnest face, recollecting the boy's father who he had heard being sentenced to death all those years ago.

"Who did that to you?" he asked with concern.

"A thug. On behalf of someone who didn't want me prying into the past," he replied.

"Interesting. You get any name?"

"Creane. 'No-one does that to a Creane.' That was his mate's parting shot. I imagine he's still in Taunton Hospital. I put a baling hook into his leg," Cal replied coldly.

"A baling hook. You don't do things by halves, do you? I'll check the name out and get back to you, see if we can find out who was behind it. Being an ex-cop I have tentacles in every town," Chauncey responded. "Now let's get down to business. You need to know where I stand on all of this."

"You arrested my father when he went to his bike in the bike sheds. And found the girl's knickers in the saddlebag," Cal replied. "I've read all the papers."

"Yeah. But the reason that I'm digging around now. You don't know about that."

"Go on."

"When Mr Walgrave died I received a letter from the solicitor handling his estate. Enclosing a cheque for a couple of grand. Asking me to poke around a bit. As far as the money would take me," he explained.

"Why you?"

"Because when the jury was out in the trial Mr Walgrave and I had a quiet chat. Off the record. I liked Mr Walgrave. I thought he'd got a raw deal off that bastard of a Judge. Making him do a case like that without a QC and trying to bully him around the Court. And I had an uneasy feeling about the whole case."

"Can you explain?"

"No. Not really. I was as wet behind the ears as Mr Walgrave, but something didn't feel right. Mind you, I'm not saying the jury got it wrong. I got to tell you that all I'm saying is I wasn't sure. I'm not here 'cos I'm convinced your dad was innocent. Perhaps he was, perhaps he wasn't. That's all I said to Mr Walgrave. And then, all those years later I had that letter. I was retired. Living on a Sergeant's pension.

My wife left me five years back. I had time on my hands. So I decided to start with Amy Beckett."

"Why?"

"Because I never believed her. Either when we first spoke to her at the school or when she gave evidence at the trial. It was obvious that she and Louise Donovan were pretty loose. I mean, look what she's doing for a living now, she's a hooker."

Sipping slowly at his orange juice Chauncey then recounted in detail the strange tale about his trip to Las Vegas and his meeting with Amy Beckett or Tammy as she called herself now.

"So sooner or later someone's got to take another crack at her, but go about it in a different way," Cal concluded.

"I've been thinking about that. She's a tough nut and I reckoned we might have to get in an American private detective. Las Vegas is teeming with them. But now I've met you I'm not so sure. Thing is, you see, apart from the actual colour of your skin, you remind me of your father. Way you hold yourself. Facial expressions. And Amy'll remember him clearly. He wasn't many years older than you are now when it all happened. Seeing you in the flesh might shake her up a bit," Chauncey declared.

"I didn't know my father was black until yesterday when I saw a press cutting with a picture of him," Cal responded ruefully. "Did it affect the trial?"

"He wasn't full black. But coloured nonetheless and there weren't that many coloureds in England in those days. Certainly not many who were schoolteachers and even fewer who were married to a white woman. Truth is I don't know if it affected the trial, but if you asked me straight I'd say one or two of the jurors at least showed signs of prejudice. Mutterings and looks and stuff like that. It's the fella who turned out to be the foreman who struck me most. Mean looking bastard. Seemed to enjoy saying 'guilty' when the time came."

"So you think it should be me who tries to nail her, even though it means an expensive and long journey?" said Cal.

"I went on a cheapie charter trip from Gatwick. Five days. Flights and hotel all in. It worked out at only a few hundred quid. We could ask Mr Walgrave's solicitor if the estate might help a bit as you're on a tight budget."

"I'd have to talk to George and her mother," Cal responded.

"That George. A real chip off the old block she is. Wish I was thirty years younger," he smiled.

"Well, I am, Mr Chauncey," Cal came back smartly.

"Graham," interrupted Chauncey brusquely. "Now tell me what happened when you tracked down Vishney."

"He had a full file in his room. Chronologically arranged. On the second press report Vishney had written a local Batford telephone number. Remember at that time my father hadn't even been charged . . . ," Cal began.

"But Vishney wouldn't have come into the case until after charging, a Magistrates Court's appearance and a committal to the High Court," Chauncey interrupted.

"Exactly, yet he was already noting a local Batford number and here it is," replied Cal warming to the task and thrusting a piece of paper with the number on it into the retired officer's large hand. "George said you'd probably have ways and means of checking it out."

"I'll give it a shot. Like I said, tentacles in every town," Chauncey replied tucking the paper into his wallet. "Let me get you a refill and then I'll explain why I asked to meet you in Wandsworth."

"Actually, it's getting busy now and it's too smoky for me. Can we carry on the discussion outside in the fresh air?"

It had started to spit with rain and the sky was a steely grey as the two men walked slowly along the littered side street towards the main road. Chauncey had unfurled an umbrella and was gallantly endeavouring to hold at least part of it over Cal's head as the rain intensified. Near the corner stood a dingy looking betting shop and the two men ducked inside to continue their conversation in the dry.

A sprinkling of shabbily dressed men stood around the poorly lit interior, staring at the racing sheets pinned to the walls or watching the build-up to the next race on the television monitors. Chauncey nodded towards an empty table strewn with discarded betting slips, screwed up balls of paper and pencil stubs.

"This is a bit tricky," Chauncey began, once they had seated themselves on the hard, red plastic chairs. "I don't want to cause you any more grief but with any capital case, or a case resulting in a life sentence, they never throw away the exhibits."

"You mean they're still stored somewhere?" enquired Cal.

"Exactly. And that's why I suggested meeting in Wandsworth. I've made a few enquiries. The storage facility is in a Home Office warehouse five minutes from here. As I was an Officer in the case I can get access. And we may just spot something that was missed all those years ago. Everything was much more amateurish in those days and it's unlikely that anyone's looked at those things since the execution. But you may find it very distressing," Chauncey explained.

"I probably will. But that's no reason not to take a look. What will we see?" Cal replied.

"Each item will have been put into a separate transparent bag and sealed. Then all the bags will have been put into a large brown paper sack and stacked somewhere in the warehouse. We'll be able to open the sack and look at the exhibits through the transparent wrapping. We won't be allowed to take anything out of its individual sealed bag," Chauncey explained. "But none of the scientific samples, swabs or slides'll be there. They're retained at the lab."

"OK. I'm up for it. Can we get in today?"

"Yes. I've arranged an appointment. They've already checked I was involved in the case. But you'll have to lie about your identity. They won't let you in if they know you're the son of the Defendant. I've told 'em I'm coming in with a youngster who's about to start work with the Prosecution Service. That'll be you."

"I thought policemen never lied," smiled Cal.

"Only in a good cause," came the wry response, "but you should realise that in that bag will be your father's clothes. Every stitch that he had on when I arrested him in that bike shed and took him to the cop shop. You may find that difficult."

"Let's do it," said Cal.

Half an hour later, under the watchful eye of an elderly female civil servant who stared suspiciously at Cal's injured face and positioned herself sentry-like in the narrow doorway, Graham Chauncey solemnly untied the piece of string from around the neck of the brown paper sack and tipped the contents on to the table. The box cubicle into which the parchment-dry lady had shown them, led off a huge storage area where similar looking sacks were stacked from floor to ceiling. Bags of human wreckage.

A number of separate packages stared blankly back at them, displaying clothing through the transparent plastic wrapping that had guarded any secrets inside for the best part of thirty years.

Sad, crumpled items. Victim's bra. Victim's socks. Victim's blouse. Item by screwed-up item, each with its own label and reference number.

Defendant's shirt. Defendant's socks. Defendant's jacket. Cal could see parts of the brown check sports jacket with leather patches sewn on the elbows.

Defendant's pen. Defendant's wallet and contents. By manipulating the outside of the plastic, Cal now saw a passport-size photograph formed part of the wallet contents and he bent down to study it. His mother's innocent face as a young woman stared back at him. This was Ma before her suffering began.

"That packet's not sealed," Chauncey remarked to the woman, pointing to a large brown envelope sitting amidst the bags.

"Photographs," she snapped back. "They never seal them. The idea's to protect clothing from the air and human contact. It doesn't matter if you touch the photos. But it's all you can touch. "

Chauncey pulled back the one chair in the cubicle and eased himself into it as he pulled the albums from within.

"I've seen a few photographs in Mr Walgrave's file of the scene after the body had been removed," Cal said.

"There's far more than just the scene here," Chauncey replied, setting out five separate albums on the table. "We've got the scene with the body still in place, the post-mortem, pictures of your father and photographs of the two sets of clothing now stuffed into these bags."

Cal leant over his shoulder and nervously watched the thick fingers turn the pages. "Black and white," Chauncey grunted as he stared at the contorted shape of the plump female body lying in the bushes at the side of the tenth hole, covered by a few twigs and leaves.

"She's still got most of her clothes on," Cal grunted. "How could the killer have wrenched her knickers off without tearing them? You can see in the photographs that there's no damage."

"I suppose it's just about possible," Chauncey responded. "And do you see some kind of faint white marks on her wrists and neck in the photograph?" "It may just be an effect of the light, but I don't think so."

"Just more unanswered questions," Cal sighed.

"We need to have a forensic scientist actually examine the clothing and the photographs," said Chauncey.

"You can't do that without Home Office approval," interjected the female officiously.

"OK, we understand all that. Cal, I'm going to open the post-mortem album, now," said Chauncey. "You may not want to look at this."

"If I can survive Creane I can deal with this," Cal replied.

The white body, already showing lividity discolouration where the blood had settled static within, was stretched out on the pathologist's slab, stripped of all dignity and yielding little by way of clues. The only visible trauma was very slight reddening to the front of the neck and, in the later photographs, the pathologist had sliced away the skin and tissue to indicate the absence of internal injury to the neck structures.

"Vagal inhibition," Chauncey breathed. "I remember the Pathologist explaining all of that to the jury. Short-lived pressure on a sensitive nerve in the neck. Stopped the heart."

"How was Mr Walgrave meant to understand all of this complicated medical stuff?" asked Cal. "He had no medical knowledge. He had no expert to advise him."

"I can assure you that he did understand it," Chauncey replied. "I suppose he must have read up on it. But it didn't seem to matter much to his defence. The case wasn't about how she died but who killed her. His job was to show it wasn't the man in the dock."

"Look at her fingernails," said Cal, as Chauncey turned to the next group of photographs which concentrated on the deceased's hands. "She couldn't have scratched the skin off a rice pudding with those."

"And there are those white marks on her wrists again. And on her neck. Can't fathom those," muttered Chauncey.

"What about the scratch marks to the Defendant's back," enquired Cal. "Let's see those in the other album."

"They're so slight you can hardly make them out," replied Chauncey, showing him the photograph of the broad, dark-skinned back of his father.

"Time's up," interrupted the sharp female voice from the doorway. "Your appointment was for fifteen minutes. If you've more to do you'll have to come back another time."

"Right," replied Chauncey, closing the albums and replacing the bags in the large paper sack. "We've seen enough for today. Next step is an expert and, like you say, we'll need approval for that."

"And you won't get it," retorted the woman with a tone of satisfaction. "No-one's going to risk showing an innocent man was hanged. I doubt he was innocent anyway."

"And how the hell do you know?" Cal barked at her. "You know nothing about it."

"They're all guilty. They don't put them in the dock unless they're guilty. That's all I need to know," she replied angrily.

"Come on," Chauncey interjected. "We're on our way."

"In more ways than one," Cal responded, staring at the sour-faced woman now ushering them out of the cubicle and back towards the main exit. "We'll be back."

Chapter 13

It was well past midnight when he swung the Mercedes into the farmhouse driveway. The sky was clear and he could see the Plough in the cold English sky. He missed Australia. The sky was different there. He missed his mother. Despite his English roots he felt nothing for England. From what he'd seen of the woman at the depositary and Vishney he didn't care much for the English. Chauncey was retired, eking out life on a pension, bored and rather liked the intrigue, but Cal suspected that was probably as far as it went. Ambiguous about the situation. He'd have a go, take a trip to Vegas, fill his time, spend the two thousand and then put it all back into the furthest recesses of his mind where it belonged.

The English legal system had put an innocent man to death and, as it so happened, that man had been his father, but he felt little connection with his father. When Chauncey had been turning over the photographs which showed his father under arrest in the police station he had seen a total stranger. A dark-coloured man from another place and another time, neither of which still existed. George was far closer to the harshness and injustice than he was and was driven by a sense of duty to her father.

There was no sign of any sinister vehicle lurking in the shadows and no interference from Nero as he approached the house which was in darkness. George had suggested that he leave the car at Bristol Station and take the train to London, which he'd done, and so he'd quietly slipped the car keys through the farmhouse letterbox before heading up to his room in the barn. Still nervous about Creane, he'd taken a torch from the car's glove compartment and its beam flickered eerily in the stillness of the barn, the farm equipment lying silent.

Placing his weight on the sides of the wooden steps, he tried to keep the inevitable creaking to a minimum and, before opening the bedroom door, he pressed his ear to it, but could hear nothing but the odd light scuffle from some mouse sniffing his way through the hay below.

The torch immediately picked out the body lying stretched out on its left side on top of his bed in jeans and a heavy knit pink jumper. Her deep even breathing was so soft as to make virtually no sound. The curtains were open and the light of the moon picked out her clear complexion as the light brown hair lay in disarray across the white pillow.

"It's me, George," he said gently.

Slowly, the long, lithe body turned on to its back and one of the almond-shaped eyes half-opened.

"Oh! I came up to wait for you to hear what happened and must have fallen asleep," she whispered.

"That's OK," he replied, switching the bedside lamp on as she swung her legs round on to the floor and sat there blinking at him, as she adjusted to the harshness of the light.

"So what did you make of Chauncey? How did you get on?" she pressed, now returning to full alertness.

"I'll fill you in," he replied, sitting down on the bed alongside her. "But first I have to tell you, George, I'm not really connecting with all of this. I feel once removed from the reality of it. And, present company excepted, I'm not very struck on the English. I think I'm losing my way a bit. Driving back from the station I was reflecting on whether I shouldn't call it a day."

"You can't," she insisted. Like I told you in Tanna, you and I have to make sure our fathers can rest in peace. I can't do it alone."

"I reckon you can, George. You've got a passion in you that I just don't have. I've suffered the shock of learning I'm partly black. I've been done over. I've seen the face of the English system up in London where Chauncey and I went. And I've seen Vishney. I'm losing heart here."

Taking his right hand in both of hers, she squeezed hard. Her hands were cold but he could feel the fire coming from within. "Do you know what they call the cause of death in an execution?" she asked brutally.

"No."

"The Hangman's Fracture. They put a hood over his head, tied his arms and legs, anchored the knot of the noose under his jaw and pulled the lever. Fracturing his spinal cord and neck at the third vertebra. That's the Hangman's Fracture. Done to your father. Terrified. Screaming. And innocent. Don't ever tell me you're losing heart," she declared angrily.

"How do you know the details?" he asked.

"I looked them up at the library. I saw pictures of the leather straps. The gallows. The metal eyelet and the rope. In my mind I smelled the inside of the hood. I tasted it," she answered defiantly.

"I've never met anyone like you, George," he announced in a voice filled with admiration.

"And it's easier now," she added, ignoring the involuntary compliment.

"Why?"

"Because originally we only had my father's belief and some oddities in the evidence. Now we know for sure it was someone else. Why else would someone be using extreme violence to warn you off? That killer's still out there, Cal. And, one way or another, I'm going to nail him. I can't make you come along any further. That's your call. But I'm going the distance. However long it takes."

Cal made no reply, but gently extracted his hand from hers. She was now clutching it so hard that it was beginning to hurt. Filled with a certainty by the fervour and courage of this remarkable young woman, he did what he had wanted to do ever since he had first espied her climbing into the Land Rover in Tanna. Putting his arm around her he kissed her and, instantly, she returned his kiss with the same fire and passion that she had put into her words. For the first time in his life Cal realised the human being he had in his arms was not just some pretty young girl encountered on an Australian beach, but a woman of extraordinary intensity. Like Chauncey had remarked, a chip off the old block.

Suddenly England didn't seem so bad after all.

Chapter 14

The man in the white coat which seemed too small for him walked purposefully along the rubber tiled corridor of Taunton Hospital, heading for the Day Room in Orthopaedics Ward 12. His feet were angled at ten to two and he was carrying too much weight around the beam. The face was heavy and the eyes were deep set and hard. Once upon a time he'd been a fairly useful trooper to have on the front line, but those days were long gone, although he still fancied himself for the occasional task now and again and, on this little job, the odds were stacked heavily in his favour.

Being a copper in Somerset for thirty years meant you could spot a gypsy blindfold at a hundred feet and, as his informant had implied, Lanny Creane was alone in the brightly lit room. Sitting uncomfortably in a rigid-backed chair, supported by pillows, with his right leg in a plaster cast extended straight out in front of him and resting on a solid plastic foot stool. A pair of crutches was angled against the side of the chair. Wrapped in a white hospital dressing gown worn thin at the elbows, he was staring with a blank expression at the TV screen flickering on the wall. The ugly face was puffed and red, the bulbous nose tinged with purple and the hair lank and unkempt.

The white-coated man slipped quickly into the room, pulling the blind down over the window in the door and covering the few paces to the outstretched leg in less than a second. Creane's puzzled and angry face looked up at the man and, in the split second between realising that this was not a Doctor but an intruder, the man, moving with remarkable speed for his weight and appearance, kicked the foot stool from underneath the leg whilst grabbing one of the pillows behind Creane and thrusting it over his mouth so as to stifle the scream of agony as the leg hit the floor and a thousand steel blades again sliced through the innards of Creane's knee. The whole body was shaking, the head trying to pull back from the ton weight of pressure being applied to his face but Creane was as helpless as a baby and the man felt the resistance die as the first wave of pain passed over and Creane succumbed.

"I'm gonna shift the pilla now, Lanny," a rasping voice declared. "If you call for help or try to reach the emergency button on the wall, then I'll stamp on your fuckin' knee. I weighed nineteen stone last time of asking. You get my drift?"

Under the pillow the head tried to nod and the man lessened the pressure sufficiently for Creane to breathe. Gasping for air and almost crying in pain, he gulped down lungfuls of precious oxygen.

"I've only got one question for you, Lanny," the man continued in the same flat, rasping tone. "And I'll only ask it once. I want the answer immediately and then I'll be gone. You just get the one chance or I'll 'ave yer leg. You with me, Lanny?"

"Wot you fucking want?" grunted Creane through his pain and fury.

"Who paid you to duff up the Aussie kid?" demanded the voice, already lifting his leg and placing it on top of the plaster cast, ready to strike and ensuring Creane felt the pressure threatening the leg.

"Dyer," came the breathless reply. "Dixie Dyer. You can check the Visitors List at Wakefield."

"You're out of your depth on this one, Lanny. As soon as you're kicked out of hospital, collect yer rag band and move on. The kid's gone. If I get wind of any more tricks from yer I'll tell Dyer who grassed him. Then you won't have no legs, will ya?"

Lifting the pillow from the face, the hard eyes stared down at the reddened face etched with pain. Creane slumped back in the chair, his eyes tightly closed, still sucking in air. The Doctors had just about saved his leg once. He could only pray that further serious damage hadn't been caused by this ex-copper. Because that was what he was.

Filth. He reeked of it and Lanny Creane sensed a copper like a shark sensed blood. But this time Creane had nothing left. He didn't even lift his head as the man in the white coat slipped quietly out of the room and away.

Chapter 15

Like the chameleon which can change its colour according to its current environment, Dixie Dyer prided himself on his ability to adjust to the times. In the early days he'd served his apprenticeship as a common or garden fence. Buying stolen goods off the burglars and handbag snatchers. Then he'd moved up to deal with the big boys. The robbers. He'd fenced cash stolen in wage snatches and the contents of boxes stolen at gunpoint from Securicor vans. He'd established an impressive network of contacts, a big-boned, brassy wife and a five-bedroomed house in Holland Park. Then he'd got caught. Ten years inside. Served nearly six with good behaviour.

When he came out, the brassy wife had moved North and the house had gone South. Armed robbers had become passé. The risks were too high. Almost every crime on the books was connected with drugs. So, like the chameleon, Dixie adjusted to the new environment. But this time around he was a little less ambitious and a lot more crafty. Lived in a modest council house in Peckham with a faded red front door. No wife. Kept a healthy distance from the big players, the ones the police would watch. Bought exclusively off the trusted inner circle and in small quantities. Only dealt in high-quality coke. Only sold to people who weren't bottom feeders. Businessmen, managers, housewives. All people with a fair bit of money and a lot to lose. A chameleon, happy in his new sandy terrain. The fact that the Old Testament description of the chameleon classified it as an unclean animal was not known to Dixie. He wouldn't have liked that.

It was one of his classy customers, who had mentioned that he had a problem that needed sorting, which had led to the away-day ticket to Wakefield. Dixie knew all of the real heavies and their prices. He'd told the punter it was a five grand job. Four grand for the bruiser and just the one grand for yours truly, as a special favour to a valued customer. So he'd given Lanny two and pocketed three. As he kept reminding himself, learn from nature, follow the ways of the chameleon.

When he answered the knock on the red front door in Peckham a few hours after Lanny Creane had received a hospital visitor, there was no-one there and he slammed the door in irritation. Council estate kids. No discipline. Not like he'd had to endure on his estate. His old man would give him a smack round the ear just for wanting sugar on his corn flakes. Turning back up the narrow hall, he suddenly heard a heavy metallic clonk and all the electrics in the house went out. Someone had thrown the mains switch in the kitchen cupboard above the sink. Dixie may have preferred to hire others to dish out the GBH, but you didn't travel his road without knowing how to cut the mustard. The six inch blade of the flick knife was exposed and poised for action before the last glimmer in the hall light bulb had died. Pressing himself against the flock wallpaper of the hall, he suppressed his breathing and stood stock still. In his game you made enemies and one of them had crossed the drawbridge.

Up until that afternoon the old police truncheon had been lying, covered in dust, on the top shelf in the garage, behind a battery charger and a selection of plastic flower pots. Now it was in the gnarled fist of a retired officer whose nickname on the Force was 'Ulna'. They called him that because his speciality was smashing the ulna, at wrist level, of resisting villains with his truncheon. And sometimes they didn't even have to resist. He knew just the right spot. Excruciating pain, six weeks in plaster, three months physio and a solid dose of arthritis as a reminder in the years to come. Dixie never heard him nor saw the truncheon arcing through the air. But when it splintered his ulna he felt it and he opened his mouth to let out a scream which would have brought the neighbours running, except that a leather gloved hand was clamped over his mouth forcing his head backwards and stifling all sound, except for a deep inner whimpering as the shards of bone and nerve endings communicated themselves to Dixie's brain and his flick knife fell harmlessly on to the shabby carpet.

"No need for any more suffering, Dyer," declared a disembodied voice from out of the blackness, as Dixie's knees gave way and he sank towards the floor, clutching at his shattered arm and desperately seeking to drag air in through his nose as the gloved hand across his mouth followed him down.

"You hired Lanny Creane. Who hired you?" spat the voice, lifting the glove off the mouth half an inch.

"You're talkin' crap, I don't . . ." Dixie began, before the glove clamped itself back over the mouth and an arm as thick as a telegraph pole hooked itself round Dyer's neck and dragged him along the hall into the kitchen and up to the sink where it pulled him up to his feet, grabbed the distorted wrist and held it under the water tap. As the waves of agony intensified still further, Dixie felt cold water on his wrist. The smell of the leather of the glove and his spittle upon it was filling his nostrils as he struggled to breathe. Then he felt the water getting hotter. And hotter. He writhed and kicked and screamed a silent scream.

"Last chance," whispered the voice, slightly reducing the pressure on the mouth and moving the wrist an inch to the side of the now scalding stream.

"Hollister. Kyngora Bank," Dixie breathed.

"You understand you may be called upon to grass him up to the police? Or I'll be back," the voice declared.

"I understand," Dixie groaned. "I've got the message."

The stranger released his hold and Dyer collapsed to the floor, writhing in agony, cursing and sobbing. But the man had gone. He hadn't even stayed long enough to turn off the hot water tap.

Chapter 16

When Cal awoke the next morning George was gone but, before he even had the chance to lever himself out of the warm bed into the chilled English air, there was a banging from the bottom of the steps and a woman's voice was shouting up to him.

"Cal. There's a phone call for you. Won't leave a message and George has already left for Benniston Farm."

"Coming, Mrs Walgrave," he shouted back, jumping up and starting to pull on a jumper and a pair of jeans.

By the time he reached the bottom of the steps the woman had retreated back into the farmhouse. She had been pretty remote with him as soon as he'd arrived, but she'd grown even more frosty when she'd seen the state of his face after Creane's handiwork. Cal very much doubted that George's absence from her own room for most of the night had gone without maternal observation and censure. As he let himself in through the side door into the farmhouse there was no sign of her.

George had already shown him the office lined with books on farming, art and aviation, but devoid of law books. The receiver of the phone was lying abandoned on the blotter of the old mahogany desk. Cal supposed that this had been where Mr Walgrave used to work, gazing out of the picture window with its sky blue floral curtains across the hills of Somerset and frequently anguishing over a man he believed to have been wronged. Now the man's son from a faraway land was seated in Mr Walgrave's leather chair looking out at the same view.

"This is Cal," he breathed down the phone.

"It's Graham. I've got some news. Can you talk?"

"Sure."

"Most important of all, I think you should leave the Walgraves," he began earnestly. "I've checked out Creane. He's very dangerous."

"But he'll be laid up for a long while. I'll be back in Sydney before he can try anything," Cal responded.

"Oh, yeah, you laid him up alright. He'll be out of the game for months. But he's from a large gypsy family. The police'll move 'em on as soon as Creane is discharged from hospital, but if Creane thinks you're still there any of 'em can pay you a visit," Chauncey explained. "He's been told you've gone and he's been warned off, but he's scum and my advice is to find a room of your own away from there."

"I'll talk to George. But I always check the road when I go in and out of the gate. You can see a long way in each direction. And forewarned is forearmed. And I mean armed," said Cal defiantly.

"You know my advice. Take it or leave it. Anyway, the man who hired the heavies is Hollister," Chauncey declared.

"Bloody Hell," came the astonished reply. "The same Hollister who Amy Beckett said she saw smoking a cigarette behind the tree on the edge of the school drive and the golf course."

"One and the same. William Hollister. Now a merchant banker with Kyngora Investment Bank but with a criminal connection to a coke dealer who supplies to the upper end of the market. Name of Dixie Dyer. Draw your own conclusions. Dyer brought in Creane."

"Is Kyngora based in London?" asked Cal.

"Yes. Mayfair. Hollister has a townhouse in Belgravia. 44 Welston Gardens."

"How on earth did you dig all of this up? And so quickly?"

"I told you yesterday. Tentacles. And I've got more."

"What?"

"*Batford 789657.*"

"Yeah?"

"The number still exists. Obviously it has a numeric prefix now, but the number's the same," said Chauncey.

"And?"

"It's a large country house. Been in the Hollister family for generations. The old man still lives there."

"Graham, you're a genius. You told me yesterday that you weren't convinced that my father was innocent. Yet you've done all of this."

"I'm still not convinced. But, whether he did it or not, something stinks. And here's the best bit. Old man Hollister, back in 1963, was Lord Lieutenant of the County," Chauncey added.

"What's that mean?"

"It means that, amongst various other civic duties, he used to dine with the High Court Judges," he declared with a note of triumph.

"Vishney," breathed Cal.

"Sir Eustace Vishney. Vicious Vishney. Bastard of the Bailey," Chauncey grunted.

"I owe you a big apology, Graham," Cal responded. "I had you down for luke-warm. Filling the time. Doing the decent thing by Walgrave. I was wrong."

"Maybe it started off that way, but, like I said, something stinks."

"Well, it's my turn now to put in some hard yards," Cal said.

"Meaning?"

"Meaning it's about time I opened an account at Kyngora."

"Yeah, I think that's the way to go. We need to ratchet up the pressure. See what pops out," Chauncey responded. "And I can up the stakes as well."

"How?"

"The press, Cal. Never underestimate the power of the press. Take care."

Chapter 17

Blonde hair down to her waist. Six feet one. Angular features heavily made-up. And naked as a jay bird, writhing around the steel pole and thrusting her flat belly, generous breasts and long buttocks into the man's face in equal measure in what was supposed to pass as being in time with the screaming, tuneless music. The air was blue from a combination of the filtered lights and the cigar smoke. Only the best Havanas. At the end of the long night her hair would reek of the stuff and she would try to wash it away together with the images of the sickly stale champagne breath, leering, sweating faces and clamouring hands. If you wanted to rack up a hundred quid an hour that was the price you had to pay. Plus the after-hours extras, but with this middle-aged creep she didn't intend to trade for less than five hundred.

It was after three when the cab drew up outside his place and she insisted that he hand her the cash before they let the cabbie go. Inside the living room was a thick-piled purple carpet, an exquisite Louis XVI cabinet, a Steinway baby grand, a dulled leather sofa which was as big as a king size bed and countless treasures of silver, onyx and ivory strategically placed on table-tops and shelves.

In the centre of the room was a low, solid block of granite, smoothed and shaped into a rectangular coffee table on which stood silver caskets, cut glass bowls brimming with fresh fruit and a variety of pornographic magazines scattered across its surface.

"Weighs half a ton," he remarked, in his clipped upper-class tone, catching her looking at it through eyes that measured everything in pounds sterling. "Needed a forklift through the French windows to get it in. Belonged to Freddie Mercury." He watched the mascara flap up and down as soon as he said that. Nothing turned them on like celebrity.

Disappearing out of the room for a few minutes, he returned with an ice-bucket and a bottle of vintage Veuve-Cliquot, which he expertly popped and poured two glasses, before nestling up beside her on the giant sofa. While she sipped from her glass, he leaned over to one of the silver caskets, opened it, extracted a transparent polythene bag filled with a white powder and laid out two lines on one of the magazines. They snorted the coke with all the grace of a Russian factory ship hoovering up a shoal of mackerel.

Despite his excesses he tried to keep himself in reasonable shape. He needed to. Not quite as tall as the girl, but broad-shouldered and, although now in his mid-forties, still with a thirty four inch waist. As he pulled off his clothes she could see that there was still a fair amount of muscle tone and, as the coke drilled its way into her bloodstream and up to her brain, she felt that rush deep within that heralded the raw sexual activity at which she excelled. The fact that these rich creeps had to pay her excited her even more. She wore no underclothing and so her dress was off and she was on him faster than a hyena on its prey. High quality cocaine always made these sessions last longer and, as the coupling intensified, so did he change. Suddenly flipping her over on to her back he drove into her with a brutality that shocked her and began to frighten her. In a second he had seized control and his hands came swiftly away from her hips. His right forearm went across her throat and his left hand went across her mouth and nose and he pressed. She could neither breathe nor scream and she was powerless against his dead weight. All she could do was show the terror in her eyes, now streaming with tears and running mascara, and buck her body and legs like a rodeo bull. And the more she bucked, the more excited he became and the more he pressed on her throat. Hovering on the edge of complete blackness, her lungs heaving and her head exploding, he reached his climax and lifted his forearm from her neck.

Gasping and retching she scrabbled at his face with her nails, but he just laughed and smacked the point of his elbow into the angle of her jaw.

"Don't make me really hurt you," he snarled. "You're getting five hundred quid for this."

"You bastard," she spat at him as her breath and her senses returned.

He moved his weight off her and reached again for the silver casket. "Yeah, but I'm a rich bastard, that makes all the difference. Come on, let's fire up again," he laughed, "there'll be another couple of hundred quid in it for you before the night is done."

When he dragged himself into the Bank the next morning there were dark circles under his eyes and his skin was taut and pallid. His secretary was already at her desk outside his office and recognised the tell-tale signs only too well. Now approaching sixty, the partners had transferred her across to him, insisting that he could only be trusted with an older model. It had cost them forty thousand pounds to sit on the sexual harassment claim by her predecessor. They had threatened him that either he accepted the old biddy or take the post in Bucharest where the bank was seeking to harness some of the new Eastern European funds that were up for grabs. Even the dried-up Miss Carpenter was preferable to six months in the Romanian hinterland.

"Mr Dijak is due in half an hour," she announced curtly. No good-mornings or good-nights any more. He couldn't stand the sight of her but was stuck with her and she despised him for his debauchery, worn on his face like a flashing neon sign.

Erich Dijak was one of the new Romanian connections. Kyngora was handling the purchase of a shopping precinct in Sheffield for his company. The transaction was all being conducted at arms length on each of the three sides. Dijak's company had a Bulgarian nominee. The Arab consortium that owned the Sheffield site was operating through a French agency and Kyngora was streaming the funds through an offshore organisation whose company headquarters was in Luxembourg. The deal had involved negotiation and calculation in three separate currencies and, just at the moment, sterling was undergoing a strengthening against the US dollar. Dijak was presently holding sterling and for every cent that the pound went up, he was saving tens of thousands pounds. One deadline had already been successfully delayed and Dijak wanted another week's postponement. The French agency was already ripping off the Arabs, like the French always do. They couldn't help themselves. But now the Arabs had dug their heels in. On the last call he had made before leaving the Bank for the joys of the pole-dancer the previous evening, the final position was completion within seventy-two hours or they'd give their lawyers the green light to turn it really ugly. He'd accepted the seventy-two hours on Dijak's behalf but didn't tell Dijak, letting him believe that time ran out today.

Hanging his Saville Row jacket on the art nouveau coat stand in the corner of his office, he slouched into his red leather top-of-the range executive chair on the window side of his matching executive desk with its two telephones and worked on the angles, chewing the end of his designer fountain pen and occasionally letting his mind wander back to the moment when last night's girl was about to pass out and then reared back into life again.

The large office had a sofa and two armchairs where the hard discussions took place. The Bank psychology was to strike from ground level, not attack from the conventional dominant position across the desk. Pouring himself a cup of black coffee from the cafetiere he moved on to the sofa, the coffee sharpening him up and his appearance lifted by the crisp white French-cuffed shirt and lemon tie.

By the time that Miss Carpenter showed Dijak into his office the excesses of last night were consigned to history, colour was returning to his cheeks and his brain was moving into full operational mode.

The squat figure presented as all grey. The hair, the moustache, the face, the suit. All grey. And so was the personality. Grey, but as hard as the granite of Freddie Mercury's table.

"I want another week," Dijak began, slurping noisily from the coffee cup that the old biddy had set down in front of him as he leaned forward in the comfortable armchair.

"Can't be done, Erich. You must leave us the signed papers this morning. I've pushed them to the very margins. I spoke to them last night. If you piss them about any longer they'll pull the plug," William Hollister replied crudely.

"Given the present currency movements, another week is at least another couple of hundred thousand dollars, maybe more. I don't like giving away that kind of money to anyone, least of all Arabs. Get me a week," demanded Dijak.

"It won't wash. This is the end of the line. You'll have to sign the papers while you're here today and we'll get them faxed off immediately," Hollister insisted.

"Try," snapped Dijak.

"I've tried."

"Try again."

"It's pointless."

"I'll make it worth your while," Dijak declared brazenly.

Hollister smiled. It had taken him less than two minutes to get the offer of cash he was awaiting. With someone like Dijak there was no subtlety. No finesse. No need to stand on ceremony.

"I'll have to offer the Frenchman a slice."

"Do it," the Romanian demanded.

"Kyngora mustn't know."

"You think I'm a fool, William?"

Hollister levered himself up from the sofa, walked slowly across to his desk and picked up the telephone on the right hand side of his desk. The direct line that didn't light up on Miss Carpenter's phone outside. Rapidly punching a number into the system while Dijak continued to slurp his coffee he caught the Romanian's eye after he'd finished dialling and held up two crossed fingers.

"Pierre, William Hollister. I have Mr Dijak with me as we speak. He's very nearly ready to sign."

There was a long silence at the London end before he spoke again.

"One week," he breathed, immediately shaking his head in response to what he was apparently hearing from the other end and then breaking into fluent French, spoken at breakneck speed. Hollister had already checked. Dijak spoke no French.

His voice grew louder and angrier before he removed the phone from his ear, covered the mouthpiece and reported back to the Romanian.

"It's getting rough. But he thinks he can get you forty-eight hours. He wants ten thousand US dollars. I'd want the same," he said softly.

"So twenty grand altogether. I want four days for that," he barked back.

"Quatre jours," Hollister drilled back into the phone.

There was a moment's pause and then a further report from Hollister with the mouthpiece muffled.

"Seventy-two hours. Fifteen grand for him. Fifteen for me. Final offer. I'm convinced of that. Take it or leave it, Erich. I can't risk pushing it any more or the whole thing will explode."

"Take it," Dijak grunted.

"It's a deal, Pierre. I'll keep your funds in my personal safe. Collect them next week when you're in London," Hollister concluded, replacing the receiver with a smile.

"Check the exchange rate," demanded the Romanian.

Hollister pressed a remote control on his desk and a television screen in the wall lit up showing the raft of exchange rates flickering across the screen like a humming bird's wings.

"Up another twenty points, Erich. You've more than covered your thirty thousand while you've been sitting there. I'd be grateful if you had the cash delivered to my house tonight. I'll be home by seven," Hollister smiled at him. "And you have to be back here in three days time to sign."

"It'll all be taken care of, William. It's good to see that English merchant bankers are no straighter than Romanians," he observed.

"Don't forget the French. We couldn't have done it without Pierre," Hollister replied with a chuckle. It was a particularly cynical chuckle, because the only sound at the other end of the telephone call had not been a Frenchman, but the engaged signal of his own office direct line. These Eastern Europeans had such a lot to learn he thought to himself as he showed Erich out. Thirty thousand dollars in his back pocket and it wasn't even time for elevenses.

By the time his last appointment of the day arrived he was flagging. The excitement of the morning's events had been followed by some humdrum phone calls and meetings and, on his return from lunch, he was less than happy to learn that the old biddy had booked him a five thirty appointment with a Charles Rolston while he had been out.

"You know that it takes a week to get an appointment with me. What do you think you're doing fixing an appointment on the same day as the first enquiry?" he shouted at her when she informed him.

"He said he was a potential investor and was only in London for a couple of days and wanted to deal with you," she replied icily.

"I've never heard of him. And I'm not doing five-thirty. No-one does five thirty any more. They've all gone home by five. Phone him up. Reschedule it."

"He said that he was sure you'd accommodate him once you knew who had recommended Kyngora," she added.

"And who was that?" he asked.

"The Vishney family. He had been recommended to consider investing via Kyngora only because of you. Apparently the Vishneys held your family in very high esteem. That's what he said. Do you still want me to reschedule him?" she enquired.

"No. Leave it. I'll see him. But don't box me in like that again. I don't appreciate it," he growled at her. Old man Vishney might be sitting in a bath chair in an old people's home somewhere but the next generation was still friendly with his father and carried a fair bit of clout. He didn't want to be seen upsetting any of the Vishneys.

Pursing her thin lips she looked down at her work and ignored him. She despised everything about him but something in his eyes always frightened her and silence was the best reaction. Let him have the last word.

At five-thirty prompt Miss Carpenter ushered Mr Ralston into Hollister's office. George had lent him a tie, her father's full length navy blue Crombie overcoat and his dapper trilby and Cal had bought a pair of ready-readers at the station's newspaper kiosk. With the benefit of the glasses and the hat at the right angle some of the impact of the facial bruising was softened and, although he felt a bit like a Chicago mobster, at least it gained him passage into the lion's den. Once in he had no intention of beating about the bush. Hollister was standing in front of his desk as Miss Carpenter closed the door behind her.

"I suspect you have an alarm on your desk, Mr Hollister. I advise you against using it. I'm not going to hurt you or attack you and I'll only be here for a few minutes. If you don't hear me out, I've already got enough to ruin you," Cal began.

As the Aussie twang registered and the bruising to the face stood out more clearly when Cal removed his hat and glasses the realisation spread across Hollister's face and the blood visibly drained from his cheeks and lips, but he made no move towards the red alarm button hidden on the other side of his desk. The two men stood staring at each other before Hollister broke the silence.

"Who are you?" he barked aggressively in a weak show of pretence.

"You know exactly who I am. I'm here to get the truth off you about Louise Donovan."

As soon as he voiced the name a shiver went down Hollister's spine and the left hand side of his upper lip nervously twitched in panic. Cal pressed home the initiative.

"I said I'd got enough to ruin you. Let me spell it out. You have a serious and expensive coke habit. Your fellow directors know nothing about it. Your supplier is a man called Dixie Dyer. He's already served ten years. I doubt the directors will take kindly to that sort of criminal association."

"You're full of bullshit," responded Hollister unconvincingly, walking slowly over to the sofa and sitting down. He wasn't sure his legs could continue to support his weight. Cal followed him and seated himself in the same armchair that had housed Dijak while Hollister had deftly relieved him of thirty thousand dollars. Cal was carrying a green Harrods bag and he placed it carefully at his feet as he continued to watch the other man like a hawk.

"When you learned from Georgina Walgrave that I was coming over to have a serious poke around you paid Dyer to have me warned off. See this," Cal spat out, pointing to his damaged face. "That's down to you."

"And just how do you propose proving any of this?" Hollister asked, in the type of English patrician accent that so irritated most of the population of Australia.

"Easy," replied Cal. "Dyer will tell the police if I give the say-so. He's been visited . . ."

The sentence remained unfinished as, after a quick knock on the door, Miss Carpenter came into the room. However much she despised Hollister she still had a job to do and Mr Charles Rolston had struck her as a rather strange-looking character.

"Is everything alright, Mr Hollister?" she asked, taking in the spectacle of the two men sat bolt upright in their seats and with an obvious sense of hostility in the air. Mr Rolston's face was angled away from her so she could not see the left side of his face. "Can I get you anything?"

"No. We're fine, thank you," Hollister replied reassuringly as the woman turned and left the room.

"There's more," Cal continued as soon as she had closed the door behind her, swinging the Harrods bag off the floor and up on to the table. "As you can see, I've been to Harrods."

"Get to the point, Stanton," snarled Hollister, terrified at what might be coming next.

"It's not Stanton. It's Stewart. I went to the curtain department this morning. Got the assistant manager's business card. Then called in at 44 Welston Gardens. Nice place you've got there. And I particularly liked this," he continued, plucking an antique silver casket out of the carrier bag and placing it carefully on the table.

"Burglary. You've burgled my home. This is a matter for the police . . . ," began Hollister, reaching across to grab the casket before Cal's hand swooped down and whisked it away.

"Feel free to phone them," he responded. "It's crammed full of cocaine. They'll be very interested in that. I told your cleaning lady I was from Harrods. Come to measure for the new curtains. I gave her my business card. She got on with her cleaning while I measured."

"What exactly do you want?" demanded Hollister, getting up and pacing around the room.

"I told you. I want the truth about Louise Donovan. But just one more thing your directors might be interested in. These . . ." he snapped, putting his hand back inside the carrier bag, extracting some photographs and tossing them on to the table. Some of them slid across the surface and fell on to the floor.

"You've been in my bedroom," Hollister exclaimed, desperately scrabbling to gather up the pornographic pictures of numerous call girls in various indecent poses.

"I've kept some for the while. In case I need them," Cal threatened. "So now you can see that I've certainly got enough to cost you your directorship and probably got enough to get you prosecuted for drugs, having me attacked and maybe a bit of porn. So let's be hearing about Louise Donovan."

Hollister walked back to the sofa and perched on the thickly padded arm. Sweat had gathered at the nape of his neck and he could feel it running down his rib cage from his armpits. His lunch was threatening to eject itself from deep within his stomach and he could taste the acid bile. But his eyes were blazing with anger. No-one treated a Hollister like this. For the moment he recognised that this dangerous bastard had the initiative. Somehow he had to retain control, give out the barest minimum of information and get rid of him. Then he needed time to think. The stakes were higher than ever. With time he could put this bastard right where he belonged.

"Why did you tell my secretary that you were a friend of the Vishneys?" he demanded.

"I had my reasons. And my evidence. I've seen Vishney's files but I'm saving that for later in the game. I've given you enough to know you're in deep trouble. Whether you murdered Louise Donovan is still an open question. So, start persuading me that you didn't and we'll see where we go from there."

"It's twenty-seven years ago for Christ's sake," he declared.

"Listen, Hollister. Cut the crap. Cut the excuses. I want the hard facts. If I don't get them here and now or, if you lie, then that silver box of coke, which will be smothered with your prints, and the other photos I've kept will be delivered to your Chairman tomorrow morning. Then I'll go to the cops with Dyer's information," Cal threatened, watching the effect of his words sink in.

"So what happened between you and Amy Beckett on that day?" he demanded.

"Like she said, she saw me smoking a cigarette behind the tree where the drive ran along the golf course. That's all there was to it. I never saw Louise or Stanton," he mumbled.

"I don't believe you. You wouldn't have brought in the heavies if that's all there was to it. You're lying," Cal concluded, putting the casket back into the carrier and starting to rise to his feet. "You'll be thrown out of the Bank before lunchtime tomorrow."

"Wait," he grunted, clutching at Cal's arm. "I know nothing that has any bearing on the murder. Ruining me won't help you. Just give me my stuff back. I'll pay for all the aggravation. I can send you back to Australia a rich man. Cash. US Dollars. Name your price."

"I've seen your porn. Women tied up. You in the middle of it. And now I've seen you in the flesh. It's in your face. You're a perv. I can smell it. And, at sixteen, your twisted hormones would have been in full flow. Something was going on between you and Louise. I want the truth, not your money. And, if I can ruin you in the process, then I'll enjoy every minute of it. Last chance, you warped bastard. Last fucking chance," he spat.

"OK, OK. I know a bit more," he whispered.

"Like you were the boy Louise had arranged to meet?" suggested Cal.

Hollister said nothing. His eyes angled down. He moved off the seat of the sofa and slumped on to the cushion, his head now in his hands.

"She was up for it," he finally mumbled. "By the time I met her on the golf course she already had her pants in her hand. She was winding me up. Showed me them. Laughing."

"Go on."

"She called me a toff. Everyone knew our family had money. She said she wouldn't do it there but she'd meet me that night and do it. Pushed the pants into my face. Told me posh girls could never do it as well as her."

"But you didn't want to wait, did you?"

"No. But that wasn't the point. She wanted money. She wanted fifteen quid. Said it'd be the best fifteen quid's worth a young toff like me had ever had. Take as long as I liked. I agreed to meet her at eight o'clock at the back of the cinema. I walked off. Left her there. That's the last time I ever saw her."

"And Amy Beckett knew it was you Louise had arranged to meet?"

"Yeah."

"And you got her to keep you out of it?"

"I told you, it had nothing to do with the murder," he insisted.

"What else did you get her to keep you out of?" Cal demanded.

"Nothing."

"Did you get her to invent seeing my father coming off the golf course?"

"No."

"You'd have wanted it there and then. The rich man's son. A worthless girl. Fat. Poor family. With her pants in her hand. You wouldn't have waited. You'd have taken it."

"No, damn you. No," Hollister shouted.

"Then why hire the heavies when I show up?" asked Cal.

"I panicked. We'd kept my part out of it. I'd done nothing wrong but I didn't want anything coming back to haunt us."

"Who's the 'we and us' you refer to? You and your father?"

"Me, really?"

"But your father knew?" Cal pressed

"Yes. He gave me a thrashing. I had to tell him."

"And he got Vishney to roller-coaster the whole show along at breakneck speed so you could never feature?" Cal suggested.

"I know nothing about that. My father spoke to Vishney the day after it happened."

"And then Vishney made sure some lawyer who was still wet

behind the ears got the defence brief," Cal concluded. "The Gentry Protection Act."

"The bottom line is that I had nothing to do with the murder," Hollister insisted, banging his fist on the table.

"Bang your fist or stamp your foot. I still don't believe you, Hollister," said Cal contemptuously.

"So what are you going to do?"

"For now I'm going to hold fire," announced Cal, collecting the carrier bag and standing up. "I'll keep your silver box and the coke while I do some more poking around. I'm getting bloody good at it. I promise you this Hollister, if you're the killer, I'll get you for it. I know a perv when I see one and you fit the bill."

As Cal moved towards the door Hollister followed him with eyes that were burning with hatred. This piece of Australian flotsam represented a threat to everything. Once he'd had more time to think he'd know how to deal with him. At least Stanton seemed to have decided to wait a while before making any revelations. The door slammed behind the Australian and Hollister was left alone to scoop up the Polaroid photographs that still lay scattered across the table. He looked at the top one which showed him naked, genitalia exposed and erect, tethered by the neck to a black girl with enormous breasts who was leading him to a bed upon which lay a naked white girl with her legs wide apart beckoning to him. Even in the midst of the danger that Stanton represented, Hollister, wholly without shame, felt the beginnings of arousal.

Chapter 18

It had taken another seven years of misery before Liz Lancaster eventually summoned up the courage to divorce her vile husband. From the night when his cronies had smashed every pane of glass in Len Goldberg's factory, to the day that she had packed a few belongings in a suitcase and escaped to the Battered Wives' Refuge in Chesterfield, he had never held down a job again. His reputation as a troublemaker in the workplace went before him and employers learned to find excuses not to hire him. Whilst he became dependent on State Benefits she had managed to get a couple of cleaning jobs up at the nice houses on the western side of the town. It was one of the ladies for whom she worked who had finally persuaded her to leave him. Seeing the frequent bruises and the signs of depression the lady had obtained the details about the Refuge.

More and more of his time had been spent at his "political" meetings and when they formed their own party he was away from home virtually every weekend. That had proved to be a blessing because, when he was home, his bitter frustration at having rendered himself unemployable was taken out on her. Not just with his vicious, whining barbs, but with his fists. On the fateful day that she had heaved her suitcase on to the train which took her up to Chesterfield her only consolation was that they had never had a child, for what kind of life would a child have endured under his roof.

The Refuge had helped with the divorce papers and had arranged for a burly, male Social Worker to accompany her back to the house in Wealdstone to collect the few belongings that she had not been able to cram into the suitcase. The house had been rented. There were no matrimonial assets. All she wanted was a few personal possessions of her mother's and the rest of her clothes. He had been waiting for her when they arrived in the Social Worker's car and he had launched his tirade of emotional blackmail upon her, explaining how he had tried to find her and how wicked she was to leave him abandoned. When emotional blackmail failed he had resorted to venom which was the usual prelude to violence, but the Social Worker's presence made him realise that even one blow would land him in court.

As they drove away from the house she looked back and saw him standing at the front door, his face contorted with fury. His fair hair was now worn so short as to be almost shaved and he'd taken to growing a tightly groomed beard and moustache which emphasised the downward turn of the corners of his mouth. Since she'd left he'd had three letters tattooed on the side of his neck, just above the collar. She'd kept her eyes averted from him throughout the visit and didn't see exactly what they were. Of course, his black boots were shining. The Social Worker was also watching him in his rear view mirror. "You married a thug, Mrs Lancaster," he pronounced, shaking his head. "Life can only get better."

The last time she saw him was at the County Court when she had obtained the decree nisi. The court staff kept him well away and the Judge found her allegations of cruelty proved in less than fifteen minutes. In the twenty years since she had never heard from him or about him. Making a life for herself in Chesterfield, she had worked as a cleaner in the local hospital for the next eight years, eventually meeting a male patient there who had suffered a heart attack. Ten years older than she was. Widowed. Their daily banter until his discharge had led to a trip to the cinema together and then the odd night at the pub and then marriage. It suited them both. She doubted that he loved her, but he was kind to her, had a medical pension from his firm, owned his own tiny house in a Derbyshire village not far from the Dales and loved his garden. In return, she worked part time in the local florists and looked after him. It was the best she was ever going to get.

Two days after William Hollister had received a visit from a certain Charles Rolston, Liz Duncombe, as she now was, had just finished wrapping a begonia plant in yesterday's copy of The Daily Mail. It was not the type of newspaper that she would ever read but, by a simple quirk of fate, page sixteen was wrapped around the flower pot at such an angle that the bold print caught her eye. It was only a few lines, but sufficient to send a chill of fear and disgust down her backbone as she remembered her ex-husband's feverish satisfaction at the charade in which he had so enthusiastically participated all those years ago.

Retired Cop To Challenge Hanging
Reporter : Don Tamlyn

> 27 years ago Graham Chauncey arrested the schoolteacher-murderer, Henry Stanton, and watched him go to the gallows. Bored with retirement, Chauncey is now heading an unofficial review of the case as pieces of evidence are unearthed that he thinks may render the conviction unsafe. The 16 year old victim, Louise Donovan, a pupil of Stanton's, was found strangled on a golf course adjacent to the school. Only 6 months passed between the offence and Stanton's execution and Chauncey believes that justice was too hurried. "I've always felt uneasy about this one for a lot of reasons. I aim to get at the truth, whichever way it falls," Chauncey told our reporter yesterday. Anyone who may have information is asked to contact him via this newspaper.

Mrs Oliver who owned the florist's shop noticed her tearing a piece from the newspaper, but Liz had no intention of discussing it with her, passing it off as an advertisement for a mail order dress she might send for, and tucked it safely away in her jeans pocket. At home later that night she stood in the kitchen ironing Tommy's shirts and thought long and hard about it, re-reading the article several times and becoming increasingly agitated. It had always been her decision never to refer to her former life. Those years had been sacrificed, abandoned and were beyond any redemption. Tommy wandered into the kitchen from the lounge where he had been watching the television and she never even heard him. Staring into space with the iron held in the air poised above his best shirt and the tatty little piece of torn newspaper resting innocuously on the ironing board.

"Penny for them," he laughed, startling her into a renewed attack on the shirt and a hurried retrieval of the scrap of newspaper which she clumsily slipped back into her pocket.

"Daydreaming, love. It happens," she smiled, but her embarrassment remained unmasked.

"What's the cutting?" he asked, nodding towards her pocket.

"Nothing," she lied uneasily.

"Then don't look so worried," he remarked. "The world isn't about to end. You haven't killed anyone."

Despite herself, she couldn't control the sudden intake of breath and she heard her own gasp hanging in the kitchen air as he inadvertently touched the nerve. From such stray remarks destinies may be changed.

"I think I'm going to tell you, Tommy," she announced, standing the iron on its end and turning off the switch. "I've done nowt wrong but I'm fretting. I need advice."

"Come and sit down in front room. You look worried to death," he replied with concern.

The twelve by twelve room was hopelessly overcrowded, with an old oak table under the laced-curtain window where they ate each evening, a bulky television in the one corner, a chintz two-seater sofa in the other corner and his special armchair, with its worn, sagging cushion, almost in the middle of the room, but angled to get prime view of the television screen. On every surface, small ornaments of turtles were clustered, staring out into the badly lit room. Carved wooden turtles, glass ones, plastic ones, every colour and every shade. The first Mrs Duncombe just had a thing about turtles.

Unusually, she sat in his armchair, sinking low into the hollow, adding to her image of insignificance, while he perched expectantly on the edge of the sofa and listened to her description of life with a bigot, leaving her to speak without interruption, but unaware of where she was going.

"He went away to some weekend rally," she continued. "When he came back all he could talk about was some bloody case in America. Down in one of them southern states. A white man had shot a defenceless black and the jury let him off. Bob thought it was bloody wonderful. A message for us all, he used to say."

"But you're rid of him, Liz. What's got you so upset about it now?" he asked.

"Soon after his crowing about that American case he got called up for jury service. The bloke they tried was black and Bob had him for guilty as soon as he looked at him. Got himself made foreman. Bullied anyone who didn't agree. Judge had 'im hanged," she explained, her voice shaking.

"The Judge wouldn't see an innocent man hanged. He must have done it. You can't go worrying about all that," he insisted.

"You're missing the point, Tommy. Bob never really cared whether he did it or not. In fact, he used to crow about it later, saying he didn't really think the bloke had done it. He just wanted to see a black man hanged. Claimed it'd stop a lot of other blacks from killing whites, like the bloke in America had said."

"Seems to me the one with the problem is Bob. It's too late for the fella they hanged. But none of it's got 'owt to do with you," he declared emphatically.

"It hadn't. Until I saw this bloody cutting," she answered, pulling the screwed up piece of newspaper from her pocket and thrusting it at him and then watching his face as he carefully read the short article over to himself.

"Ah, I'm with you now," he nodded. "You think this retired copper should know the hate stuff that the bastard was spouting."

"How could he ever have had a fair trial with someone like Bob on the jury? Let alone as foreman. But I'm frightened it'll bring him back into our lives," she continued.

"Sometimes you gotta stand up for what you think is right. He don't frighten me. He'll never find us anyway. If it was me, I'd tell this ex-copper what you just told me. Besides, if the black bloke didn't do it, then someone else did. Walking free," he said.

"I keep thinking about his wife. The bloke had a wife. Bob told me she went into the witness box and lied. 'Any white woman who went with one of them ain't got any morals anyway' was what he used to say. If he was innocent how could she ever get over it?" she asked, wringing the front of her apron in her hands as she voiced aloud for the first time the worries that had gnawed away at her over the years.

"OK, Liz. Get the writing pad out of the table drawer. We're going to write a letter to this Chauncey fella and send it to the paper. We'll say we insist that our name's kept out of it. But you'll feel better for getting it off your chest once and for all," he announced decisively.

Pulling herself up out of the armchair, she busied herself finding the writing paper, envelopes and a pen and then they both sat down together at the oak table in the window. They wrote it out in rough first, then altered the odd word here and there, before she rewrote it in her best writing while he addressed the envelope. They kept a book of stamps under the green china turtle on the mantelpiece and, as soon as the stamp was in place, she hurried down the road to the letter box at the side of the church. As she heard it drop down the chute and out of sight she felt a wave of relief. It probably wouldn't make a scrap of difference but she felt confident that she had done the right thing. That's what mattered most.

Chapter 19

Four years previously they had reopened the Grand Hotel on the Brighton seafront after the IRA detonated a bomb there in an attempt to blow up Margaret Thatcher and The British Cabinet. Five people were killed when the bomb exploded at three o'clock in the morning, shredding the bathroom where Mrs Thatcher had been two minutes previously. On her insistence, at nine thirty sharp the next morning, she recommenced the next session of the conference.

Eustace Vishney had immediately suggested that they should meet at The Grand for tea when Neville Hollister had telephoned him on receipt of Vishney's letter outlining the disturbing visit paid to him by that dreadful Walgrave girl. The teas there were every bit as delicious as at The Ritz. Cucumber sandwiches, a four-tier stand of fresh cream cakes and a large china pot of Darjeeling. Best of all, he would make sure that Hollister was landed with the not-inconsiderable bill.

Dolphin Glen had its own mini-bus, painted chartreuse green and magnolia. Vishney hated being seen in it, stuffed inside with all those inconsequential geriatrics like some Darby and Joan outing, but it saved him a taxi-fare and he made sure it dropped him off at The Grand early, well before Hollister was due.

Even though tea service was not due to begin for another half an hour Vishney could only see two tables left in the window of the glorious front lounge directly across from the seafront. Pointing imperiously at one of the window tables the liveried waiter, plainly some kind of foreigner, led the old man, bedecked in a three-piece suit which was conservatively one decade out of date and possible two, towards the chosen table..

"No. No," snapped Vishney, pointing to the other seemingly

available window table which was just further along at the end of the row. "I want that table, not this one," Vishney demanded.

"But, Sir, that table is . . ." began the waiter respectfully.

"Don't you understand simple English?" Vishney barked out, causing other heads to turn and observe the patrician's handling of the underclass. "I want that table, there."

The waiter gave a Gallic shrug and walked Vishney towards the table at which Vishney was pointing, only to reach a mirrored wall. The table that Vishney was demanding was a reflection of the very table to which the dutiful waiter had been leading him.

"Stupid man," hissed Vishney, trying to cover up his own foolishness as some of the other guests realised what had happened and were openly sniggering. Vishney slipped on his pince-nez and picked up the menu.

"Why can't they get English staff?" Vishney announced loudly as the waiter eased him into a chair and went off for a snigger of his own.

The long head stared out of the window across to the grey sea beyond. A few stragglers had braved the chill wind and were pretending to enjoy struggling along the promenade. It didn't seem very long ago to Vishney that a black limousine had whisked him along these South coast roads to Lewes and Winchester to preside over some weighty trial. How important he had felt in those days. How important he had been, he reminisced, a half-smile briefly diluting the customary sour expression, as the glorious memories flooded back, until he was abruptly jolted back to reality by the cut-glass accent of Neville Hollister.

"How are you, Eustace? It's been a long time," he declared, holding out a podgy hand and seeking to manoeuvre his portly frame into a chair.

"You're not here to enquire after my health," came Vishney's acid reply, as he assessed how many extra stone Hollister had acquired since they last met.

"No. Your letter was not good news. And there's been a bit of a development on our side since your incident. We'll just order tea and I'll bring you up to date."

"I would suggest we have the full English cream tea," Vishney said. "It's extremely good. Mind you, your waistline will suffer."

Hollister was well aware that his Michelin Man shape was beyond redemption, as was his high-blood pressure and blotchy red face.

"Two full English teas," Hollister called across to the waiter who had now donned his white gloves and was approaching their table with a tray bearing the teapot and accessories. As soon as he had turned up their china cups and poured the tea Vishney demanded the news.

"What's this development, then?"

"William had a visitor at work. It was Stanton's son," Hollister replied.

"I see. I believe it was him who was with the wretched girl when she came here the other day," said Vishney. "This needs stamping on."

"It gets worse," Hollister continued. "Apparently he tricked his way into William's house."

"Outrageous," exclaimed a shocked Vishney.

"But we can't report it to the police, can we? Open up a can of worms."

"What did he take?"

"Some photographs," began Hollister gingerly and then pausing. " . . . I gather of a rather compromising nature."

"So William's still unable to control himself, is he? That's how this whole bloody thing began," Vishney responded angrily.

"Stanton's threatening to send them to the Board at the Bank. And maybe the police. Unfortunately, one of William's friends had left some kind of drugs there as well and Stanton found the stuff. Making similar noises about that. Ah, here's our cream tea. Looks splendid," he added, as the waiter set down a plateful of thin triangular-cut cucumber sandwiches on brown and white bread and a cake stand overflowing with éclairs, scones, puff pastries and vanilla slices.

Vishney's hand snaked out and seized four of the white bread sandwiches and the two men fell silent while they devoured the fare. *Dolphin Glen* charged enough, stretching his judicial pension more than somewhat, but the food was like school meals. Tea at The Grand at someone else's expense was a treat to be savoured. His hand reached for the cake stand and the long fingers closed on one of those exquisite small éclairs bursting with fresh cream. Hollister was watching him, clearly resenting the premature attack on the cakes whilst he was still on the sandwiches.

"You say he's threatening," Vishney said, breaking the silence as he took a quick break between éclairs. "Either he's going to report it or he isn't. Which is it?"

"At the moment it's just a threat. Stanton says he'll make his mind up when he's poked around a bit more," Hollister answered, having now cleared his plate of sandwiches and moved on to a thick vanilla slice, whilst calling for the waiter to refill their teacups.

Vishney had piled his plate up with a scone, covered in clotted cream and jam and a renewed supply of the sandwiches. He leaned back in his chair, taking the side plate with him, and continued the exchanges in between mouthfuls.

"What am I meant to do about this, Neville? I did nothing wrong. I hurried matters along and helped avoid some embarrassment for your boy and the family name. But as far as Stanton was concerned, the jury heard the relevant evidence."

"There was a bit more to it than that, wasn't there, Eustace? Still, I'm not here to rake over old coals. We just need to decide how to warn these awful people off. Did you read yesterday's Daily Mail?"

"Of course not. Rag. I've only ever read The Times. Since Oxford days. Why?" asked Vishney.

Neville Hollister put his hand into his inside jacket pocket and withdrew his wallet which he opened up, extracted a cutting and handed it to the old man who, replacing his plate on the table, held the piece of paper between his thumb and index finger like it was a tramp's sock and read it over to himself. Twice. Without eating. "Pissing in the wind," he announced finally, handing the cutting back.

"Maybe. But William thinks we should do something about it. He thinks Chauncey, Stanton's son and the girl are obviously in this together and reckons if we can warn Chauncey off, then the other two will fall away. Amateurs," Hollister declared as he moved on to a scone.

"That's for you and William to grapple with. There's no evidence that I did anything improper. No evidence at all. I just want an assurance that I hear no more about this. I've told the staff that the security must be improved. Should never have got near me," he whined.

"There's more to it than that, Eustace. When Stanton confronted William he told him that he had seen your files. Obviously, we don't know what that means. But you will," Hollister said, watching closely for Vishney's reaction.

The old man's face drained of blood, the gaunt cheeks were sucked inwards and his lips were tight and drawn, exposing the artificial whiteness of his dentures. Hollister was reminded of a Victorian death-mask.

"My file of the whole case has been mislaid," he replied acidly. I checked after that girl had left."

"What was in it?"

"Nothing."

"Are you sure?"

"It was only press cuttings. No notes. Nothing."

"Can you be sure that you didn't write anything on the cuttings that may link you to me?" Hollister demanded.

"No. I can't be bloody sure. It's twenty seven years ago. I haven't looked at them since 1963. As far as I remember there was nothing," Vishney replied angrily.

"So Stanton's bluffing," concluded Hollister.

"It would seem so. But Stanton isn't your problem, is he? Like you said, he's an amateur. So's the girl. Her father was useless. The one to worry about is that retired officer in the newspaper report. He'll know how to dig," Vishney observed, now moving into a final assault on the few remaining cakes on the stand.

"It's just the family name, Eustace. That's all I'm seeking to protect. William was very stupid," Hollister explained weakly.

"And has remained so," Vishney added tartly.

"But we know it was Stanton who was the murderer, don't we?" asked Hollister, seeking reassurance.

"And we shall continue to say so," answered Vishney, now beginning to see a way forward.

"So what do I do about this Chauncey fellow?" Hollister asked.

"Give him something more important to worry about. Cut his legs off," Vishney spat.

"What does that mean?"

Vishney had filled his belly to the point where he could eat no more. All that was left on the table was one sandwich and two puff pastries. Picking up his paper napkin and looking around to check that the waiter was not in view, he wrapped them within its folds and carefully slipped the parcel into his jacket pocket before explaining the solution to Hollister, whose expression of disapproval made no impression on the old Judge.

"Policemen are like Judges," Vishney began. "The longer they do the job the more they become obsessed by the pension. Go into any Judges' Dining Room at lunchtime and all they talk about is their bloody pension. Same with the police."

"So you think if he's told that playing around with old cases, trying to upset the apple cart, is unprofessional, outside the code and all that. Could lead to the loss of his pension. . . " Hollister reasoned out loud.

"Exactly," Vishney interrupted. "Disciplinary breach. Putting him in breach of contract. Threaten to get the lawyers on it."

"But don't I need some top brass to issue the warning?" Hollister asked.

"That's the easy part."

"Ah," sighed Hollister. "I'm with you now. Maxcroft."

"Of course, Maxcroft. Big noise at the Met. Top of the tree. Dragged up in the gutter and greedy for the trappings of the upper class. Craves a title. Bends the knee to every Judge, High Sheriff and Lord Lieutenant in the land. Putty in your hands," Vishney concluded.

"I thought you were out of touch down here in Brighton, Eustace," smiled Hollister.

"It's in the blood, Neville. You only lose it when they carry you out. Good afternoon," declared Vishney, pushing his chair back, offering a quick handshake and then moving away, leaving Hollister to pick up the tab.

Chapter 20

George had convened a council of war on Saturday morning. They decided that Salisbury was about half way between Taunton and Canterbury and by midday she and Cal were walking across the Close, the wide green spaces that surround the seven hundred and fifty year old Cathedral. Chauncey was late and so they went inside the medieval masterpiece.

Cal was overawed by the details of the construction which were outlined in the literature on offer. Built within a single generation with a spire at over four hundred feet which was the tallest in England, weighing six thousand four hundred tonnes. Inside was an original version of the Magna Carta and the oldest mechanical clock in the world. Hundreds of pillars of dark Purbeck Marble and windows beyond counting. They sat on a pew in silence and absorbed the atmosphere which had not changed in all the centuries of the Cathedral's existence. By the time that they emerged Chauncey was standing at the main gates. George had spoken to him numerous times on the phone but this was the first time that they had met face to face and it fell to Cal to make the introductions. Chauncey seemed ill at ease and not keen to go to a pub or a café but to get down to business immediately and so they sat on a bench near St Ann's Gate, surrounded by ivy-coloured Georgian and Victorian houses. There was a hint of early spring in the air and thin rays of sunlight slanted across the roofs. George positioned herself between the two men, slipped her pink jacket off her shoulders and then proceeded to set out the agenda.

"All roads lead to Hollister," she began. "He paid Dyer to set a heavy on Cal. We now know he'd met Louise on the golf course and he's still lying about what actually happened."

"And he's a kink," Cal added. "I've kept some of the photographs."

"We're slowly building a case but I think our priority is to try to get the original exhibits re-examined, particularly with a view to DNA. Big advances are being made. I've read about it. Am I right, Graham?" George asked, turning to look at him.

Chauncey nodded in agreement but said nothing.

"I managed to speak to Littleton on the phone last night," Cal volunteered. "He's a vicar in Newcastle. Spoke for half an hour. He's absolutely sound on the times, even after all these years. My father would have had to move like greased lightning to rape and kill the girl and still be back in the building when Littleton saw him."

While Cal and George grew more animated as they listed the developments, Chauncey became increasingly sullen, shifting uncomfortably on the bench.

"What's your take on the way forward, Graham?" Cal asked directly.

There was a long silence. Chauncey got up off the bench and stood facing the pair of young faces looking expectantly up at the senior member of the team. He put his hands in his pockets and looked out towards the Cathedral that must have witnessed a million human dramas in its formidable history. This was just another little one in the great scheme of things.

"I'm afraid I've got to pull out," he eventually announced in a flat voice.

"Pull out. Why?" George demanded. "Without you we're lost. You know the rules. We know nothing."

"I've been railroaded. Standard police technique. As you know, I got an old contact at the Daily Mail to run that piece. It provoked five replies. Three were from nutters. Par for the course. But one was a phone call yesterday morning. Directly to my home, not via the newspaper," he explained.

"How did they get your number?" George asked.

"Very easily," came the immediate response. "It was Ian Maxcroft.

Top brass in the Metropolitan Police. Sees himself as the next Commissioner. That means a knighthood. I know officers who worked with him in his younger days. They called him Max Crafty. Sly, back-stabbing, manipulative."

"What did he want?" asked Cal.

Chauncey moved back to his seat and crossed his arms. He was hating this. He was being weak. These two youngsters depended on him. He had the time. He had the inclination. But he didn't have the strength. Nor did he have the bank balance.

"To advise me to leave well alone," he eventually answered. "He said it was highly unprofessional for an Officer to try to undermine a conviction in one of his own cases. Yarnell would be turning in his grave. Then he delivered the real message. If I continued he'd institute proceedings to confiscate my pension."

"Can he do that?" George exclaimed in horror.

"Oh, yes."

"He's been nobbled," Cal said.

"Of course," Chauncey replied.

"Vishney and Hollister," announced George.

"Probably," Chauncey agreed. "But look at it from my point of view. I've had two ex-officers take very serious liberties with Creane and Dyer. If Maxcroft got wind of any of that he'd go for me big time. Might try to prosecute me."

"But he doesn't know about that does he?" Cal asked.

"Not yet. But he's been sniffing. He discovered I went to the depository at Wandsworth. Claimed I wasn't entitled. But more importantly said I'd lied about who I took. The Prosecuting authorities denied all knowledge of any prospective member of their staff going. Maxcroft said he knew it must be you. Exposing original exhibits to the hands of the convicted murderer's son. It's enough to do for my pension," Chauncey told them, now leaning his head in his hands.

"And do you think he's right?" Cal enquired.

"Yes. I know he's right. That old biddy at Wandsworth would identify you in five seconds flat. I could hardly survive without my pension. I've got to phone Maxcroft tonight and give him my decision."

"You've got to pull out. I can see that," George declared sadly.

"I've still got some of the money your father's estate left me to pursue the enquiry. I'll send that straight back to the solicitors," Chauncey insisted.

"No," George responded immediately. "Dad wouldn't want that. You've already helped us along the way. We'll have to press on alone but you can tell us now which way to go."

"In my opinion, Amy Beckett. Tammy," Chauncey replied. "She's a key to all of this. Cal, you've got to blast your way over there and put the fear of God into her. You'll have to confront her away from her minders. Find out where she lives. Get her isolated."

"If you failed, what chance do I have of getting anything out of her?" Cal countered. "What do I do? I can't beat her black and blue in the hope she cracks before I end up in a Nevada Penitentiary."

"No, you can't. And she's been on the wrong end of hard-fisted men all of her life. She punched me in the mouth. You've got to terrify her mentally. Petrify her. I'll tell you everything I learned about her in the short time I was with her."

Chauncey then spent ten minutes going over all she had said to him in the Riviera Hotel and how she had behaved, while Cal absorbed every last detail. When Chauncey could remember nothing further to help, George took him back to when he had first mentioned the article in *The Daily Mail.*

"You said the newspaper article provoked five replies," she reminded him. "Three nutters. Maxcroft. That's only four."

Chauncey stood up again and his hand went to his inside jacket pocket and emerged holding an envelope.

"It's a letter from the divorced wife of the foreman of the jury that tried your father," he said, thrusting it into Cal's hand. I'll leave you to read it. All I ask is, if you decide to use it, then get her to write a similar letter to one of you, leaving me out of it, so that Maxcroft can't blame me for it. She'll co-operate. Even if her name comes out, which obviously she doesn't want. I rang her up and explained."

Then, with his head down, muttering his apologies, he shook hands with each of them and walked away under the shadow of one of the greatest Cathedrals in Man's history. Shoulders drooped, all pride and self-respect stripped away.

George brushed away a tear and then took the letter from Cal's hand and read it out loud.

Dear Sir,

My ex-husband, Robert Lancaster, was foreman of the jury that heard Mr Stanton's case. After they found him guilty, Robert used to say that he didn't really think Stanton had done it but he wanted to see a black man hanged, to stop other blacks from killing whites. Robert hated black people. He'd been to a rally where they talked about a case in America where a white man shot a black man but the white jury cleared him. Robert thought this was wonderful and a message for all white people. He said he stood no nonsense off any juror who didn't agree with him. He used to shout at me and beat me up and he could be very frightening so I understood how hard it was to stand up to him. Mrs Stanton was a witness for the defence and Robert hated her for going with a black man. I can assure you, having been married to him for many years, that he never gave Mr Stanton a fair hearing and it has worried me ever since. My new husband and I would ask you to keep our names out of this, as I don't know what Robert would do if he knew I had told you all of this.

Yours sincerely

L. Duncombe (Mrs)

When she had finished reading it there was a long silence as the two of them stared at each other in a combination of disbelief and renewed hope.

"It's absolutely devastating," Cal eventually exclaimed. "How can the Home Office or Court of Appeal ignore that?"

"No fair minded person could fail to see that he didn't get a fair trial with a racist bigot as foreman of the jury," replied George. "This is a whole new line of attack."

"There's so much to do, George. And not much time. I only have three weeks left," said Cal, putting his arm around her and holding her close. "I hate the idea that I'll soon be on the other side of the world from you."

George looked up at him and kissed him gently on the cheek. "We'll find a way," she assured him. "We've got energy. We've got youth. And, at least for the moment, we've got each other. This evening we'll prepare a brief. Like Dad used to get from the solicitor. Putting all of this together. Listing our evidence. I'll phone Tim Sprackley, Dad's old barrister friend. Ask him to review it and submit it to the Home Office. I know he'll help. We'll argue that they must re-examine the exhibits, particularly for DNA and give us leave to appeal."

"And I suppose I've got to make a flying visit to the Bright Light City," Cal responded. "And find some way to crack open a street-hardened tramp."

"We all have our weaknesses," said George. "And you'll find hers."

Chapter 21

As culture shocks go, they don't come much bigger than four in the morning in rural Somerset and eleven at night in Las Vegas, Nevada. George drove him to Gatwick along deserted motorways, leant over from the driving seat outside the Terminal and held him tightly in her arms and then, suddenly, she was gone. After hours of mind-numbing airport queuing and automatism, he was strapped into a narrow seat with his knees in his chest for another nine hours until the sardine-can charter aircraft put down in Bangor, Maine for immigration, customs and refuelling. Cal only had one small rucksack which he carried as hand-luggage, so more empty hours before the reloading and six airborne hours to McCarran Airport, Las Vegas. Out of the blackness of the sky, a canopy of brilliant lights had suddenly materialised below and, within minutes, he was in a cacophony of heat, noise, neon, glitz and bedlam that made four in the morning in Somerset seem like it was on another planet in another time.

Wrung out, mind-blown and suffering from a severe case of lack of reality, he had somehow found his way across a sea of green baize, bells, screaming one-arm bandits and fat Americans shouting and whooping, to the check-in counter at The Sahara Hotel. Given the budget price he was paying the room was palatial but he had little energy to appreciate it and just pulled his travel-stained clothes off, collapsed into the king size bed and passed out, dreaming of aircraft engine noise, plastic food and flashing neon. Somewhere out there, working the bars and the lounges, was another piece of the jigsaw. Tomorrow he would track her down.

The gold velvet curtains were so heavy that they needed long rods to open and draw them and they cut out all light. When he awoke, the room was in pitch darkness and he picked his way carefully towards where he remembered the window to be, located a rod and pulled back the curtain. The whole panorama screamed white heat. His room looked out across the Strip towards the purple mountains encircling the vast bowl. The metal of cars was shimmering and the white concrete was blinding. He couldn't find his watch and in Vegas clocks are a rarity. Time is an irrelevance. Turning on the TV, he learned it was eleven fifteen and the temperature was already ninety-nine degrees.

A power shower. Shave. The face looking much better. The colour fading from dark blue to off-yellow and the swelling had subsided. Clean clothes. He looked human again. Down twenty floors in the elevator and into absolute bedlam. Bells, shouting, jostling, flashing lights. Blundered across the casino floor and, eventually, espied some glass doors on to the street. As he walked out of the air-conditioned hotel and on to the wide concrete pavement of the Strip the blast of heat was like Lanny Creane landing an industrial glove right between the eyes. The traffic was virtually stationary and the pedestrians were ten wide on the sidewalks and in football crowd volumes. Every few yards the spot men were slapping concertinas of cards on their hands and thrusting a card into any passing male's hand. Pictures of half-naked girls. White, black, oriental, Asian, yellow. You name it. Every one with a phone number.

Cal fought his way down to the next intersection and cut east towards Paradise Road where the crowds quickly fell away and he felt like he could breathe. A coffee shop loomed into view and he ducked through the doors into a thirty degree temperature drop and slid on to a red plastic stool at the counter. A waitress with dead eyes smacked a glass of iced water in front of him and then poured him a mug of coffee.

He went for the Slam. Two buttermilk pancakes with maple syrup, three scrambled eggs with Cheddar cheese, two bacon strips, hash browns and rye toast. And more coffee. The fourth mug shrugged off the last vestiges of Gatwick Airport, the drone of aircraft engines, vague drifting recollections of Bangor and fitful sleep in a blacked-out room twenty storeys over a desert floor with ringing bells, flashing lights and half the world's population. He was ready for action.

Back in the football field-sized foyer of The Sahara Hotel were a few car rental desks. He chose the one manned by the prettiest girl and arranged for a medium range sedan to be delivered to the hotel. It would be delivered within the hour, so Cal wandered in to the heart of the casino to pass the time. Broad phalanxes of one-armed bandits stretched as far as the eye could see; men in garish Hawaiian shirts clustered around blackjack tables, scratching the green baize with their cards in silent demands for the stone-faced dealer to turn them another card; obese women with voices like foghorns spread their chips across the roulette tables, leaning so far across the table to get their bets on that their cleavage virtually spilled out on to the Middle Dozen. All the while the steel eyes of the pit bosses watched every move, every gesture, every win and every loss. But the real action was gathered round the half a dozen craps tables where the crowd was three and four deep, shouting, whooping and urging the thrower on.

Cal knew as much about playing craps as he did about neurosurgery. In fact neurosurgery looked less complicated. But ignorance can be bliss. Pulling a twenty dollar bill from his pocket he thrust it at the man with a rake pulling in the dice after each throw.

"That's the Stick Guy, pal. You get chips off the dealer," a Brooklyn accent wrapped in a Danny Devito covering bawled out at him.

In three seconds flat his twenty dollars was changed and a bald man in a silver suit and no shirt pressed the red dice into his hands. "Now you're the shooter, greenhorn, let's watch you throw," he yelled, while Danny Devito ordered him to put half his money on the "Pass Line". Cal rolled the dice down the table, bouncing them off the walls like dodgems at a fairground.

"Six," shouted the Stick Man while two dealers placed chips on the table and the dice were being pushed back at Cal by the long stick.

"No sevens," said the suit. "We want a six before a seven."

And Cal threw a six. And another six. And the crowd roared. And Danny took over Cal's betting. He threw eight more times. Two sixes. An eight, two nines, a ten and a twelve. The crowd grew thicker around the table. This kid was hot. Danny was turning purple with excitement. Cal threw a seven. The dice passed to another shooter.

"You did great kid," said the suit.

"Nice throwing," agreed one of the dealers, pushing a pile of black chips in Cal's direction and leaving them standing directly in front of him.

"Whose are those?" Cal asked Danny.

"Yours," came the reply. "Six hundred bucks. You shoulda bet more. I made a grand."

Wandering away from the madness at the table he lined up at the cage to cash his chips in. Twenty dollars had become six hundred in twelve minutes flat. This was a million miles from the reason why he was really here. Went for a cup of coffee at the bar where video poker machines were set into the counter top. A young girl in a black suit, tights, stilettos and bright red hair slipped on to the adjacent stool. Green eyes as vacant as the Mojave desert. Cherry lip gloss, still glistening from a renewed application in the last sixty seconds. Purple fingernails. Face that had seen it all, done it all and just kept wanting more. She must have watched his run of luck at the craps tables. That's what she did. Hunted a winner like a leopard stalked the antelope and then she would bring it down. Lurched into her routine, the glossy lips moving while the face remained on auto-pilot. Cal told her he was meeting his wife in twenty minutes. The black-waistcoated barman, his bullet head sweeping his terrain like radar on top of an airport control tower, told her she might want to take a hike. Cal played a few hands of poker on the machine. Had a refill of coffee. Lost twenty dollars. Time to get the car.

It had been valet parked and the car jockey ran to retrieve it. 1990 Dodge Dynasty sedan automatic. Two-tone grey. V6 engine. Square back. Rows of lights. Drove like a Centurion tank with an enormous turning circle, but functional and anonymous. Ideal. The air-conditioning was already on full blast and the radio was pretuned to the Country Music station where Garth Brooks was considering what might happen "If Tomorrow Never Comes." It took him half an hour, driving around the sections of Vegas that the tourists never see, to get a true feel of the car and the tempo of the roads. Then he turned to the serious stuff.

West on Sands Avenue, then Spring Mountain led him into Industrial Road. *Ellie's Exotic Escorts Agency* was easy to miss. It was no more than an industrial unit in a side street at the back of Industrial Road and across the railroad tracks. A wide alleyway ran alongside the building with a row of parking places. In the blinding sunlight of early afternoon the neon of the sign in the window was not at its most eye-catching. Only three vehicles were parked, presumably belonging to the girls and any telephonist. Cal surmised that early afternoon was off peak in the flesh trade. Opposite the alleyway on the other side of the road was *Alonso's Plumbing and Heating*. An untidy, fenced off yard with a narrow office front and half a dozen parking bays. Cal reversed into one of the vacant bays and turned the engine off. There were two street lights within fifty feet of the alley.

Alonso's would be closed at night and from this vantage point he could see anyone entering or leaving *Ellie's* and going to any parked vehicle at the side. Time to head for South Decatur Boulevard and *Delicate Daisy's Floral Delights*. Tammy was to receive a magnificent bouquet of flowers, delivered by *Delicate Daisy's* refrigerated delivery service to *Ellie's Exotic Escorts Agency* office, with a card inscribed with the thanks of last night's unnamed gentleman client. Cal would be paying the florist in cash.

By his reckoning there was no way she would be wrapping things up for the shift before midnight and so, after a long rest behind the drawn golden curtains and a New York strip steak in the Caravan Coffee Shop at the Sahara, he set off for a Ralph's supermarket at half-past eleven. In Las Vegas the supermarkets, with their own one-arm bandits, never close. A polystyrene ice box, a bag of ice, four cans of Coke, three bananas, some turkey breast, cream cheese, a French stick sandwich and small knife to put it all together got him change out of a ten dollar bill and he headed for the vigil at *Alonso's Plumbing and Heating*. He was in position by ten past midnight with a clear view of the alleyway opposite. Seven vehicles were parked there, well illuminated by the street lighting as he'd anticipated. There was little traffic and not a soul to be seen on foot. The vigil began.

It was hot in the Dodge, even with the windows open. He'd brought a pillow from his room and stuffed it against the driver's door, swinging his legs up on to the passenger seat and sinking low into the seat. Gradually, he worked his way through his supplies as two hours ticked by. Occasionally, a cab would draw up, depositing some under-dressed female who would enter *Ellie's* for a while, before another cab would draw up and take her away. At three o'clock a girl walked out of the office and went to a red Chevrolet in the alleyway and drove away. He was on his last Coke. But she was not carrying a bouquet of flowers.

At half past three another cab drew up with three girls in it. They went inside and then one emerged alone and headed for the parked vehicles. She was carrying an impressive bouquet of flowers. Cal could even see the motif of a big yellow daisy on the wrapping paper. A mass of dyed blond hair, aquamarine blouse, dark blue skirt. Good legs on high heeled shoes which fitted into the panorama of Industrial Road and the railroad tracks like a Big Mac at a Vegetarian's convention. Into a brown Ford F-150 pick-up and on to the road. She slipped on to the Freeway, out past the Airport and then hit US 95 South. In twenty minutes they were virtually the only vehicles on the road and he had to drop way back in case she got suspicious. Following her remained easy as he could see her lights in the clear desert air from a mile back. After another thirty five minutes they arrived at a crossroads with a traffic light in the middle of nowhere. He finished his last banana. Searchlight, Nevada. She turned left. No street lighting. Less than a mile down the road she swung the pick-up off the road and stopped. He jammed on the anchors. The interior light of the pick-up came on and he caught a glimpse of the blonde hair and the white wrapping paper. He slipped out of the Dodge and, silent in soft desert boots, ran towards her vehicle. The moonlight was good. Half a dozen permanent trailers backed up to a rock face. Well spaced out. All in darkness. Save one where a light came on as he watched and a blonde head appeared at the window and closed the curtains. Tammy was home. Cal spent half an hour walking the area, driving in and out of the excuse for a town, getting his bearings. He was nearly ready.

Chapter 22

The next morning Cal stopped at a sex shop. There were plenty of those in Las Vegas. Then to a hardware store, where he bought a MagiLite torch and a roll of duct tape, before barrelling the V6 engine up Interstate 15, exiting west on Cheyenne Avenue before turning north on Decatur until just after the junction with Route 215 where he hit open desert country, away from the immediate effects of the concrete and the neon. After a few miles he spotted a tired advertising hoarding with faded paint pointing west up a dirt road. *Escobarga's Desert Zoo* read the board. *Patron : Cesar Escobarga.*

Bouncing the Dodge over the potholes, he travelled up the track for half a mile before arriving at a cluster of trees and vegetation and a couple of dilapidated outbuildings. An old camper van, a Chevvy pick-up truck and a jet black Harley-Davidson FXB 1340 Sturgis stood outside under shanty awnings, thinly covered with straw to fend off the fierce direct sunlight.

Pulling up alongside the Harley Cal climbed out of the car and was immediately hit by the overpowering stink of animals and their dung. It smelled like an Indian circus. On the far side of the awning was a wooden kiosk with a sign saying *Hours 10–6. Ring Bell.* Cal pressed the red button underneath the sign and heard a muffled buzzing somewhere deeper inside the compound. After a couple of minutes a figure emerged down a path leading from amongst the vegetation and walked up to where Cal was leaning on the kiosk. The man was about five-six tall, but nearly the same width. A greasy, blue spotted kerchief was tied around his head and a grey pony tail hung down at the back. Thick grisly hair poured out from the top of his threadbare Harley T-shirt while Maori warrior legs in shin length biker boots held up the human cube. The face was from the south-eastern flank of Chiapas, where the Mexican tropical jungle is at its densest, eyes lost in the leather creases and wrinkles and a mouth that barely moved when he spoke.

"Five bucks entry," he grunted.

"Are you Mr Escobarga," Cal asked tentatively.

"Who's askin'?" came the surly reply.

"I called you. About the snake," said Cal.

"Oh, the Aussie. Yea, snakes. I'm Escobarga. Venga," he responded in an accent as thick as the foliage, ushering Cal through a crude gate at the side of the kiosk and down a narrow path.

The path wound around to the front of the outbuildings and Cal could now see that they were cages and obviously the main source of the overpowering smell. On the floor of one of the inadequately sized structures a tiger was lying asleep amidst piles of its own hardened deposits, surrounded by a flotilla of horseflies. The animal's coat was dull, matted and lifeless. The adjacent cage housed two monkeys, perched up in the roof on a crude little shelf and cowering in a corner as Escobarga led Cal past their filthy abode and then disappeared inside a large shed which made a sauna bath seem arctic. The shed contained a series of tanks with various depths of green water, slime and rotting branches. A wooden barricade, about four feet high, separated the tanks from the boards where the paying punters would stand and try to spot the odd lizard, snake or turtle from within the seething mass of decay.

Escobarga walked to the far end of the shed and armed himself with an implement that was longer than he was and had a hook on the end, before approaching one of the tanks and leaning over the barricade, the eyes now so narrowed as to become invisible while he scoured the green for the creature he was seeking. Suddenly, he plunged the hook into the vegetation and, with a flick of his thick wrists, landed his prey, plucking a five-foot diamond back from its hiding place and swinging it over the barricade and on to the floor, slamming his biker boot on to the snake about nine inches below the head and pinning him down, as the reptile writhed for a few seconds before lying still, considering its next move.

"Western Diamondback rattlesnake," Escobarga mouthed. " How long you want him?"

Cal stared down at the creature, still malevolent, but stripped of all dignity. Its skin was grey to brown but dry and cracking, with diamond blotches down its back. Two stripes ran diagonally from its eyes across its face and its tail was just like that of the racoon and, as if on cue, the whole tail lifted skyward and the sound of its rattle shot across the shed like electric current.

"Kill me if he could," Escobarga laughed. 'But he can't. He's been cut."

"What do you mean?" asked Cal, as the snake had another surge of energy and fought to lift its head from under the punishing boot of its captor.

"In the jaw they have a gland. Venom gland. It's been cut out. Can bite, but no venom. You wanna know the name of the gland?" he enquired.

"Yeah"

"Duvernoy," the Mexican replied. "The gland of Duvernoy."

"I want him for tonight. Just 'til the morning," Cal said. "How do I handle him?"

"Tongs. Big leather gloves. And, for extra bucks, I give him a shot of calm."

"What's a shot of calm?"

"A drug. Isoflurane. Just before you collect him I give it him. Make him sleepy. Awake but sleepy. Easy to handle," Escobarga explained.

"How much? With the Isoflurane?" Say I pick him up at midnight and return him by ten tomorrow morning."

"What you want him for?" the Mexican responded, now lifting his boot and re-hooking the snake, so that he was dangling off the ground.

Cal took a step backwards to make sure he was out of reach, but the snake seemed to anticipate that he was on his way back into the tank and, with another flick of the thick wrists, Escobarga tossed him back into the stinking vegetation and turned to look carefully at Cal, waiting for his reply.

"I want to play a joke," Cal replied unconvincingly.

"I think not," Escobarga grunted in disbelief. "I just need to know he don't get hurt."

"I can promise you he won't be hurt," Cal assured him.

"A hundred bucks to rent him. And another two hundred insurance. Cash. Bring him back safe I give you the two hundred back. Also I hold your passport until he come back. And name of your hotel in town."

"OK. I'll bring my passport and three hundred dollars. Midnight tonight. I'll want the tongs and the gloves," he insisted.

"Done," muttered Escobarga, now heading out of the shed and back towards the entrance. "I give him shot when you arrive. So it lasts. Put him in sack. One other thing."

"Yeah?"

"You hurt him, I hurt you," he said with a smile that suggested he hadn't had his Duvernoy's gland cut out.

"I'll keep him safe," Cal repeated. "He'll probably enjoy a night on the town."

Chapter 23

At just after nine the Dodge swung into Industrial Road, up towards the railroad tracks and along the side street which housed *Ellie's Exotic Escorts Agency.* It was dark and the neon sign was flickering brightly in the office window. Driving past the front of the office, Cal slowed down to look back up the side alley where the girls parked their cars and, on the spot nearest the office door, stood the tired brown Ford F-150 pickup. An early start to work might mean an early finish so he aimed to be in place before two.

Cutting back towards The Strip, he passed a white stucco building proudly advertising itself in green neon as *Celia's Cocina* with pick-up trucks slewed everywhere on the parking lot, indicating that the locals must rate it, so he U-turned his way back. Inside, it was teeming with Latinos and blue collar workers, the hard-beat Mariarchi bands were blaring from the giant speakers and there wasn't a tourist to be seen. Squeezing himself in at the bar, he downed a couple of stinging Margaritas. Patron Silver Tequila, triple sec and fresh-squeezed lime. Dynamite. They found him a table for one at the back and brought him a plate piled high with steak quesadillas. Flour tortillas crammed with tender steak, cheddar cheese, chile poblano, red bell peppers and succulent sautéed onion. The garnish was guacamole, lettuce, tomato, sour cream and roasted salsa. Washed down with three ice-cold Tecate beers he felt a million dollars. Then his brain reminded him why he was really sitting in the middle of the Nevada desert about to collect a rattlesnake in a sack.

Back at the wheel, he pointed the Dodge towards *Escobarga's Desert Zoo*, listening to Willy Nelson singing "Crazy." Another legend. It was pitch black when he turned on to the dirt road but, as the ground rose, he could see the vast pall of light in his rear-view mirror hanging over Vegas like a mystical cloud. Underneath it, invisible human hoards were clamouring to self-indulge in all of man's most base activities. Greed, liqor, sex and lucre. Perm any four from four. In any order you choose.

When he reached the excuse for a car-park Escobarga was waiting for him by the Harley, no doubt having watched the headlights on high-beam picking their way up the track. A bottle of Pacifica was in his hand and a laden, brown Hessian sack lay at his feet.

Cal turned off the engine and lights and got out. The smell was less pungent in the cooler night air. Escobarga was dressed in the same clothing as earlier and, in the poor illumination thrown out by the Dodge's interior light, looked like some ancient Aztec warrior.

"You got the green?" he demanded, exuding fumes of beer and tequila in Cal's direction.

"Count it," Cal replied, thrusting a thick Sahara Hotel envelope into the gnarled, brown fist. "Three hundred and my passport. Room 2022 at The Sahara."

The Mexican leant inside the car and slowly counted his way through the money with his thick fingers and then studied the passport details and the photograph.

"What you really up to, kid?" he asked. "What you want with a drugged-up rattler?"

Cal didn't answer but nodded downwards towards the sack. A long pair of metal tongs and heavy leather gloves lay alongside it.

"Has he had his shot?" he enquired anxiously.

"Yea. No problem. He travel in the trunk. No problem," replied the Mexican, picking up the sack, gloves and tongs as Cal popped the trunk lid open.

Escobarga threw the tongs and gloves into the trunk, but then spent a long time nestling the sack carefully into a position where nothing was digging into its cargo, whispering in Spanish to the snake. By the time he snapped the trunk lid closed Cal was back in the driver's seat and ready to roll.

The Mexican came round to the open driver's window and rested his granite chunk of a forearm on the sill.

"Hold him about a foot below his head. You got that?"

"Yeah."

"And remember. Ten o'clock, kid. Don't make Escobarga come after you," he warned, his words hanging menacingly in the desert air.

"I got the message," Cal answered as he fired the ignition.

"You forget something," grunted the Mexican.

"What?"

"You don't know his name."

"I didn't plan on any conversation," Cal responded.

"Chac. His name's Chac. Mexican God."

"Of what?"

"Lightning. And rain. The body of God has scales. Like a snake. You speak to him. You call him Chac. Don't forget," the Mexican shouted as Cal slipped the automatic transmission into reverse and pulled back, heading for Searchlight.

Within twenty minutes he was again pointing south on an almost deserted US 95. Nevertheless, with a live rattler in the trunk and a couple of Margaritas and Tecates on board, he didn't want to be stopped by a stray Highway Patrol Officer and so kept well within the speed limit. An hour later he arrived at the traffic light and headed down towards the lake. The trailer was just about a mile off Cottonwood Cove Road and it was hard for even a stranger to get lost in Searchlight.

Parking in the shadows where he'd parked the night before, he headed for the trailers. All six were in total darkness. His eyes rapidly adjusted to the darkness. There was something about the desert terrain and clear, dry air that seemed to lend the night sky a kind of translucence and even though he was sixty miles away from the Vegas Strip, he still sensed the trillions of watts being projected skywards. A lone dog was barking somewhere back towards the town and a distant screech owl announced it had clawed some hapless prey from the desert floor. As he neared the trailers, he could hear the sound of air conditioners pumping their relief into the trailers and, in the trailer furthest to his right, he could see the blue flickering of a TV screen from within. Without using the MagiLite he made it to her front steps. There was a washing line running from a hook on the metalwork adjacent to the door to a pole a few yards away. A couple of T-shirts, a bath towel and a pair of jeans were hanging motionless in the still air. The lock on the door was deceptive. At first it appeared flimsy and insubstantial, but it proved surprisingly resistant to both force and an amateurish attempt to slide it open with a credit card. So he moved to the left side of the trailer where the air conditioner was droning relentlessly away. It looked new, and as if it hadn't been properly fitted as it was crudely lodged in a window, resting on the sill and held only by the pressure of the window frame above, leaving gaps on either side.

A dirty plastic crate lay abandoned next to a bucket with a hole in it. Standing on the crate, and holding the air conditioner unit firmly in his left hand, he pushed up on the frame with his right and the window rose as sweetly as a well-oiled piston. Ensuring that the unit stayed balanced, he felt his way in with his right leg, followed by his shoulder and then his whole body. He was standing on a footstool. Safely re-anchoring the unit under the window frame, he turned on the pencil torch. He was in the sitting area. A small couch, a TV on a wall stand, a table with a few magazines and a dirty plate and a vase containing his flowers on it, an ugly lamp with a Cactus Jack glass shade and a wet towel on the floor. Moving further inside he came to the kitchen/bathroom area, with a sink to the right and a narrow door to the left giving on to the shower and toilet. Then, the front door and then her bedroom. A door opening to the right, a double bed, a small chest to the side of the bed and a built-in wardrobe along the left wall. Clothes lay abandoned across the floor. Turning the torch off plunged the room into perfect darkness.

Slipping out of the front door and ensuring that he did not fully close it behind him, he hurried back to the Dodge where he collected his gear and struggled slowly back to the trailer. It was a good job there was no-one around to hear him puffing and straining. That sack was heavy.

Back inside he set himself up in her bedroom, behind the door and waited. The air conditioner was pretty efficient and, after half an hour, he was cold. He hadn't bargained for that and so helped himself to a light blanket off her unmade heap of a bed. Through all of this he had remained nerveless. A soldier on a military mission. The demands of the next step overshadowing any emotion. Coming over from Australia, planning discussions with George, meetings with Chauncey, even the trip to Nevada had seemed like an exercise in a duty, but now he was faced with as bizarre a situation as he had ever known, involving breaking into some wayward female's home with the intention of sending her to the edge of a cardiac arrest. She'd better hurry up, he thought, Chac was beginning to smell.

Hovering somewhere between semi-consciousness and sleep, he was jolted back to razor alertness by the trailer shaking. He hadn't heard her vehicle, or the front door opening, but she'd closed it hard and that was what had brought him round. A light went on in the sitting area and then he heard her noisily relieving herself in the bathroom with the door open. A fridge door opened and closed and liquid was poured into a glass. Elastic snapped and clothes were thrown on the floor. She belched and passed wind. Then the light went off and her steps approached the bedroom and she moved towards a light switch he'd observed and noted on the left side wall. That's when he struck with a ferocity that surprised even himself.

She had no inkling of danger. Although the room was dark, its familiarity meant she was at complete ease when a gloved hand violently rammed itself across her mouth and an arm of steel anchored itself across her throat from behind and lifted her six inches off the ground. Amidst the blind panic she tried to drum her airborne heels into the assailant's groin, but they bumped harmlessly against solid legs in rough material. Her eyes watered, she whimpered and snorted and he felt her mouth working beneath the thick glove, desperately seeking some flesh on which to purchase, but he just pressed even tighter and the stink and taste of dead rodents from the glove added to her sense of nausea. When she tried to reach back with her hands to punch or tear flesh with her nails or elbow the intruder, he simply lifted her further off the ground and arched her backwards so she felt that her spine might snap. By now her resistance was already zero, but the fact that she was stark naked reduced it to a minus and she fell still, dangling like a rag doll. That's when, in a flash, he threw her on to the bed on her front and whipped a length of duct tape across her mouth from behind, effectively gagging her. Before she had the presence of mind to make any effective use of her liberated hands, he had them pulled up behind her back and she felt restraint manacles snapped on to her wrists. Some items stocked by sex shops have uses beyond carnal knowledge. Then, he rolled her over and wound more duct tape around her mouth, trapping and pulling at her dyed, disheveled hair in its adhesive as he made a job of it. Finally, he pinned her legs down and wrapped the tape around her ankles, before turning on the light and reviewing his handiwork.

Her naked breasts and her flat belly were heaving as she stared at the dark figure with the bruised face, sweating from his exertions and dressed like a marine on a combat mission. She squeezed her thighs together in a forlorn attempt to reduce the humiliating exposure produced by her nakedness and subjugation.

Cal knelt over her and saw abject horror in her eyes. Even eyes designed to measure everything in dollars and cents can be terrified. The make-up had run and the fleshy cheeks were red and tear stained. At close quarters Cal could see the hard lines running down the sides of the face and disappearing beneath the grey duct tape.

"You're going to give me the truth about Louise Donovan," he spat. "You'll only get one chance. If you scream, or lie or don't deliver, I'll make him sink his fangs straight into your pussy."

His own threat disgusted himself, but at least he knew it was a bluff. She didn't. He watched her eyes frantically darting left and right to see what he was referring to. Then he got up, went to his paraphenalia behind the door, picked up his tongs and eased them inside the sack before pulling the drowsy diamond head out on to the floor. Fixing the tongs about a foot below the rattler's head, he heaved him up on to the bed, letting the scales rub across her naked thighs and breasts, slowly bringing the head up to her face. He saw her gag, her stomach convulsed and the duct tape around her mouth puffed out as she must have vomited. Her eyeballs went up in the sockets, leaving only the whites and he realised that she had passed out. Putting the listless snake on the floor, he lifted her head and wrenched off the duct tape, taking chunks of hair with it, but allowing the vomit to be exhaled. The stink of her sickness and terror mingling with the rank stench of the snake was overpowering and he felt himself gagging. Her fainting lasted only seconds and the eyes fluttered back to recognition in a face whiter than the sheets she lay on while her breathing came in ragged gasps.

Sitting astride her, but without putting pressure on her, he picked up the tongs again and leant over to grab the snake. This time, as he heaved it upwards, he kept the head further from her and avoided any contact with her body. She was whimpering and snivelling. He was ashamed that he had the capacity to behave like this.

"Who had Louise arranged to meet?" he barked.

Her eyes met his. For the first time he saw more than just fear. There was intense hatred for what he was doing to her. But he didn't care. He shook the tongs so that the snake's head threatened and he could see that, despite the creature's drugged listlessness, its eyes were open and the cruel, elliptical pupils were taking in its surroundings. He moved the head nearer towards her and then, in a voice barely audible, she spoke.

"Who are you?" she whispered.

"I ask the questions. I want the answers or you get the rattler. Who had Louise arranged to meet?"

"William," she replied. There was no fight left. All the hardness fell away. "He promised her money."

"What for?"

"What d'you think?"

"Where was he afterwards when you saw him?" he asked.

"Coming off the golf course. Nearer to where she was found than I said. I saw him stop and light up."

Cal let the snake down slowly on to the floor and threw a sheet over the woman. There was no pleasure for him in her humiliation and fear.

"I asked him if they'd done it," she continued. "He said it was worth fifteen quid. That was a lot of money for us back then."

"Did he look like he'd just been in a struggle? Or had just attacked her?"

"Red-faced. Flustered. But actually seemed quite proud of himself," she replied, her voice now calming. "When we heard later in the day that Louise was dead, he found me after school. Said I was never to repeat what I knew. Swore he hadn't killed her, but no-one'd believe him. Promised me a hundred quid to shut up about him."

"Did he give you the hundred?"

"Yeah. And more over the next couple of years. 'Til I came out here. I had to say I'd seen him in the drive, 'cos I had, but I was never to tell about the rest of it."

"What about seeing Mr Stanton come off the golf course and walk near the bike sheds. Was that true?"

"I did see a man come off the course and go towards the sheds. Before we left school that day we heard Mr Stanton had been arrested 'cos Louise's knickers had been found in his saddlebag. When I heard that I just put two and two together," she sighed.

"And made five," he snapped.

"Maybe. Maybe not. Listen, I've had enough. You've got what ya come for. I feel sick. Just get that fucking snake out of here. I'm gonna throw up again."

"OK," he replied. "I'll get rid of it. But you're going to write out what you just told me. I'll put the snake in its sack and put it outside the trailer while you write it. Then I'll go."

She nodded and lay quietly, still shaking, under her sheet while he got the snake back into the sack and then put it outside her front door with the rest of the stuff.

Back in her bedroom, he released her, turned his back while she put a robe on and watched her sit on the bed and write it all out. It didn't take her very long.

"If you call the cops, or do anything about this, then I'll deny it. You have no proof. You're not hurt. And you'll make even bigger trouble for yourself with the UK authorities. I'm not after you. I'm after Hollister," he explained, relieved at learning what he had, but deeply uncomfortable at how he'd achieved it.

"Who are you?" she breathed.

He didn't answer her, but got up, walked to the front door, down the three steps and carefully picked up the sack.

She was standing in the doorway, watching him, her composure returning. The hideous experience was just becoming another chapter in the endless abuse men subjected her to. She hated them all.

"Who are you?" she repeated, as he set off for the Dodge with the sack held well away from his body.

"His son," he answered coldly.

"I thought so. You look like him. I hope you rot in hell, just like he's doing," she shouted, slamming the door and dropping the latch.

Cal popped the trunk of the Dodge open and put all the stuff including the snake inside, before slipping into the driver's seat and firing the Dodge up. That's when he felt the cold steel of a rifle barrel shoved into the back of his neck.

"Turn the fucker off," a rough male voice demanded.

Switching off the ignition, he glanced furtively in the rear view mirror. *Giants* baseball cap, thick beard, old, a few yellow teeth, snarling. Looked imbecilic. Seriously dangerous. Still pressing the barrel into Cal's neck, the man kicked open the rear passenger door and shouted out.

"Tammy. It's Pete. Get your ass out here."

Cal sat in silence, weighing the options. The old man was pushing harder with the rifle, actually hurting Cal's neck where the steel was rubbing against the thin skin on the hard bone.

Tammy appeared at the open car door, still in her bathrobe but with her face washed. She looked like a Shakespearian harridan, but spoke like a Vegas tramp.

"Trash him, Pete. He used a fucking rattler on me. Trash him," she spat out.

"Did he bite ya?" Pete asked.

"Nah. But frightened the shit out o'me?"

"I saw him come out ya door and dump a bag. Took a look. Diamond head, but drugged to the eyeballs. Reckoned I'd check 'im out. Who is he?"

"It don't matter. Hey," she barked at Cal, "give me that fucking piece of paper back. He's got a paper of mine," she explained to Pete, who pushed even harder with the rifle to emphasise the woman's demand.

Cal pulled the paper from his pocket and held it up. The old man snatched it from him and handed it to the woman.

"You really want me to trash 'im, Tammy?" he asked.

"I won't be telling on ya, Pete," she answered. "Bodies out here are like flies on shit."

"Drive," snapped Pete. "Real slow. Push her over walking pace and I'll take yer head off."

"Looks like ya'll reach hell even sooner than I thought," Tammy snarled as she slammed the door and the Dodge edged gently forwards.

After a few hundred yards across black, deserted scrubland, the old man told him to turn off to the left along a single-track dirt road, pot-holed with deep craters. Each time the car lurched over a rock, the barrel dug deeper into Cal's neck and he waited for the old man's finger to jerk the trigger, either by design or by accident.

The car headlights picked out an iron gate and crude railings cordoning off an area at the end of the track. As the Dodge came up to the gates Cal could see what it was. A cemetery. In the middle of absolutely nowhere.

"Stop," barked the old man. "And get out. Real slow. With your hands on top of your head."

Cal did as he was ordered. With one amendment. Within his right hand on top of his head was the small kitchen knife from Ralph's supermarket which had been on the central console under a map from the car rental company.

"Straight through the gate. Turn left," the voice directed, accompanied by a sharp prod in the small of the back from the gun.

This was higher ground and completely exposed. The moonlight was stronger than up by the rock face where the trailers stood. He could see that the terrain was rock and stone. No earth. The graves were hewn not dug. It took machinery to get down six feet. Cal wondered who ended up out here? Locals? People from the desert military bases? Was it still used? Exactly how was he going to avoid adding to their number?

He reached the railings at the far side. Large mounds of rocks and stones were piled high around an empty hole. Someone was expected. He stopped at the edge.

"Only dug it yesterday," the old man cackled. "Funeral tomorrow. Bury him in five foot 'stead of six. No-one'll know the difference. You'll be in the bottom foot."

"None of this is worth killing me for," Cal reasoned. "I'll pay . . ."

"Shove it," he interrupted. "Life here ain't worth shit. Mess with Tammy and you mess with Pete. Now drop in there. Not often a man climbs into his own fucking grave."

Cal's heart was racing. There was a fine line between some small town idiot trying to put the frighteners on him and actually killing him. Until now, Cal had not fully realised just how fine that line was. A muffled shot in a deep grave in the middle of nowhere. A layer of rocks. Tomorrow a coffin laid on top and no-one would be any the wiser. Ever. And no-one would probably waste too much time looking. The barrel was now pushing hard into his back. The man was very close. Cal slowly lowered himself to the edge of the grave, as if to drop into it as ordered, and the rifle pulled away. Cal crouched, put his left hand on the rocky edge and, in a lightning move swung his right hand around and plunged the knife into the foot of the gunman above, simultaneously throwing himself headlong to his right.

There was a piercing scream and an explosion that made it feel as if his head had been split open. He felt burning on the side of his face as the explosive rocketed from the barrel. It scorched his cheek and deafened him. But it missed him. By a cat's whisker. Old Pete was in his Indian moccasins and the blade of the knife passed through the thin leather like it was paper. If the terrain had not been so hard the knife would have impaled his foot to the ground as it went straight through, slicing through small bones, vessels and tissue. Cal jumped to his feet. The man had dropped down and was clutching the knife in his foot, wrenching it out, still screaming. Cal kicked the rifle out of the man's hand and heard it clatter into the grave below. Then he kicked him in the ribs. Very hard. Twice. Pete stopped screaming and lay there gasping for air and retching. Cal left him and ran back to the Dodge and away.

Such was life in Searchlight, Nevada in the spring of '90.

He drove back down the dirt track and on to the paved road, past the trailers. He reflected on the fact that he'd threatened a woman with a live diamond-back, that he'd nearly had his head blown off by a cretin in a desert cemetery and that Hollister had lied to him last week about not having sex with Louise. No doubt the Hollisters had continued to buy Amy's silence about William's shameful admission and all that would have entailed for the Hollister family name. And the likelihood was that Amy had also lied about it being his father she'd seen going from the golf course to the sheds. That was the totality of what he'd learned.

In terms of hard evidence for the Court of Appeal he'd come away from Searchlight with zip. Zilch. Nada.

Chapter 24

As soon as he first set eyes on her, he knew that she needed to be taken. It was not as if he was at that time in the cycle when he had even started looking. This was simply a chance encounter. Destiny, as he saw it. Later, when he was eating her thigh, he realised that this final animal ritual of consumption was a dimension of the condition that had never been able to express itself, because his work had always been hurried and conducted in the open air. Seclusion and a slower pace produced a fulfilment which carried the experience on to a higher plane.

Work that day had involved a journey which passed along the A37, once the route of the Fosse Way, that Roman masterpiece of civic engineering which had cut a swathe from Exeter to Lincoln. Set in a fold in the Mendip Hills stood the ancient market town of Shepton Mallet, where he had stopped to break the long journey home. Parking his car in a side street, he called in for something to eat at a café in one of the narrow lanes near to the market place. Bangers and mash. Opposite the restaurant was a public house with a well-lit steep flight of stone steps leading up to its entrance. That's where he had seen her. Relaxing over a coffee at his table for one in the window he had been satisfying himself by surreptitiously belching and passing wind when she had emerged from the pub doorway and, in yellow high-heeled shoes, had started to pick her way down the steps, from a height which was probably twenty feet higher than where he sat. Initially, his vision was filled by her legs, disappearing into an above-the-knee yellow pleated skirt, providing enticing flashes of inner thigh as she made the descent. The legs were short, heavy in the calf and the flesh of the thighs wobbled, contained in ecru tights. That was the crucial moment when he had realised the new direction in which the craving was destined to take him.

Hurriedly paying his bill, he started to follow her through the streets. It was already nearly dark. Her buttocks were stretching the skirt provocatively as they moved from side to side, making her gait cumbersome. Her upper body was wrapped in a waist-length, loose-fitting, mock suede jacket with grey and white synthetic fur running down the edges of the lapels. Standing about five feet four with crudely dyed blonde hair, showing dark roots easily visible under the street lighting, he tracked her from behind, keeping in the shadows as she inelegantly trundled her way across the market place on those cheap yellow shoes.

The fact that he had still not seen her face heightened the excitement, but he knew he had to move with great caution as this mission, unlike all its predecessors, had received no planning. He was still wearing the same clothes that he'd worn all day, he had no equipment with him, he was unaware of the local geography and the risk of leaving clues was significantly increased. She arrived at a main road on the north-west side of the town centre and suddenly stopped, taking him by surprise, until he realised that she was at a bus stop. Slipping into a shop doorway he could now see her clearly, about twenty-five yards away, turning back to look down the road and presenting her face towards him. There were still plenty of people about and her eyes did not linger in his direction. A sullen face, thin eyebrows, snub nose, hollow cheeks but thick, glossy purple lips with a ring fixed in the centre of the bottom lip. It was far too dangerous to get on the bus with her but, as he stood and considered his options, the jacket fell open and he could see that there was a band of exposed flesh between the bottom of her tank top and the top of the skirt. The flesh was lily white and spilled generously over the waist band of the skirt with a silver pin glinting from her navel. He knew that nothing could stop him from acting, even if the risks were high.

Emerging from the shop doorway he broke into a trot, heading back the way they had walked and towards where his car was parked.

The bus would run along the main road. If he could reach his car and get back to the area of the bus stop while she was still waiting it would be easy. If she had gone, then he would have to catch up with the bus and hope she was still on it. As soon he turned the corner he started to run and within two minutes was at the wheel of his car, retracing his route back to the bus stop. The adrenalin was pumping and he was acutely aware of his own agitated breathing. As he turned left on to the road where he'd left her, a single-decker bus was pulling away from the bus stop. There was no sign of the girl. She had to have just got on. He let a couple of cars get behind the bus and then followed.

After a mile the buildings were thinning and the street lighting was of lower intensity. It was another mile before the bus stopped for the first time. A small agricultural village called Croscombe. A school, a pub, a church but no girl in a yellow skirt and yellow shoes. The road seemed to be running parallel with a narrow river on the north side, with the occasional cluster of houses and the odd road. Dark and rural. There was now no other traffic and he had to drop back sixty yards to keep a respectable distance from the bus. Then, its brake lights came on, it stopped and yellow shoes and a yellow skirt stepped off the platform and the bus pulled away. No other cars or people. Poor lighting. A few houses. He jammed on the anchors and switched off the lights. He could see her yellowness quite clearly, crossing the road and turning up a side road towards the river. As she disappeared from view he drove down the main road without lights. A risk, but the area was deserted. He turned right, without indicating, and saw her ahead, walking in the middle of the road. There was no pavement, just a muddy verge. He stopped. There was a building just ahead of her on the left. It was in darkness. As she neared it, she veered towards it and disappeared from view. He heard a door bang closed. A few seconds later a downstairs light came on. She was home. He just needed to check that she was alone.

Chapter 25

Forty miles away Georgina Walgrave was in trouble. The cow Theodora was in the back barn with a prolapsed uterus. Cal had been due back at Gatwick from America that afternoon but had telephoned from Maine to say that the flight had been delayed by at least six hours, so she'd booked him into a bed and breakfast in Horsham. He'd have to trek cross-country by train tomorrow and she'd pick him up from Taunton station. Meanwhile, her energies were concentrated on trying to save Theodora. One of the old hands, Billy Bracknell, who'd been with her father for fifteen years, had been working late and came racing in from the lower field to tell her that it looked like Theodora was about to calve and he was uneasy about the way she was walking. Billy's vibes about cows were seldom wrong. George believed that they had a breach on their hands and they'd somehow urged the cow up to the back barn and anchored her head in the head gate expecting to have to pull the calf out. George had the ropes ready to tie to the calf's feet and start tugging, but suddenly the calf emerged and so did the uterus. Billy released her from the head gate and, amidst the slime and the blood, left her to the skills of George while he attended to the calf.

The chances were that the calf would survive, but it was quite possible that Theodora might bleed to death. It was a certainty that they could not risk her calving again. They already had buckets of water laced with iodine and George bathed and washed the expelled uterus with copious amounts of it, before embarking on the process of re-introducing the organ back inside the cow. Still washing it, she pushed and manoeuvred, while Theodora continued to push in the opposite direction. Billy left the calf on the straw and brought an eight foot plank in from the yard which he slotted through the steel bars of the pen, placed on the cow's back and applied downward pressure to prevent her from pushing. With sweat pouring down her face and blood and mucous covering her from head to foot, George eased the uterus back into place. Now she had to sew the cow back up. It was a grisly business for a pretty girl.

An hour later, showered and with her wet hair hanging loose, she was in the kitchen eating a sandwich of fresh salmon, cream cheese, celery, shredded carrot and mayonnaise on rye bread, half-watching the TV when something moved outside the window in the yard. At first she thought it might be Billy, but then she remembered that he had left before she'd finished sewing Theodora up. Her mother was upstairs in her bedroom, working on some correspondence for the village church. Placing the glass of Chardonnay down on the kitchen counter, George pulled her boots on over her jeans and got her father's side by side Purdey 12 bore shotgun from the safe in the cellar. Slipping a cartridge into each breech and a handful of spares into her parka pocket, she threw the metal switch positioned by the kitchen door and stepped out into the yard, now illuminated by the floodlights she had just activated.

Billy had left the tractor out, parking it alongside the Mercedes by the barn. A few bales of hay were scattered about and a drake and mallard were waddling away back towards the pond, having been disturbed by the light. A row of metal bins ran along the outer barn wall, filled with various types of feed and a variety of empty five gallon containers were lined up awaiting collection by the disinfectant suppliers. Immediately alongside the last container stood a thick-set man, bald, pebble glasses and wrapped in a filthy coat down to his ankles, tied in the middle with a rope. He made no attempt to hide himself and nor was he alone. Another man was sitting at the wheel of her Mercedes, door ajar, one leg in and one leg out.

"Who are you?" George shouted, although the man's appearance left her in little doubt as to his connection with the previous attack on Cal.

The man didn't answer but started to walk towards her.

"One more step and I pull the trigger," she shouted, her voice firm and calm as she brought the gun up and pointed it directly at the man's midriff, causing him to hesitate.

"I want to pull it," she spat. "I can see who you are. Keep coming. I won't think twice."

"Where is he?" the man demanded, showing a toothless mouth and an over-sized tongue. "Where is the bastard?"

The other gypsy had now emerged from the Mercedes and had slowly walked towards the other thug, stopping sideways on to George. Younger, also bald, with tattoos on the side of the neck she could see. Thin, mean, wearing a loose-fitting camouflage jacket, mud-splattered jeans and black knee-length boots with high Cuban heels. George thought of her father meticulously cleaning the upholstery of the Mercedes every Sunday morning and pictured this sewer rat wiping his filth over those same seats.

George swung the gun from one to the other. A pair of vermin. She was quite prepared to shoot them in the legs if they made a move and her eyes were communicating the message. Loud and clear.

"He's gone. Left the country. And won't be back," she said. "Not only are you trespassing, but you're threatening. The police'll be delighted if I blast you to hell. And, like I said, I want to. It'll be in the front, not in the back."

"Bullshit," grunted the younger one. "You haven't got the bottle to take on the Creanes . . ."

The rest of his sentence was drowned out as George pulled the trigger and the explosion filled the farmyard. The ducks scattered, birds in the barn roof screeched and left their roosts and every dog in the valley started barking in unison. The two men turned tail and lurched off down the drive and back towards the road, unsure whether or not either of them had been filled with shot. On the paving stone in the yard where the younger one had stood, a lone, shattered Cuban heel lay on its side, blasted from the boot as cleanly as if it had been done by the village cobbler.

George was shaking and bumped into her agitated mother as she turned to go back into the kitchen. Mrs Walgrave was becoming increasingly disenchanted with the trouble that seemed to follow Cal Stewart to their house and George knew that, whatever gloss she tried to put on it, her mother would not want him back here again after this latest episode. Despite all her efforts, Mrs Walgrave insisted that she report what had just happened to the police and had made the call herself, demanding that a police car be sent round immediately to check that the intruders were no longer in the area. As soon as she replaced the receiver, the telephone had rung and she answered it. Cal was on the line.

"Tell him," demanded Mrs Walgrave as she handed the phone over to her daughter. "Tell him that he can't stay here."

"We've just had another visit from the Creanes," she announced. "I dealt with it. But mother doesn't think you should stay here."

"Are you OK?" he asked with concern.

"Fine. I saw them off. Me and Purdey, that is. Where are you?"

"I'm in that b and b you booked. They ran a pick-up service from the airport. I'm exhausted. You know most of what happened in Nevada from what I told you when I called you. I'll fill in the gaps tomorrow in person."

"I don't think it's wise for you to come back here," replied George, staring at her mother who had remained defiantly in the kitchen and was openly listening to every word. "Mother is worried. The police are coming any minute."

"My funds are starting to run a bit low. I've got nearly two weeks left here," he answered.

"I know all of that. I've got a solution," she said, turning her back on her mother and whispering into the phone. "Phone me at eight in the morning."

Then she calmly replaced the receiver.

"He's not coming back here, Georgina," she declared. "Your father became obsessed with this whole affair. And now it's passed to you. I want no more of it. Thugs at my door. A gun being fired. The police. I won't have it."

"It's alright, mother. I've got the message. I've told him he can't stay here any longer."

Picking up the Purdey, she unloaded the unused cartridge and headed back towards the cellar, bolting the kitchen door as she passed it. Her nerves had settled now. It was the first time she had ever pointed a loaded gun at another human being, let alone pulled the trigger. Perhaps her mother was right. Perhaps she too was becoming obsessed with this fight for justice. The trouble was, when she had fired the gun, in her deepest inner soul, she had wanted to hurt that gypsy. Really hurt him.

Chapter 26

His car was neatly parked in a row of cars in a side street on the edge of Shepton Mallet. He was down to shirt, trousers, the pair of gloves from the console and a dark-blue woolly hat. In a carrier bag was a spare shirt and a pair of jeans. No means of identification on him. Nothing in his pockets, save for the screwdriver from his tool kit and the cut throat razor. Finest Sheffield steel. Hand ground with carbon steel blade. Ebony handle.

The two red plastic containers carrying two gallons of petrol each had already been taken from his boot and secreted in the bushes near to her house, awaiting later collection. Closer inspection had disclosed that it was an old one-storey stone-built cottage, probably originally for a farm labourer. Two bedrooms. A narrow path up to the front door with no porch. An unkempt front garden and an even worse rear garden with abandoned chunks of metal, an old pram and grass that hadn't seen a mower in years. Stealing a look in to the kitchen from the rear, he had seen her pouring water from a kettle into a cup. In her underwear. Lemon-coloured. Large breasts overflowing from the brassiere. Rippling as she moved. And that large expanse of white belly. The silver pin beckoning him from her navel. Calling. Her make-up had been removed. The cheeks were puffy. The lips were no longer purple but pink and full, the ring protruding and, for one exquisite second, her tongue had slipped out and stroked it. He only dared risk a few seconds watching her, but the promise was beyond his wildest dreams. He could taste her. He felt the sweat heavy across his own upper lip and the trickle down his back. The nearest property was more than a hundred yards away. He'd watched the house until the lights went out just after midnight. No-one else had arrived. Periodically, he'd crept back up to a window and looked through.

He'd only ever seen her, no-one else was there. Once the lights were out, he'd retrieved his car from the isolated lane where he'd left it with its nose tucked up tight against a hedge and its rear number plate smeared with mud, rendering it illegible to any casual passer-by, of whom there appeared to be precisely none. A quick drive back into the town. Found the parking place. Exactly two point eight miles back to where she waited for him.

Walking briskly out of town, carrying his carrier bag, he passed a row of terraced houses with side alleys running between every set of eight. It was in the alley alongside number forty-one that he saw the bike. Black. Anonymous. A few gears. Nothing fancy. Unlocked. Just over two miles on a bike. Maybe ten minutes. The excitement now approaching fever pitch. It was the thought of touching the flesh. The fatness of the flesh. Loose and white. But young flesh. It was its youth that gave it that special sensation. Destiny had chosen her for him.

When he'd watched her through the kitchen window he'd noticed that the upper transom had not been fully closed. Leaving his carrier in the long grass, he quietly leaned the bike under the kitchen window and hauled himself up on to the saddle, screwdriver poised and, like a sculptor shaping an angle, he popped the window stay in the transom, reached through and eased the handle of the main window backwards. His prize was now so tantalisingly close.

The kitchen smelt of old microwaved meals, bacon grease, discarded take-away containers and rotting rubbish. It was very dark. Little moonlight found its way into this cell of grime and he picked his way with the utmost care towards the outline of the door that led into a small hallway. Cut the phone wires. Opposite was the sitting room, its door wide open and the screen of the television attracting such little light as forced its way in through the front window. As he stood, silent and motionless, he could hear her. From the room to his left. Maybe within a dozen feet of him. Snoring. All those folds of blubber now at rest. Probably on her back. The neck, soft and exposed. Eight feet. Six feet. Door wide open. A single bed with the headboard directly under the window. Cheap, thin curtains. He was right. She was on her back, dirty blonde hair on the pillow. Air sucked noisily in through the ugly snub nose and, as she exhaled, those thick lips gave a little shudder and, ecstasy, she still wore the ring through her lower lip. The bedclothes were up to her chin and, in the poor light, he could see nothing of her neck. Joys yet to come.

At the side of the bed, now within two feet of her, his presence communicated itself to her. Like some feral animal, the intensity of his craving and the fever of his desire must have created their own odour and, through her sensory glands, sent the warning of danger. The eyes opened and Diane Pierce, shop girl, daughter of a single mother who was away visiting her own mother in Blackburn, saw the face of the man who yearned to end her life. There is a nano-second between sighting the danger and reacting and it was too fleeting for her to do more than draw in the breath for agony's scream and pull up her knees in animal reflex. His gloved left hand snaked across her lower face, his entire bodyweight was upon her, his face was three inches from hers. Kicking, twisting, squirming, screaming, shouting were all beyond her physical resources as the dead weight pressed all air from her body and the face smiled. He was watching the terror in her eyes. She whimpered and snorted. Still he just watched. Then she felt the weight lessen for a split second as his right fist came up and into view, clutching an object within. Bringing his right hand to his mouth, his teeth tugged at the edge of what lay hidden within and she saw the silver glint of a blade which would slice open her throat like a machete in a pineapple.

Growling, whimpering, contorting and thrashing about, she tried everything she could, but it was as if she lay beneath a two ton whale. She sensed the coldness of the blade on her neck and felt the steel pass through her flesh, arteries, veins and cartilage. Slowly. He sliced so slowly. Working by feel. Never taking his eyes from hers. Kissing and licking her cheeks as the warmth of her own blood gushed from her severed throat. It took her a minute to die. He took the ring in her bottom lip into his mouth and savoured it, then sipped blood from her throat. He pulled back the sheet. She was naked. Every young girl has some physical virtue. Even an ugly one has something. This one had white, clear skin. He folded the blood-drenched razor and returned it to his pocket. For the only time that he was in that house, he removed his right glove and caressed that flesh he had lusted after in the street and through her window. Folds of her belly in his hand. Probing her vagina, squeezing her breasts and then, the glorious act of rape as what had, until now been the ultimate defilement. But this time there was more. With her legs spread-eagled and the red inner tissues of her neck exposed from the gaping wound, he reopened the blade and sliced a chunk of white flesh from the inside of her left thigh. It came away like bark from a tree. Then he turned her over and raped her again from behind, before hacking off a chunk of flesh from her right buttock and repositioning her on her back.

Carrying the two strips of flesh in his re-gloved hand, he returned to the kitchen. The cooker was run on propane. He'd seen the large container in the back garden. He found a cheap cigarette lighter and ignited the front ring, located a frying pan in a cupboard, some kind of margarine from an otherwise almost empty fridge and dropped the prize into the sizzling fat. He watched it turn from white to a light brown and he leaned his head directly over the pan to inhale the smell, an aroma like he had never experienced before. Then, carrying the pan and its contents back into the bedroom, staring in fascination at the corpse, he sat on the bed and ate her meat, savouring the juices and biting deep through the cooked flesh. The taste of erotica. A whole new sensation. That was the moment when he realised this was the dimension of his condition that had always previously eluded him. This was the final ecstasy. He couldn't quite eat it all, but he was fulfilled.

Then he moved into the final phase of the operation with military precision. Found her pants on the floor at the side of her bed. Put them aside to take with him. Wrapped the sheet around her. Out through the back door and retrieved the containers of petrol. Emptied two gallons on the corpse on the bed. Scattered it over every surface in the kitchen and the hall. The whole place reeked of gasoline, making his eyes stream with tears. Removed his shirt and trousers and drenched them in petrol and placed them on top of the already drenched corpse. Went over the whole area again with the other two gallons until he had turned it into a powder keg. Retrieved his carrier bag from outside and slipped on the clean shirt and jeans. Some blood transference, so he'd dispose of those by burning when he got home, together with the gloves. Picked up the lemon pants. But this time he wanted more. A special memento. Pulled out the razor and hacked off her little toe. Fat feet. Burgundy nail polish crudely applied to her toe nails. Wrapped it in the pants and into his pocket.

Got the cigarette lighter and started the inferno. Waited a second to see his clothes in a mass of flame, a whoosh of sound and heat, into the kitchen, turning on all four gas rings as he passed, out through the back door which he closed behind him and on to the bike. Like lightning down the lane, he could hear the fire tearing through the house. As he turned on to the main road he looked over his shoulder and saw the sky lit up. No-one around. A few critical minutes of frenzied pedalling. Woolly hat worn low. Not a soul. Not a vehicle. A minute later an explosion. The propane tank. Seconds now and he would be safe. He could slow down. Appear normal. No-one. There it was. Number forty-one. Bike back where he'd found it. Hurry. A quick wipe of the handlebar grips with the outside of his sleeve. A casual pedestrian passing through the shadows. To the sanctity of his car. Unstoppable. He could feel her pants in his pocket, containing the extra memento. He could still taste the sweetness of her thigh. Ecstasy.

Chapter 27

Detective Chief Inspector Bill Tedstone had served most of his time in Taunton. He remembered the days when a murder would have dominated the news for weeks but, nowadays, with Bristol just down the road, they were commonplace. Invariably down to drugs or sex or both. Shootings, stabbings, blunt instrument across the skull. Never had a poisoning. Would have liked one of those before he reached the end of the road. Unlikely now, only three months to go before the gold watch. Couldn't come fast enough as far as he was concerned. The job had nothing left for him. Everything was computers, databases, form-filling, political correctness. He'd had a bellyful. Just wanted to keep his head down and get out.

The routine was nearly always the same. Phone call at home in the middle of the night. Hear the wife's groan followed by her rolling over and going straight back to sleep. All fifteen stone of her. Pull on the night gear. The thick, polo neck maroon jumper, brown corduroy trousers, green Wellington boots, heavy navy blue overcoat that she'd given him as a birthday present ten years ago and the tweed cap. He was in the habit of keeping a couple of tubes of mints in the pocket of the overcoat. Freshened the mouth when he was talking to the people at the scene. Always the same cast of characters. Scene of Crimes bods, pathologist, uniform bobbies, a couple of potential witnesses and the gawpers.

Arson to destroy the evidence was increasingly coming into fashion. The villains were reading about DNA making its way into the Courts and were very nervous of it. Cars used in crime were now commonly burnt out and torching the scene of a crime was flavour of the month. It looked like the maniac in this murder had set out to remake *Towering Inferno*. Odd thing about fire was that when accelerants like petrol were used, sometimes the petrol consumed itself and left underlying material less damaged than might be anticipated. The propane tank in the back garden had exploded. Must have sounded like a bomb going off. Several householders in the vicinity had immediately dialled 999 with the result that the Fire Brigade from Shepton were there remarkably quickly. Extensive fire damage of course, but the team would salvage enough to pluck a few clues from the wreckage. Not that he was too bothered. The chances of solving this one in a hurry didn't look too good, so it would be someone else's problem not his.

Tedstone walked slowly across the metal footplates that the SOCO fellows had put down and picked his way into the bedroom. Still only half-awake. Perhaps this would be the last time he'd have to drag himself off to one of these scenes from hell. He could still feel the heat. What was left of the walls and floor was sodden from the firemen's hoses. Blackened timbers exposed in what was once the roof space. It was the smell that got to him. The acrid smell of smoke, burnt wiring, furniture and the ruined fabric of a house. This one had an extra ingredient. A partially burned body. Still lying on its back on what had been the bed, but now just a mound of burnt wood and mattress stuffing. The springs stared up at him. A blackened corpse lay silent, contorted in a death of indescribable brutality. Floodlit by merciless, crime scene high-intensity lighting.

Photographs could never really capture the impact of a dead body, still in situ, displaying the true extent of the violence that one human being was prepared to do to another. This woman now had no face. Just black crepe paper and vacant sockets. Her legs were spread wide and Wesley Spicer was bending over her, so engrossed in what he saw that he never even heard Tedstone approach from behind.

There were two Home Office approved pathologists used by the police on this Division. It was a matter of luck which one was on call when the body was discovered. Steven Hedgecombe was one of the new breed. The Murder Squad detectives despaired of ever getting a firm opinion from him about anything. In Court he agreed with almost any proposition put to him. Now known as Steven *Hedgebets* because of his weak indecisiveness, he was viewed as a peril to navigation. Tedstone was relieved when he saw that they'd got Spicer. Old school. Took a look at the body at the scene of the crime. Got a feel for what had happened. Places where a human life had been violently extinguished developed their own aura. Spicer could almost smell what had happened. Then, back to the morgue where, in his skilled hands, the body spoke to him. He'd open it up and feel the victim's pain. Then he'd tell you what happened and stand by it. The old coppers called him *Spicer, the slicer*. All of this would mean less aggravation for Tedstone in handling the enquiry.

"What you got, Dr Spicer?" Tedstone asked, causing Spicer to turn his head over his shoulder.

"Oh, didn't hear you. Come and take a look. I'll show you," Spicer replied, moving over to make room for the lumbering figure in the familiar overcoat and cap.

Tedstone crouched down and stared at what had once been the woman's inner thighs, genitalia and pubic region but was now blackened, shrivelled chicken skin, with some partially intact areas of flesh and exposed bone. As he got down to the same level he felt a wave of nausea start in the pit of his stomach and force its way up his digestive system and he swallowed a small mouthful of vomit, hoping that Spicer had not observed the reaction. The taste of his own sick was added to the lingering stink of the charred body and the sodden debris.

"It's hard to be sure, but I think some of the flesh of the left thigh has been removed, rather than burned. You can see the effects of the flame and the kind of partially charred tissue that remains. Then, when you look here," Spicer said, running his finger along the inner surface, "there's absolutely nothing. Been removed."

"What's that telling you then?"

"I won't know 'til I get her on to the table, but your boys found that at the side of the bed," he answered, pointing at a frying pan. "It's an odd place for a frying pan. And it's got the remains of something in it. Something that looks remarkably similar to the burned flesh you can see on the body."

"Bloody hell. You don't reckon we've got a flesh gorger on the patch, do you? That's all I need. But perhaps the woman was eating something from the pan in the bedroom."

"Possible. Except your boys looked in the kitchen. And in the fridge. There was no meat, no poultry, nor the remains of any. Anywhere," Spicer replied as his eyes moved down the body towards the feet. "And there's something else."

"What?"

"She's had the little toe of the right foot taken off. Look. Despite the burning you can see the crude hacking of the bone. I'll be able to tell better when I've examined her properly with all the instruments, but my first impression is just what you said," Spicer declared.

"A flesh gorger?"

"Exactly."

"I've had one before," sighed Tedstone as he pulled himself upright. "Must be twenty years ago. A woman. Put a five iron over her lover's head while he was asleep. Half a dozen times. Then hacked bits off 'im and scoffed 'em. And I ain't going to tell you what bits."

"Insane?"

"No. The quacks said it was sexual revenge. No basis for insanity or diminished responsibility. Abusive father, boyfriends and so on. Calculated revenge. Pleaded guilty to murder. Probably out by now, working in a cake shop."

Shaking his head, Dr Spicer pulled off his rubber gloves and put them back in his metal case with all the other paraphernalia of death that he carried around with him. "Wouldn't fancy buying my custard tart off her," he grunted. "You can get the body into the bag now. I've done all I can here and the photographer's been and gone."

"OK," said Tedstone, beckoning across to one of the Paramedics, lurking in the hall. "Where you going to do the PM?"

"Bristol. Ten in the morning. You'll be there, I take it?" Spicer replied as the Paramedics began the grim task of lifting the body and sliding it slowly into the long plastic body bag.

"S'pose so," Tedstone acknowledged. "Hopefully the last one I'll . . ."

"Hang on," the pathologist interrupted, as he watched the Paramedics at work. "Just hold her in that position for a minute. Look, Chief Inspector, the body was lying on its back directly on the bed. The back was much more protected from the fire. Less damage. Look at the right buttock. Very limited fire damage."

"And he's sliced a chunk off her arse," Tedstone said with a groan of disgust. "It gets better by the minute. A nutter decides to invade my bloody patch when I've got three months to go. Make sure you keep all this cannibal business away from the Press. They'd have a field day. Last thing I want is a national sensation."

Chapter 28

Sirens, fire-engines and police cars had raced up and down the main road for nearly three hours, constantly waking Colin and Sue Earnshaw as they tried to get a decent night's sleep. Six o'clock in the morning was a tough enough time to get up anyway, particularly with a four mile commute on a pedal cycle to start the day. Colin Earnshaw was now foreman at the carpet warehouse, with four staff working under him, and he considered it an important matter of principle to arrive at work before them. Over a hurried bowl of cereal, he learned from the local radio news that there had been a major house fire just outside Croscombe with a fatality. Foul play was suspected. So that explained all the sirens and traffic during the night.

Hurrying out of the side door of the house, he emerged into the dark alley where he always kept his bike only to discover it was not where he had left it. No-one had stolen it because he could see it further down the alley, maybe five feet from where he always left it, its handlebars resting against a black metal down-pipe. Lifting it away from the wall, his hand felt sticky and he noticed knots of long grass and weed lodged at the back of the chain guard and under the mudguard. Colin was furious and stormed back into the kitchen to get a damp cloth. His wife was standing at the sink, filling the kettle.

"That bloody Nelson kid has been on my bike again," he raged. "Looks like he's been over the fields on it. Sticky stuff on the handlebars, grass everywhere. . . ."

"No," Sue interrupted. "They're away. Went yesterday. Whole family. Gone to Ireland for a funeral."

"Well, who else round here would have taken it, used it and then put it back?" Colin asked. "And what's this bloody stuff on the handlebars?" he asked, holding up a dirty, sticky hand.

"You don't think it might have something to do with that fire, do you?" his wife enquired with a note of concern.

"Don't be bloody stupid. Some lunatic used my bike to get down to Croscombe and back?" he replied, lifting his hand to his nose and sniffing. "Bloody hell," he exclaimed, pushing his hand under his wife's nose. "Bloody hell, smell that."

"It's petrol," she whispered after a pause. "I don't like it, Colin. They might think it was you what started the fire."

"Don't be barmy, girl. Mike Cottrell was still here watching the video when them sirens started last night. And then I was in bed with you. We'd best phone the cops. If I run, I'll catch the six twenty bus. You can deal with 'em and they can speak to me after work," he said.

Chapter 29

Still jetlagged, Cal took the train from Horsham up to London and then the Northern Line tube to Belsize Park. It was a steep walk up Haverstock Hill and then across to the Mews in Hampstead where George's sister, Katie, had a studio flat. That had been the solution to which George had referred but did not want her mother to know about. The problem was that Katie was on a two week course in Edinburgh and, whilst that left her flat empty and available, she needed to be persuaded that some strange Australian, on a bizarre mission and already the subject of one serious assault, should be given the freedom to intrude into her seven hundred square feet of London space. Where George was bold and imaginative, Katie was dull and cautious. One like the father, the other like the mother. Of course, Katie knew everything about the Stanton story and its effect on her father and whereas it inspired George to right the wrong, Katie wanted precisely nothing to do with it. Such had been the size of the task confronting George as she tracked her sister down by telephone at the crack of dawn the next morning, whilst ensuring that her mother had no idea what she was about.

As Cal trekked up the hill he was ignorant of the battle that George had fought with her reluctant and sulky sister. If he had known that it had cost George two hundred pounds to persuade Katie to let him stay there for the remaining six days of her absence then he would have declined the offer. But, of course, he didn't know and he collected the spare key from the downstairs tenant, climbed the staircase to what once had been the upper section of a stable block, and let himself into the studio. Minimalist. A central living area with a breakfast counter and a tiny open-plan kitchen behind it. A narrow floral patterned sofa that turned into a bed with a tall lamp on a pink metal base alongside it. Bathroom and shower, leading off the kitchen recess. Modern art all over the walls, pristine white carpet so he immediately kicked off his shoes, a television, CD player and a few books about art and design sitting on the coffee table with an empty Dartington glass vase.

Placing his bag on the counter top he removed the cushions from the sofa and pulled out the bed section. The bed was made up and he lay down on top of it. The next thing he knew was that the phone was ringing. It was afternoon. George was at Hammersmith Bridge. Tim Sprackley had been in touch. He'd heard from the Home Office in record time. Bad news. He wanted to buy them dinner and explain it all to them. She'd be at the Mews in half an hour.

It seemed like a hundred years since he'd seen her. The Nevada experiences were but a dream, lacking all sense of reality. It was hard for him to believe what he had done with that snake. And Escobarga, with his face of leather, became a caricature from a long-forgotten fantasy. But, as he and George lay on the sofa bed, limbs entwined and passion spent, he gave her the flavour and detail of a Desert Zoo, Searchlight, an Americanised tart and a bearded cretin in a Nevada cemetery. In turn she recounted her dealings with the Creanes. Guns, violence, rattlesnakes, Establishment resistance to justice. A cocktail of ingredients from a world in which they were no longer strangers.

Tim Sprackley's chambers had moved out of the Temple and were in Covent Garden. By eight o'clock the parking spaces in the basement of his building were empty and he was waiting by the gate to let them in as George swung the Mercedes down the ramp. She hadn't told Cal very much about him except that he was a friend and a contemporary of her father's, but one glance at him was enough to see that he was locked in a time warp. Tall and thin, he wore a brown gabardine mackintosh, a bowler hat and carried an impeccably furled umbrella and a battered leather briefcase.

At close quarters an abbreviated brush moustache became visible and, as George ran up to him, his kindly eyes lit up with pleasure and he bent the long body downwards to hug her, still clutching his briefcase and umbrella. His voice was clipped and like dry leaves crunching underfoot. As George put it later he was 'as decent an old stick as you could ever hope to meet'. The problem was, as Cal appreciated within thirty seconds of talking to him, he was completely ineffectual. Well-meaning, adoring of George, solid, reliable, but just too nice, too decent ever to represent a serious threat.

They dined at *The Roast Tomato*. It was throbbing with young people in smart designer outfits, drinking expensive cocktails and enjoying being young in a free country and with money in their pockets. Tim Sprackley, incongruous in his black jacket, waistcoat and pinstripe trousers, sat opposite George and beamed at her. The daughter he never had. His wife had died on their fifth wedding anniversary in the late sixties after an asthma attack. They had no children and he had never remarried. As Cal watched him, he saw the sadness in the lines of the narrow face. Just like his mother's. They all ordered the same starter, spiced fish cakes with chilli and ginger. Tim chose a classy Pinot Noir and, when their main courses arrived, Cal tried to steer the conversation towards the news from the Home Office, but their host declared that the depressing business of the day should wait until coffee, so Cal concentrated on his outstanding venison and beef pie with leeks and redcurrants.

Their table was in a quieter corner of the restaurant so they could comfortably hear themselves talk. When three cups of espresso coffee arrived, Tim Sprackley leaned down to his feet and pulled up the old briefcase with its tired straps and worn out handle. A working lifetime of transporting briefs had produced those effects. Who knows what sadness, debauchery, meanness and deceit had travelled in paper form within that battered bag? Now it was about to disgorge another cargo of disappointment and anger.

"I'm so sorry," Tim declared, as he handed them each an A4 sized brown manilla envelope. "I put the case as strongly as I possibly could. I'm sorry. I made a copy for each of you."

"We know you'll have done everything you possibly could," George replied, resting her hand on his and looking up into his long, lugubrious face. "Shall we read this now?"

Sprackley nodded and sat back in his chair, sipping his espresso as the two youngsters slit open their envelopes and digested the unsavoury contents.

Regina v Henry STANTON 1963/T/463

Requested Reference Back To The Court of Appeal (Criminal Division)

Dear Mr Sprackley,

The Home Secretary has received your correspondence and documentation in respect of the above requested reference and, after appropriate advice and consultation, has concluded that there is no basis upon which the Court of Appeal should be invited to consider that this conviction has been rendered unsafe.

The Home Secretary appreciates that you are acting pro bono and that the son of the deceased convicted offender has travelled from Australia to the United Kingdom to pursue this matter and, accordingly, I have been directed to expedite this response.

The reasons for the Home Secretary's refusal are set out below.

Yours faithfully,
Nigel Plunkett CBE
Case Referrals Secretariat

The Secretary of State's Reasons for Refusal To Refer

1 The original conviction was subject to an appeal. That appeal was fully argued in the Court of Appeal in 1963 and the appeal was dismissed. None of the material recently submitted to the Home Office raises fresh evidence capable of undermining the conviction.

2 The Court of Appeal in 1963 was fully satisfied that the evidence could sustain a conviction. The Judge directed the jury properly in law. There was no suggestion of any material irregularity at trial.

3 The new assertions now made against William Hollister are without merit. At the time of the original enquiry there was no evidence of his involvement in the murder. The current references to:

[a] His alleged possession (unsupported by any tested evidence or report to the police) of Class A drugs in 1990 is of no evidential value at all in respect of the murder.

[b] His alleged possession (unsupported by any tested evidence or report to the police) of pornographic material in 1990 is of no evidential value at all in respect of the murder.

[c] A recent alleged assault on Cal Stewart (son of the convicted offender) alleged to have been initiated by Hollister (unsupported by any report to the police) is dependent upon the evidence of Dyer and Creane, both convicted criminals. The assertions of each of those two individuals is not considered to be worthy of belief.

[d] Cal Stewart's unsupported hearsay assertion that William Hollister had recently admitted seeing the deceased, Louise Donovan, on the golf course shortly before her death and discussing possible sexual liaison at a later time, even if true, is not evidence of his involvement in the murder.

4 The alleged impropriety between the trial Judge [Sir Eustace Vishney] and Neville Hollister [father of William Hollister] is without any evidential foundation. William Hollister was neither a suspect, nor even a witness at the trial. The fact that the Judge had noted the Hollister family home telephone number on press cuttings of the case imports neither proof of when he did this, nor of any impropriety. As Lord Lieutenant of the County, part of Neville Hollister's civic duties demanded that he establish and maintain social contacts with the Judiciary.

5 The evidence of Littleton is exactly the same as the evidence he gave at the trial. The jury heard it and saw him and concluded that the convicted offender still had time to commit the offence and return to the school building by the [approximate] time that Littleton claimed to have seen him.

6 DNA evidence is in its infancy in terms of forensic application in criminal investigations and criminal trials. Nevertheless, last year, three capital cases in which the offender had maintained his/her innocence were selected for forensic review in the light of advances in DNA profiling. This case was one of those selected and various swabs, samples, clothing and exhibits were subjected to DNA testing and profiling and other scientific examination. Attached hereto is the detailed report. In summary, no DNA profile was raised of the convicted offender, nor of any identified or unidentified male and the only DNA profile raised and identified was that of the deceased Louise Donovan.

7 The alleged perjury/unreliability of Amy Beckett is unsubstantiated by any independent evidence.

8 The alleged racial bias by the Foreman of the jury is without merit for these reasons :

[a] It is dependent upon the word of an ex-wife who was

party to an unhappy marriage and an acrimonious divorce. She never made any such allegation either contemporaneously, nor in the subsequent twenty-seven years. The potential for malicious fabrication is high.

[b] Even if her allegations were true, a jury consists of twelve people and the other eleven would not have tolerated such an approach without protest to the trial Judge. No such protest was made. The verdict of guilty was, as it had to be in 1963, unanimous.

[c] Even if her allegations were true, the English process of jury trial demands free and reasoned debate by a jury, safe in the knowledge that their discussions are secret. No English jury would have tolerated racial prejudice of this sort, nor allowed it to influence their verdict.

Enclosure: Scientific re-examination of exhibits. Findings, notes and conclusions.

"I've never read such sanctimonious rubbish," George declared angrily, tossing the papers on to the table. "The other jurors would have complained to the Judge! There was a bigot in the jury room and the Judge made it clear that he thought Henry was guilty. Who are these people who make these decisions?"

"They're the Establishment, my dear. They run the country," Sprackley explained patiently. "I have seen many examples of jurors behaving with hostility towards a Defendant because of race. A white juror making it obvious he despised a black Defendant. An Asian juror behaving similarly towards a white Defendant. Any number of permutations you want. And I've never heard any complaint from any of the other jurors in nearly thirty years of practice."

"What I don't understand," Cal observed, "is how your system can allow a person to sit on a jury without anything being known about him. Lancaster was as extreme as a member of the Ku Klux Klan. Yet no-one knew. And when it is exposed the Establishment, as you call them, close ranks to protect the system."

"I agree. And if anyone ever dares to complain to the Court of Appeal or to the Home Office they'll be met with the kind of jargon you've just read," Sprackley answered.

"Straight off the word processor," George added. "No enquiry into any blatant prejudices in a juror. It's madness."

"And from what I've told you over dinner about what I wrung out of Amy Beckett there's nothing new to add to our case, is there?" Cal asked.

"I'm afraid not. She retrieved the piece of paper. And there's no chance of getting her to make a statement. Unless you get something else on Hollister, or on anyone else for that matter, then I'm afraid we're snookered," Sprackley concluded.

"There's something I don't follow," said George thoughtfully. "According to Hollister's admission to Cal, he agreed to meet Louise later for sex and to pay her fifteen quid then. According to Amy Beckett's latest version, Hollister admitted actually having sex with Louise on the golf course and giving her fifteen quid. But the fact is that Louise's body did not have fifteen pounds on it when it was discovered. She had less than a pound. So that would support Hollister's version."

"No, not necessarily," Cal replied. "I've been thinking about that. If Hollister paid her and then killed her he's very likely to have retrieved his money. It would have left too many clues. The fact she had so much money. Fingerprints. That kind of thing."

"And if it wasn't Hollister?" asked George. "If it was your father. Or someone else. Would they have taken the money?"

"Well, we know that the evidence from the list of possessions on arrest showed that Henry Stanton only had three pounds on him when arrested," Sprackley reminded them. "But that doesn't mean he couldn't have hidden the fifteen pounds somewhere in the school."

"All we've succeeded in doing is producing more and more questions. No answers," Cal observed. "I didn't read through the scientific examination document in the Home Office letter, Tim. It looks detailed and technical. Does it give us any ammunition?"

"I don't think so. Take it away and read it through with care. You'll understand it. But I couldn't see anything of use," Sprackley replied.

"So where do we go from here?" asked George, searching only for the next step forward and never contemplating defeat.

"Back to Australia," Cal replied emptily. "I can't think of any other line of attack. We've pulled out all the stops and ended up with nothing."

"Not exactly," said Sprackley, beckoning to the waiter for the bill. "Everything you've done tends to suggest that your father was not guilty. Proving he didn't do it is a different question from identifying the actual killer."

"But we've shown that he didn't get a fair trial," George protested. "That should be enough."

"But it isn't enough, George. We know that from this Home Office whitewash letter. I think Tim is really saying that we're stuck with the verdict and stuck with the public injustice, but privately we can feel that my father was not a killer. We may have to settle for that. Have I understood you correctly, Tim?"

"You're a perceptive young man, Cal. That's exactly what I was saying. Fred Walgrave knew your father was innocent. Fred's judgement was always sound. Live your life knowing that you're not the son of a murderer. And move on," the old man advised, tucking his credit card back into his wallet and rising slowly to his feet. He had taken the youngsters as far as he could and done everything he could to honour the affection in which he held his departed friend. Now they all had to move on.

Driving back to Hampstead George was silent. Once she had got the bit between her teeth, nothing would deter her. That's why she had travelled all the way to Tanna. It was not in her nature to give up. But Cal's time in England was now running out and they had each gone to lengths beyond anything they would normally have contemplated in a desperate attempt to right a horrendous wrong. Despite all of this, they had been contemptuously brushed aside by what Tim called 'The Establishment' and she had no idea where to turn next. Chauncey might have come up with something but he had been blackmailed out of the equation with consummate ease.

Cal was also silent and depressed, glancing in the poor light from London's lamp posts at the West Country newspaper George had bought as she left Taunton that afternoon. The headlines were about a murder of another young girl. Nothing changed. Young girls were still getting murdered by ruthless men.

"Did you read this?" he asked George, breaking the silence. "Girl murdered in her own bed and then the house being torched? Croscombe. Near Shepton Mallet. That's not far from you, is it?"

"Forty odd miles," she answered. "It's all over the news. The house was badly burned and so was the body. But the news said that the pathologist had enough left to be sure she'd been murdered before the fire was started."

"How?"

"Her throat had been cut so deep he found knife marks on the bone at the back, the upper spine."

Cal shook his head in disbelief. "I think it's time for us to get back to our lives," he concluded. "Take Tim's advice. We've had a bellyful of murder, violence, the ugly things. We've done what we could. Both our fathers would have recognised that. It's time to move on."

"Never," George barked. "Never." She swung her head round to stare at him in defiance and, even in the half-light, he could see her eyes flashing.

"We go back to the flat. Open a bottle of wine. And we go over it all again. Somewhere we'll find something. We can start by reading the scientific report. I couldn't even begin to take that in while we were in the restaurant."

"I haven't got your energy, George," he replied quietly.

"Then I've got enough for the two of us," she responded.

Back in the flat George inspected her sister's wine collection in a wooden, red rack in the corner of the kitchen.

"Katie's into Italian this month. It's Valpolicella or Chianti," she announced glumly.

"Either," Cal replied, lying on the unmade sofa-bed and already deeply immersed in the complex terminology of the scientific report.

George poured two glasses of the Valpolicella, sipped hers and pulled a face. "Il cheapo," she remarked, before slipping on to the bed alongside him and picking up her copy.

An hour later they had finished.

"Clean as a whistle," Cal declared. "No DNA, hair, fibres. Nothing."

"It happens," George replied. "Tim explained all of that to me. Particularly with swabs and exhibits as old as these."

"One thing caught my eye," said Cal. In the photographs that Chauncey and I looked at in Wandsworth you could just about make out white marks around the girl's wrists and neck. The scientific report confirms they were present and contained some kind of hydrated lime and lead pigment."

"What does that mean?"

"The report doesn't take it in any further. It just says the quantities were so small as to prevent any more useful analysis."

"Like everything else," she sighed, pouring the last of the Valpolicella in to his glass and snuggling up against him. "Just more questions."

"I'll be back in Sydney soon," he said, voicing an ever-deepening concern. "Where's that going to leave us?"

"You mean 'us' as in 'you and me' or 'us' as in injustice?" she asked.

"Both," he replied.
"Early days in the first," she responded.
"And ancient history in the second," he added.
They looked at each other and laughed. It was better than crying.

Chapter 30

By five in the morning George was heading west on the M4 back towards Taunton. There was little traffic and the Mercedes purred along. Tom Wilde, who had a large dairy herd near Fivehead, needed half a dozen beasts innoculated and she was due to arrive at eight thirty. It would be a close call. Driving allowed her to think. She slipped a Paul Simon disc into the CD player. *Diamonds in the Soles of Her Shoes, Slip Slidin' Away*. The brain could really work against that kind of background.

By eight o'clock she was well off the motorway and within thirty miles of Tom's farm. Paul Simon gave way to the local radio. The usual diet of weather reports, traffic conditions and the news. She was only half-listening. *The Croscombe Cremation* was mentioned more than once. It rang a bell and then she remembered. Croscombe was the village Cal had referred to when he was reading her paper in the car. The murder of a young girl. Diane Pierce. Just nineteen. She listened to the details. Throat cut, probably raped, and then the whole house set ablaze. The police wanted to know if anyone had seen a man riding a pedal cycle in the vicinity in the early hours of the morning. A cycle had been examined. Trapped grass and weeds recovered from it matched the grass and weed in the back garden of the burned house. Smears of blood had been found on the handlebars. They were of the same group as the victim's. Traces of some kind of white hydrated lime had also been identified on the handlebars, perhaps transferred from a rider's hands. Dynamite. George stopped the car. She had to phone Cal.

The phone call to Cal from the petrol station where she stopped took only two minutes. They both agreed that she should contact the police. As soon as she got home she went directly into the office and called the Murder Incident Room, demanding to speak with the Senior Officer in charge of the investigation, indicating that she had some important information to assist the enquiry. The officious young Detective Constable Staines who took her call told her that Chief Inspector Tedstone was a very busy man and it would be better if she provided the information on the phone immediately and, if appropriate, it would be passed on to the Chief Inspector. She replied that her information was extremely sensitive and that she only intended to divulge it to the Senior Officer. Giving Staines her name and address she saved the threat until the end.

"Tell Mr Tedstone that unless I speak with him personally in the next hour I'll take my information to the Press. And I'll ask them to print that you told me Tedstone was too busy to listen to what I had to say. That should do your promotion prospects a power of good."

Staines' message had reached Tedstone while he was reviewing the day's progress on the case. Fifty three phone calls from the public. All useless. No sightings of anyone on Earnshaw's bike. No DNA on the handlebars of the bike except the victim's, doubtless transferred by the gloved hand of the killer. No help from the hydrated lime. Earnshaw never handled that kind of stuff so it probably linked to the killer but led nowhere. Diane Pierce had no enemies. No current boyfriend. Little money. Nothing of value in the house. Probably raped but Spicer couldn't be certain. Had roped in a couple of the local nutters. Waste of space. In short, zero progress. At least he'd kept the flesh-eating out of the news. If that got out he'd be under siege. Chances were with this type of killing that it wasn't a local at all. Drive in on the motorway from anywhere in the country. Watch the girl. Strike. Out on the motorway to anywhere. You could be in Birmingham, Manchester, Newcastle in a few hours. This kind of maniac would have done his homework and would probably strike again. And when he did it would be somewhere else in the country, making it a cross-divisional problem and by then he'd be playing lawn bowls down at the club every afternoon. After twenty years of trying they'd made him Club Captain at last.

Then this Walgrave woman's message reached him. "Extremely sensitive information which she was threatening to take to the Press." He didn't like the sound of that one little bit. Had she got wind of the flesh-eating? It sounded like she might have. Summoning Belgrave, he pulled on his coat, marched out to the car park and headed for the Walgrave farm.

George let them in while her mother fussed around getting increasingly agitated, so George showed them into the office and despatched her mother to make them a cup of tea, coming directly to the point as soon as the two men were seated and the door was closed.

"I heard on the news that a bike was probably used in this murder," she began.

"That's the likelihood," replied Inspector Belgrave. Tedstone always expected the junior officer to do most of the talking, calling it 'information-gathering strategy'. Belgrave put it down to idleness and disinterest.

"And that somehow the murderer may have transferred hydrated lime on to the handlebars," George continued.

"Again, a likelihood," Belgrave nodded.

"Well, take a look at this," said George, thrusting her copy of the Home Office letter and scientific report on the Louise Donovan exhibits into Belgrave's hands.

"I'll take that," Tedstone interposed, making sure the girl understood who actually called the shots.

"I've highlighted the sentence that made me get in touch," George explained and then sat back while Tedstone read the report of traces of hydrated lime and lead pigment on Louise Donovan's wrist and neck.

Tedstone seemed to take forever and was working his way through all of the paperwork. He was still reading it when Mrs Walgrave came back into the room with two cups of tea and clucked around finding places to put them, before George managed to manoeuvre her back into the kitchen.

Belgrave, an unhealthy-looking, prematurely balding beanpole, sat sipping his tea, awaiting his turn to read the papers that were pre-occupying his Chief Inspector. Eventually, Tedstone handed them over to him and turned his attention to slurping his tea, in which he'd asked Mrs Walgrave to put no less than three spoons of sugar.

Belgrave seemed to get the point rather quicker than his boss. "What's your connection with this Stanton case, Miss Walgrave?" he asked.

"Stanton was wrongly convicted," she replied assertively. "My father was a barrister. His defence counsel."

"And where is your father?" demanded Tedstone. "Doesn't want to get involved, I shouldn't imagine."

"He's dead," George snapped back, staring angrily at him. "Now what are you going to do with this information. It's an odd thing to find in two murders. Hydrated lime."

"I only read your paperwork quickly," Belgrave interjected quickly in an attempt to soften Tedstone's insensitivity. "But when was this other murder?"

"1963," replied George.

"1963," Belgrave repeated. "It's ancient history. Hardly likely to have any connection with a 1990 murder."

"Not if Stanton was innocent. It would mean Louise Donovan's murderer was still at large," she asserted.

"Hang on, Miss, we're talking twenty seven years ago, anything could have happened," said Tedstone, putting his cup and saucer down on top of her father's precious Atlas which sat on a side table.

George jumped up and grabbed the cup and saucer, openly trying to wipe away the ring that Tedstone's thoughtlessness had created. Tedstone ignored his gaucherie and ploughed straight on.

"Firstly, we are to assume that Stanton was guilty. The jury said so. The Court of Appeal said so. The Home Office say so. That would knock any connection on the head. Secondly, even if it wasn't Stanton, then the murderer could be dead or in Timbuktu."

"We think we know who really murdered Louise Donovan," George announced starkly.

"Who?" snapped Belgrave.

"A fellow pupil of hers, William Hollister," George replied.

"He's referred to in that paperwork from the Home Office," Tedstone observed with irritation in his voice. "It says that the accusation against him was without merit."

"But if you interview him, search his place thoroughly, you may find something that connects him with this murder in Croscombe. That would change everything," George told them forcefully.

"When you just said 'we' think we know who really murdered Donovan, who exactly did you mean by we?" Tedstone enquired.

"Me. And Cal Stewart, Stanton's son," she answered.

"The Home Office lists the reasons you gave for being suspicious about Hollister. They conclude the suspicions are groundless," Belgrave pointed out.

"There's more," George explained. "Amy Beckett has admitted that Hollister was boasting about having sex with Louise in the minutes before she must have been murdered. Hollister has been lying about this for years and when we tried to check it out he arranged for Cal to be attacked."

"That depends on the word of a couple of villains who the Home Office say wouldn't know the truth if it hit them between the eyes," Tedstone said.

"Anyway, we're very grateful to you for getting in touch and I can assure you we'll make some enquiries in the light of what you've told us."

"Yes, very grateful," Belgrave repeated, as the two men got to their feet.

"You think it's rubbish, don't you?" declared George angrily.

"Not at all," Tedstone assured her. "Like I said, we'll check it out."

"Then why haven't you even asked for a copy of the report," George snapped back in frustration.

"Just about to do that," Belgrave insisted. "Can you give us a copy now?"

"Take that one," George muttered. "I'd already done a copy before you arrived. And I've written Hollister's home and work addresses in London on the back so that you can go and arrest him."

"We need evidence to arrest someone, Ma'am," Belgrave said pointedly.

"Then you'd better start looking," George barked back. "His house is full of coke and porn."

"We'll check it out," Belgrave replied.

"That letter from the Home Office, Miss Walgrave. It mentions Stanton's son coming over to the UK. Presumably you haven't just spoken to him on the phone. I take it you've actually met him?" Tedstone probed.

"Yes," George replied defensively.

"Where?"

"Why do you ask, Chief Inspector,"

"That's what I do, Miss. Ask questions," Tedstone replied, his policeman's nose sniffing a little more to this than met the eye. "Where did you meet?"

"Here. He's stayed at our house to work on the case," George replied, not mentioning her trip to the other side of the world.

"I see," said Tedstone.

"I'm not sure that you do. His father was hanged for a murder he didn't commit," George responded. "I've shown you a possible link between that murder and the Croscombe murder. How do I know that you're going to act on what I've told you? You don't seem very interested."

"It'll all go in the file and we'll action some enquiries. You have our word on that," Tedstone assured her as they came to the front door and a worried Mrs Walgrave loomed back into view.

"Thank you for the tea, Ma'am," said Belgrave. "We'll be in touch, Miss Walgrave. I'll phone you personally and tell you what happens with Hollister."

George watched them walk back to the anonymous black car in which they travelled and set off down the drive.

"Useless idiots," she announced to her mother. "They think I'm just on a frolic of my own, 'cos of Dad."

"I'm sure they'll check out anything that may be of use, my dear," said her mother, wondering to herself whether the case of Henry Stanton would ever go away and leave her family in peace.

In the police car ambling back to Taunton, Tedstone was offering his opinion on the worth of defence barristers.

"Their clients are never guilty," he declared. "They strung this one up and he's even got his daughter running round years later on a wild goose chase claiming he was innocent."

"But what if he was innocent?" Belgrave asked.

"If my grandmother had wheels, she'd be a bloody bicycle," retorted Tedstone dismissively. "Her father's fed her the line for years. Now Stanton's son is over here trying to make a fuss and no doubt screwing little Miss Walgrave at the same time."

"Can't blame him for that," Belgrave observed. "She's a looker, alright."

"Maybe. But she sees a chance to give their hopeless campaign a lift on the back of a bit of inconsequential nonsense in our case," Tedstone continued. "A woman on a mission. Avoid them like the plague."

"Wise words," Belgrave nodded.

"Born of experience, I can tell you," said Tedstone. "Last thing I want is her using our case to shout from the rooftops that the coppers topped the wrong bloke twenty seven years ago. We don't want to be linked to that kind of bullshit. We'd be all over the nationals."

"On the other hand, what if it was Hollister who'd done both? And we cracked it wide open inside forty-eight hours. You'd want to be in the nationals then, wouldn't you? Going out with a bang, I'd say," Belgrave observed.

"You live in cloud cuckoo land, Belgrave. Still, we're going to have to interview this Hollister bloke. Day trip to London for you and me tomorrow. Early start. Get a warrant to search his drum. Now stop at the next pub. I need a drink. I've had enough of this bloody case for one day."

Chapter 31

Miss Carpenter was shocked when two police officers presented themselves at her desk unannounced and without any appointment. One was extremely tall, thinning mousy hair and pock-marked skin while the other was much older, heavy-featured, wearing a navy blue overcoat that looked like it had seen war service. Crimean War that is. Either her boss had sexually assaulted one of the office juniors or he'd been caught taking illicit backhanders was her instinctive analysis when the tall one demanded to see Hollister.

"He's not in yet," she announced. "And he's got meetings booked all morning. You'll have to make an appointment."

"We'll wait, he'll see us," the older one said, settling himself down on the visitor's couch in her office. "Couldn't fix us a cuppa, could you?"

"For what purpose do you wish an appointment with Mr Hollister?" she snapped back, ignoring the request.

"Police business, madam," the other one replied. "And a cup of tea would go down very nicely. We've driven a long way," he added, with a poor attempt at a smile.

"Where from?" she asked, intrigued.

"Get us a cuppa, dear, then I'll tell you all you want to know. Three sugars for him, two for me," he said, the smile widening and exposing the crooked upper canines.

With a show of reluctance she walked out of the door into the corridor where the executive staff free drinks machine was located. The machine didn't cater for three sugars, so she just pressed extra sweet and carried the white polystyrene cups back into her office. Neither of the men was present but the door into Mr Hollister's office was not fully closed as it always was in his absence.

Putting the cups down on her desk she barged angrily into his office to find the tall one standing over Mr Hollister's desk, starting to look through his appointments diary which was on top of the desk, while the older one had opened one of the filing cabinets.

"Just what do you think you're playing at?" she shouted.

"Oh, sorry if we're out of order," the older one replied. "Thought we'd save a bit of time if . . .

"Who are these men, Miss Carpenter?" an angry male voice suddenly demanded, as Hollister walked swiftly into the room.

"We're police officers. I assume you are William Hollister," Belgrave responded, moving back round to the client's side of the desk.

"Police," Hollister repeated, the wind taken out of his sails. "And what's your business?"

"Better if we have a bit of privacy, Mr Hollister," Tedstone interjected. "This is Inspector Belgrave and I'm Chief Inspector Tedstone. Could we ask your secretary to give us a few minutes?"

As Miss Carpenter withdrew, closing the door behind her, Tedstone walked round the desk and lowered himself into Hollister's executive leather chair, leaving Hollister standing at the side of his own desk like an errant schoolboy awaiting discipline from the teacher.

"We're here about a few things, Mr Hollister. Mainly murder," Tedstone began.

"What murder?" Hollister spluttered, the face of Louise Donovan looming back into the forefront of his memory, alongside the angry features of Stanton's son uttering his threats about the coke and the dirty pictures.

"Two choices," Belgrave declared. "We can start discussing things here which may or may not lead to your arrest and leaving your office building in handcuffs. Or you can agree voluntarily to help us with our enquiries, which means we can go off to the police station in a nice, civilised manner, chatting and smiling as we pass through the building. Your choice."

"I want my solicitor," Hollister said.

"Of course," Tedstone replied.

"Let me get at my phone then," Hollister retorted, reaching towards the black multi-line box with its array of flashing lights, until Tedstone's hand suddenly came down firmly on top of his.

"Just think it through first, Mr Hollister. We want you to come with us to help us with our enquiries. Just to the local police station here. Ten minutes away. It may never come to more than that. If you make us arrest you, get the lawyers in before we've had time for a chat, you may make it look a whole lot worse here at work. Like my colleague says, it's your choice."

"And at the police station I can send for my solicitor at any time I choose?" Hollister enquired nervously.

"Absolutely," Belgrave nodded. "Shall we go? Our car's directly outside."

Walking past Miss Carpenter's desk where the two plastic cups of tea still stood, Hollister told her with a forced smile to cancel his first appointment, but he intended to be back for the second. As soon as the door closed behind the three men, her hand grabbed the phone as she prepared to pass on this juiciest piece of tittle-tattle.

Sitting in the back of their car and now away from the office, Hollister became more assertive.

"What the hell's this all about?" he demanded.

"Murder. Maybe two. We believe you may be able to assist us," Belgrave replied.

"What murder?"

"Just wait 'til we get to the station. Better that way," Tedstone observed. "Things said in police cars tend to get misinterpreted."

"What do you mean?"

"Well, we want to see if you can help us about a murder. We don't want to have to start talking about Class A drugs or dirty pictures, do we? If you get my drift," said Tedstone.

Hollister went silent as he tried to think it all through.

"See, it's like this," Tedstone began, turning right round in his seat so that he was facing Hollister head on. "We can get the lawyers in, cover the drugs and the porn allegations and then move on to the questions about the murder. Or we can cut out the crappy stuff, and the lawyers, and go straight to the questions we're really interested in. About the murder. You may prefer that."

The rest of the journey passed in silence.

Chapter 32

INTERVIEW RECORD

PERSONS PRESENT:

Detective Chief Inspector Tedstone
Detective Inspector Belgrave
William Neville Hollister

Tedstone: You're here to help us with our enquiries. You're not under arrest. You're free to leave whenever you want. However, if our enquiries lead us to believe that you're hiding something, we'll come back later in the day and arrest you. Do you understand?

Hollister: Yes.

Tedstone: Although this is not an interview under caution it is being tape-recorded. You can have a lawyer here if you want one.

Hollister: How long will that take?

Tedstone: I've no idea. Depends on whether you know one or the Duty Sergeant has to arrange one for you. Depends on where they are. When they're available.

Hollister: What exactly are you going to ask me questions about?

Tedstone: A murder three nights ago. Near to Croscombe, Somerset.

Hollister: Are you going to ask me questions about anything else?

Tedstone: Yes. I'm going to ask for your consent to search your home. I've got a warrant but I'd prefer to carry it out with your consent.

Hollister: I'll want our family solicitor present at that search. But here in the police station. In this interview. Are you intending to ask me questions about anything other than this Somerset murder?

Tedstone: Yes. I may ask you if you had anything to do with the murder of Louise Donovan in 1963.

Hollister: Right. I've no intention of answering any questions at all about a 1963 murder until I have been advised by a lawyer. I'll answer anything you want about the Somerset murder.

Tedstone: OK. I'm content with that. In this interview we'll confine our questions to the Croscombe murder. In the meanwhile your solicitor can be contacted and we'll arrange to meet him later at your house. You'll come with us. At the end of that search, if we have more questions for you, then they'll be conducted in the presence of your solicitor. Are you content with that?

Hollister: Yes.

Tedstone: Write down your solicitor's name and we'll get the Sergeant to contact him and make the arrangements while our interview progresses. Quicker that way.

Hollister: OK.

Tedstone: Did you know Diane Pierce?

Hollister: No.

Tedstone: Have you ever been to Croscombe, a small village in Somerset?

Hollister: No.

Tedstone: Have you ever been to Shepton Mallet?

Hollister: Never.

Tedstone: Have you had any contact in any way with hydrated lime?

Hollister: I don't even know what it is.

Tedstone: Ground up limestone, often diluted with a chemical fluid or with a pigment.

Hollister: No.

Tedstone: Can you ride a pedal bike?

Hollister: Of course.

Tedstone: When were you last on one?

Hollister: Probably ten years ago.

Tedstone: Are you married?

Hollister: No.

Tedstone: Do you live with anyone?

Hollister: I live alone.

Tedstone: Can you say where you were three nights ago?

Hollister: Three nights?

Tedstone: Yes.

Hollister: As a matter of fact I can.

Tedstone: Where?

Hollister: At a corporate dinner. I proposed the vote of thanks to the host company at the end of the affair.

Tedstone: What time would that have been?

Hollister: About midnight.

Tedstone: Was this affair by chance anywhere near Shepton Mallet?

Hollister: Not exactly. It was in Aberdeen.

[*Silence*]

Tedstone: I see. How many people were in attendance when you thanked the host company?

Hollister: About a hundred and fifty.

[*Silence*]

Tedstone: Can you give me the name of someone who could confirm this?

Hollister: In my pocket I've got the business card of Sir Nigel Tomms. Managing Director of Silicove. Here it is. It's got his phone numbers on it. Get your henchman to go and phone him. Now. Then we can bring this bloody charade to an end.

Tedstone: I'm suspending this interview while Inspector Belgrave leaves the room to telephone Sir Nigel Tomms.

[INTERVIEW SUSPENDED 9.54 am]

[INTERVIEW RESUMED 10.36 am]

Tedstone: I'm resuming this interview. Your account of your whereabouts has been verified. We are satisfied that you can no longer assist us in our enquiries in this matter.

Hollister: And what about the heavy stuff you were dishing out in the car. False allegations about drugs and pornography. Threats. You haven't mentioned that, have you?

Tedstone: Nothing improper occurred in the car, Mr Hollister.

Hollister: And now you want to search my bloody house, do you? With firm evidence that you're barking up the wrong tree. I'll see that you regret this. My father. . .

Tedstone: It will no longer be necessary for us to search your house.

We'll contact your solicitor and cancel immediately. You're free to leave. Unless you have something further to say I intend to turn off the tape recorder.

Hollister: No. Nothing.

INTERVIEW TERMINATED

Chapter 33

Neville Hollister was in a fury. They were expecting Lord and Lady Wolston and the newly appointed Circuit Judge and his wife for dinner that night. Moreover, after several frustrated attempts, he'd managed to persuade Oliver Bethstone to accept his invitation. Bethstone was a complete empty head but, by one of those extraordinary quirks of irony that only the Labour party could achieve, he was Shadow Minister for Housing. If the Conservatives fell at the next election, which was looking increasingly likely under the trapeze artist's son, then Bethstone would be the man deciding which parts of the Green Belt were to be re-zoned for residential or commercial building. A relationship to be nurtured. Now, with all the arrangements to be made, William had phoned with the news that, despite Maxcroft's threats to Chauncey, the pressure was still being applied.

William had reluctantly explained that he had been forced to confess to Stanton's son that he was in possession of drugs and pictures that could do some serious damage to the family name and Stanton's son had plainly provided this information to the police.

When William had been bullied into revealing all that had passed between him and the police, Neville had raged at him down the phone. His appetites just grew stronger not weaker with the years and it always ended up with him looking to his father to bail him out of trouble. The more the father shouted, the more the boy continued to whinge and whine.

It took another embarrassing call to Maxcroft, dragging him out of a meeting with the Chief Constable, to register the complaint. Either Chauncey was still active or it was all down to Stanton's son and the girl. Either way, the pressure on William had to be stopped.

Maxcroft assured him that he'd check it out with the officers who'd seen William that morning and get back to him as soon as he could.

Now, with less than half an hour to go before the guests were due to arrive, Hollister had heard nothing. Sitting in a wing chair in the library, attired in black tie, he was already on his third large Scotch when, at last, the phone rang.

"Hollister," he barked.

"Ian Maxcroft. Sorry it took so long. I had trouble tracking down Tedstone, the senior officer who dealt with William. He'd disappeared off the radar."

"Yes"

"His information came from the girl. Nothing to do with Chauncey. Said he had to follow it up. Recognised she'd got an agenda of her own."

"Yes."

"He's satisfied that William is nothing to do with this Somerset murder. Cast iron alibi. He'll tell the girl that himself. He'll pay no attention to these drugs and pornography allegations. He's been given no hard evidence and isn't interested. William'll have no more trouble from his end."

"What about the old murder?"

"They're whistling in the wind. The Home Office has told them there's no basis on which the case can be reopened. I've checked that and now seen the correspondence. Their case is hopeless. Stanton's son goes back to Australia in a few days. It seems under control."

"I hope so. But I expect you to keep your eye on it."

"Of course."

"Thank you, Ian. Good evening."

Neville Hollister drained the remains of his glass, his ill-temper now beginning to abate. But how many more times did the boy expect him to extricate him from the mire? He felt exhausted and there was an evening's important networking ahead. Preparing the ground for the next favours.

Chapter 34

Bill Tedstone hadn't disappeared off the radar. It was just that he recognised trouble when he saw it and Georgina Walgrave spelled trouble. He could see the determination in her face and so he wanted to ensure that she was made to feel absolutely satisfied that he'd made all proper enquiries, hadn't ignored her information and that Hollister could not possibly have had anything to do with this murder. Then she would be left with precisely nothing to take to the Press. Besides, he had a sneaking admiration for the girl. So, after the long drive back from London, he'd gone over the material that had come into the Incident Room in his absence, which didn't amount to a row of beans, and then taken his own car and driven out to the Walgrave Farm alone. Belgrave had clocked off.

Just before he left the Station the call had come in from Maxcroft. Why top brass in London should be showing an interest was beyond his comprehension and he certainly wasn't going to ask. But it certainly vindicated his decision to go and out and talk to the girl personally.

This time she was out in the barn, sleeves rolled up, rubber boots sliding in the straw and the slime, hair tied back, wrestling with a frightened white calf, trying to drive a long needle into its flank. He leaned on the metal bars of the stall and watched her, lithe and strong for a girl. Belgrave was right, she was a real looker. During the struggle she became aware of his presence, acknowledging him with a wave of her hand.

After a few minutes the deed was done and she came over, red in the face from her exertions.

"Tougher than arresting a burglar who's legging it," he said.

"Enjoyed the show, did you?" she responded tartly.

"I came personally to tell you, Miss Walgrave, that, contrary to your impression yesterday, I took your information extremely seriously."

And?"

"My colleague and I have been to London today. We went to Hollister's place of work. We took him to a local London police station and interviewed him at length. We covered your allegations and your suspicions in no uncertain terms."

"And?"

"Obviously, I'm not at liberty to recite chapter and verse, but I am able to tell you that, as sure as I'm standing here, Hollister could not have had anything to do with the Croscombe murder."

"How can you be so sure?"

"Because within an hour or two of the time Diane Pierce was being murdered, Hollister was making a speech to a hundred and fifty business men in Aberdeen. He's not the man."

"And you've checked this?"

"Oh, yes. It's kosher. I've no evidence to pursue the drugs and the dirty pictures and, if I can speak frankly, it's the murder that I'm interested in, Miss. I'm sure you can understand that."

George sat down on the edge of a barrow that stood alongside the stall. The calf was now settling and her day's work was done. She felt flat. Both she and Cal had been so convinced that Hollister was in the thick of the Donovan murder and the chances that the common ingredient of hydrated limestone should appear in both murders had seemed beyond coincidence. Now Tedstone's news had reduced it to ashes.

"I don't think there's much more I can do to help," he said, looking down at her crestfallen face. "We're grateful for your help and you have my word if there's any change in what I've told you, then I'll call you myself. And I'd be grateful if you backed off Hollister and my enquiry. Good evening, Miss."

The edge of the wheelbarrow was starting to dig into George's shapely posterior and she pulled herself up, staring intently into the tired eyes of a man who was plainly counting the days, but seemingly had followed up on the information that she'd provided.

"Before you go," she began, "give me your take on this. You've probably been a policeman for longer than I've been alive. What do you make of hydrated lime appearing in both cases?"

"I haven't a clue. And I don't know very much at all about the Stanton murder. Only thing I can tell you is that down at my bowling club the stuff they mark the boundary lines with has got hydrated lime in it. Some kind of whitewash. Should think it's got a thousand uses," he replied.

Before he'd even finished his sentence it hit George between the eyes like a thunderbolt. Why hadn't she worked it out for herself? She'd even done Advanced Level Chemistry. Suddenly, she saw the connection, although she wasn't proposing to show more of her hand to Tedstone than was absolutely necessary. But he had access to extensive resources which could make all the difference. She needed his help.

"Have you got a few minutes, Chief Inspector?" she asked, her tone now stripped of its earlier edge of hostility.

"I'm tired," he smiled, rather warming to the girl, despite the aggravation she might have represented. "What is it you want?"

"Come into the house. Have a glass of something. I won't keep you long, I promise."

Picking up the vaccine case and her instruments, George led him into the house, attentively sat him down at the long pine table in the warm farmhouse kitchen, poured him a glass of her Dad's best Glenfiddich and asked him to do her a favour. Just to humour her.

Chapter 35

The next day George was committed to attending the horse sales on the far side of Trowbridge with Dolly Levett. Dolly bought, sold and bred thoroughbreds and always took a vet along with her to any sale that she attended, paying handsomely for the service. Any animal that she contemplated purchasing would have to be examined and assessed by George before Dolly would bid. It would be a long day and so George was anxious to get an early night. Accordingly, her call to Cal was short and to the point, informing him of Hollister's seemingly solid alibi for the Somerset murder and asking him to do some particular research tomorrow. When she'd finished at Trowbridge she'd drive up to London, stay the night and they could take stock.

At the sales Dolly Levett bought two yearlings and a foal. In all, George had to inspect a dozen animals, some of them likely to attract bids involving considerable sums of money. It had rained a miserable, thin rain for most of the day and much of her work had been carried out in the open because of the poor stable accommodation at this particular sale and she felt chilled through. Dolly Levett, who George thought rather looked like a horse, with hair worn far too long for her age, and big, yellow teeth was a very demanding lady. She wanted to know every last detail about any horse that took her fancy. By three o'clock George was feeling the strain. Fortunately, so was Dolly's chequebook and George's duties were over. She had done the drive from this sale to Katie's flat a few months ago and knew it was about a hundred and ten miles and so, London traffic permitting, she hoped to be there by six. It was important that she was there before seven, as that was the time that Tedstone had promised to phone her at the London number and she wanted to be the one taking the call.

She sailed along until a few miles west of Windsor on the M4 when the traffic ground to a complete standstill. Tuning to a radio station with traffic bulletins, she learned there had been an accident on the eastbound carriageway at the Heathrow exit. Chaos. There was some slight progress on the inside lane so she forced her way across and took the first exit off the motorway, eventually picking her way round the roundabout at the slip road and blundered her way across Southall, Hanwell and Ealing, eventually ending up on the Westway, through to Elgin Crescent and into North West London. As the nose of the Merc swung into the Mews, her car clock already showed ten past seven. The long day, the rain and the tension of the late dash had left her with a splitting headache and, as soon as Cal had let her in and given her a hug, she searched through Katie's medicine cabinet for some Extra-Strength Anadin and downed a couple with a glass of tepid water, flopping down on to the sofa. Tedstone hadn't phoned. Perhaps he never would. He'd only said he'd do what he could. It was now outside the ambit of his own murder enquiry. Cal started to tell her the results of his research when the phone rang and she grabbed it.

Cal was leaning on the kitchen counter watching her. He'd spent a couple of hours in the local library and had clear cut answers to the questions George had asked him to research. In her phone call to him last night she'd made it very clear that she didn't want him answering any call from Tedstone and, now she'd arrived, she was bossy, distant and seemed to have taken over the whole project. Her fingers were pressed to her forehead and her eyes screwed up, as she obviously listened intently to what Tedstone had to say to her, before thanking him and replacing the receiver. The call had probably lasted no longer than forty-five seconds.

"Of any interest?" he asked.

"Oh, yes," she replied. "But give me your information first."

"Easy. Hydrated lime has any number of applications, but its most common everyday use is in whitewash," he answered.

"Go on."

"It can be used externally. Often found on sports pitches to mark boundaries, touch lines, that sort of thing," he continued.

"Any more?"

"Yes. In the sixties, when it was used for pitch marking or wall painting, it often had a lead pigment ingredient. That became environmentally unacceptable and so gradually that pigment was excluded. Other stuff was often put in. Does any of that help?"

"Oh yes," she answered, getting up and coming over to the counter next to him. "It's dynamite. But I knew last night that it would be."

"You do cryptic very well," Cal remarked. "Let's see you do some plainspeak."

"Right," said George, pouring herself another glass of water from the tap but, this time, getting some ice from the fridge and putting it in, and then sitting on the one bar stool that Katie had brought from the farm. Why had she only got one stool? Didn't she ever have company for breakfast? George's mind switched back from her sister's social life to murder.

"We're agreed, aren't we, that your father was almost certainly not guilty?"

"Yes."

"And we're agreed that the real murderer must have taken Louise's pants, then panicked for some reason and slipped them into a saddlebag in the sheds?"

"Yes," he nodded. "I've thought about that a lot. I imagine the particular bike was probably chosen at random. So they could have ended up in any of the saddle bags in the bike sheds that afternoon."

"And we're agreed that the candidate that has dominated our whole approach, for seemingly very good reason, is Hollister?" she continued.

"Yes. With very good reason. Look at what I found in his house and what kind of person he is. You've never met him. I have. He's still a major suspect," Cal declared forcefully.

"OK. But let's move on from there. Do we both agree that it's a remarkable coincidence that hydrated lime should appear in both the Donovan murder and the one in Somerset?" she postulated.

"Of course."

"So we needed to link Hollister either to hydrated lime or the Somerset murder," she continued.

"But we can't," Cal declared flatly.

"No, we can't. And, armed with Tedstone's interrogation of him, we can go one further. Unless he's got a private supersonic jet we're forced to categorically eliminate him from the Somerset murder," George reasoned.

"So, either the 1963 murderer and the Somerset murderer are two different people and the hydrated lime is simply coincidence. Or, if it is the same murderer, then it can't be Hollister," Cal concluded.

"Yet, the two murders have this seemingly compelling link, the hydrated lime," George summarised, getting off the stool and disappearing in the direction of the bathroom, returning after a moment with a couple more tablets in her hand.

"You've only just taken some Anadin," Cal remarked, pouring her another glass of water and leading her back to the sofa where George immediately downed the pills.

"I've caught a chill at that bloody sale. I need to get a few of these down me and go to bed," she responded. "But let's just talk this through first. It makes a big difference to say it aloud and bounce it off someone who knows the facts as well as I do."

"Right," Cal agreed, sitting down beside her. "It seems far more logical to me that it should be the same killer. Perhaps he's got a job in which hydrated lime is handled."

"Exactly," exclaimed George. "And you've just told me that lime is a sports pitch boundary marker. Now, ask yourself, what sport is linked to Louise Donovan's murder?"

"Golf," he snapped.

"And whereabouts on the golf course was she killed?"

"Near the boundary with the school drive," he responded.

"And, given what you know now, how might the out of bounds line have been marked?"

"With whitewash."

"By whom?"

"The ground staff, green keeper, whatever they're called," he answered slowly.

A long silence followed as Cal mulled it over. He kicked off his shoes and put his feet up on the coffee table, his hands behind his head.

"You're telling me that Louise's murderer may have been the green keeper who said he found the body," he finally declared.

"I'm telling you it's a serious possibility. Which we should try to explore. If he'd just been marking the out of bounds line, or had touched whitewash recently, then his hands or gloves could have transferred the hydrated lime to her wrists and neck. It hit me as soon as Tedstone told me that his bowling club used that stuff to mark the grass," she explained.

"What chance have we got of finding him? Chauncey never found him. He'd completely disappeared. He could be dead."

"True. But Chauncey didn't have access to the same resources that my new friend has?"

"You mean Tedstone?" he enquired.

"I do. He's about to retire. Originally he saw me as someone who could land him with a lot of aggravation. Talking to the Press. Cause celebre. Linking it to the 1963 murder. He didn't fancy any of that kind of aggravation, unless, of course, it could lead to him solving two murders in twenty-four hours. So we went through all of that," she explained.

"And then he was quickly convinced that Hollister couldn't possibly be the Somerset murderer," Cal observed.

"Yes. I was no longer any kind of threat to Tedstone after that. In fact, seeing how deflated I was, I think he felt a bit sorry for me," she continued.

"And no doubt you turned on the charm," Cal smiled.

"Use what you've got. That's what Dad used to tell me. So I talked Tedstone into doing me a favour. He could access other databases including the passport office. I doubt Chauncey could."

"And what's he come up with?" Cal asked, leaning forward and looking into her face.

"Walter Mangan left the UK in 1964. He emigrated. That's what Tedstone just said."

"Where to?"

"Australia. Got an assisted passage for ten pounds."

"Bloody hell. Where to in Australia?"

"Place called Albury. He'd got a job down there. That's as much as the records show," she answered. "Tedstone said that's all there is. He couldn't help any more."

"Maybe not," Cal observed. But perhaps I can. Have you heard of Albury?"

"Never," George replied.

"Well, I have. It's on the Murray River. A few miles north-west of Melbourne. Beautiful spot," he explained.

"I don't see how you can help by knowing Albury, Cal. Walter Mangan's name has never come up again. Not since he left. He's never been heard of in the UK again. Certainly no Walter Mangan of the appropriate age group appears on the major databases that Tedstone accessed. So it would seem to blow our theory that it's the same murderer on both occasions."

"You're missing an alternative possibility," Cal suggested.

"What?"

"That he came back to the UK at some point. Under a different name. Perhaps took Aussie citizenship and had an Australian passport. My Ma did."

"I see," said George. " So you're suggesting that you might be able to help by checking this out from the Australian end when you get home, whereas Tedstone certainly won't get further involved?"

Cal got up and paced around the room, trying to analyse the limited information that they had now amassed before responding.

"Do you know what the Murray River is famous for?"

"No," said George.

"Golf courses," he answered. "The river is the dividing line between Victoria, where Melbourne is, and New South Wales. In the sixties and seventies there was no gambling in Victoria, and so at weekends they'd all cross the river to gamble. That led to golf courses being constructed. And flourishing. And they had the river to keep the fairways green."

"So presumably there'd be plenty of jobs for anyone who'd worked on an English golf course," she remarked.

"For sure. Thing is, George, I've got a pal in Sydney, Dek Karpinen, he's a golf pro out at Parramatta. Known him for years. The golf world's a tight little world. A lot of them know each other, know the other pros, know the green keepers, know the course managers."

"So?"

"Well, his dad, Barry was also a pro. That's how Dek got involved. And, if I remember this right, when I first met Dek, his dad had just got transferred to a course in Sydney from one of the Murray River courses. Had been there for years. His dad just might have come across Mangan."

"I see. It's well worth a shot. You'll have to get on to it as soon as you get back."

"No. I can do better than that. It's already early morning in Sydney. I'll leave your sister the money for the call. But if I call Dek now, he can have a word with his dad. We'd know soon enough."

"Do you know his number?"

"No. But Directory Enquiries will. There won't be many Dek Karpinens in Sydney," he replied.

"Do it," she replied enthusiastically. "Do it now. Tell him to phone us back at this number and reverse the charges. We'll leave Katie the money. Tell him to call even if it's the middle of the night. This may be worth getting up for."

"There's another angle, George," he added thoughtfully. "Dek has an older brother, Rod. Married. Lives in Melbourne. I've only met him once when he visited Dek in Parramatta."

"Yes?"

"Well, Rod is an Officer in the Victoria Police. Dek could ask him to check out if there were any unsolved murders in the general area of Melbourne and Albury after 1964. The victim will be a young girl, almost certainly sexually assaulted, killed by some kind of violence to the neck. It'd be interesting to know," he said.

"You've missed something out," she added. "It's a pound to a penny that her pants'll be missing."

"I'll make the call," Cal responded immediately. "Like your Dad used to say, use what you've got."

Chapter 36

The lithe, black girl sat on the edge of the leather sofa, her bare toes kneading the thick-piled purple carpet, like a cat testing the ground, while the man was seated at the Steinway, playing Chopin's Moonlight Sonata. Of course, unless it was Acid House or Milli Vanilli, she wouldn't have the slightest idea what he was playing and couldn't have cared less. Where she came from they didn't know the difference between Beethoven and Liberace.

In front of her, on the solid chunk of rock that had once belonged to Freddie Mercury, sat five hundred pounds in twenty pound notes and a glass of champagne. The taxi had only just dropped her off and the man had settled up as soon as he'd let her into the magnificent house. Her immediate reaction was that if she played her cards right then she might be leaving in the morning with considerably more than the agreed rate. The photographs he'd deliberately left lying about on the extraordinary table indicated he was a man of varied tastes.

As he got up from the piano and moved over towards her the front door bell rang and he excused himself to answer it. Two minutes later, he returned, white-faced and nervous, followed by a handsome, dark-complexioned young man, carrying a Harrods carrier bag, who took one look at her and summed up the purpose of her mission at the same velocity that light travels.

"If you're going to play games again, Hollister, then this'll take a long time and she'd better go, taking her bunce with her," Cal barked, nodding in the direction of the pile of cash.

"I ain't exactly earned it yet, baby," the girl replied. "Still, if William agrees, I've got a very nice friend I could send for if. . . "

"Shut up, Chloe," Hollister interrupted. "Take your drink and wait in the kitchen. This won't take long."

The girl slid off the sofa, her long fingers seizing the money and tucking it down her cleavage as she sidled by the two men, her buttocks swaying provocatively in her body-hugging black dress.

"Nothing changes, does it," Cal observed, watching her leave the room.

"What do you want?"Hollister demanded.

"I've got your things in this bag," Cal replied, holding it up. "This is decision time for you. I've seen Amy Beckett. She's turned out as debauched and corrupt as you. But, there again, she didn't have your advantages in life did she? She didn't have a Lord Lieutenant in the family. Anyway, she told me a few things."

"What?"

"That's for me to know and you to worry about," Cal responded, lowering himself on to the sofa where the girl had been sitting. "Either you give me the whole story or I take this stuff into your offices tomorrow morning. If you satisfy me it's the truth, then I'll hand it over now. Things have happened. Like I said, it's decision time."

"I suppose you're the reason the police interviewed me about some other murder," Hollister spat back at him, moving over to the piano stool and perching on the edge of it. "Well, you destroyed your credibility there alright."

"So, you do want to play games," Cal said menacingly.

"No. I don't. I'll tell you exactly what happened. But I want your promise that I get that stuff back as soon as I've told you, your assurance that you've made no copies of the photos and that this will be an end of it," he replied.

Although Hollister was pale and obviously nervous, Cal noticed that there was more self-assurance about him this time. Fortified in having the perfect alibi for the Somerset murder and seeing the prospect of bringing Cal's threats to an end, he seemed almost anxious to rid himself of this enduring burden. Immediately after Cal had made the call to Dek Karpinen, George had retired to bed feeling ill and had cancelled her morning's appointments. It had still been early and Katie's flat was so small there was nowhere for him to go without disturbing George, so he had pulled Hollister's dirty little collection out of the cupboard and set out to bring this part of the story to a head. His conviction that Hollister had murdered Louise had taken a heavy knock but he was not letting him off the hook unless and until he was sure. So, knocking on his front door unexpectedly was worth a shot. If Hollister tried anything then Cal would have taken great pleasure in laying him out on his best quality Wilton.

"Done," said Cal. "Now talk."

"Louise was a scrubber. Overweight. Crude. A tease. She'd been on at me for weeks about how many boys she'd done it with, but she'd never do it with me," he began, his eyes looking over Cal's shoulder into the middle distance as he obviously dredged back memories from another time.

"Go on."

"Then, the day before she was killed, she came up to me after school. Rubbed herself against me. Said she'd seen something in town she wanted to buy. If I gave her the money, then she'd . . ."

"What?"

"I can remember her exact expression. It was so crude. Remember, I was just sixteen. I'd never actually been with a girl properly."

"Don't look for the sympathy vote, Hollister. Just get on with what happened," Cal shouted back at him.

"She said for fifteen quid, she'd shag the arse off me," he blundered out. "It excited me to hell. I didn't have fifteen quid. I stole it out of my father's wallet that night. Three five pound notes. The next morning I showed her the money. We arranged to meet in those trees by the tenth hole during the lunch hour."

"And?"

"What I said to you at the office the other week was partly true. She was waiting. Pants in hand. And a condom. I gave her the fifteen quid. We did it. It was horrible. She laughed at me. I was no good. I got up and walked off. She was still lying there when I left. I could see her pants. Navy blue. Thrown to the side on the grass. I kept in the bushes and went down to that tree Amy talked about and lit a fag. I felt so embarrassed. I expected Louise to spread it all round the school that I was useless at it. So, when Amy came over, I pretended I was pretty pleased with myself, told her I'd shown Louise a thing or two."

"So when you left her she was alive and well?" Cal pressed.

"She was laughing at me."

"If that's right, then what happened to the fifteen pounds? It wasn't on the body, nor was it in my father's possession when he was arrested?" Cal asked aggressively.

"I've thought about that a thousand times. I thought the police would find it and it would lead back to me. We knew about fingerprints and that kind of thing. That's part of the reason I swore Amy to secrecy and paid her off then and over the years. I admit to that. But all I could think of was that someone must have been in those bushes. Watching us. As soon as I'd gone he must have moved in. Done for Louise. Taken the money and pants and gone off towards the school drive. Panicked and dumped the pants. I've told you all I know."

"No. There's more. Where does that bastard Vishney fit into this?" Cal demanded.

"I told you at my office. My father thrashed me. Realised I'd taken the fifteen quid. Got the whole story out of me. Gave me the money to keep Amy quiet. Once they'd arrested someone for the murder he phoned Vishney. Hurried the case along. Kept me out of it."

"So you all sat back and let an innocent man hang," Cal spat at him.

Hollister swung his legs round under the piano and put his head in his hands. Cal could see his shoulders heaving as he sobbed. In silence.

"I didn't know he was innocent. I still don't know. I just knew that I was innocent. I've never allowed myself to think beyond that," he eventually whispered. "Our family name had to be protected. That's why I wanted you warned off."

"Your family name stinks, Hollister. So does Vishney's," Cal shouted, getting to his feet and throwing the carrier bag on to the chunk of granite, its contents half-spilling out. "Here's some more of your dirty secrets, you filthy bastard."

"There's no proof Stanton didn't do it," Hollister protested.

"If he didn't, then you and your family and Vishney have left a murderer on the streets for twenty-seven years. Even shit like you may find that hard to live with," Cal replied, walking over to Hollister and grabbing a handful of his white and blue striped designer shirt. "And tell Vishney, when this is over, I'm coming after him. His name's going to stink as much as yours."

"What do you mean?" Hollister asked, as Cal released his grip on his shirt and headed towards the door.

"The Press, Hollister. They'll love it. Innocent man hanged. Lord Lieutenant's son had just paid for sex with the victim. Judge railroads case along to hush up Hollister family embarrassment. Appoints inexperienced barrister to defend. You be sure to tell Vishney what's coming his way."

"You promised that if I told you the truth that would be the end of it as far as I was concerned," Hollister protested, getting up from the piano stool and following Cal to the door to the hallway.

"The end of me taking the coke and porn to your Bank. No more than that. And I want Vishney. I want him badly. You belong in the gutter. Get your latest tart back in. You go well together." Cal shouted, as he marched down the hallway towards the front door, catching a glimpse of a black face peering out of a doorway at the other end of the hall.

"He's all yours, darling," he called out to her. "Throw him back in the gutter when you're done."

Cal stormed out of the house, slamming the front door behind him. The English Establishment. The morals of alley cats.

Chapter 37

When the phone rang at ten past eight the next morning both George and Cal were still asleep. George groaned and turned over. She felt awful. Cal had taken himself off to a pub after his encounter with Hollister and tried to suppress the disgust with several pints of English bitter. He didn't feel too good himself, but he lurched out of bed, grabbed the phone and accepted the reversed charges call.

Dek Karpinen was a man of few words.

"Barry knew of a Mangan," he began, ignoring the niceties. He'd always called his father by his first name.

"Ground staff on one of the smaller Murray river courses. Barry never worked with him. Met him a few times. Miserable bastard. Loner. But played a bloody good game of golf himself. That's why Barry remembered the name. The clubs had staff tournies. Mangan always did well."

"When was this?" Cal asked.

"Sixties. But may not be your man. Limey alright, but this joker was Craig Mangan. Not Walter. Barry's sure about that. Ugly bugger, stuttered, Barry said."

"What happened to him?"

"No idea, mate. Barry thought he just got tired of the place after five or six years. Heard he'd gone back to England."

"Thanks Dek, I owe you one when I get back," Cal said warmly.

"Not so fast. I also spoke to Rod," Dek continued. "I waited 'til he called me back before I phoned you."

"Yeah?"

"1968. Albury girl. Found floating in the Yarra ten miles downstream from Melbourne. Strangled. Never caught the bastard. You think it was this Mangan guy?"

"Don't know. Could be. One last thing, Dek. If he came back to England. Looked for the same kind of golf job here. How would I find him? Is there a register or anything like that?" Cal enquired anxiously.

"Nah. But like I said to you when you called me. In the golfing world everybody knows everybody else. Gossip like a lot of bloody women. The club that Mangan worked for on the Murray was attached to a hotel. You need to speak to a pro in England who's worked the hotel courses," Dek concluded.

"You don't happen to know one, do you?" Cal asked.

"Nah. But I know a guy who does. Mark Gevinson. Chiltern Hills Golf Club. Near Reading. Mention my name."

"Great stuff, Dek."

"One more thing, Cal."

"Yeah?"

"The kid in the Yarra."

"Yeah?"

"Fully clothed. Except . . ."

"No pants," Cal anticipated.

"You got it in one, pal. So long."

Cal climbed back into bed and lay on his back thinking, while George drifted back to sleep, occasionally groaning and sniffing. With George out of the game for the day he would have wheels. He'd phone up and check Gevinson was working that day and then drive down to the Chiltern Hills Golf Club and speak to him face to face. The real question was whether or not to tell Tedstone all that he now knew. Did it amount to enough to make them look for Mangan? Would it persuade them that they should reopen the 1963 case? His conclusion was that the answer to the first question was probably 'yes', but the answer to the second question was almost certainly 'no'. So, whilst his information might assist them in the Somerset murder, it would leave little chance of getting them to rake over the 1963 coals. On that analysis, at least to begin with, he decided to go after Mangan alone. By nine o'clock he was driving west on the M4. Gevinson had agreed to see him for a coffee in the clubhouse at ten thirty. He'd left a note for George outlining what Dek Karpinen had told him.

Chiltern Hills Golf Club was only an hour's drive from London, yet it might have been a world away. Set in the midst of rolling English countryside it was carved in the valley formed by two hills. A magnificent five star hotel stood at the end of a long, tree-lined drive and, on the west side of the hotel, stood the palatial club house and the course itself. Parking in the middle of the collection of Porsches, Jaguars, Mercedes and Range Rovers, Cal had wandered along the thick-carpeted corridors, passing the designer golf-wear showcases and into the lounge and bar where all the seating was covered in deep-burnished leather and onward to the Snead Coffee Lounge where Gevinson had suggested they met. The Snead Coffee Lounge permitted casual dress, whereas the Palmer Restaurant was strictly formal.

Mark Gevinson looked nothing like he sounded on the phone. Quite short, with broad shoulders and chest, he had wrists and fore-arms that rippled with power, but his face was that of a scholar. High forehead, rimless glasses, light blue eyes that exuded intelligence and a very serious manner. Nor was he alone, for, as he slipped into the booth in the corner of the restaurant which Cal had already occupied, another man immediately appeared and sat down alongside him.

"I'm Mark Gevinson," he announced without a smile. "You'll be Cal Stewart?"

"Sure," Cal replied, offering his hand across the table and feeling the strength in Gevinson's grip as he responded.

"I've asked Mitchell Ormsby to join us," Gevinson continued, as the other man held his hand out. "He's our club manager and has worked at dozens of courses in the UK."

"Fine," Cal replied, acknowledging the overweight figure with a walrus moustache and thread-veined cheeks. Cal had his number before he even spoke. Eater. And drinker.

"Coffee's coming," Cal said "It's very decent of you to see me. I'll try not to take up too much of your time."

"I've got a lesson at eleven. I'm OK 'til then," Gevinson answered, as the elderly, prim waitress arrived with a jug of coffee, fresh cream and a selection of biscuits. The coffee cups were already laid out on the table.

"Put this on the corporate entertaining tab," Ormsby said to her, as Gevinson poured the coffee.

"In case you don't know, I owe Dek Karpinen a big favour," Gevinson began.

"I didn't know," Cal responded.

"No. Dek's not the kind of guy who'd have said anything. Fact is I did a year as a pro at his course out in Parramatta. I had a bad car accident. Not my fault. The other driver was drunk. But a passenger in his car was seriously injured and it all got very ugly. Threats. Phone calls in the middle of the night. That sort of thing," Gevinson explained. "Dek sorted it all out. Saved me a lot of worry and a lot of aggravation. So, if I can help a pal of his out in any way, I'm delighted to do so."

"OK," Cal nodded. "Like I told you on the phone, I'm looking for a man who's been connected with golf courses since at least 1963. Groundsman, green keeper, probably moving up into course maintenance and management. I know he left the UK for Australia in 1964. Took up a position with a club in Albury, near Melbourne."

"Lots of clubs and courses round there. Murray River," said Ormsby, already helping himself to his third biscuit.

"Probably stayed there until about 1970," Cal continued. "Seems he then came back to England. Now under the name of Craig Mangan. I suspect on an Australian passport. Never heard of him since. But, from what I've picked up, his job down in Albury was for a large hotel which had a golf course attached. Dek thought he may have approached similar organisations over here when he was back in the UK looking for a job."

"Well, he might and he might not," said Ormsby. "And from what you say, he may still be a fairly low-grade course employee. With those kind of jobs they tend to take anything, anywhere. The plum jobs at the quality clubs or with the fancy hotels, like this place, are hard to get. They're very choosy when it comes to hiring staff."

"Apparently Mangan wasn't very popular. Dek's dad described him as a loner and a miserable bastard," said Cal.

"But Barry calls all Limeys miserable bastards," Gevinson laughed.

"But he was probably right about this one," Cal smiled. "And there's another factor that might help trace him. Barry said he was a classy player in his own right. Used to play for the club staff in their tournaments and was pretty handy."

"What do you want with this guy?" Ormsby enquired. "Or shouldn't I ask?

"It's probably better if I don't say," Cal replied carefully. "I may risk doing him an injustice. But I can promise both of you that I'm not wasting your time on something trivial. The reason I need to find him is very important."

"Is it a police matter?" asked Gevinson.

"Maybe," Cal answered. "If the time comes when there's really something fit to go to the police, then I'll call them in. But, like I said, I may be barking up the wrong tree. Talking to Mangan is the only way I'll find out."

"What do you think, Mitchell?" Gevinson asked, turning towards the fat man. "Have you got enough to check it out?"

"Not really," Ormsby answered. "Have you got any kind of description of him?"

"All I know is what Barry told Dek," replied Cal. "And this, of course, is in the late sixties, so it's over twenty years ago. But he described him as ugly and having a stutter. That's all I've got."

"I know most of the major hotel courses in the UK. I've worked at a lot of them. Nowadays, many of them are chains. One corporation will own four, five or more. I can start to put the feelers out. Make some calls. If he's working for one in the south-east I've a good chance of finding him. The further north you go, then the fewer my contacts and, frankly, if he's in Scotland, I'm out of touch up there," Ormsby explained.

"It's a lottery then," Cal observed.

"Absolutely. But I'll try. Give me your phone number. I'll have a good idea by the end of the day and I'll give you a call," said Ormsby, forcing his bulk from between the table and the bench seat and getting up.

"If you think you might know something by the end of the day then, if it's alright with you, I'd like to hang around here. Catch up with you later when you know the score and when it's convenient for you," Cal responded.

"Sure," said Ormsby. "But what will you do all day? I'm not likely to know anything before late afternoon."

"He can play a round of golf, Mitchell," Gevinson interjected. "I'll fix him up with some clubs and shoes and a partner. Someone who I'm confident will beat him. Can't have an Aussie coming out here and winning, can we?'

Chapter 38

Before he set out to the first tee in borrowed shoes and with a spare set of Mark Gevinson's clubs, Cal phoned George. It rang out for a long time before she answered, sounding awful. Headache, cold, shivering. She thought she'd probably got the flu and had cancelled all of her work for tomorrow. There was food in the fridge but she wasn't hungry and she planned on spending the rest of the day in bed. Giving him her approval to hang on to the car, he updated her about his visit to Hollister's and the enquiries Ormsby was putting in hand and promised to phone later. Today, George was out of the game.

Mark had fixed him up to play a round of golf with a retired business man who was a club member and always looking for a fresh challenge. When Mark had told him that the fellow was retired he had looked around the locker room for a grey-haired old man, only to find that Tony Medina was the right side of forty. Bronzed, fit, handsome, just back from a cruise round South America and playing off a six handicap, Cal learned a lot about him in the three hours it took them to get round the difficult course.

Son of a greengrocer who used to be at the market every morning by four and then ran his shop in Gillingham until six in the evening, Tony had determined to find a better way to earn a living. Leaving school at sixteen, with no proper qualifications, he went to work in a builder's yard and watched the inefficiency, pilfering and surliness that permeated the running of the business. Traders were kept waiting for hours while stock was searched for in the warehouse and yard, expensive items disappeared into thin air and most of the staff behaved as if they were doing the customer a massive favour to even bother to talk to them. So Tony decided to "go silver", as he neatly put it. Armed with a bank loan which his father secured, he rented a small yard of his own on the edge of the town where rents were low and there was plenty of parking. He hired two old age pensioners as his staff. Buying small amounts of stock at first, he devised an accounting and locating system which meant he knew where every screw, washer and plank of wood was stored and it could be retrieved within a minute. His two trusted retirees were attentive, knowledgeable, honest and delighted to be back at work. They cared. And the word quickly got around that service would be quick, efficient and delivered with a smile.

In two years he had a staff of twelve and had trebled the size of his yard. His stock control system was so efficient that not only did it eliminate loss, misplacement or running out of goods, but it was also wanted by other organisations. He patented it and sold it. And he gave his employees shares in the business with quarterly dividends if profits went up. Six years later he had trading centres in four other towns in the South-East. Ten years later he went public and, after three consecutive years of record trading, he was bought out by a national combine. Then he retired and took up golf and had got his handicap down to six. That's the kind of man he was.

Despite recounting his life story to Cal, Tony Medina made absolutely certain that he won their match and, in the bar afterwards, let Cal buy the drinks. But then he took him into the Snead Coffee Lounge and treated him to a very late and very lengthy lunch which was still going on at half past four when the bulky figure of Mitchell Ormsby loomed into view. Spotting Cal at the table with Medina, he raised his index finger and pointed to an isolated table on the other side of the restaurant and took himself off in that direction. Cal explained that he had matters to attend to with Ormsby and bid his gracious and entertaining host farewell. Medina shook his hand firmly and looked him in the eye.

"You got some kind of problem that brings you over here?" he asked pointedly.

"You're a perceptive bugger, Tony," Cal laughed. "It's a long story, but I'll sort it. I think I'm nearly there."

"Well, remember this. I can spot a decent kid when I see one. And you're one. If ever you need a hand, you give me a call. I don't say what I don't mean," he said, thrusting his business card into Cal's hand. "But you need to improve your swing," he added as he walked away, chuckling to himself.

After the strain and intensity of the ongoing battle, the interlude had provided a few hours of light relief for Cal and a valuable reminder that, when this expedition was finally over, there was another more normal world to which he would be returning.

Ormsby had ordered a pot of tea and a piece of apple pie. Cal settled for just the tea.

"Did he beat you?" asked Ormsby, pointing in the direction of the departing Tony Medina.

"Of course," Cal replied. "He's that kind of guy."

"Heart's in the right place, though," Ormsby continued between mouthfuls of apple pie and ice cream. "We had a young pro here, contracted some disease. Had to have his leg off, below the knee. Just married. Won't ever get a job as a pro again. Tony heard about it. Arranged a tournament to raise some money. Got some celebrities down here. Hundred grand it raised. Except when Tony handed over the cheque it had become a hundred and fifty. He'd put fifty grand of his own in."

Cal poured himself a cup of tea and observed the spectacle of Ormsby ordering and devouring a second serving of apple pie and ice cream, his eyes twinkling as he savoured every morsel. When he'd finished, he leant across the table and grinned impishly at Cal.

"I've cracked it," he announced proudly. "I'm even better than I thought I was. You know what they call it?"

"No."

"Networking. Who you know. Each contact leading you to the next. Very satisfying," he smiled.

"Are you going to order another helping of apple pie or are you going to put me out of my misery?" Cal asked.

"Right, yes, sorry. I spoke to managers I know at four of the larger hotel groups who have their own golf courses. Obviously, they had to go off and make their own enquiries with the heads of course maintenance, promising to phone me back if they came up with anything."

"Yes?"

"Only one did call back. Donald Spencer. Course Supervisor at Moonlight Country Hotels in Hampshire. They've just had a new green keeper join them from their hotel near Bishop's Stortford. They have a large staff because they own six hotels right across the southern part of the UK. From Wales across to Cambridgeshire. They move the staff around. Donald said the green keeper didn't recognise the name, but he did remember a particularly unattractive guy on the ground staff. Right age group. Stuttered and a bloody good golf player."

"Promising."

"Yeah, so I phoned the clubhouse at Bishop's Stortford. Said we were thinking of running a staff and management intra-hotel tournament next year. Said we'd like to invite a couple of their course maintenance staff to play in it. Did they have any who had a decent handicap? He came straight back with two names. Tommy Lester and Craig Mangan. Said I'd like to write to them. Write to the Hotel's Personnel Department, he replied, they'd pass the letter on. I suggested it was more personal to write direct to their homes. Hang on, he said. Give me a minute."

"And?"

"He came back with the addresses. Here's the one you're interested in," Ormsby announced triumphantly, producing a piece of hotel notepaper out of his trouser pocket.

Cal looked at the address. "Harlow," he said. "Where's that?"

"Essex. About ten or eleven miles from the Bishop's Stortford course," Ormsby replied.

"And how far from here?" Cal enquired.

"Best part of eighty miles, I should think. Take you at least a couple of hours at this time of day," Ormsby answered.

"Tell me, Mitchell, do you know this hotel chain well?"

"Oh yes. Quality organisation. Courses are high standard."

"Do you know where each of their hotels is located?" Cal continued.

"I think so."

"Do they have one anywhere near a town called Shepton Mallet?" Cal asked, his eyes riveted on Ormsby as he awaited the answer.

"You bet," Ormsby responded. "In the Mendip hills. Beautiful place. Accommodation in small blocks around the course. I've actually stayed there."

"I can't tell you how helpful you've been," Cal breathed. "How do I ever thank you for this?"

"Easy, Cal. Two ways. One, come back some day and take me out for a meal. I never say no to food. Secondly, and more seriously, watch yourself. Hope I'm not stepping where I shouldn't, but I don't much like the sound of this Mangan fella," he replied with obvious concern in his voice.

"I'll be fine. And I'll let you know what happens," said Cal, already up on his feet and moving towards the corridor where the public phones were. He had to phone George.

When Cal phoned the flat it simply rang out and he became concerned. After waiting five minutes, he tried again and this time George answered on the first ring.

"Was that you a few minutes ago?" she asked. "I was in the bathroom. You'd gone when I picked up."

"I was worried when you didn't answer. Are you feeling any better?"

"Not really. It's obviously the flu. I can't get rid of the headache and I can't get warm. A good night's sleep and I'll be on the mend. What's your news?"

"It's a long story. But the bottom line is I've found him. He works for Moonlight Country Hotels. A chain of six hotels with golf courses. He's at their course near Bishop's Stortford. They've got another one near Shepton Mallet, so draw your own conclusions," he explained.

"It's enough to bring Tedstone in, isn't it?" asked George.

"Probably. But how heavily is Tedstone going to go after him for what we're interested in. If they can get him for the Somerset murder he'll never be released anyway. Will they see much mileage in trying to overturn a conviction from twenty seven years ago? I'm not convinced."

"Well, you've made serious progress. Come back to the flat and we'll decide how to go about things in the morning," George said. "Get yourself something to eat on the way back. I don't want anything and I'm going to take a couple of sleeping pills that are in Katie's medicine cabinet."

"OK. Get your head down. We'll speak in the morning," Cal replied, already plotting his route to Harlow.

Chapter 39

Seventy-five miles later he turned off the A414 and picked up a parallel road running east called Edinburgh Way. Stopping at a depressing pub for an almost inedible cheese sandwich, made of yesterday's sliced white cardboard and tasteless cheddar, he got directions to Cranmer Avenue off a middle-aged barmaid whose eyes looked in different directions. Half an hour later, having left the Mercedes parked on the main road, directly under a street lamp, he turned left and walked into the street which he believed would mean the end of this traumatic journey. In his hand was a torch with a heavy rubber casing and up his sleeve was a tyre lever with a chisel edge for removing hub caps. As he walked down the pavement, passing identical small town houses with ugly facings of white wood, paint peeling off and different coloured front doors, he reflected that on that fateful afternoon on that magnificent South Pacific island, he could never have anticipated that the story might find its conclusion in a sad little estate in a soulless Essex town.

Throughout the drive from the Chiltern Hills Golf Course he had tried to work out in his mind exactly how he was going to play this, considering a straight confrontation or perhaps sleeping in the car, waiting until Mangan left for work in the morning, and then trying to get inside the house. By the time he was approaching number 23 he was still none the wiser as to exactly what he would do. His heart was now beating much faster. Every fibre of his being told him that Mangan was going to turn out to be the killer and he knew that he must be extremely dangerous. Far more dangerous than Lanny Creane, and that had been one of the most terrifying experiences of his life. It was dark and the street was poorly lit. He was only wearing a cotton shirt and a thin jumper. Suddenly he was aware of the cold and began to shiver, recognising that part of this was brought on by nerves.

The road curved to the right as he reached number 17 and number 23 was just out of sight beyond the bend. A youth loomed out of the dark and startled him. He must have come out of one of the houses just ahead. Cal let the end of the tyre lever slip down his sleeve into his palm and gripped it tightly. Dressed in a three quarter length anorak, the youth wore the hood up, deliberately suggesting menace and, as he passed Cal, he stared at him, weighing him up, ready for trouble but moving on by. It was that kind of street. The youth was black and Cal shrugged his shoulders at the irony.

Each house had a very short drive leading directly to the front door. The drive was the width and length of a car with a small garden to the side. In most of these driveways stood a car and other vehicles were parked in the road and on the pavement itself. There was no garage. Some cars were without wheels, standing on bricks. Broken bikes lay on untended grass. Overflowing dustbins and bags of rubbish were everywhere. Harlow Man had taken a new town and turned it old and dirty. Slowing his pace, Cal turned the corner and set eyes on the nest of the rat. Tension eased rapidly from Cal's body as he saw that the house was in complete darkness and there was no car in the drive, nor was there one directly outside the house. There was a light in the downstairs front room of number 21 but number 25 appeared as deserted as Mangan's. Cal continued walking, staring in through the window as he dawdled by. Net curtains denied any view of the interior, but he could see that the house and garden were poorly kept, with a black front door that had splashes of white and yellow paint upon it. A dog was barking inside a house on the opposite side of the road and nobody was making any attempt to shut it up. Blue flickering of television screens appeared through some of the windows and the sound of tuneless music escaped through the odd open window as he carried on walking down the road.

When Cal reached number 41 there was a break in the pattern.

An unpaved dirt track ran down the side of the house to a row of garages and Cal immediately turned down it. The track opened up into a square of derelict land with a row of garages made of concrete block on three sides of the square. By keeping to the left of the garages Cal was able to follow a rough path which brought him on to some open land, allowing him to turn left again and pick his way over waste land which ran directly behind the houses in Cranmer Avenue. Counting them down from 41 he reached the ninth house. The back was also in darkness. The three panels of cheap fencing that separated the wasteland from the overgrown back garden were leaning drunkenly in their shallow foundations. Cal had forced himself between two of them in the blink of an eye. A white plastic chair lay on its side in the weeds and knee-high grass. Bricks and chunks of concrete were scattered about. There was a kind of path up the centre, constructed out of slabs which had cracked and splintered. A hutch with chicken wire, containing some kind of creature, was pressed up against the back wall of the house. Bits of rotting vegetables were stuffed in the holes in the wire and it stank like a cess pit. Lines of wire strung between concrete posts separated the house from its neighbours. Bending low, Cal hurried up to the house, his eyes seeking an open window, but in vain. The creature in the hutch scurried through the straw, making Cal jump as he reached the back door. He tried the handle but it was locked.

Cal could now sense the end of the road. He was closing in on a killer. A massive injustice was about to be exposed and the corruption within the English system laid bare. As he weighed up the options one face, above all others, kept flashing through his mind. Not his father nor George nor Hollister. It was the patrician face of Vishney, with his pince-nez perched on the edge of his nose, and that supercilious sneer. That bastard's compliant race to conviction had destroyed as many lives as had the murderer. Decisions were now making themselves.

Cal had no doubt, despite the enormity of the risk, that he intended to break into that house. Although he was still shivering, he was also sweating from the tension. The cold steel of the tyre lever once more pressed against the palm of his hand, but this time he pulled it completely from within his sleeve and crouched by the back door. Music floated from the window of a house several doors down the street and snatches of dialogue from some old film on a television nearby drifted in the air. A car drove down the street too fast and occasional bursts of barking by that same dog from earlier, now distant, punctuated the other sounds.

The sharp chisel edge was now forced between the frame and the door itself and Cal was slowly applying pressure to the shaft. There was a creaking as the steel of the lock pressed hard against the frame, followed by a louder sound of splintering wood. Cal stopped, taken aback by the volume of the splintering sound in the night air. Sweat poured off his brow as he remained crouching, the quadriceps aching with the strain of the position. A long minute's wait. Then he reinserted the chisel edge and pulled back in one solid movement on the lever and, with a crack, the lock wrenched its container from the wooden frame and the door sprang open. Standing stock still in the doorway, he waited to see if the noise had provoked any reaction. The music still played. The wretched dog still had bursts of barking. There was no other movement. No shouts. No footsteps. Cal Stewart, house-breaker. He was in.

Masking the full glare of the torch with his hand and keeping the beam low, he examined the kitchen. Dirty washing-up piled high in the sink, a wooden table with a red formica top and a seat for one in the corner. A bottle of tomato ketchup, its top encrusted with dried sauce, stood on the table alongside an empty tin of mandarin oranges with a dirty spoon resting within. Linoleum tiles on the floor, cracked with patches missing. Filthy cooker. Empty bottles of cheap, unbranded whisky on the window-sill, next to a rusty can of fly-killer. The whole area reeked of stale water and drains.

A door led into a narrow hallway. To the right were the stairs and to the left a doorway into the lounge. Cal switched the torch off in the lounge as the window looked out on to the street, but he could see enough to make out a television, couch and old newspapers strewn over the thin carpet. Back in the hallway Cal walked the couple of paces to the front door. A dozen or so letters and circulars lay on the floor, suggesting that the householder had not been here for at least a couple of days. Cal bent down and picked up an envelope marked British Gas. It was addressed to C. Mangan of 23 Cranmer Avenue, Harlow.

The stairs were carpeted but still creaked. They turned on a quarter landing and another short flight took him to the upstairs landing. The front bedroom was reasonably illuminated from the street. Single bed. Unmade. Clothes all over the floor. An old free-standing wardrobe which Cal opened. Men's clothes on bent wire hangers, dirty mud-encrusted shoes and underwear on the bottom shoe-rack.

In the corner, leaning against the wall, stood a set of golf clubs in an old, tatty bag. Ignoring the bathroom, Cal stepped across the landing to the second bedroom at the back of the house.

The door was closed and he cautiously opened it to reveal a small room with red-painted walls. Red velvet curtains were drawn closed, shutting out all external light. The floor was laid out with tiles depicting oriental shapes and signs. There was no overhead light, just an Asian lantern atop a gold pole in the corner of the room. Nor was there any furniture save for one extraordinary piece. It was an ancient Chinese, Ming style prayer altar, carved from finest elm wood with gold inlay. It consisted of a central cabinet, about four feet high, with two full-length doors, and shorter attached side cabinets with three drawers on each side. Obviously, the holy books would have been placed on the top platform whose edges curved upwards. Pointing the torch at the doors, Cal could see how carefully the piece had been maintained, highly polished and revered, in stark contrast to every other miserable piece of furniture in the house. This was Mangan's shrine. His Holy Place. Slowly opening the doors revealed eight slim drawers ranged vertically. Attached to the inner side of each door was a piece of white muslin, each bearing a pair of oriental hieroglyphics in black print, which Cal recognised from time he'd spent in Singapore. They were the Chinese symbols for death, reflecting the philosophical links between death, sexuality and rebirth.

But it was the eight drawers on which he concentrated the beam of light from the torch. Each had a paper label stuck to the outside with writing in a crude hand upon it. The label of the top drawer read *Louise Donovan*. The bottom drawer was labeled *Diane Pierce*. Each of the other six drawers was labelled with a girl's name. With a shaking hand, Cal pulled back the top drawer. It was crammed with newspaper cuttings covering everything to do with the 1963 murder. Cal picked them up and scanned them, recognising some from the counterparts he had seized from Vishney's file. Underneath them was a sheet of paper and glued to it was a faded picture from a glossy magazine. Plainly, the picture had once depicted a glamorous young female, modelling lingerie, but Mangan had simply cut out the section from navel to thigh, displaying her shapely figure clad in a pair of navy blue knickers.

The second drawer, labelled *Kerry Baker* was similarly filled with newspaper cuttings from Melbourne newspapers in 1968 about the discovery of a girl's body in the Yarra River. But the contents of this drawer had an added ingredient. A pair of girl's pants. Once pink, now faded and stained along the crutch.

Each of the other drawers had its name, its cuttings and the pants. The seventh drawer was *Carol Dobbins. Warwick December 1989*. Stained, stinking pants.

Number eight. *Diane Pierce.* Fresh, still-white newspaper cuttings. Lemon knickers, extensively bloodied. But this drawer had even more. A glass jar, the size of a small jam jar, full of a clear liquid, with a tight-fit metal top and lying on its side. Cal picked it up from where it lay and shone the torch directly upon it. Within the liquid, now sinking to the bottom as he held the jar upright, was a brown object. Cal stared in disbelief as he slowly recognised it for what it was. A severed little toe, the nail still bearing a smudge of what once had been burgundy nail polish.

Sickened to the pit of his stomach, Cal returned the jar to its place, closed the drawers and doors of the cabinet and hurried downstairs. Slipping the tyre lever back up his sleeve and shining the torch at his feet, he decided he would leave by the front door. When he'd turned off the main road into Cranmer Avenue he'd noticed a public phone box on the corner. In less than two minutes the police could be informed and enough evidence to clear his father, solve another seven murders and lock Mangan up for the rest of his life, would be safely in their hands. The destination was finally in sight.

That's when he came face to face with Walter Mangan, psychopathic serial killer. So engrossed had Cal been in the gruesome discovery in the back bedroom that he had neither heard a car arrive in the drive, nor heard Mangan entering the house by the back door. It was always Mangan's habit to use the back door and, on espying the splintered frame and bits of wood on the floor he was forewarned and forearmed. And forearmed meant exactly that.

The knife was an American fighting knife with a razor-sharp blade of high-quality carbon steel edge. The handle was constructed of wood, but with the addition of a die-cast zinc grip moulded to it, which contained four finger holes for firmness of grip. Designed to combine balance with wicked sharpness it was as deadly a weapon for use in close-quarters combat as could be found. Mangan was in the perfect position, weight distributed evenly on each foot, knife held out ahead of him in his right hand and with the benefit of surprise. Cal had absolutely no chance against the first strike which was a quicksilver thrust aimed just below the left rib cage, at an upward angle so as to slice straight through the major arteries and into the heart. The damage to the arteries would be clean cut, so that loss of consciousness and death would be rapid. If he missed the heart and only succeeded in tearing the arteries then the artery might contract and slow or stop the bleeding. This knife would not tear, it would slice and sever. Terminally. It was scientifically intended as a death blow.

Cal saw the strike, heard the feral intake of breath as the killer delivered it and actually saw the glint of the steel as it flashed through the air. Instinct made him draw both arms across his chest and body and, like the soldier whose cigarette case saves him from the sniper's bullet, the blade drove straight into the rubber casing of the torch he was carrying in his left hand. Although Mangan immediately wrenched it free, Cal had been given a precious life line and he kicked straight ahead, at just below-the-belt height, and felt heavy contact with the man's groin, followed by a grunt of surprise and pain. But Mangan still kept coming forward, this time slashing wildly downwards with the knife and, as Cal tried to step to his right to avoid the blade, he felt a searing pain across the top of his left shoulder followed, in an instant, by the full bodyweight of the attacker crashing into him, knocking him backwards into the hall and on to the floor. Mangan dived on top of him, left forearm across his throat, one knee on his right arm and the other on his chest, swinging the knife round at the side of Cal's neck. Death was a nano-second away when Cal snaked out his left hand, aiming for Mangan's wrist but, instead, taking the point of the knife in the palm of his left hand. The blade sliced through the middle of his hand and out the other side, cutting his face on the jaw line. Cal screamed as Mangan pulled out the blade and pressed his knife arm across Cal's mouth so as to stifle the scream. The flat of the blade, extending from Mangan's hand, now pressed against the side of Cal's jaw. He could feel the blood pouring from his hand and shoulder and face but, for some reason, the most pain was in his hand which was pumping out blood.

In the hall there was a half-light through the glass of the front door and the open lounge door and, for the first time, he got a view of the killer's face. Mangan saw the fight as over. Cal was badly wounded, motionless and pinned to the floor by a man armed with a lethal combat weapon. But before delivering the death blow, which he was now actively relishing, Mangan wanted to know whose life he was about to take. He doubted that he was dealing with a casual burglar.

"Who th-th-the fuck are you," he stuttered, his face less than a foot above Cal's. His hair was dark, thick and worn long. The face was thin with hollow cheekbones and pockmarked white skin, eyes unnaturally close together and, even in the poor light, Cal could see them darting from side to side, like an animal, poised above its dying prey, ever-watchful for theft of the carcass from other predators.

As he spoke, exposing small yellow teeth and bloodless lips, the foulness of his breath filled the air, making Cal gag. He had lifted his hand an inch upwards from Cal's mouth to allow him to answer, but poised to slam down again if Cal tried to scream. As the hand lifted, the point of the blade was right against Cal's clavicle and Mangan deliberately jabbed it a few centimetres downwards so it pierced the skin and was in actual contact with the bone.

"I'm Stanton's son," Cal whispered.

The hand went back down on the mouth and the point of the knife lifted away from the bone as Mangan absorbed the revelation.

"That one was a m-m-mistake," he snarled. "I was m-m-marking the out of bounds line. Watched them from the b-b-ushes. Fucking tart. Got fifteen quid outta her h-hand. When I had her she just went d-d-dead. Thought I'd b-bin seen. Dumped the pants in the saddle-bag." As he spoke, he shifted his weight to the left and the pressure on Cal's right arm was reduced.

Cal's breathing was becoming increasingly shallow as he was losing so much blood and his strength was ebbing away. Mangan was on the verge of inflicting the fatal blow and Cal had to try to make one final move. He was aware of the tyre lever up his right sleeve but, in his present position, he couldn't pull it out. Mangan was tall and thin but not very well-built. In ordinary circumstances Cal would have had a chance of throwing him off. But these weren't ordinary circumstances. He would almost certainly have to take one more strike with the knife in any attempt to escape. It would be a matter of pure luck where that blow landed. But Mangan wanted one thing more from his victim. To ask the question that he could never have asked of anyone before this attack on his home.

"Did you s-s-see my shrine?" he stammered, self-congratulation seeping from every syllable.

Cal moved his head up and down to signify that he had and the thin lips parted in a smile of satisfaction and Cal took his chance. Whipping his right arm round and upwards he drove his index and middle fingers towards Mangan's close-set eyes. Only the index finger hit its target and Cal felt the whole of the first joint compress the eyeball and enter the socket. At the same time Cal had thrown his head and upper body as far away from the knife as possible and tried to catapult Mangan over on to his side. As Mangan screamed in agony and his left hand clutched at the savaged eye he swung the knife and Cal took the blow that he realised would be unavoidable.It went straight into his lower left abdomen. But Mangan's weight was off him and he hurled himself across the floor towards the front door and on to his feet. Mangan had one hand to his eye and was struggling to his feet with the knife pointed out in front of him. Cal brought back his foot and kicked the right elbow with all the force at his command and the knife flew out of Mangan's hand. Now free to pull the tyre lever from his sleeve he was the one armed and he crashed it across the same elbow, shattering the bone as Mangan screamed in agony and collapsed on his back on the floor. Cal kicked him viciously in the ribs on the right side and then kicked him equally viciously in the same place on the left. Mangan was finished. But Cal was not. The red mist had descended. Now, in his mind's eye, he did see an image of his father, and in that terrible second he brought back the tyre lever over his right shoulder and smashed it down on Mangan's skull. He executed him.

Chapter 40

When he came to he was in a hospital bed attached to more tubes and wires than a NASA computer. A middle-aged nurse with a disapproving expression was standing over him, watching him slowly opening his eyes.

"You're in Intensive Care, Mr Stewart," she explained in a firm voice, unsmiling.

"How bad am I?" Cal breathed.

"You've had major abdominal surgery. And surgery to your left hand. You have a bad injury to your shoulder and a serious cut to your face," she answered coldly.

"How bad?" Cal repeated.

"You'll live. The Doctors will give you the details," she responded, rearranging the bolster size pillows so that he was propped up in the bed.

"How long will I be in here?" he asked, wincing as he readjusted his position on the pillows.

"A few days I should think. I'll tell them you're awake."

"Tell who?" he enquired, hoping it would be George.

"The police of course," she answered, heading for the door. "The other man's dead. The police are outside."

A moment later two young uniformed police officers walked hesitantly into the room.

"I'm PC Horcher. This is my colleague PC Buswell."

"I want to see Georgina Walgrave."

"You're seeing no-one. You're under arrest for the murder of Craig Mangan. You don't have to say anything, but anything you do say will be taken down and may be used in evidence against you. Do you understand?"

"Are you crazy?"

"An officer will remain outside your door until the Doctors release you. Then you'll be taken to the police station for interview. That's what DCI Colley has instructed us to tell you."

"How did I get here?

"I've told you all I can."

"Where's Georgina Walgrave. I know she'll have come to the hospital."

"I've told you all I can," Horcher repeated, walking to the door and out into the corridor.

PC Buswell lingered a few seconds before following his colleague, but, on reaching the door, turned back over his shoulder and spoke softly.

"She's outside, mate. She has been for the last thirty-six hours."

"Let me see her," Cal shouted after him, but he shook his head, quietly closing the door behind him.

After another twenty-four hours they moved him out of Intensive Care and into a windowless side ward with six beds in it. Except he was the only patient. Imprisoned. The doctors came and went and slowly his strength began to return. A uniformed police officer sat outside the door. Shift by shift. Sometimes Horcher. Sometimes Buswell. Sometimes a face without a name. No visitors. They allowed him a phone call from his mother. Bemused, crying, elated at the prospect of her husband's case going back to the Court of Appeal, but frightened that Cal had come so close to death. He chose not to tell her that he was under arrest, in the expectation that once he was fit enough to be medically discharged, then the police would ask a few formal questions and let him go. Initially, the abdominal injury hurt like the devil but, after a couple of days, began to ease. The shoulder injury was healing nicely and although his face looked a mess, he was assured that the skilled suturing would leave only a thin scar running along the line of his jaw. But his hand was a worry. There was considerable damage and his grip was as weak as a baby's. Months of physiotherapy lay ahead.

On the fourth day a small man, in his late fifties, with gold-rimmed spectacles, virtually no hair, a briefcase and a dark grey suit was ushered into the room and introduced himself as a solicitor by the name of Oliver Newcombe. He explained that the Consultant had informed the police that Cal was fit to be discharged tomorrow and that the police intended to take him to Harlow Police Station to be interviewed. George had been persistently demanding to see him and had been refused and she had contacted his firm. Oliver Newcombe was the senior partner of the firm who had handled Frederick Walgrave's estate and George wanted him to attend at any interview and advise Cal. Seated on the edge of the empty bed next to Cal's, Newcombe set about explaining to Cal what he thought was going on.

"I've been kept incommunicado," Cal protested bitterly. "What the hell are they playing at?"

"They're playing at political correctness," Newcombe retorted disdainfully. "Trouble is, political correctness can lead to political decisions. You need to be careful."

"How do you mean?"

"They're in a hole. An innocent man was hanged. The system left a murderer out there who continued to kill. They never made any enquiry about him. You came along and, in a few weeks, solved eight murders. They're acutely embarrassed," Newcombe began.

"And?"

"And you then killed Mangan. They suspect you didn't have to. You went beyond what was necessary to defend yourself and simply took revenge. They don't want people taking the law into their own hands. Least of all when that person is already showing them up as institutionally incompetent."

"So where does that leave me?" asked Cal.

"At real risk of being charged with murder," Newcombe replied sombrely. "I've spoken to an Inspector Pendell. Unpleasant fellow. Aggressive and self-righteous. Watch him. He's deliberately declined to release any details about Mangan's responsibility for all these murders to the Press until after he's interviewed you. He's waiting to see which way you're going to play it."

"What do I do?"

"Don't admit to breaking into Mangan's house and don't tell them the sequence of blows," Newcombe urged anxiously.

"You mean don't tell them that I clobbered him over the head with a piece of iron after he was down and out," said Cal with disarming candour.

"I didn't hear you say that," Newcombe replied emphatically. "That's tantamount to an admission of murder. I didn't hear it and never say it again."

"So what do I say?"

"You'll have to give me some instructions now. Then I'll be able to advise you properly. But the general flavour must be that you were fighting a dangerous, armed psychopathic killer in a fight that went to the death. You or him. All you can say is that you did your best to make sure it wasn't you. Do you understand?"

"Yes."

"Right," said Newcombe, picking up his briefcase and extracting a blue notebook from within. "Let's get started."

Chapter 41

6.43. Alarm clock. Shower. Corn flakes. Half a cup of milk. Earl Grey tea. Shower again. Left sock first. Right shoe last. Blue shirt on a Tuesday. Nine hundred and forty four steps from the front door to the station. Exact change for newspaper. Sit or stand facing the engine. Arrive at work by side door. Wash hands. Start work.

The routine was everything. Unless the routine was followed to the last detail there would be a disaster. The routine protected him from danger. The routine kept his life in order. Everything had to be precise. The pens laid out on his desk like soldiers on parade. Files immaculately stacked. Answer the phone after three rings. Straighten files again. Never stray beyond the established routine. A crime is committed. Evidence meticulously gathered. Culprit caught. Interviewed and confronted with his crime. Punished. The Law controls the natural order.

It had been her final taunt hurled at him as she slammed out of the house for the last time. "Find yourself a woman who can live with OCD," she had screamed as she struggled down the path with the heavy suitcase towards the car where her lover nervously waited, anxious to avoid a confrontation with a police inspector whose wife he'd been screwing for the last eighteen months. He hadn't understood what she'd meant so he'd asked around. Obsessive compulsive disorder. The use of rituals to control anxieties. His anxiety had only ever been to maintain the natural order. She had destroyed that order by infidelity. She was responsible for producing the very condition that had rent them asunder.

Since her departure his symptoms had worsened. There were no children. He had no interests outside his job. So now all of his mental energies were directed into his duties as a police officer. Inspector at

32. Assigned to Major Homicide. Gather the evidence. Catch the killer. Confront him with his crime. Punishment. Restore the natural order.

They'd been waiting for five days to interview this vigilante who'd caved in Mangan's skull. Of course Mangan was a serial killer. A monster. But he should have been confronted by the authorities of the State. Interviewed. Tried. Punished. Through the system that imposed the regime under which civilised man must live. Stewart could have called for the police before he entered the house. He could have sent for them when he had defeated Mangan in the fight. But he'd deliberately chosen to defy the natural process. Succumbed to the mentality of the lynch mob. Selected himself as Judge and jury. Appointed himself as executioner. His crime had undermined the natural order. He must pay the price. Realign the files. Straighten the row of pens. Wash hands. To the Interview Room. Restore the order.

INTERVIEW RECORD

PERSONS PRESENT:

Detective Chief Inspector Nicholas Colley
Detective Inspector Joseph Pendell
Cal Stewart
Oliver Newcombe [Solicitor]

Pendell: You've been brought to this police station under arrest on suspicion of the murder of Craig Mangan. You've been cautioned. This interview is being tape recorded. You've been in hospital for five days, but the doctors have assured us that you're now fit enough to be detained in a police station and asked questions. If you feel unwell at any stage then say so and I'll immediately suspend the interview.

Stewart: Right.

Pendell: As you know, Craig Mangan was found dead in the hall of his house at 23 Cranmer Avenue, Harlow on Friday night of last week. He had bruising to the groin, multiple fractures to his ribs on both sides, fractures to his elbow and forearm, a gouging injury to his left eye which probably blinded him in that eye and a compound, depressed fracture of the skull. Are you responsible for any of those injuries?

Stewart: I'm responsible for them all.

Pendell: You were found lying unconscious outside the back door of Mangan's house by police officers who were despatched when a neighbour made a 999 call reporting screams coming from that house. You were taken by ambulance to Harlow Hospital and operated on for a knife injury to the abdomen which had severed the intestine, knife injuries to the shoulder and hand and a facial wound requiring thirty two stitches. How did you suffer those injuries?

Stewart: You know damned well. Mangan.

Pendell: We recovered a torch with rubber casing which seemed to have been cut by a knife. Whose was that?

Stewart: It was from Georgina Walgrave's Mercedes. The one I drove to Harlow in. That torch saved my life. It took Mangan's first strike with the knife. Have you seen that knife?

Pendell: We did recover a knife from the hallway. It's been identified as a modified US Marine Corps knife with finger hole grips. Who did it belong to?

Stewart: Mangan.

Pendell: We also recovered a tyre lever. It's been scientifically examined and found to have Mangan's hair on it. Whose was that?

Stewart: It was from the Mercedes.

Pendell: It's right to tell you that we're wholly satisfied that Craig Mangan was responsible for a number of murders, so we're under no illusions as to how dangerous he was. However, we want to hear your account of what you were doing in his house and how these various injuries occurred.

Stewart: Frankly, you make me sick. Telling me now you're satisfied that he was a serial killer. And then arresting me. Your lot did bugger all about catching him in 1963. You did nothing about checking what he'd been up to in Australia. You did bugger all about comparing seven similar unsolved murders over the years and likewise with the eighth in Somerset.

Pendell: That's your opinion. I want to know how he came to be killed. In this country we live by the rule of Law not by lynching. You don't just walk into someone's home and kill them because you think they're guilty of some crime. Why did you kill him?

Stewart: Because he tried to kill me.

Pendell: How did you get into his house?

Newcombe: I advise you not to answer that question.

Stewart: Why not? Mangan's responsible for my father being hanged. An innocent man. I suppose you'd call that the rule of Law would you, Pendell?

Pendell: How did you get into his house?

Newcombe: Don't answer.

Stewart: Have you examined his bloody shrine? Have you looked in his little jar in the bottom drawer? Do you really think any decent person gives a toss that he's dead?

Pendell: That's not for me to answer. Our job is to enforce the Law. Preserve the proper order. Investigate whether you've broken into his house. And whether you have killed him as an act of vengeance. If you fractured his skull, which was the fatal injury, after he'd suffered those other injuries which would have rendered him defenceless, then we want to know. You've no right to take the law into your own hands. Which injury was the last injury you inflicted? Was it the blow to the skull?

Newcombe: I advise you not to answer.

Pendell: Did you use that tyre lever to fracture his skull as the hair deposits suggest?

Newcombe: I advise you not to answer.

Stewart: I've been attacked by a psychopath with a wicked knife, suffered serious injuries, including having that blade plunged into my belly, and all you want to know is when I hit the bastard over the head. What did you expect me to do? Ask him if he felt OK?

Pendell: How do we know that the knife wasn't yours?

Stewart: 'Cos I'm telling you. Have you done any bloody detective work to find out where Mangan got it from, had it adapted? I doubt it. You haven't lifted a bloody finger to catch him since 1963. Why change the habits of a lifetime?

Pendell: Just calm down, Mr Stewart. We don't take kindly to the vigilante mentality over here. You're not helping yourself and you're not helping us get to the bottom of this . . .

Stewart: I've had enough, Mr Newcombe. I've led them to a serial killer. Nearly got myself killed in the process and I'm forced to listen to this self-important jerk telling me that I'm not helping them get to the bottom of it. Can we stop here and now. Let the bastards do what the hell they want.

Newcombe: You're not obliged to answer any of their questions. And, frankly, Chief Inspector Colley, the hostile manner in which this interview is being conducted is unacceptable. I'm advising him not to answer any questions unless Inspector Pendell changes his tone.

Colley: May I ask everyone to cool the temperature. We just want to get Cal's account of what happened. Once we do, we can move on. Now, Cal, please tell us how the fight started.

Stewart: Don't patronise me. Don't call me Cal.

Colley: Very well. How did the fight start?

Stewart: He came at me with that knife.

Colley: Inside or outside?

Newcombe: I advise you not to answer.

Stewart: I'm sick of this, Mr Newcombe. I don't care admitting I broke in to his house. The cops had done nothing about catching him and so I was looking for evidence. And I bloody well found it. I was leaving the house to dial 999 from the phone box on the corner.

Pendell: So you admit breaking into Mangan's house?

Stewart: Yes.

Pendell: Your duty was to call the police

Stewart: I wasn't acting out of duty. I was trying to see if he was a killer.

Colley: Was he in?

Stewart: No. He appeared in the hall as I was leaving and there was an almighty fight. To the death. It was him or me.

Pendell: At what point did you deliver the fatal blow to the head?

Stewart: No comment.

Pendell: Why is it that question that you choose not to answer?

Stewart: No comment.

Pendell: Is it because you delivered the fatal blow when he was already badly hurt and unable to defend himself?

Stewart: No comment.

Pendell: You just finished him off, didn't you?

Stewart: No comment.

Pendell: It's obvious. He had nothing left. But, instead of leaving it to the police and the courts, you took revenge because of your father. That's what happened isn't it?

Newcombe: I'm asking for this interview to be suspended. I want to talk to my client. And I'm formally complaining about the way in which you have interviewed him. He was only discharged from hospital yesterday and you, Mr Pendell, have gone about this like a bull in a china shop.

Colley: I think it is sensible to terminate the interview. We'll let you know by noon tomorrow if we intend to conduct a further interview. In the meanwhile we intend to keep him here. In view of the fact that he's only just been discharged from hospital we won't put him in a cell. We'll find a room and have a doctor on call in case he feels unwell.

Stewart: In the whole of this interview you've never once mentioned what you intend to do about my father's case. I want to know what's going to happen.

Colley: That's not our decision. It's all in the hands of the Home Office and the Director of Public Prosecutions. I also intend to liaise with him immediately to decide whether or not you should be charged with any criminal offences arising out of breaking into Mangan's house and his death.

Stewart: You've stopped Georgina Walgrave from seeing me. That's about as low as you could get. Now I've met you, Pendell, I realise who would have made that decision. When can I see her?

Colley: Not at this stage.

Stewart: I'd like to place something on record.

Colley: What?

Stewart: The Judge who helped do for my father. Vishney. I'll have a lot to say about him soon. Now's not the right time. But he's a corrupt bastard. While he's a corrupt bastard you two are just bastards. Plain and simple.

Pendell: That's it. Civilised rules mean nothing to you. You'll be detained here. You had your chance to speak. The interview's over.

Chapter 42

Within half an hour Inspector Pendell had arranged to visit Sir Eustace Vishney at Dolphin Glen in Brighton at four o'clock that afternoon. When he arrived, the staff had been instructed to take him to the card room which would not be in use at that time. Vishney was seated at one of the card tables, playing a complex variation of solitaire, whilst he awaited his visitor. Four other unoccupied card tables, a sofa and a desk with a telephone on it made up the rest of the furniture in the room.

Given that a police officer wished to speak with him, Vishney had dragged out his old black jacket and pin stripe trousers from the back of the wardrobe. The cut of the lapels was out of date, the trousers were too tight round the waist and both smelled of mothballs. He looked what he was. Yesterday's man, waiting to die. Pince-nez in place, he looked up as Pendell was shown into the room and took the seat opposite him across the table.

"I'm Detective Inspector Joseph Pendell," he began. "We've got a man named Stewart in custody. He's the son of a man you tried in 1963 . . . "

"Stanton," Vishney interrupted.

"Yes. Stewart broke into a house in Harlow where a man called Mangan lived. There was a fight. Mangan ended up dead. We're presently considering whether or not to charge Stewart with murder," Pendell explained patiently.

"What does that have to do with me?" Vishney barked, gathering up the cards and returning them to their box.

"You may be able to help us in our understanding of what happened in 1963," Pendell replied.

"How?" Vishney responded, a note of unease creeping into his voice.

"I would ask you to treat this next matter as confidential until we release it to the Press, Sir Eustace," said Pendell. "But we are now satisfied that the murderer in your case was Mangan, not Stanton."

"What?" exclaimed Vishney. "What? Rubbish. Stanton was the murderer."

"No, Sir, I'm afraid not. The conviction was a mistake. The Prosecution will have no choice but to concede the appeal. Mangan was the killer," Pendell declared firmly, causing Vishney to unwind his long body from the chair and walk ponderously to the window. He felt ill. Everything he'd done to help Hollister had been done against the firm understanding that Stanton was guilty. This could spell disaster and humiliation for him in the newspapers.

"How do you know you're right?" the old Judge barked across the room.

"We have the evidence, Sir. But what we want to know is this. Obviously Stewart would be hostile to you because you were the Trial Judge and his father was convicted and hanged. But did anything happen beyond that which caused the boy to hate you even more? Did you do anything at that trial which might have been misinterpreted? Anything which would make the son so full of hatred against you personally?"

"Of course not," Vishney replied, going hot and cold. "His father was convicted on sound evidence. I find it hard to believe he was not the culprit. The victim's pants were found in his saddlebag. I presided over a fair trial with a fair result."

"Not according to what the son said to us today in interview. I'll quote you the relevant extract," Pendell responded, pulling a copy of the transcribed interview from his inside jacket pocket and reading out loud.

"The Judge who helped do for my father, Vishney. I'll have a lot to say about him soon. Now's not the right time. But he's a corrupt bastard."

"Outrageous," Vishney breathed unconvincingly.

"Forgive my bluntness, Sir Eustace, but we really need to know. Did you do anything which could explain that observation by Stewart?" Pendell enquired.

"Outrageous," Vishney repeated, evading the question and returning to his seat.

"Tomorrow we face the difficult decision of whether Stewart should be charged with murder. If we don't charge him, he obviously has in mind to say quite a lot about the 1963 murder. We need to know if any of it may have a bearing on his state of mind when he was involved in the fight with Mangan which resulted in Mangan's death. So I would welcome an answer to my question."

Vishney remained silent.

"Did you do anything which might lead Stewart to believe that you had been corrupt or unfair in the conduct of that trial?" Pendell asked for the third time. "Of course," he added diplomatically, "we realise it would have been a misinterpretation."

"Most convicted prisoners believe their trial was unfair, Inspector. You know that as well as I do," the Judge eventually responded.

"Yes, sir. But Stewart's anger towards you appears cold and reasoned. It may well be part of the build-up for any attack on Mangan. We need to know so that we can tell the Director tomorrow when the decision of whether or not to prosecute will be made," Pendell explained.

"My conduct of Stanton's trial was exemplary," declared Vishney. "I don't want you to allow Stanton any opportunity to say anything against me personally, do you hear?"

"That will be far easier to achieve if he's charged with murder. His credibility will be undermined in the eyes of the public and, assuming he's remanded in custody, he won't get the opportunity to speak to the Press. I'm sure you follow, Sir."

"Only too well," Vishney answered. "So I trust that you will be able to find sufficient reason to charge him."

"We'll do our best. He has defied the natural process. Appointed himself as executioner. But I don't want any surprises. That's why I wanted your assurance that his accusation has no substance. You've been very helpful. Thank you for your time," Pendell responded, returning the copy of the interview to his pocket and getting up to leave.

"This Mangan fellow; who you now believe was the murderer. What's the evidence he did it?" Vishney asked nervously.

"We're not releasing any of the evidence about Mangan until after we've made our decision about whether or not to charge Stewart," Pendell replied.

"You have my word it will remain in confidence. I am a retired High Court Judge, you know," Vishney persisted.

"Very well. Mangan told Stewart that he killed Louise Donovan. He said it was an accident. Short-lived pressure on the neck in the course of sexual activity. You'll know better than us what the pathologist at trial said about the mechanics of the death. We don't have a transcript of the evidence. But, in addition to that, we recovered the pants of seven other murdered girls from Mangan's house. All murdered after Louise. And a picture of a model wearing navy blue pants in a drawer marked *Louise Donovan*. Fairly convincing, don't you think?"

Vishney sat in silence, staring at the pack of cards, ignoring Pendell and working out his next move.

Pendell left the room, but did not fully close the door and positioned himself so that he could still see the Judge. After a couple of minutes, Vishney's hand dived inside his black jacket and emerged with a small diary which he thumbed through, before moving to the desk where the telephone sat. Laying the open diary on the desk he lifted the receiver.

"Sir Eustace Vishney, Room 9. Get me 019354288," he said, obviously speaking to the Dolphin Glen operator, and then waiting in silence for the connection to be made.

"Yes. Good afternoon. Sir Eustace Vishney here. I wish to speak with Mr Maxcroft, please. Yes, certainly, I'll hang on," he said.

"Ah, Ian. Eustace here. A matter upon which I would seek your advice. That problem we had with that Chauncey fellow. Another development. A man called Mangan is suspected of the original murder. I doubt it's right. Evidence against Stanton was overwhelming. But Mangan is dead. By the hand of Stanton's son. And there's a meeting with the Director tomorrow to decide if the son should be charged with murder, which of course he should be . . . "

Pendell slipped quietly away from his listening post. He'd heard enough. When Stewart had called Vishney a corrupt bastard Pendell had been watching him like a hawk. Looking into his eyes. Stewart had some good reason for making that accusation. Listening to Vishney on the phone had confirmed Stewart's diagnosis, but Pendell enjoyed pulling the strings. Vishney's desire to suppress his secrets about his conduct of the Stanton case had just added another powerful ally to the camp in favour of prosecuting Stewart. The natural order would be restored. It would be interesting to see what tomorrow had in store.

Chapter 43

Four men and two women were seated around the mahogany boardroom table in the Director's office. A whiteboard, with blue felt tip writing still upon it from discussion about some other case, occupied half of a side wall. An easel with a flip-chart was alongside the window and the entire back wall was a brief library, consisting of shelves stacked with files, briefs tied in pink ribbon and other papers. Six cups of coffee on a tray had just been deposited on the table by a young girl who was now quietly withdrawing, closing the door behind her.

The elder of the women was at the head of the table. Iron grey hair. Austere. Unsmiling. Unmarried, judging by the left hand, and as sensitive as a witch's broomstick.

"As you know, I'm Winifred Drew. Under the Director's protocol my department is authorised to make the decision of whether or not to institute proceedings in this case and many sensitive cases," she declared dryly, her eyes moving from one person to the next as she weighed up the likely formations of alliances. "It would be sensible for everyone to introduce themselves," she continued, nodding firstly in the direction of Colley to whom she had already spoken on the phone.

"Detective Chief Inspector Nicholas Colley, Senior Investigating Officer in the arrest of Stewart and the death of Mangan," he announced.

"Detective Inspector Joseph Pendell. Second-in-command to Mr Colley."

"Detective Chief Inspector Bill Tedstone. Officer in charge of the Diane Pierce murder which we now know was committed by Mangan. I've also spoken with Superintendent Ruskett who can't be here this morning. As you all know, he's taken overall charge of all the Mangan murders."

"I'm from Harlow's local Prosecuting Office" the other female stated. A small lady, shapeless hair style, tortoiseshell glasses which didn't suit her and a noticeable moustache. "I'm the Senior Solicitor there and my name is Margaret Blick."

All eyes turned to the remaining male at the table. Only Winifred Drew knew who he was. An enormous barrel-chested hulk of a man. Probably six foot seven. Sandy, thinning hair. Freckled skin and broad, ugly nose with the kind of nostrils that angle themselves for internal inspection. "Ian Maxcroft," he announced loudly. "National Policy Department. Based at the Metropolitan Police."

The hint of a smile appeared at the corners of Pendell's mouth and then quickly evaporated.

Behind Winifred Drew, in a chair right up against the wall, sat another man. Grey suit. Grey hair in strands flat across his head. Glasses. Pale, smooth skin. Silent. He never introduced himself. He never spoke. Never moved. But everybody knew who he was. Downing Street was institutionally incapable of keeping its fingers out of any pie.

"We've all been given a copy of the report compiled so helpfully by Detective Inspector Pendell. So I believe we can immediately get down to the making of actual decisions. Perhaps you would therefore start us off Inspector, by summarising any evidence which exists against Stewart of any offence," Winifred Drew suggested, producing a fountain pen from her plain, brown handbag and pulling off its cap.

"He broke into Mangan's house. Armed with a tyre lever," Pendell began. "Mangan had bruising to the groin, his ribs were extensively broken on both sides, probably by kicks, his right elbow and forearm were smashed and the left eye was so badly gouged that the eyeball was probably beyond repair. Those injuries would have rendered him completely incapable of representing a threat to a five year old child, let alone a young man of Stewart's physical characteristics. Then his skull was caved in with the tyre lever. Dead on the spot. I would therefore suggest that he is charged with murder."

"You said that the skull was 'caved in'. It was a compound, depressed fracture at the side of the skull, wasn't it?" Tedstone asked.

"I've seen the skull," Pendell replied tersely. "On the pathologist's slab. Looked like a walnut. After you've stamped on it."

"How are you able to suggest that the skull fracture came last in time?" Drew enquired.

"The pathologist can't say," Colley intervened.

"No," Pendell responded. "But what she can say, and she's the best neuro-pathologist in the business, is that the skull fracture was a catastrophic event. It terminated life there and then. So either Stewart carried on gouging an eye, fracturing ribs, an elbow and an arm on a corpse, or the blow to the skull was delivered last. On a defenceless man. A jury's entitled to conclude that it was the latter scenario."

"But how can you know that, for example, he didn't inflict some of the injuries and then deliver the blow to the head and then, within a second or two, inflict the rest?" Tedstone persisted.

"A jury would be entitled to look at the whole picture and conclude that Mangan was kicked in the groin, had his eye gouged, his arm smashed, went down, ribs kicked and then, lying defenceless, Stewart finished him off. You've read our interview of him. He wouldn't answer our questions on that main issue. Jury'll know why he didn't answer," Pendell insisted.

"Because he did just what Inspector Pendell has analysed," offered Margaret Blick.

"What about the dreadful injuries that Stewart suffered?" Winifred Drew asked. "Aren't they powerful evidence Stewart was defending himself against a lethal attack?"

"We don't know who the knife belonged to," Pendell replied. "It was a vicious weapon. Could've been Stewart's. But, to be fair, it's far more likely to have been Mangan's. So you're right, Stewart was probably defending himself against an armed attack. But he won the fight. And then took the Law into his own hands and became Judge and jury."

"I'd like to say something, ma'am," Colley interposed. "Inspector Pendell is probably right in his analysis. But we have to live in the real world here. Mangan was a homicidal maniac. His crimes are grotesque. We've all read Mr Tedstone's report on the Pierce murder. A jury is not going to want to convict anyone of murder when Mangan was the victim. Let alone Stewart. Whose father was hanged for one of Mangan's murders. And when Stewart was himself seriously injured."

"Hear, hear," said Tedstone.

"But isn't our duty to prevent people, whatever the horrendous background, from taking the Law into their own hands? The sympathy may go to Stewart one hundred percent. But the Law is against him. A Judge would have to tell the jury that," reasoned Winifred Drew.

"Exactly," Pendell agreed. "Legal process. Not vigilante revenge."

"And," interposed Margaret Blick, "if the jury thought that the provocation that led Stewart to deliver that final, fatal blow was so intense, then they could find him not guilty of murder but guilty of manslaughter."

"Just what I was thinking," Drew nodded. "In the end this is a decision for my department. But I am very keen to take your opinions into account. Shall we go round the table and see where we are?"

"Before we do," said Colley, "you state that the ultimate decision is for your department. But what about Prosecuting Counsel's opinion?"

"Mr Colley. Times have changed," Drew retorted. "The balance of power has shifted. Barristers want our briefs. We'd listen to any advice Prosecuting Counsel offered at trial, but we make the decision as to whether to charge or not. Do you agree, Margaret?"

"Oh, yes," Blick agreed, beads of perspiration now glinting within the fine hairs of her moustache.

"Right," said Pendell. "I would propose that he be prosecuted for murder."

"So would I," said Blick.

"And I would not," Tedstone responded. "He killed a killer. Let common sense prevail."

"I'm afraid I have to disagree with my own Inspector," Colley said slowly. "I think Mr Tedstone has summed this case up in four words. 'Let common sense prevail.' Let the lad go back to Australia. Close the book on this whole dreadful business. The Law let Stanton down and let all of Mangan's victims down. Let's not start preaching about the Law as a reason for prosecuting a young man whose father we wrongly hanged."

"That just leaves you, Mr Maxcroft," observed Winifred Drew, as all eyes turned to the giant who had not, as yet, uttered a word.

"Without the Law we are nothing. Public policy is involved here. If we don't prosecute him it sends out a message. Official approval of lynch mob justice. My Policy Unit bases all of its decisions on the Law. Stewart should be prosecuted for murder," Maxcroft declared.

"Very well, thank you all very much," said Winifred Drew, rising from her chair to signify that the meeting was over. "My department will contact you individually by two o' clock this afternoon with our decision. Whatever we decide, Mr Colley, the details of the Mangan murders and the enquiry can no longer be withheld from the Press. I suggest you arrange a news conference for late afternoon."

"I agree, ma'am," Colley replied. "We'll provide all relevant information and I'll incorporate your department's decision into that release."

As the various participants left the room, the grey man, Donald Castleton, got up from his chair and came over to the table where Winifred Drew had now re-seated herself and was filling a glass with water from the carafe.

"Prosecute him," he ordered. "For murder. To be tried at the Old Bailey. Before Mr Justice Froyd."

"Of course," Winifred Drew replied with a hollow smile. "Did you ever think I actually cared what any of them had to say? Really, Donald, I had hoped that you knew me better than that."

Chapter 44

Uniformed officers brought him in a police van with blacked out windows. Packs of press photographers were milling about outside the massive solid metal gates that led into the yard at the back of the Magistrates Court. They jostled each other and leaped in the air like desperate salmon hurtling upstream to press their lenses against the tinted window in the hope they'd got a shot, but Cal was seated on the hard bench with his head between his knees so that there was no prospect of them getting anything worthwhile. The officers escorted him in handcuffs across the yard and into the cell area. The smell of burned sausage and reheated bacon floated along the passageway as the prison staff ostensibly prepared breakfast for their incarcerated guests but, in fact, wolfed most of it down themselves. As he was led to a cell of his own, other prisoners stared at him through the bars. They knew exactly who he was. There is no better process of communication than between men who are caged. Cal was profoundly angry but also afraid. He was still weak from his injuries, on medication and with little strength in his left hand. If he ran into trouble with other prisoners he would be easy meat. Yesterday, when Oliver Newcombe had come to tell him that they had decided to charge him with murder he had been sick. Pendell had sent in a bucket and mop and told him to clean it up himself and then walked him to the Custody Sergeant's desk and charged him with murder.

Declining the offer of any breakfast he accepted a warm, weak cup of tea out of a chewed, yellow plastic cup. Two hours passed. At least he had a cell to himself and he lay on the hard, wooden slats in the same position that thousands of other incarcerated souls must have done over the years. Only the faces changed. The theme stayed constant. The frailties of Man.

When they led him along the passageways, up the stairs and into the raised dock in the middle of the Courtroom, he blinked in the sunlight pouring through the skylights and gazed ahead at a sombre figure on the Bench, dressed in an ordinary suit. Recognising the back of Oliver Newcombe's head, seated in the front row, he then saw Pendell, standing with his back against the wall, staring at him, distaste and superiority written all over his face. This was the arena in which Pendell could really deploy his power. He could try to get him remanded in custody until the trial which could be months later.

As Cal attuned to the light and atmosphere, he turned to look behind him. That was where the public were accommodated and the gawpers and ghouls had queued up for seats. The story had been plastered all over the papers and television ever since Colley's press conference yesterday afternoon. But Cal didn't really take any notice of them because his eyes had been transfixed on the lovely looking girl in the middle of the front row. It was the first time he'd seen George since leaving her ill in bed on that fateful morning, seemingly so long ago. How he longed to walk over and hold her. Tell her that everything would be alright. Tell her how much he loved her. But iron bars separated them. He felt belittled. Humiliated. As if he was some wild animal that could not be trusted to have any contact with civilised society.

George was trying to smile, but she was crying. Her eyes were already red, her cheeks were pale. Perhaps it was his imagination, but she looked thinner and smaller and so vulnerable. Half-lifting his hand to acknowledge her, the Dock Officer tugged him round to face to the front as his name was called. As he turned he suddenly realised who was sitting next to George, staring earnestly at him. It was Tony Medina, his doughty opponent from Chiltern Hills Golf Club. The charge of murder was read out to him and then he was told to be seated. A woman sitting on the same row as Newcombe introduced herself to the Court as Margaret Blick and asked for the case to be committed for trial at the Old Bailey and for the prisoner to be remanded until then in custody. She called Detective Inspector Pendell into the witness box and he took the oath before reciting to the Magistrate that the Defendant was viewed as determined and dangerous, having come from Australia on a mission of revenge, with no known ties to this country and therefore presenting a high risk of absconding.

Oliver Newcombe protested loudly, clearly and eloquently, requesting that Cal should be admitted to bail. He answered all of Pendell's objections and handed in a written list of conditions that could be attached to bail, including living at George's, the surrender of his passport, daily reporting at a police station and sureties that could be provided. Thirty seconds after Newcombe sat down, Cal was being pushed back down the dock steps into the cells below. Remanded in custody. Next case.

They took him to a prison somewhere in Oxfordshire. In the middle of nowhere. The reception procedure felt more intrusive than the surgeon's scalpel. On the first day he was held on the wing which contained other men facing murder charges. Most of them smelled. Most of them were either dangerous or psychologically damaged or both. They all knew who he was. But none of them were hostile to him. The very reverse. His extermination of Mangan had gained the Murderers' Union seal of approval. Whilst it was a relief not to be on permanent guard against inmate attack, which was the lot of most prisoners, their endorsement of his actions unnerved him. Given his own cell, he was trying to adjust for the first time in his life, to the night-time sounds of a man's prison, bursting at the seams, full of foul odours, pungent chemical disinfectants, screaming, expletives and an overall aura of menace.

Suddenly, in the middle of the night, it felt as if Mangan had plunged his blade back into the abdominal wound and he cried out for help. It didn't come very quickly, but when it did, they acted with efficiency. He was taken immediately to the hospital wing, a prison doctor was summoned, the sodden dressing over the suppurating abdominal wound was removed and he was immediately driven to the local hospital. The wound had become infected. His low, depressed state had weakened his resistance. The wound was cleaned. He was put on intravenous drips and told that he would remain in the hospital for at least seventy-two hours. His right wrist was handcuffed to the iron bed head and, eventually, he fell asleep.

Five days later he was back in prison and, at least physically, he was feeling much better. At two o'clock in the afternoon, an officer came to his cell and told him he was wanted in the Visitors' Area. They kept him for half an hour in a holding room. They put an orange bib over his neck with a number on the front and back. He was number eighteen. Then, the double doors opened and he walked into a large hall. There were twenty tables, each with a number painted on the table-top and with four chairs around each table. Three of the chairs were yellow. For visitors. The fourth was purple. For the prisoner. On a yellow chair alongside table eighteen was George. He hurried towards her, arms outstretched but, as she rose from her chair, a female prison officer with thighs and a rear end that would have done credit to a front-row forward, appeared from nowhere and stood in between them. "No touching. At any time. Or I terminate the visit," she barked. George sank back on to the hard, yellow chair and Cal, deflated and humiliated, averted his eyes and lowered himself on to the purple seat.

"It's like a nightmare," said George. "But I have to say something to you immediately. Oliver Newcombe warned me that when the police have a weak case and there's a lot riding on it they often bug prison visits."

"You mean we're probably being recorded?" Cal responded incredulously. "They'd go that far?"

"Almost certainly, Oliver said under no circumstances were we to talk about the facts of the case. They'd trawl through the tapes afterwards and if ever you'd said anything that might damage you, then they'd use it."

"I don't want to talk about the case anyway, George. We both know that Mangan was a psychopathic murderer who tried to kill me and I defended myself, there's not much more to say is there? It's you I want to talk about. How are you bearing up?" he asked.

"It's been quite dreadful," she responded. "It's been all over the papers. On the TV. They did a poll. Eighty three percent of the people say you should never have been prosecuted."

"But there's only twelve that matter, aren't there? And we won't know who they are until the trial starts. Are you keeping up with work?" he enquired. "You don't look too clever."

"I'm coping. But it's a nightmare. I'm so ashamed that our country can treat you like this."

"You don't upset the British Establishment without paying a price," he replied. "We're paying it. Both of us. Big time."

"They only returned the Mercedes to me yesterday," she complained. "Said it had to be scientifically examined. They found it within an hour of the fight. You had the keys in your pocket with the registration number on the key ring. And they've deliberately held on to it until yesterday."

"That'll be Pendell's doing," he told her. "The one you saw in Court claiming I'd run away back to Australia. He's been a bastard from the very beginning. Obsessed with order and control."

At the next table a child was causing a disturbance, running round the chairs and trying to sit on the inmate father's lap. The woman from Stalag 4 reappeared and delivered a final warning.

"How are you surviving in here? With all this pond life," George asked, looking round at the selection of murderers, rapists and burglars.

"The regime strips you of all dignity and all privacy," he explained. "That's hell to deal with. But the other inmates don't bother me. I'm approved of. There was a worry that the Creanes might have someone in here with a brief to do me over. But I've been told they've checked it out and there's not a problem."

"What's the timetable?" she enquired.

"It's in for Plea and Directions next week. I'll have a QC appointed by then. And he'll make another application for bail. Oliver said the chances are better before the Trial Judge than they were before the Stipendiary Magistrate, who wouldn't have the bottle to stand up to Pendell."

"About the QC. I spoke to Tim Sprackley. He gave me some names. I've sent them to Oliver's office. I'm going to speak to mother tonight about raising the money to pay . . . "

"No. No," he interrupted. "I don't want you paying. Oliver says I'll get Legal Aid."

"But then you won't get the best QC," she retorted.

"Let's see what kind of job he does when he applies for bail next week, then we can make an informed judgement", he suggested.

"OK. Now one other thing about Tim," she said tentatively.

"What?"

"He told me that it is a racing certainty that your father's case will be listed in the Court of Appeal very quickly and that the appeal will be immediately allowed. He said that the Prosecution will not resist it and that the authorities will want it hurried through in an attempt to minimise the fall-out," she explained.

"We want the truth spelled out. Not some fast-tracked whitewash," he retorted angrily.

"Tim says we'll have no control over when it's listed and it will be soon. But we need a barrister to do it who will be prepared to spell it all out. The truth about Vishney, Hollister, Lancaster. He said the

Appeal Court Judges will try to suppress most of that and that some barristers, even a QC, might give up. Not wanting to offend the Establishment. Their own careers to think of and all of that kind of stuff."

"So who do we get?" he asked

"Him," she replied nervously. "He's desperate to do it."

"Tim? He's a lovely man, George. But he's kind and gentle. I'm afraid he's ineffectual," he responded, not wanting to hurt her feelings.

"Well, we're going to spend the rest of this visit discussing that, Cal. It'll be your call in the end but I want you to hear me out."

"OK. OK," he smiled. "Let's talk it through."

Chapter 45

At the Plea and Directions hearing at the Old Bailey, Mr Justice Froyd, who had been allocated the trial, was unable to attend. His trial at Winchester had overrun by several days and therefore, for the purpose of this formal hearing only, the case had been transferred to another High Court Judge who worked on the overriding principle that no-one, but no-one, was ever entitled to bail if they were on a murder charge. He dismissed every argument of Charles Purmort QC, recently instructed by Oliver Newcombe as Cal's Leading Counsel, with a shake of the head and a muttering of "not on a murder charge."

The hearing of the appeal against Cal's father's conviction had, just as Tim Sprackley had predicted, been expedited and was due to be heard in ten days time. Purmort argued weakly that Cal must be allowed to attend that hearing, even if it meant that bail should be allowed for just those few hours. "Not on a murder charge," came the repost. The last throw of the dice was that Cal should be taken to the Court of Appeal in custody so that he could be present. The Judge was not interested. Purmort gave up too soon. The hearing was a complete disaster. George was in tears. Purmort sent a message to the cells that he would come to the prison and discuss matters in detail the day after the appeal. Oliver Newcombe was furious. Cal sent a message back to Purmort that he wasn't up to it and he didn't want him to do the trial. Detective Inspector Pendell looked on and smiled. The natural order was being restored.

Chapter 46

Heavy oak walls lined with law reports up to the ceiling. Microphones dangling from wires for the barristers. A caged but empty dock pinned on a side wall like a box at the theatre, although the usual occupants were seldom given to applause. At the far end, three thrones, high on a giant platform, from where the Appeal Judges could look down at the advocate targets and decide whether to snipe with single shots or open up with a full machine-gun barrage.

The public sat behind the barristers and solicitors in long rows of hard, creaking seats, invariably overawed by the clinical aura of remote, dispassionate iciness that the courtroom engendered. The fabric of this place had absorbed tragedy, death, injustice, insanity, and every known frailty of the human condition, producing an atmosphere of stillness and hopelessness.

When the three Appeal Judges entered the room and were helped on to their thrones by a clerk each, all movement stopped, all voices were rendered mute and it was as if creatures from an alien planet had descended to declare whether earthlings should perish or survive. The acute intelligence from the three pulsating brains lasered down in one direction, poised either to deliver ten thousand volts into the barrister's heart or to spare him.

Tim Sprackley had earned a decent living at the Bar, but he'd never really quite made it. The big cases had always slipped away. He didn't have the killer instinct. Despite his shortcomings, George had won the argument at the prison visit discussion with Cal. She had promised faithfully that she would report back to Cal every detail of what happened and every nuance of how Sprackley did his stuff. He had been Frederick Walgrave's trusted colleague and friend and was the closest they could get to Frederick conducting the appeal himself.

He adored George and had done everything he could to support her in her pursuit of the truth, even during the days of darkness.

Of course, this was an appeal against conviction which he could not lose. The Prosecution had no basis on which they could or would resist the appeal. There was powerful evidence in Mangan's shrine that he was the killer. Sprackley's brief was to make sure that he exposed in public the other sinister dimensions of the Stanton trial. The actions of Neville Hollister in contacting Vishney, the deliberate appointment by Vishney of inexperienced defence counsel and the race to conviction, the failures of the police and the recent refusal of the Home Office to act on the racist bigotry of the jury foreman. Sprackley's battle would be with the Judges who would seek to sideline those issues and simply allow the appeal on the basis that the chance discovery of Mangan's shrine undermined what had otherwise seemed to be a justified conviction.

The public gallery and Press benches were packed to the rafters. George was two rows behind Sprackley, with Oliver Newcombe to her left and Tony Medina to her right. In the back row sat Mark Gevinson and Mitchell Ormsby. In the row immediately behind Counsel was a young girl, shorthand notebook and pencil poised, despatched by Ian Maxcroft to get a record of everything that was said, both for his own purposes and to provide a copy for Sir Eustace Vishney, presently sitting in the window at Dolphin Glen, keenly aware of events in The Royal Courts of Justice and terrified of what may be said.

Lord Justice Sellister, in his black robes, was the central commander. A double first from Cambridge, Law and Mathematics. A brilliant commercial practice. Overtly disdainful of anyone whose intelligence did not reside in the stratosphere and a slavish defender of the system. He loved English Law. It was his life. It was as near perfect as the human condition would allow. Of course, very occasionally, mistakes would happen. Always for a reason that no system could really have seen at the time. Defender of the Establishment. Today's target? Some lanky barrister who he'd never heard of before. Not even a QC. Obviously never really had it and, whatever he might have had, now past it.

Under his wig, Sprackley's lugubrious face looked more apprehensive than ever and his brush moustache twitched with nerves. Sellister's milky blue, unblinking eyes peered at him through rimless glasses, weighing him up at turbo speed and concluding that a single bullet should take him out.

"Mr Sprackley, we have been informed in writing that the Prosecution do not intend to resist this appeal. The evidence against the Appellant in 1963 must have appeared very compelling. An unfortunate and almost unforeseeable error has occurred. That is your case isn't it?" Sellister declared.

"No, My Lord. Our case is that the trial that led to the Appellant's execution was corrupt, inept, biased and an outrage," Sprackley responded, his words delivered in his dry, clipped voice, but reverberating around the Court like static electricity.

George nudged Oliver Newcombe and whispered excitedly to him, "This is it. Tim's going to produce the performance of his life. I told Cal that I thought the miracle might just happen."

"Emotive words, Mr Sprackley but are they not rather wide of the mark?" Sellister snapped back, unable to control the irritation in his voice. "The lower underwear of the victim was found in the Appellant's saddlebag. In the event, another explanation emerged many years later but, at the time, seemingly potent evidence of guilt."

"With respect, Your Lordship is overlooking the fact that significant white marks on the victim's wrists and neck were never investigated. If they had been, a potential link to Mangan would have been disclosed at that time. Further, Your Lordship is ignoring the role of the Trial

Judge in the charade of a trial that took place and the fact that the jury foreman shared the same moral principles as the Grand Wizard of the Ku Klux Klan."

George heard her own intake of breath and a few heads turned to see from whom it had come. After a professional lifetime of unrelenting ordinariness, Tim Sprackley's moment had come. He was riding his stallion over the prairie, out of the stirrups, hair flowing in the wind, young again, heart bursting with the sheer joy of being alive and no force in the world was going to stop him. It was as if he had been born for this minute, to carry the standard of Frederick Walgrave and Henry Stanton into battle and slay the enemy massed on the far side of the hill.

"I do not approve of that kind of analogy, Mr Sprackley," the Lord Justice replied, coating every syllable with judicial venom.

"Mr Stanton's case is that he did not approve of being hanged for a crime he did not commit, My Lord. I respectfully submit that is rather more important than any choice of analogy," Sprackley retorted.

Although the rest of the Courtroom was in total silence, every time Tim Sprackley hit back at the Judge the air was filled with silent cheering. It was tangible. The people knew that they were witnessing a momentous event. A terrible injustice had been done. The two men who had suffered the most were now both dead. But their ghosts were here. In this Courtroom. And a quiet, diffident, ordinary man had become, for these unique few moments, their champion, soaring to heights that, until this very second, he himself had never realised he could reach. To stop this latest Establishment creature on the Bench from suppressing the enormity of the wrong that had been done. To stand up to him. Sprackley's gown had become the cape of Superman. Sprackley was invincible.

"The public should know, My Lord that Mr Stanton was of coloured extraction. That the jury foreman was an active member of an extremist party and vowed to see Mr Stanton convicted because of his colour. The public should know that Mr Justice Vishney was in direct contact with the father of an important potential witness with a highly relevant secret about the . . ." Sprackley continued.

"Enough, Mr Sprackley," a booming baritone voice bellowed from the Judge on the right. "How dare you attack a retired Judge, unable to defend himself and on such spurious grounds. You know your appeal is going to be allowed. You will leave it at that."

"No, My Lord. With respect, it cannot be left at that. Mr Justice Vishney is still alive. Mr Stanton is not. It is Mr Stanton who cannot defend himself and rail about spurious grounds for being wrongly convicted of murder. It is Mr Stanton who cannot shout from the roof tops that the Judge who ordered him to be hanged by the neck until he was dead had deliberately chosen a young inexperienced barrister, without a solicitor or QC, to defend him."

Despite herself, the tears were running down George's face. Tim Sprackley was inspired. He was flying. He was at the pinnacle. He was unstoppable.

A thin whining voice emerged from the Judge on the left. "Mr Peere-Havingham," he intoned in the direction of Counsel for the Prosecution. "Would you please state publicly the Crown's position on this appeal."

A short man, rather too heavy for his height, but with an open face and lively eyes pulled himself to his feet. How he had enjoyed Sprackley's tour de force. He'd never met him before, but the enormity of what had happened to Sprackley in these few moments was not lost on Nigel Peere-Havingham QC. After this was over, he intended to take Sprackley across the Strand to his club and share a bottle of champagne.

"The Crown's position, My Lord? Certainly," Peere-Havingham replied. "We do not resist the appeal. Mr Stanton was wrongly convicted. It should never have happened. Not only do we not resist the appeal, we support it. As Leading Counsel for the Crown, I support every word that my learned friend, Mr Sprackley has uttered. Every word. Can I be of further assistance, My Lord?"

No-one spoke. The two Judges on the sides got up, gathered around the Lord Justice of Appeal's throne, conferred in whispers for a couple of moments and then resumed their seats. Lord Justice Sellister cleared his throat.

"This appeal of Henry Francis Stanton against a conviction for murder in 1963 will be allowed. The conviction emanated from an unfortunate evidential error. The conviction will be quashed. A full Judgement will be delivered at some later date."

"Court rise," called the usher, as the Judges filed solemnly out.

Tim Sprackley lay back in his seat, his eyes directed upwards to where he knew Fred Walgrave was watching. He was shaking, but he was fulfilled.

With the Judges now gone, a short, dark-complexioned man with brown curly hair, twinkling eyes, a cheeky face and the shoulders of a barn door, sitting towards the back of the gallery, began to clap and, in an instant, the whole Courtroom was applauding and cheering Sprackley, none more enthusiastically than Nigel Peere-Havingham. He realised, like George, that he had witnessed a miracle.

Chapter 47

The following day Oliver Newcombe arrived at the prison for a conference. Passing through the tedious security procedures he eventually arrived in the small conference room where Cal had been placed to await his visit. News of the momentous events of the previous day in the Court of Appeal had already been relayed to Cal in the telephone call he had been allowed to make to an elated George last evening and his mood was sky high when Newcombe bustled through the door. But before Cal could even begin to discuss the Court of Appeal hearing with Newcombe another figure materialised from nowhere and sat himself straight down at the table.

"This is Mr Bahr," said Newcombe. "He's the replacement for Charles Purmort QC."

Bahr was dark complexioned with brown curly hair, short in stature, brown twinkling eyes, quite handsome in a cheeky sort of way, broad-shouldered, probably forty-five and exuding self-confidence.

"I'm Mickey Bahr," he announced loudly. "I'm not a QC. I was born and brought up in Hackney. I can turn a cockney accent on and off like a tap, and I do, depending on who I'm talking to. I didn't go to university. I qualified by going to Law College while I worked in the fish market. They'll never make me a QC because I never give up and can be quite insufferable. Most Judges hate me because I won't stand for being pushed around. I'll defend you with everything I've got. Oh, and most important of all, the reason I'm here is because I've been friendly with Tony Medina since we were boys. He knows how good I am. And he's paying my fee which, I hasten to add, is very considerable," he concluded, pausing momentarily for breath.

"If you noticed, George had sat next to Mr Medina at Harlow Magistrates Court and got in touch with him as soon as we decided that Mr Purmort was not suitable for this case," Newcombe explained.

"Bloody hell," said Cal. "What a speech. But don't you know that this whole sorry story started when a barrister who was not a QC was thrown into a murder case which ended in tragedy?"

"Of course I know. I've read all the papers. And where do you think I was yesterday? Watching a soccer match? In the pub? No! I was in the Court of Appeal. Cheering for Sprackley, God bless him. I know all about Vishney. You're frightened of history repeating itself, are you?"

"Wouldn't you be?"

"Of course. But do you know what the other barristers call me? Mickey Crowbar. You've met Tony Medina. We're the same breed. Would you like him at your shoulder when the going got rough?" asked Bahr.

"Yes," Cal replied without hesitating.

"Well, I'm his choice. I won't be offended if you want a QC. The Prosecution'll have one for sure. Take me or leave me. It's the market place. You're the punter," said Bahr.

"I'll take you," Cal replied immediately.

"Right, let's get down to business," Bahr declared, swinging his briefcase up on to the table and unloading the papers from within. Cal could see that yellow highlighting appeared everywhere, copious notes were written neatly in the margins and, when Bahr produced his blue Counsel's notebook, it was already completely filled with handwritten notes in a beautiful hand.

"You've got nice writing for a fish porter," Cal observed.

"Don't be fooled, Mr Stewart. I might have a lot of front. But I learned early on that froth wasn't enough. Tony taught me that. Substance was needed. Writing nicely, reading extensively and working like a Trojan. Those are the kind of things that really matter. Now, to business," Bahr announced decisively, "I'm going to start with the question that you're never going to answer. When did you hit him with the tyre lever?"

"After he'd . . ." Cal began.

"No, no, no," Bahr interrupted. "Listen to me. That's the question you're never going to answer. Do you understand? Never. You'll be asked it a dozen times. You're never going to answer."

"So what do I say?" Cal asked.

"You're a bright fella, I can see that. "You've got a brain. You solved eight murders in a few weeks. The police hadn't solved any of them in twenty seven years. So use your brain. Whatever words you like. But you never answer that question. If you do, you'll be convicted of murder," Bahr stated grimly.

"And then what would happen?" Cal enquired.

"You'd get life imprisonment. You'd serve a minimum of twelve years, maybe more," came the sharp answer.

Cal remained silent.

"Mr Newcombe gave you sound advice at the very beginning of all this," Bahr continued. "You have to get over the message that you were in a life and death confrontation. Against a man with a lethal knife. You knew he had killed eight people. You knew he was trying to kill you and very nearly did. All you can remember is a pitched battle. Who did what and when and how . . . all of that detail . . . you can't possibly say. You fought for your life. One of you was going to come out dead. Tell the jury that. Keep telling them that. Whatever the Judge says or does, keep telling them that. Whatever Prosecution Counsel asks or suggests, keep telling them that. You get my drift?" he grinned.

"I'm beginning to," Cal replied.

"Had you better explain about manslaughter, Mr Bahr?" Newcombe asked. "He needs to understand that very clearly."

"Yes. Your defence is that you were defending yourself. If you were, then you're not guilty of murder or manslaughter, you walk," Bahr explained carefully.

"And what if the jury decide a stage was reached where Mangan was beaten and I was no longer defending myself?" Cal asked.

"That's murder," replied Bahr. "But murder can be reduced to manslaughter if the jury think you may have been provoked."

"What does that actually mean?" Cal enquired.

"That Mangan's previous murders, and then his attack on you, so provoked you that you lost your self control and so would any reasonable person in your position. That's manslaughter," Bahr explained.

"Is that a possibility in this case?"

"Yes. It is," Bahr answered directly.

"And how long would I get?"

"Four or five years," came the immediate reply. "Better than murder, though."

"I don't want to serve one day for that bastard," Cal told him. "It's bad enough I'm in custody at all."

"I agree," Bahr nodded, "and I do have some better news for you about that. The case has been given a date. Your trial starts in eight weeks time. I can assure you that is very fast indeed."

"Why is it being heard so quickly?"

"Because they want it over and done with. The public has a short memory. This case is a major embarrassment to them. You heard what happened in the Court of Appeal yesterday. They want the whole thing dead and buried. Preferably with you having been convicted of murder. Don't take the Law into your own hands. Look what happens. Now let's move on. That's the best damage limitation as they see it," Bahr explained patiently.

"OK, I understand. So eight weeks to the final showdown. I can handle that. I'll be fully recovered by then as well. What do you know about this Judge they've appointed? Froyd."

"I could say a lot. I've had battles with him before. Best way I can put it is, if you had a choice between being tried by Vishney and Froyd, then you'd choose Vishney," Bahr declared.

"So we've got a real battle on our hands," Cal concluded.

"To the death," Bahr replied. "But you're good at that type of battle. You certainly won your last one."

"This time I'll need help," Cal observed ruefully.

"And you've got it," Newcombe intervened. "Mr Bahr is obviously a fighter."

"But is he a winner?" Cal asked.

Bahr pretended that he wasn't listening and made some more notes in his book. For all of his self-confidence, he was worried. The kid had had a raw deal. Learning about his father as he had. Tracking down and confronting a psychopathic crazy and then ending up in the dock. He was personable and honest. Too honest. All the ingredients of a disaster. And Bahr liked him. Liking a client was dangerous. The whole case was dangerous. But, like he'd said at the beginning, he'd defend with everything he'd got. He only hoped he'd got enough.

Chapter 48

Eight weeks may be a relatively short time to arrange the logistics of a murder trial, but for Cal and George it still seemed like an eternity. She was beginning to let some of the farmers down, not keeping appointments and becoming distracted. Whilst her mother was relieved and happy at the eventual success of the appeal, she remained extremely concerned that her daughter was obviously in a relationship with a man who was languishing in prison, awaiting trial on a murder charge. Ever since Cal had arrived at the farm she had feared a disaster and had deliberately kept her distance from him. Now that George would have welcomed her support, she remained remote.

As Cal was a remand prisoner, he was allowed daily visits and his visitors were allowed to bring food into the prison for him. The prison food was disgusting and he desperately needed a balanced and nutritious diet to assist in the long journey back to health after his injuries. The prison authorities had no interest in any of that at all. So George had driven cross-country from Somerset to Oxfordshire daily, carrying high protein and high carbohydrate meals for him, then battling through the prison security procedures which sometimes took an hour to get through, surrounded by women with tattoos, screaming kids, body odour and foul mouths. Their common denominator was that they had a man locked up inside.

After a week of it, she was exhausted and Cal could see the deterioration. Moreover, despite what he felt for her, he detected that the strain was so intense that the relationship was suffering. She had lost weight, she wasn't sleeping and black shadows had appeared under her eyes. So Cal told her she must reduce her visits to once a week. Although she challenged him, her resistance was so low that she surrendered and they reached a compromise. George would arrange a support unit of people to visit. On Wednesdays, Cal spent the day in the hospital wing, having his injuries checked and doing extensive physiotherapy so he was content that no-one should visit that day. Therefore, to arrange one person for each of the other days of the week, George would need to find five volunteers.

As soon as she got home she telephoned Tony Medina. Within ten minutes he had called her back saying that he, Mark Gevinson and Mitchell Ormsby would cover a day each. Mickey Bahr and Oliver Newcombe would do another day and work on the case with Cal. She was only one short. Easy. She phoned Tim Sprackley. Two minutes later she had the full team. Together they would see Cal through. Together they would fight.

Chapter 49

Vespasian Froyd became a Law Lord and sat in the House of Lords for eleven years. Given that his father had saddled him with the name of a Roman Emperor, Vespasian had little hesitation in imposing the same absurdity on his own son, and, just as the real Emperor Flavius Vespasian had done in AD 39, Lord Vespasian Froyd called his son Titus.

Emperor Titus had ruled the Romans at the time that Mount Vesuvius erupted, destroying Pompeii and Herculaneum, and Titus Froyd was just as capable of volcanic eruption as Vesuvius. Emperor Titus was also renowned for holding some of the most expensive and spectacular gladiatorial games in the history of Rome. That was exactly how Titus Froyd saw his Court. A battle between gladiators. Where the Prosecution was the gladiator, the defence was the Christian slave and Titus Froyd was the Emperor with the ultimate power of life or death, depending on which way he pointed his thumb.

In some respects he was a good Judge. Really serious criminals had little chance of escaping conviction in his Court, and he had been entrusted with several high profile trials in recent years, every one resulting in a conviction which had no chance of being overturned on appeal. However, in certain other respects, he was an appalling Judge. He viewed himself as being bigger than the process itself, he lacked the ability to distinguish between the dolt and the villain, he viewed the fact that a man was in the dock as conclusive evidence of guilt and he treated defence barristers like lepers. Moreover, having a father as a Law Lord had instilled in him an overriding sense of protection of the system and the majesty of Law.

Nevertheless, Downing Street believed in never leaving matters to chance and, a week before the trial, Donald Castleton had been despatched to ensure that the objective was completely understood. They had arranged to meet at six o'clock by Henry Moore's carving of *Three Standing Figures* in Battersea Park, which fitted in very well with the Judge's pre-dinner walk, taking him from his house in Cheyne Walk, across Albert Bridge and directly into the Park.

From the bridge, Froyd spotted two cormorants and a grebe, also enjoying the early evening air and then walked past the black walnut trees and the Kentucky coffee trees, before slowly making his way to what he considered to be yet another example of grotesque modern sculpture. He also viewed Donald Castleton as grotesque, the face of politicians' insidious invasion of the Law, but he recognised that one word from Castleton into the ear of his Masters, changed careers, both political and judicial.

As the Moore monstrosity loomed into view he espied Castleton sitting on a bench with his briefcase neatly on his lap. Wearing a grey overcoat, a knitted grey scarf, grey woollen gloves, grey trousers, grey socks and black shoes. 'Same standard of artistic flair as Moore', the Judge thought to himself as he approached the bench and sat down alongside Castleton. Whereas Castleton was slight and anonymous, Froyd was large, red-faced, heavy-featured with a shock of black hair to which he applied daily generous amounts of Grecian hair colouring. Extreme vanity was yet another of Froyd's failings. These two stalwarts of the British Establishment had conducted other such meetings in the past in similar anonymous locations. Thereafter the case had always ended successfully. This was just another in the chain. There was no need to beat about the bush.

"About the Stewart case, Judge," Castleton began. "The Appeal Court hearing last week turned into a disaster. There is a great deal of anger at the way it was conducted. It's already been decided that Peere-Havingham will never be briefed for the Prosecution again."

"It wasn't him. It was the Defence Counsel. Never even heard of him.

He ran riot. Sellister lost control. Sellister was shafted," Froyd retorted, "He's not up to it any longer. Time for a change, don't you think?"

"Are you interested, then?"

"Of course."

"You'd certainly need a satisfactory result in the Stewart case first," Castleton declared firmly.

"And what does satisfactory mean?" Froyd asked. "Does it have to be a conviction for murder or would manslaughter suffice?"

"Stewart has become a major embarrassment to us. You know he's gunning for Vishney and that he's capable of undermining our jury selection process. If the public gets too excited about racist bigots on our juries we'll have to change the system. Questioning of jurors. Pre-trial selection hearings. Like in America. Imagine the cost to the Treasury," Castleton complained bitterly.

"So you want him discredited by a conviction and locked up until the public's forgotten all about him," Froyd observed.

"Exactly. And quickly. That's why we've expedited the trial date."

"But that doesn't answer my question. Does it have to be murder or would manslaughter suffice?" Froyd demanded.

"We would prefer murder," Castleton replied.

"That may be very hard to achieve. Whatever the legal niceties of what was actually going on at the time Stewart struck the fatal blow, public opinion is and will remain sympathetic to him. He killed a monster," Froyd pointed out forcefully.

"Do you think we don't know all of that?" Castleton answered, making no attempt to disguise his irritation. "I merely said that we would prefer murder. We'd settle for a conviction for manslaughter. You can lock him up for a few years and by the time he comes out he'll be yesterday's news."

"So it's murder if possible, but manslaughter is sufficient?" Froyd checked.

"Yes."

"Sufficient for your Masters?"

"Yes."

"And sufficient for me?" Froyd pressed.

"What exactly do you mean?" Castleton responded.

"You know what I bloody mean."

"Elevation to the Court of Appeal?"

"Yes. Does a conviction for at least manslaughter guarantee me a place in the Court of Appeal?" Froyd demanded, his face now bright red.

There was a long silence while Castleton stared unblinkingly at the Judge through his glasses. Finally, he spoke. "Yes," replied Castleton, rising to his feet. "I am authorised to offer that guarantee. And I think that concludes our business. Good evening."

Titus Froyd remained sitting on the park bench. He knew a lot about Battersea Park. He'd been brought up in the house in Cheyne Walk until his father had sent him off to Eton. That was why he knew all about the black walnut and Kentucky coffee trees, cormorants and grebes. But he also knew a good deal of the history of why the Park had been created. In the last century the *Red House Tavern* had stood on Battersea Fields, within a few hundred yards of where he was now seated. It was a den of iniquity, attracting highly undesirable elements to the locality and setting the worst of examples. Therefore, to encourage high moral conduct amongst the local populace and a respect for, and pride in, Britain and the Empire, the Park had been constructed and nurtured. He smiled to himself, for he and Castleton had just carried on the noble tradition.

Chapter 50

Traditionally, barristers operate from chambers. Shared staff and shared office accommodation, ranging from the grandeur of the Temple to low-rent converted terrace houses in outer city suburbs. Mickey Bahr, however, did not have chambers. He worked from home but, in his case, home was a refurbished Dutch barge on a residential mooring on Chiswick Pier which he shared with his stunning, flame-haired actress girlfriend, Ginny Jensen, currently resting. Barristers are obliged to have a clerk who takes phone calls from solicitors, arranges case dates and conferences and, by far the most important task of all, fixes fees. In return for these duties, the clerk either receives a percentage of the barrister's fees or is paid a salary. Mickey Bahr did not approve of the professional obligation to have a clerk. In his opinion, no-one could fix a fee better than himself and he was perfectly capable of arranging dates and talking to solicitors without a clerk. But, five years ago, the Bar Council Disciplinary Committee had been informed of his illicit way of practice by a jealous colleague and he'd had to get a clerk. Coincidentally, that was when he had met Ginny at an opening night party for a production in the West End. The show had been panned by the critics and flopped in a week. That's when she moved in to his houseboat, with its thirty foot reception room and four palatial, en-suite cabins, and became his clerk.

Thus, it was Ginny, lying stark naked on their designer Heavenly bed, imported from California, who, at nine o'clock sharp on the last working day before the trial began, received the telephone call from Cecil Kerne QC, Prosecuting Counsel in the case of Stewart, wishing to speak with 'Mr Michael Bahr of Counsel'. She had informed Mr Kerne that 'Mickey Bahr', as he insisted on being called, was currently underwater, checking the hull, but would return the call within the hour, which he duly did.

"Mickey Bahr here," he began.

"The case of Stewart. What's the name of the QC leading you? I want to speak to him. No-one seems to know his name," a cut glass voice demanded.

"Because there isn't one," Mickey answered.

"You mean you're doing the case against me on your own?" Kerne exclaimed.

"I've been losing a lot of sleep over it," said Mickey flatly.

"I see," Kerne responded, completely unable to determine whether Bahr was being sarcastic or if he meant it.

"What can I do for you?" Mickey asked him.

"Your client is plainly guilty of murder. He delivered the fatal blow when Mangan was already down and out," Kerne reeled off confidently.

"Thank you for sharing that with me," responded Mickey.

"However," Kerne continued, ignoring the riposte, "we recognise that there may be a degree of sympathy for your client, given the nature of Mangan's crimes, and so we're prepared to make a very generous gesture, a very generous gesture indeed."

"Namely?"

"We will drop the charge of murder if he pleads guilty to manslaughter."

"You mean manslaughter because he was provoked?" Mickey enquired of him.

"Precisely."

"And what's the real reason behind this? A bird in the hand?"

"Absolutely not. We would expect to convict him of murder if there's a trial. Our gesture is founded on . . . "

"Do me a favour, Kerne," Mickey interrupted. "Spare me the

bullshit. It doesn't cut any ice with me. I suggest we'll get on better with each other if there's no more bullshit."

"Perhaps you would like to take your client's instructions on my offer," Kerne responded sullenly.

"It'll have to wait until Monday when the trial begins. It's already Friday morning. I won't get an appointment for a legal visit in the prison at this late stage," Mickey informed him.

"One's been booked for you at four o'clock this afternoon."

"Who by?"

"It's been arranged," said Kerne evading the question.

"OK. In that case I'll drive up there and pass the offer on to him."

"And what will you advise?" Kerne enquired anxiously.

"I'll advise him to think about it," Mickey replied unhelpfully.

"I'd welcome a phone call this evening to inform me of his reaction," Kerne said.

"OK."

"Before seven. I'm dining out."

"I won't be back in London until about then. Late Friday afternoon traffic is chaos," Mickey told him.

"Can't you stop on the way?"

"Why are you so anxious?" Mickey asked.

"I'm dealing with very high authority in this case. They are keen to proceed with the murder case. It was my advice that, given the enormity of Mangan's crimes, we should offer you manslaughter. They're not happy about it but have agreed. So I don't want to keep them waiting," came the reply.

"How high is this authority?"

"I'm not at liberty to say."

"Right," said Mickey. "I'll call you before seven then."

"Just one other consideration that you may wish to pass on to your client," Kerne added.

"What?"

"Do you know that Froyd is trying this case?"

"Of course I do."

"He'll be pushing hard for murder. A plea to manslaughter may seem very attractive when you see the whites of his eyes. And that isn't bullshit," Kerne announced smugly.

"I'll speak to you later," Mickey said, replacing the receiver, before immediately re-lifting it and leaving a message for Oliver Newcombe to be at the prison at four.

"What was all that about?" a voice called from the cabin containing the Heavenly bed.

"The grey suits are so desperate to keep the lid on this and lock Cal up for a few years that they want to deal," he replied, walking into the cabin where his clerk still lay on the bed, naked as a jaybird, reading the latest edition of *The Stage*.

"Does that mean you have to leave immediately?" she asked, looking up at him through those emerald green eyes.

"No, I've got half an hour," he replied.

"Excellent," she said, "I'll take my commission now," throwing her paper on to the floor and rolling over on to her back.

Mickey Bahr had learned that a successful barrister always keeps his clerk satisfied.

Chapter 51

Four o'clock was outside normal visiting hours and the screening booths at the entrance to the prison were deserted. Moreover, the influence of the authorities behind Kerne meant that Mickey Bahr was eased through the security procedures like Royalty at the races. The special treatment had even extended to a special room being set aside for the conference. The table and chairs were not bolted to the floor, there was a window, albeit barred, and even a plastic jug of water and three white plastic cups. Oliver Newcombe and Cal were already seated at the table when Bahr walked in through the door leading from the public access area. Behind Cal was a separate door which led back to his cell block. Although Cal's wounds had healed and he was physically stronger, the emotional strain of being about to go on trial for murder was written all over his face. While the dark complexion acted as a partial disguise the prison pallor was apparent and the features had grown gaunt. The English Criminal Justice System was stealing Cal's youth. Visibly and rapidly. Mickey Bahr tried not to imagine what Cal might look like after even two or three years inside, let alone the twelve or more that would follow a conviction for murder.

"Why have they laid out the red carpet?" Oliver asked as Mickey took his seat.

"They want something," Mickey responded directly. "This morning I had a phone call from Prosecuting Counsel, Cecil Kerne QC, that's why I'm here. He'll drop the murder charge if Cal pleads guilty to manslaughter."

"Why? And why at the last minute?" Oliver demanded.

"Kerne started off by giving me a lot of bullshit. But by the end of the call I think I'd sussed it out," Mickey began. "The politicians, the top lawyers, most of the heavyweight cops like Maxcroft and Pendell are pushing hard for murder and only murder. But they're not the ones who have to persuade a jury to convict Cal of murdering a monster. That's Kerne's job. And he's not a fool. He thinks a jury may draw back from murder, because of their hatred of the victim. And Kerne is not blinded by the politics. So, he's obviously advised them that whilst they may get Cal for murder, they just as easily may not."

"So they offer to take a plea of guilty to manslaughter. They may not get murder anyway. This way they get a guaranteed conviction for homicide, although it's only manslaughter. Cal's locked up for a few years. He's muted. His word is devalued. The lid goes back on. By the time he comes out, it's all ancient history anyway. Have I summarised accurately?" Oliver asked.

"Absolutely," Mickey replied. "So let me spell out the practicalities of the choices, Cal. Then we can discuss them."

Cal nodded.

"If you go to trial, the jury'll have three choices," Mickey continued. "Count one, guilty of murder. Count two, not guilty of murder, but guilty of manslaughter. Provocation, like I've explained before. Third choice, not guilty of either murder or manslaughter. If they convict you of murder, you get life imprisonment. Minimum twelve years to serve, maybe more. If you plead guilty to manslaughter, you completely remove the risk of that happening."

"And, as you've told us before, a conviction for manslaughter, should mean a sentence of four or five years," Oliver confirmed.

"Yes. Less time off for good behaviour, which does not come off a murder sentence. And also, with just a manslaughter conviction, time spent on remand comes off. With manslaughter you should be out in less than three years," Mickey told them.

"I know you can't be precise," Oliver interjected, "but can you give Cal some idea of his chances before a jury?"

"I've thought about nothing else since I got Kerne's phone call," Mickey answered. "Well," he added with a smile to himself, "for almost all of the time anyway. I put the chances of the jury convicting you of murder at thirty percent. I put the chances of the jury convicting you of manslaughter at forty percent and I put the chances of them acquitting you of both murder and manslaughter at thirty percent. That's the best I can do."

There was a long silence as the three men quietly re-analysed the kind of odds that Bahr was estimating. It was Oliver Newcombe who spoke first.

"One way of looking at those odds is that Cal has the same chance of being found guilty of murder as he does of being acquitted altogether," he concluded grimly.

"Exactly," Mickey replied. "That's what makes the offer of manslaughter attractive. It's the most likely outcome anyway and the remaining gamble between acquittal and a life sentence is at even money. It's a hell of a risk to run when you can be guaranteed that, if you take manslaughter, you should be out in less than three years."

"So what is your professional advice to our client, Mickey?" Oliver asked.

"Before I answer that, I have to tell you about another factor in the equation," Mickey added solemnly. "The odds I've given you depend on the battle being fought on an even playing field. This playing field will not be even. Mr Justice Froyd will add his considerable weight to the Prosecution."

"Why?" exclaimed Oliver.

"Because he is another creature of the Establishment. Because he is ambitious. Because he is vain and arrogant. He'll push for murder. But, like Kerne, he'll recognise that securing a conviction for murder will be difficult. So, what he'll do is push for murder whilst, at the same time, making manslaughter sound like a generous and merciful compromise. He'll leave the jury with virtually no way of avoiding a manslaughter conviction unless they completely defy him. Meanwhile he'll continue to press for murder," Mickey explained to them as they both watched him with expressions of profound dismay.

"So that makes the odds even worse," Oliver concluded.

"Considerably worse," Mickey confirmed. "And I can tell you, with regret, that the occasions when juries defy Judges are rare. And, in my experience, the occasions when juries defy Froyd are almost zero."

"These are deeply depressing matters to be discussing with Cal just before we go into battle," Oliver said.

"I would never have discussed them with Cal if Kerne hadn't phoned this morning and offered manslaughter," Mickey retorted immediately. "They have maintained throughout that they were only interested in murder. The question of them accepting manslaughter was a complete non-runner. And, of course, they knew that their offer would lead to a discussion between us as depressing as this. Kerne particularly referred to Froyd. He said a plea to manslaughter may seem very attractive when we see the whites of Froyd's eyes."

"This way, they force us to our lowest point just as the trial is about to begin," Oliver declared, shaking his head in disbelief. In his modest and respectable practice in Somerset he had never been exposed to a high profile criminal trial in which the Establishment were pulling the strings. "Tell us, Mickey, what is your advice to Cal?"

"My advice is to think about the offer. Give it very serious consideration indeed. The stakes are sky high. I'm prepared to fight and will fight. But this is an enormous decision for you. Think about it. Tell us your decision on Monday morning," Mickey said.

From the moment that Mickey Bahr had walked into the room, Cal had never uttered a syllable. His worried face had turned from one man to the other. He had absorbed every word. His heart had sunk into his boots. Mickey Bahr had obviously done his best, within tight professional constraints, to weigh up the odds and offer an opinion. But, in the end, what he was saying was that it was Cal's decision and no-one else's. You can't play around with a decade of another man's life like it was a commercial decision of whether to sell some shares or float a company. It was all down to Cal. The prospects of staying in prison for another twelve years or more terrified him. The scar along his jaw line had healed but it was still pink and, in his present anguish, it had become livid and unsightly. Mangan had left his mark visibly, as well as emotionally, and now he had the capacity to rob Cal of the best years of his life, just like he had done to his father. The dressing on his left hand had only been finally removed last week and, slowly pouring himself a cup of water, he looked down at the results of the hideous injury. Whilst there had been considerable improvement in the mobility and grip he knew that the hand would never be the same again. Yet, as he saw it, the man whose crimes had caused this chain of catastrophic events over two generations was being deployed as a means of protecting Establishment interests. Their sanctimonious claim that he was entitled to the protection of the Law was a device to conceal their own appalling institutional weaknesses and deceits.

Lifting the cup of water to his lips in his damaged left hand he drank it all down before pushing back his chair and walking to the door which would take him back to the cell block.

As he opened the door he turned back and looked down at the two concerned faces that were watching him with such sadness in their eyes.

"Thank you for coming, gentlemen," he announced. "I don't need any further time to reach my decision. I'd like you to thank Mr Kerne QC for the generosity and humanity of his offer. I'd also like you to tell him that he should take his offer and shove it firmly up his arse. See you on Monday morning."

Mickey Bahr nodded. "My sentiments exactly," he said. "Roll on Monday."

Chapter 52

Cecil Kerne QC rose to his feet in the Old Bailey courtroom to open the case for the Crown. Tall, painfully thin, with smooth skin that looked like it had never needed the touch of a razor, small pig-like eyes and a cut glass accent that came from another time. The court was full. Cal's supporters with frightened faces, the hacks with pencils poised, the police, the concerned members of the public and the voyeur ghouls who feasted upon human depravity and tragedy. A jury of twelve, sworn without any enquiry as to their beliefs, prejudices or attitudes. Two of them couldn't even read the oath properly and had to repeat it after the Clerk of the Court. Cal had stood up to protest. On both occasions. He wanted his freedom to be judged by people who were at least literate. Mr Justice Froyd ordered him to sit down immediately and not to be so contemptuous of decent law-abiding people, doing their civic duty as jurors, but who were understandably nervous at speaking in public.

Kerne had three audiences. The jury, the Judge and the hacks. He had two objectives, a conviction for murder if at all possible, but ensuring that he at least got manslaughter. He had one fear; that common sense might prevail.

Of his three audiences he went firstly for the hacks, striving for the lunch edition headlines which the jurors and their families would read. "Our civilised society will not tolerate the vigilante, will not suffer the lynch mob, will not condone a burglar, armed with a fear-some weapon of steel, who broke into a man's home and caved in his skull with such ferocity that the pathologist described the injury as akin to that seen in high speed, head-on car accidents," he began.

Then he aimed for the jury. "This man faces a charge of murder. That is what lawyers call his crime. In reality, his act was that of execution. He broke into a man's home to usurp the role of the State, to override the powers of our police force, to deny his victim the constitutional right of a trial and to act as Judge, juror and executioner. He now enjoys his right of a fair trial in front of fair-minded, decent people, such as yourselves. The very right he was determined that his own victim should be denied."

Finally, his words for the Judge. "Of course, Mangan was a dangerous man, who probably had serious psychiatric problems and who should have faced trial. But he only killed women. He was no threat to Stewart until Stewart broke into his home, bent on revenge for his father. Our system of Law, honed over the centuries, imbued with the vast cumulative experience of wise Judges such as His Lordship who presides over this trial, has learned the dangers of any citizen seeking to take the Law into his own hands. Unless, rigorously and unfailingly, we enforce the Rule of Law then there can only be one result. Anarchy. Stewart's way was the way of the anarchist. Your verdict will say, this is England, we do not do things in this barbaric way."

The florid figure on the Bench, his face nearly the same colour as his red robes, edged with ermine, looked along the two rows of six, conveying with his eyes and the nodding of his over-sized head, the accuracy and sagacity of the words of Leading Counsel for the Crown.

Before he called his first witness, Kerne had one other missile to launch. His Friday night dinner had been ruined. His entire weekend had been sullied, as he smarted under the one line message Bahr had relayed to him from the Defendant in response to his offer of manslaughter. "This particular Defendant," he concluded, "plainly knew only one way of fighting. To fight dirty. The kick to the testicles. The finger gouging the eye. Kicking to the ribs when the man lay beaten and defenceless, the decimation of the elbow and forearm with a weapon and the final, armed barbaric blow to the head.

At the end of this trial you will pass your verdict on a man who, with stealth, enters the home of another, fights as I have described and seeks to defy the Rule of Law." He'd added that paragraph immediately after he got home from dinner on the Friday night.

In this absurd way the trial of Cal Stewart got under way.

R V CAL STEWART TRANSCRIPT 1990/4

Kerne: Is your name Hilary Ingham and are you one of the leading neuro-pathologists in the United Kingdom?

Ingham: Correct.

Kerne: Tell the Court your conclusions as to how Craig Mangan met his death.

Ingham: The direct cause of death was a massive blow to the left side of the skull, the impact being just above the temple. It caused extensive intra-cranial haemorrhaging and a compound, depressed fracture of the skull.

Kerne: When you examined the fracture in your laboratory can you describe what it looked like?

Ingham: Like an egg that had been smashed on a hard surface. Fractures running across the side of the skull like a spider's web. Shards of bone. Irreparable brain damage. Death would have been virtually instantaneous.

Kerne: Would you describe it as akin to an injury more usually associated with a high-speed, head-on impact in a car crash?

Bahr: I object to that question. It is an outrageously leading question and unnecessarily emotive.

Mr Justice Froyd: The jury are not fools, Mr Bahr. This eminent neuro-pathologist is describing a blow with a weapon to the head of another human being of massive proportions. Mr Kerne is quite entitled to seek words of description from the witness, in non-medical language, which conveys to the jury the enormity of what was done to the victim. What analogy would you suggest is the most helpful to the jury, Dr Ingham.

Ingham: Akin to an injury more usually associated with a high-speed, head on impact in a car crash.

Mr Justice Froyd: Thank you.

Kerne: Please describe the other injuries you found.

Ingham: An object had been plunged into his left eye. Almost certainly a finger. The eyeball had been gouged. He would have likely been left blind in that eye if he had survived.

Kerne: Carry on.

Ingham: Deep bruising to the genitalia. Of a kind I have frequently seen when a man has been kicked in that area. Fractures to four ribs on the left side and five ribs to the right. Again, consistent with kicking and, unless the assailant was skilled in a particular type of martial art, necessarily delivered when the victim was on the ground. His right arm was fractured through the ulna and the elbow was shattered.

Kerne: Setting aside the fatal skull fracture. In what condition would the victim have been as a result of all of these other injuries?

Ingham: Half-blinded. In unmitigated agony from the fractures to his arm and elbow. In severe distress from the kick to the genitalia. In pain and enduring breathing difficulties from the rib fractures. Probably with a significant diminution in his level of consciousness and, almost certainly on the ground.

Kerne: Could he conceivably, being as generous as you properly can be to the Defendant, have offered any kind of physical threat at all to the Defendant or to anyone?

Ingham: Of course not. He was wholly defenceless.

Kerne: And if the Defendant had then embarked upon the fatal blow to the head, was the victim left with any chance of taking avoiding action, or doing anything to escape its impact?

Ingham: Absolutely nothing.

R V CAL STEWART TRANSCRIPT 1990/5

Bahr: Throughout your evidence you have not been asked, nor have you offered, any analysis of the sequence of blows. Is that because, from the pathology, you cannot be sure as to the sequence of blows.

Ingham: You would need to have been present to describe the precise sequence of blows. I was not present. So, in one sense you are right, from the pathology alone, you cannot be sure as to the sequence of blows. But pathology is not blind to common sense. The overwhelming likelihood is that the blow to the head came last.

Bahr: How can you say that? For example, how can you say that Mangan was not kicked in the groin, fell and was immediately struck over the head with the iron tyre lever?

Ingham: I can't. But what I can say is that, if that was the sequence, then your client would have been gouging the eye and fracturing the arm and ribs of a corpse.

Mr Justice Froyd: Like you said, Dr Ingham, the pathology should be combined with common sense. The common sense represented by a jury.

Ingham: Exactly.

Mr Justice Froyd: And, of course, Mr Bahr, the Defendant is now the only living person who was present at this dreadful scene. So, later in the trial, he can explain to the jury the sequence of blows, so as to assist them in using their common sense.

Bahr: Am I really meant to answer that observation, My Lord?

Mr Justice Froyd: Entirely your choice, Mr Bahr.

Bahr: Despite your remarks, Dr.Ingham, is it not the case that, as the pathologist in this case, you are not able to offer a definitive, expert assertion of the sequence of blows?

Ingham: True.

Bahr: You cannot say for sure when, in the whole sequence, the fatal blow was struck?

Ingham: I cannot.

Bahr: Were you made aware of the grave injuries sustained by the Defendant?

Mr Justice Froyd: She examined the victim. Not the Defendant. How can the Defendant's injuries have anything to do with her diagnosis of the victim's injuries?

Bahr: Because the mobility and pain of the Defendant may be relevant to when, where and how blows were inflicted, My Lord.

Mr Justice Froyd: Not in my Court, Mr Bahr. I see exactly what you're about. So will the jury. Sympathy has no place in a jury trial. Thank you, Dr Ingham, your evidence is completed. We shall now adjourn for lunch.

Chapter 53

Cal was taken down to the cells for a lunch of a greasy sausage sandwich and a mug of weak, tepid tea. He couldn't force any of the sandwich down, but somehow managed to drink the tea. His mouth was dry, his head was splitting, but the prison officers refused to allow him any pills without reference to a doctor. Mickey Bahr and Oliver Newcombe dutifully went down to see him, but there was little to say, save to express their joint disgust at the behaviour of Froyd. The jury had just stared ahead, blank-faced and inscrutable, ever since the case had begun. There were nine men and three women. Neither Bahr nor Newcombe had the slightest idea if this was helpful or unhelpful. The whole charade was a lottery, where the man who pulled the tickets out of the hat had only one objective. To make sure that the man in the dock never came out the winner. Cal had caught occasional glimpses of George in the public gallery, together with other members of the support team, but he had looked away. He felt so demeaned by it all. At least the trial had started. And he had not wavered for one second over his decision to refuse the offer of a plea of guilty to manslaughter, even after seeing the whites of Froyd's eyes. Bahr had said the trial would be short. His turn in the witness box would come tomorrow. But next on the agenda was Pendell. He grimaced, but there was no-one there to see. Despite all the support offered to him, one hard truth existed. In the end, he was on his own.

R V CAL STEWART TRANSCRIPT 1990/8

Kerne: Did your enquiry ever unearth any evidence to prove which man was in possession of the knife?

Pendell: No. it may have belonged to either the Defendant or the victim.

Kerne: The jury have just listened to the tape of interview when you questioned the Defendant and he claimed that the knife had belonged to the victim. Did you find any evidence to support his assertion that the knife was the victim's?

Pendell: None.

Kerne: Did you ask the Defendant at what point he had delivered the fatal blow to the head with the tyre lever?

Pendell: I did. More than once. He never answered the question. He answered most of the others. But never that one.

Kerne: Did you give him every opportunity to answer it?

Pendell: Repeatedly. He never had the slightest intention of answering it.

Kerne: Did he ever suggest it was not the final blow?

Pendell: No.

Kerne: When you, perfectly properly, pressed him to answer such a vital question, what was his manner?

Pendell: Aggressive. He called me a bastard. Called Detective Chief Inspector Colley a bastard. And threatened to make disparaging remarks about the trial Judge who had tried his father.

Mr Justice Froyd: A Judge who is now retired. Having given many years service to the community. And unable to answer back.

Pendell: Exactly, My Lord. It was at that point that Mr Colley and I decided to terminate the interview. The Defendant had been reduced to advancing empty abuse.

R V CAL STEWART TRANSCRIPT 1990/9

Bahr: Until the Defendant led you to Mangan had the police identified any evidence themselves which might have led to Mangan's arrest?

Pendell: It was early days in the enquiry.

Bahr: Early days. Going back to 1963. Seven subsequent murders over the following decades. And you call that early days?

Pendell: I meant early in the Diane Pierce murder.

Bahr: Had anything in the Diane Pierce enquiry pointed the police towards Mangan?

Pendell: I'm not the Officer in that case.

Bahr: No. But you know the answer to my question. Tell the jury the truth. Twenty- seven years down the line and eight murders later the police were no nearer identifying Mangan as the killer than they were at identifying Jack the Ripper.

Mr Justice Froyd: Are you suggesting that the police's difficulty in solving those murders is a justification for your client fracturing this victim's skull?

Bahr: No. I'm suggesting that Mr Stewart had to take desperate measures to obtain evidence against Mangan because the police had proved themselves wholly incompetent at doing so over a period of twenty seven years and eight murders.

Mr Justice Froyd: I adjudge that to be irrelevant to the jury's task. Move on.

Bahr: In interview Mr Stewart told you that the knife was Mangan's. Are you seriously trying to suggest that it may actually have been Mr Stewart's?

Pendell: It may have been. How am I meant to know?

Bahr: But did you not know that Mr Stewart is a young man who has no criminal convictions?

Pendell: Not in the UK. We asked Australia and they said they had nothing on him. But I've no idea how accurate their records are down there.

Bahr: Do you have any evidential basis to suggest Mr Stewart has ever carried a knife?

Pendell: I know he carried a tyre lever. And broke into the victim's house with the lever in his possession.

Bahr: And Mangan? Did you not have good reason to believe he carried a knife?

Pendell: His murders did not involve a knife. They were strangulations.

Bahr: So when he sliced flesh from Diane Pierce's thigh and buttock you are suggesting that he did not use a knife, are you?

Pendell: He may have used a kitchen knife from her house.

Bahr: And when he hacked her little toe off, are you suggesting he didn't use a knife?

Pendell: I have no idea.

Bahr: Did you examine Mangan's shrine?

Pendell: Yes.

Bahr: With the little toe in preserving fluid? And the pants of his numerous female victims?

Pendell: Yes.

Bahr: And yet you tell the jury that you never had any basis to form a view as to who the knife belonged to?

Pendell: As you press me so hard, I will tell you. I actually formed the view that the knife probably belonged to the Defendant. He'd shown himself to be a liar in interview. If he said the knife was Mangan's, then my view was that the opposite was probably the truth.

Bahr: Before you just gave that answer had you ever previously suggested that you thought the knife was probably the Defendant's?

Pendell: No.

Bahr: Have you ever suggested before that you thought the knife was probably Mangan's?

Pendell: I really can't remember.

Bahr: Can't you?

Pendell: No.

Bahr: You can't remember if you've ever suggested to anyone that a knife you are now telling this jury probably belonged to Stewart in fact probably belonged to Mangan?

Pendell: No.

Bahr: My Lord, I require Detective Chief Inspector Colley to be called.

Mr Justice Froyd: Why? His evidence covers the same ground as Inspector's Pendell's. He adds nothing new.

Bahr: He is a witness in the case. I am entitled to ask him questions. I want him called.

Mr Justice Froyd: May I seek to assist you, Mr Bahr, in your difficult task. You do not solve the evidential problems that you face by merely repeating the same aggressive questions to another police officer, you know.

Bahr: I ask that Detective Chief Inspector Colley be called into the witness box.

Kerne: He is here, My Lord. I can call him. I shall not be asking him any questions myself.

Bahr: Do you accept that the evidence shows Mangan to have been a serial killer and extremely dangerous?

Colley: Yes.

Bahr: Did you have any evidential basis at all to conclude that the knife belonged to Mr Stewart?

Colley: No.

Bahr: Did you ever hear Detective Inspector Pendell suggest that he believed that the knife belonged to Mr Stewart?

Colley: No.

Bahr: Did you ever hear Inspector Pendell suggest that he believed that the knife belonged to Mangan?

Colley: Silence.

Bahr: I repeat my question. Did you ever hear Inspector Pendell suggest that he believed that the knife belonged to Mangan?

Colley: I believe I did.

Bahr: Who did he say it to?

Colley: Me.

Bahr: Anyone else?

Colley: The representative of the Director of Public Prosecutions, a Prosecuting Solicitor, Chief Inspector Tedstone and Ian Maxcroft from the Metropolitan Police Policy Unit. At a case conference.

Mr Justice Froyd: Where is all of this going? I think the jury have heard enough of it. You've made your point. Inspector Pendell's memory may not be perfect.

Bahr: I will not be deflected. Did you make any notes?

Colley: Yes.

Bahr: Where are they?

Colley: In my briefcase. On the seat behind Mr Kerne.

Bahr: May the witness's briefcase be passed to him?

Mr Justice Froyd: Why? This is all peripheral to the central issues.

Bahr: I intend that Mr Colley should read his note to the Court. Do you now have it, Mr Colley?

Colley: Yes.

Bahr: Read it.

Colley: Inspector Pendell said that the knife could've been Stewart's but, to be fair, it was far more likely to have been Mangan's.

Bahr: Thank you.

In the back seat of the public gallery a bronzed, fit looking man, smiled silently to himself. Tony Medina had known that Mickey had learned to fight in the gutter. There could be no better training than that for a battle in the Court of Mr Justice Froyd. Tony's instinct had told him that Pendell was lying and that Colley would not lend himself to the distortion. On that note the day had ended with the Prosecution case almost completed. Tony took George back to her hotel in Bloomsbury and then took her out to dinner. They made a sombre couple. There was little point in bemoaning Pendell's deceit or Froyd's prejudice. In the end the case would turn on how Cal performed in the witness box and they both knew that he was emotionally exhausted. So were they. George had booked a double room for the duration of the trial in hopeful anticipation that she would be sharing it with Cal when the nightmare was over. It was just about the only gesture left for her to make. But, as she tossed and turned, alone and lost in the wide expanses of the bed, she wondered if he shouldn't have accepted the offer of manslaughter. Tomorrow would determine Cal's fate.

Chapter 54

R V CAL STEWART TRANSCRIPT 1990/13

Bahr: Did you kill Mangan?

Stewart: I must have done. I just remember a fight of extreme violence. In the dark. Then waking up in hospital.

Bahr: Why would you have killed him?

Stewart: Because he was armed with a knife and was trying to kill me. It was him or me.

Bahr: Why had you broken into his house?

Stewart: Because I had reason to suspect that he was a murderer. Who had watched my father go to the gallows. And then gone on to kill again. I had no faith in the police, or in your system. I intended to find some evidence and then call in the police.

Bahr: And you found his shrine?

Stewart: I did. And I notice that the jury have not been provided with a photograph of it. Of course, it would not help the Prosecution case if . . .

Mr Justice Froyd: Don't tell my Court what would or what would not have helped the Prosecution case.

Stewart: Then perhaps Your Lordship would explain why they have not been shown a photograph of it. It was the most chilling and obscene thing that I have ever seen in my life. Mangan was a dangerous killer who relished causing death.

Mr Justice Froyd: I will not tolerate speeches from a Defendant or any witness. You answer questions. That is our system and I am here to enforce it.

Bahr: When did you first see Mangan?

Stewart: After I'd found the shrine and was leaving the house. I was going to phone the police. He came at me with that knife. I'd like the jury to hold it. Imagine it going into their shoulder, their face, their belly.

Bahr: What happened?

Stewart: His first strike hit my torch. Otherwise I'd have been dead in five seconds.

I kicked him in the groin. Made no difference. He came at me again with the knife. Stabbed me in the shoulder. Got me down. I carried on fighting, but his blade went straight through my hand and then I felt it slice into my face. I was pinned down. He was about to kill me. But he wanted to know who I was. I told him. I was bleeding heavily. I felt weak. I was waiting for death. But he wanted to crow. I suppose, knowing he was about to kill me, he felt safe. Never been able to crow to anyone else before. Said he'd done for Louise. Then asked if I'd seen his shrine. He was boasting.

Bahr: Did you have a weapon?

Stewart: Not as such. I had the tyre lever. But that had been to force the door open. Not as a weapon. It was up my sleeve. All I remember is that when he mentioned his shrine his voice changed. Like he was in some private world. Thinking about what he'd done. Like taking that girl's toe off. He was a madman. I saw a glimmer of hope and went for it. Tried to throw him off and all hell let loose. I must have got the lever into my hand, but I don't remember what I did. I had five inches of steel blade in my belly. Tends to dull the memory. I must have struck him a number of times. I've no apologies to offer. It was him or me.

Bahr: Why did you refuse to answer Inspector Pendell's question about when the fatal blow was struck?

Stewart: Firstly, I couldn't be sure when each blow was struck. Secondly, Pendell had no interest in my version. He'd made his mind up, whatever I said. That's why I called him a bastard. And, as the jury saw yesterday, he's a liar.

Mr Justice Froyd: Mr Bahr, control your client.

Bahr: Control him from what, my Lord? Telling the truth?

Stewart: Wait a minute. I said no apologies. One exception. I shouldn't have called Mr Colley a bastard. I withdraw that. He's been uneasy about this all the way through. But I don't withdraw calling Vishney a corrupt bastard. . .

Mr Justice Froyd: Enough. Enough. One more word of attack along those lines and I shall suspend these proceedings. Mr Bahr, I told you to control him.

Bahr: I've no more questions, My Lord. No doubt Mr Kerne will keep him under control in cross examination.

R V CAL STEWART TRANSCRIPT 1990/14

Kerne: If the tyre lever was only a means of forcing entry, why did you take it inside the house with you?

Stewart: What do you suggest I should have done? Left it at the door?

Kerne: Or put it down. Downstairs. And collect it on your way out.

Stewart: I didn't think to do that.

Kerne: So when you went upstairs, did you have it in your hand?

Stewart: It was up my sleeve.

Kerne: I suggest you took it upstairs in the hope and expectation that the victim would be in. You took it upstairs to attack him with it.

Stewart: Untrue. He wasn't in. If he'd been in, he'd have heard me force the back door.

Kerne: When you'd seen his shrine, got your evidence, why didn't you just run out of the front door and up the road to phone the police?

Stewart: I was going to. Then he was suddenly there. Confronting me.

Kerne: The truth is you heard him at the back. You went to attack him. With your fearsome weapon already drawn.

Stewart: I didn't hear him. It was a tyre lever, not a fearsome weapon. And it was not drawn.

Kerne: And is it not the truth that the knife was yours and the victim disarmed you?

Stewart: No.

Kerne: You claim that when you were pinned down, the only injury that the victim had sustained by then was a kick to the groin?

Stewart: I believe so.

Kerne: So the rest of his injuries are all in the latter stages of the fight?

Stewart: I assume so.

Kerne: Was the fracture to the elbow caused by your tyre lever?

Stewart: I assume so.

Kerne: Was the fracture to the arm caused by your tyre lever?

Stewart: I assume so.

Kerne: And the multiple fractures to his left ribs. Were they caused by your lever or by your boot?

Stewart: I'm not sure.

Kerne: You kicked him when he was down, didn't you? There was no linear bruising on his body consistent with the use of the lever on his ribs. You kicked him.

Stewart: Probably.

Kerne: Likewise to his right ribs. Kicks?

Stewart: Probably.

Kerne: Are you skilled in martial arts?

Stewart: No.

Kerne: So is it safe to assume that you couldn't kick that high on a man who was upright?

Stewart: I don't know. I can't remember.

Kerne: You kicked him when he was down didn't you?

Stewart: Perhaps.

Kerne: And when did you gouge his eye?

Stewart: I can't remember.

Kerne: Before you struck the fatal blow to the head of the victim?

Stewart: Throughout this trial you, the Judge, the pathologist, the police have referred to Mangan as the victim, as if to brainwash the jury into sanitising him. He was no victim. Diane Pierce was a victim. Louise Donovan was a victim. My father was a victim. . .

Mr Justice Froyd: The jury aren't here to listen to a speech from you. No-one's under any duty to rephrase the language of the witnesses or even of myself, simply because you do not like to hear a man you killed with an iron bar, described as a victim. You answer the questions. No more, no less. Do you understand?

Stewart: No. I don't understand. I don't understand how you call this justice.

Mr Justice Froyd: Impertinence will not help your cause.

Kerne: I suggest you were carrying out the act that you had gone to his house to perform. You were taking his life. An eye for an eye. His life for your father's.

Stewart: No. No.

Kerne:I suggest you struck that catastrophic blow to the head with a piece of iron when the victim lay helpless on the floor.

Stewart: I don't remember. He had stabbed me. I was in extreme pain. I was faced with a monster. So what if I did as you claim, what man wouldn't have done the same?

Mr Justice Froyd: And there we have it, don't we? You deliberately did what you believe any man would have done.

Stewart: I didn't mean to put it that way.

Kerne: But you have, Mr Stewart. In effect, you have admitted unlawful homicide. I have no more questions.

* * *

Cecil Kerne was cock-a-hoop. As he saw it, the Defendant had given an answer which was an admission that he had gone beyond self-defence and had struck the fatal blow after Mangan had been made helpless. So long as the jury acted faithfully on that concession, then a conviction for at least manslaughter was a certainty. Therefore, he started his final address to them arguing that their only real choice was whether they should convict only of manslaughter, or go the final step and convict of murder. An outright acquittal was no longer an option, it was murder or manslaughter. Thereafter, he spent thirty five minutes explaining why the Rule of Law demanded that they must harden their hearts and convict of murder, so that people in our civilised country should know that juries will not tolerate aggrieved people taking the Law into their own hands. He concluded, as he had opened the case yesterday, with a patriotic fervour that made his patrician voice quiver with emotion. "Your verdict will say, this is England, we do not do things in this barbaric way. That is not the English way. Murder, members of the jury. Not manslaughter. Murder."

Mickey Bahr had the lunch adjournment to gather his thoughts. Cal had done so well until the very end. Kerne had overplayed the final answer for all his worth, but, on any analysis, it had done enormous damage to the defence case. Locking himself away in a conference room on the top floor of the building, he re-jigged his notes, put extra sections in, put a blue pencil through others, until he hoped he still had some coherent argument left that they should still not convict of manslaughter, let alone, murder. But, in his heart of hearts, he recognised that Cal was almost certainly doomed on manslaughter. The inner prayer was that he should be spared a conviction for murder. There was no time for even a sandwich or a cup of coffee. It was panic stations and every moment was vital. At two o'clock, to a hushed courtroom, he rose to his feet, his notes spread out in front of him. The florid face from the Bench was watching him like a hawk, ready to pounce.

And then, Mickey Bahr surprised even himself. He picked up his notes, tossed them aside and opened up with both barrels.

"Mr Kerne has no monopoly on speaking about the English way. The English way may be represented by aristocratic principles espoused at Eton, or by plebeian principles picked up from the gutter in a back street comprehensive. Neither is necessarily more English than the other. He seeks to depict the true English way as civilised and the way of Cal Stewart as the way of the barbarian.

"May I list the deeds of the English way as they affect this case. The English way hanged Stewart's father for a murder he did not commit.

"The English way allowed a racist jury foreman to browbeat other jurors to conviction.

"The English way put a Judge in charge of that case who helped facilitate the injustice. The English way allowed the Home Office to reject such arguments as spurious.

"The English way let Mangan, described repeatedly in this Court as the victim, to murder eight people while the police failed abysmally to link those cases together or even suspect him.

"The English way led a police inspector to mislead you from the witness box as to who the police really believe was the owner of that knife.

"In his nest in Harlow, Mangan constructed his shrine, acquired his US Marine knife and was prepared to kill anyone who tried to interfere with his ritual slayings. And, when a brave man did what the police should have done twenty-seven years ago and confronted him, Mangan, with every sinew in his body, sought to make his nemesis his ninth victim, plunging that knife into Cal Stewart's face, hand, shoulder and abdomen and, by the grace only of a rubber torch, not driving it into his heart. And the English way has been to put Stewart on trial for murder.

"I submit that such a decision to prosecute was, itself, barbaric. And, at the end of it all, on words expressed clumsily in the witness box under extreme pressure, the English way is to railroad you into saying that those clumsy words represent, at the very least, an admission to manslaughter.

"I submit that the true English way is the way of fairness. To all men. Regardless of class, creed, education or colour. I submit that your verdict will bring this shameful series of events to a conclusion which vindicates Cal Stewart in the brave action he took, vindicates the memory of his father which lies at the very heart of what he did and tells our leaders, lawmakers and Establishment that we will not lend ourselves to the suppression of inconvenient and uncomfortable truths.

In this case how do you send out that message? I will tell you. Not guilty of murder, members of the jury and not guilty of manslaughter."

It was the shortest speech that Mickey Bahr had ever made to a jury. But it was, by a distance, the most powerful. Several times he had sensed movement from the Bench as Froyd prepared to dive in but, even Froyd had realised that judicial silence was, at this sensitive stage of the trial, the better option. After all, as soon as Bahr sat down, Froyd would sum the case up to the jury and he had every confidence that a few words from him would redress the balance.

Throughout both speeches the jury had sat impassive. Not a flicker of expression from any of them had disclosed what they were making of this formidable struggle. Mickey Bahr feared that, despite the Judge's many interventions, they would simply take the lead from him and be skilfully steered into convicting of murder.

Froyd slowly poured himself a glass of water from the decanter in front of him, his eyes travelling along the two rows of jurors, lingering several seconds on each one, seeking to transfix them like the cobra hypnotising the rabbit. Then he drank his water. All of it. Slowly. And then he smiled at them. A sickly, artificial smile, displaying his neglected teeth. In the back of his mind he could hear Castleton's promise. Already he was Lord Justice Titus Froyd.

"In English Law, because a man wrongs you, however grave that wrong, you are not provided with a licence to break into his home and bludgeon him to death. If you do so, that is murder and that is the verdict that the Prosecution seek.

"It is open to you to convict of the lesser alternative offence of manslaughter instead of murder if you think Mangan's conduct provoked the Defendant into killing him when he need not have done so. It is hard, if not impossible, to see how the Defendant's last answer in cross-examination, leaves him with any defence at all to manslaughter. Thus, you may think, that the real choice for you is whether to convict him of manslaughter or of murder. In so deciding, sympathy must play no part in your decision. You must convict of murder if the evidence so dictates and not take the softer course of manslaughter out of sympathy.

"I have had printed out for you the two central questions that you must determine. The usher will hand these out. One for each of you. I will then read them out loud to you."

As the usher distributed the twelve pieces of paper the Judge poured himself another glass of water, this time staring down at Bahr and watching him squirm as the next missile was primed, aimed at his client and now ruthlessly launched.

> "Question number 1 for you to consider. '*Are we sure that Stewart inflicted the fatal blow when Mangan was defenceless? If so, the verdict must be guilty of murder, subject to Question 2 below.*
>
> Question number 2 for you to consider. '*May Stewart have killed Mangan when he was defenceless because he was provoked by Mangan's previous murders and Mangan's use of the knife upon him? If so, this reduces murder to manslaughter and the verdict must be Not Guilty of Murder but Guilty of Manslaughter.*

"You will observe that there is a short, but very important, addendum to Question 2. *Namely, that the Prosecution submit that the Defendant's final answer in cross-examination is an admission to manslaughter and leaves him with no defence to this charge.*

"I will now remind you of that last crucial question and answer. Mr Kerne suggested that the fatal blow to the head was delivered when the victim lay helpless on the floor. The Defendant answered with these words '*I don't remember. He had stabbed me. I was in extreme pain. I was faced with a monster. So what if I did as you claim, what man wouldn't have done the same?*

"So, there it is, say the Crown. Manslaughter on the Defendant's own testimony. Let us now review the evidence and consider whether you should go one stage further and convict of murder."

In fifteen minutes Mr Justice Floyd reminded the jury of the impact of the evidence of the pathologist and the answers given by the Defendant when interviewed by the police, laying heavy emphasis on his refusal to answer the crucial question. He packed more venom into the fifteen minute review than an African green mamba pumps into its prey to kill it. Five minutes later they were in their retiring room considering their verdict.

Cal was in poor shape, alone in his cell, head in hands and hyperventilating. Mickey Bahr and Oliver Newcombe went down to see him and demanded that the Prison Officers send for a doctor. They were told it was just stress, they had no intention of disrupting the routine, they had eighteen courts and forty-three prisoners to deal with and that Bahr and Newcombe should end their visit. They rejoined George and the rest of the support team in the coffee bar and sat in miserable silence.

Meanwhile, the Judge was in his chambers preparing his sentencing remarks. If the jury came back this afternoon he would make the headlines of tonight's Evening Standard. His words would be splashed across the front pages of every national in the land. When he had finished drafting them he read them out loud in front of the mirror, practising an emphasis here and a silence there. When they were fully honed, he laid them aside, waiting for the usher's knock on the door to announce that his time had come. He had neatly highlighted the actual sentences he intended to pass. A mandatory life sentence for murder with a recommendation that the Defendant serve not less than sixteen years. And, for manslaughter, a savage eight years.

Forty minutes later came the knock on his door. The jury had reached a verdict. They were ready to come back into Court. Froyd frowned, perhaps just a little too quick a return to get a conviction for murder he thought to himself, but maybe not. In any event, manslaughter was a given.

When he re-entered the Court it was packed beyond capacity. People were crammed into every row, they were standing in the aisles, solicitors and barristers from other cases had filled the lawyers' benches in the well of the court and the atmosphere was electric. The prisoner was brought into the dock, eyes down, struggling to breathe and shaking. The scar on his face that Mangan had bequeathed him seemed angry and alive.

The sombre-faced jurors returned to the jury box, not one of them looked at the man in the dock, invariably the kiss of death. An ominous hush fell across the courtroom. In this desperate moment Cal thought of his father, like him, in a dock at the Old Bailey awaiting the verdict where the word 'guilty' meant the rope. And Henry Stanton had been a wholly innocent man. The foreman, an anonymous middle-aged mouse of a man stood up, clutching his piece of paper with the Judge's two questions upon it.

The clerk of the court began the ritual that had endured over the centuries.

R V CAL STEWART TRANSCRIPT 1990/19

Clerk of The Court: Has the jury reached verdicts on which you are all agreed?

Foreman: We have.

Clerk of The Court: On the charge of murder do you find the Defendant guilty or not guilty.

Foreman: Not guilty.

Clerk of The Court: And is that the verdict of you all?

Foreman: It is.

Clerk of The Court: On the alternative charge of manslaughter do you find the Defendant guilty or not guilty?

Foreman: Not guilty.

Clerk of The Court: And is that the verdict of you all?

Foreman: It is.

Mr Justice Froyd: How can that possibly be right, Mr Foreman? You heard the admission of the Defendant in cross-examination. I would assume that, understandably, in such a moment of tension, you must have made an error when you spoke. I shall direct that the Clerk of The Court repeats the taking of your verdict on manslaughter.

Clerk of The Court: On the alternative charge of manslaughter do you find the Defendant guilty or not guilty?

Foreman: Not guilty.

Clerk of The Court: And is that the verdict of you all?

Foreman: It is. Absolutely. No mistake. Not guilty.

Pandemonium broke out in the courtroom. Froyd made no attempt to control it because he was thundering along the dais back towards his chambers, his face the hue of an overripe Victoria plum. As he reached the door, he looked back at the football crowd chaos to which his precious courtroom had been reduced. Amidst the masses of animated faces, his eyes alighted on only one. A lone figure. In the far corner. Standing. Watching. Donald Castleton. For one fleeting second Castleton caught his eye and shook his head. With that gesture Titus Froyd witnessed his aspirations being ground into the dust under the heels of an Australian maverick and an inconsequential barrister who hadn't even gone to university.

Events thereafter moved with lightning speed. One minute Cal was surrounded by burly Prison Officers in a criminal dock and, in minutes, he was being thrust through crowds, carried along corridors and jostled across hallways until suddenly, he was out in the fresh air and blinking in the sunlight. He was standing at the top of a flight of stone steps leading down to the street. Beneath him the crowd stretched as far as he could see. A sea of faces stretching endlessly in each direction. They were cheering. He'd had no idea of the extent to which his case had become a cause celebre. Isolated in his cell, he had not realised how many of the decent English public had really cared and now there was an outpouring of relief and joy. An attractive girl somehow managed to get right up alongside him, whispering urgently in his ear that she was from one of the national tabloids and was authorised to go immediately to six figures for an exclusive on his story. He shook his head and she moved away.

There were banks of microphones, live outside broadcast cameras, reporters, all pushing, jostling, tugging and demanding. An interview. A statement. A quote. Anything. Looking behind him he observed that, by some miracle, his team had gathered in a solid row behind him. They were all there. Flanking him. Tony Medina. Mark Gevinson. Mitchell Ormsby. Mickey Bahr, still in his winged collar and bands. Oliver Newcombe. Tim Sprackley in his brown gabardine mackintosh. And, of course, George.

"I do have something to say," he announced, leaning close to one of the microphones, shocked at hearing his own voice amplified and echoing off the surrounding buildings. His voice sounded strong. The crowd stopped cheering. They were right across the street so that no traffic could move. For this moment a whole section of London fell silent. And Cal Stewart delivered.

"I'm not rejoicing," he began. "I'm a very angry man. And let's get one thing straight from the start, I'm not looking for financial compensation for my father, my mother or myself. I'm not selling my story to the newspapers. I'm just telling you that you have elements in your social and criminal justice systems that stink, and I'm intending to name a few names and then get the hell out of here.

"In 1963 my father was hanged for a murder he didn't commit. William Hollister, now a merchant banker with Kyngora Bank, had just paid the schoolgirl victim of that murder fifteen pounds to have sex with him. That same afternoon my father was arrested for murder. Hollister's father, Neville, Lord Lieutenant, was frightened that a detailed investigation and a painstaking criminal trial conducted by experienced defence lawyers would expose their family name to shame. The next day he telephoned Judge Vishney, now living in Brighton, drawing his judicial pension. Hollister corruptly encouraged Vishney to get the case tried in his list, as rapidly as possible and for my father to be represented by an inexperienced barrister. Vishney obliged, unfairly appointing young Frederick Walgrave to defend my father.

"Let it be said, Frederick Walgrave did everything in his power to expose the truth. No man could have tried harder. But the odds were stacked against him. Vishney pushed ahead at breakneck speed, interested only in securing a conviction. The evidence against my father was weak. My father was of mixed blood. Half black. The foreman of the jury was an active member of a fringe extremist party whose aspirations were the same as the Ku Klux Klan. Frederick Walgrave's daughter, Georgina, and I obtained powerful evidence of this bigotry and reported it with other complaints to the Home Office. We were told that the other jurors would not have tolerated any racism without protest to the Judge and they would never have allowed their verdict to be influenced by a bigot. This was sanctimonious claptrap. As long as you allow criminal cases to be tried by jurors of whom you never ask a single question, then your system will remain at risk of doing to others what it did to my father.

"My father was executed. My mother's life was ruined. Frederick Walgrave was haunted by the injustice until he died. Meanwhile, the real killer, Walter Mangan remained free. He had tasted murder, savoured it and lusted for more. His crimes grew worse. He has committed a number of other murders of young girls in this country and at least one in Australia. Mangan was a psychopath. He grew more sophisticated in avoiding detection. If there had been a proper investigation in 1963, and not the headlong race to secure a conviction against my father and get the case buried, Mangan may well have been identified as the killer in 1963 and all these other lives would have been spared.

"When Georgina Walgrave and I recently started to press to have this case reopened, Vishney and Neville Hollister brought pressure to bear on a policeman who tried to help us. In that activity, they had the corrupt assistance of Ian Maxcroft, a senior Metropolitan Police Officer. And William Hollister paid a thug to have me so seriously beaten that I would give up and go back to Australia.

"In the end Georgina and I found Mangan. And we found the evidence of his guilt of the 1963 murder and many more. He tried to kill me. I wiped him out. Like you would wipe out disease-ridden vermin in your home. And I was prosecuted for murder. I don't know if Maxcroft or Vishney or Hollister had anything to do with that outrageous decision, but one thing is for sure, despite every word I am uttering here, I won't be in receipt of any writs from any of them for slander. They wouldn't dare.

"And Pendell, one of the officers in charge of my case. He's just like Maxcroft. Self-righteous. Self-seeking. And, as I told him face to face, a bastard by nature.

"It's over. Frederick Walgrave and my father are vindicated. Your jury selection system stinks. Your criminal justice system is corrupt. When my father's case eventually came up before the Court of Appeal for them to state publicly that they'd got it wrong, I wasn't even allowed to attend. They kept me in custody. But Mr Sprackley, despite efforts to mute him, bravely spelled out the enormity of the outrage. And do you know what the Court of Appeal said? It was an unfortunate evidential error. That's what I got from them.

"Have you learned anything from all of this? Of course you haven't. Anyone who has sat in Court during my trial and listened to Mr Justice Froyd would realise that he is merely the modern version of Vishney. Hell bent on a conviction to protect the system. No doubt seeing personal advancement as part of the eventual pay off. He's welcome to sue me as well. I'd enjoy meeting him in Court on even terms, instead of when the dice are loaded in his favour.

"As a people I respect you. But your Establishment stinks. Your system stinks. It's up to you whether you do anything about it or not. Frankly, I no longer care. I've no more to say."

Beneath him the crowd remained in a shocked silence. Turning round, he shook hands with all of his new friends in turn. The steel grip of Mark Gevinson, the beaming face of Mitchell Ormsby with its walrus moustache stretched by the breadth of the smile, the bronzed good looks of Tony Medina and finally his legal team, Oliver Newcombe and Mickey Bahr. Last in line was Tim Sprackley, but Cal did not shake his hand. Instead he threw his arms around him, his head only coming up to Sprackley's shoulder and his face pressed into the gabardine of his out of date, brown mackintosh. He hugged Sprackley as he would have hugged the father he never knew and he spoke softly so that only the tall, thin man, whose eyes were now moist, could hear.

"George told me everything," he whispered. "Every word, every gesture. My father was dead and I was in prison. But we heard you. We heard you."

Tim Sprackley raised a hand and patted Cal ineffectually on the back. He didn't know what to say or do. All he knew was that, at last, he had championed a freedom and that life had purpose and that life was good.

Cal put his arm around George and strode down the steps. Forcing his way through the still stunned crowds on the pavement he reached the black cab that stood waiting for them, its door held open by a uniformed police officer. Helping George in, he turned round to take one last look at the Old Bailey, the crowds, his friends. His eyes happened upon a figure standing on the fringe of the crowd, watching everything. It was Pendell. Cal raised his fist in triumph and punched the air. Pendell melted away. He had become an insignificance.

Just as Cal was bending to get into the cab himself, someone tapped him on the shoulder. It took Cal a second or two to realise who it was and then he recognised him as the foreman of the jury. He was smiling and offering his hand which Cal accepted and then ducked into the cab. The juror had never spoken but, as Cal pulled the heavy door closed and the taxi moved gingerly away, forcing a passage through the crowds, he became aware of a piece of a screwed-up paper that the juror must have pressed into his hand as they shook hands.

"What is it?" asked George as he opened it up.

"That man, he was the jury foreman. He slipped it to me," Cal replied. "It's a copy of the questions that the Judge gave the jury," he continued, as he began to read it. With George leaning over to read it with him, they were taken on a secret trip into the jury's retiring room.

THE JUDGE'S QUESTIONS FOR THE JURY

> *1 Are we sure that Stewart inflicted the fatal blow when Mangan was defenceless? If so, the verdict must be guilty of murder, subject to Question 2 below.*

Alongside this question appeared twelve ticks in black biro.

2 May Stewart have killed Mangan when he was defenceless because he was provoked by Mangan's previous murders and Mangan's use of the knife upon him? If so, this reduces murder to manslaughter and the verdict must be Not Guilty of Murder but Guilty of Manslaughter.

[The Prosecution submit that the Defendant's final answer in cross-examination is an admission to manslaughter and leaves him with no defence to this charge]

Alongside this question appeared twelve ticks in black biro.

However, although the Judge's printed questions for the jury had stopped at that point, the same black biro had written out further questions below.

3 Are we all sure that the Judge was unfair in the way he conducted this trial?

Alongside this question appeared twelve ticks in black biro.

4 Are we all sure that Inspector Pendell was a bastard, just as Stewart said at the end of his police interview?

Alongside this question appeared twelve ticks in black biro.

5 Are we all sure that Mangan deserved everything he got?

Alongside this question appeared twelve ticks in black biro.

6 Are we all sure that, despite our answers to the Judge's Questions, we have absolutely no intention of convicting Stewart of anything?

Alongside this question appeared twelve ticks in black biro.

Cal started to laugh. And then George joined in. They laughed for the first time in many weeks. They laughed so hard that the cab driver turned round and started to laugh with them. He didn't know why he was laughing. But they did. It was the laughter of freedom.

Chapter 55

George had somehow managed to deal with Cal's mother, stopping her from coming over for the trial. It would likely have killed her. But now Mrs Stewart could confirm the Qantas flight to Sydney for tomorrow. Cal's neatly packed rucksack, containing his few belongings that had been left in Katie's flat, stood just inside the door of the hotel bedroom in Bloomsbury. They had dinner sent up to the room. Neither of them was hungry. They never turned on the television. Nor did they speak very much. They were no longer the same people. The Establishment and the system had taken two young, happy lives and wrung them out. Now they had to shake themselves down and start again. As different people.

Before going to bed, Cal stood in the piping hot shower for thirty minutes, trying to scald away the insidious, microscopic germ cells that prison had injected into his pores and into his spirit. He realised that complete sanitisation would take a lot longer than half an hour.

Eventually he went to bed where George was waiting for him, naked beneath freshly laundered sheets, appreciating how difficult this would be for him. He had not felt the softness of her skin for three months and when he did, he thought of his father, denied forever the touch of his mother. When George gave herself to him he was ashamed because, although he had no doubt that he loved her, his possession of her was borne of hunger and felt base. George understood. But her very understanding made it harder, because she surrendered herself selflessly, only anxious to give to him and not to take for herself. When he fell asleep, she did not. Although she had dreamed of sharing this bed with him and now that dream had come true, she was still alone.

In the morning she lay silently while he took another long shower, emerging from the bathroom in clean clothes, shaved and steeling himself for whatever lay ahead. He came over and sat on the bed, holding her hand.

"I want you to go home," he began, "wind up your affairs and come down to Sydney and be with me. There's plenty of jobs for vets, particularly for those specialising in large animals. It's the new world, a new life together."

There was a long silence before George replied, her eyes misty and her voice shaking, but Cal recognised the finality in her tone.

"No, Cal. I've thought very hard about it. You and I were brought together for a specific purpose. We've achieved that purpose. We've each of us laid our fathers to proper rest. Wherever their spirits are, they are now at peace. That was our mission. It's the pinnacle of anything we could ever achieve together. It can never be any better or more fulfilling. Our lives will always be enriched by the momentous thing we did together. That's where it should stay. That's where it should stop. I think that we both know that."

By the time she had finished, the tears were running freely down her cheeks, but her eyes never left his and her determination never faltered. Cal bent down, kissed her gently on the cheek and then turned away. He never spoke, for he knew that his voice would have let him down. George was the most remarkable person he'd ever met or was likely to meet and he adored her and wanted only to be with her. But, even as he picked up his bag, quietly closed the door behind him, and walked out into the free world again, taking that first step on the long journey back to Australia, he knew that what she had said was absolutely right. She was wise beyond her years. Their mission was complete. It had been on a level of intensity that neither of them would probably experience again. A normal relationship between them had likely been rendered unattainable in the process. So they should end on top of the mountain, always able to look back and look down and remember what they did for their fathers and what they had offered each other. It was the saddest moment Cal had ever endured, but it was also the proudest.

* * *